MW00939702

REAGAN'S REDEMPTION

BOOK EIGHT IN THE *BODYGUARDS OF LA COUNTY* SERIES

CATE BEAUMAN

Reagan's Redemption
Copyright © January 2015 by Cate Beauman.
All rights reserved.
Visit Cate at www.catebeauman.com
Follow Cate on Twitter: @CateBeauman
Or visit her Facebook page:
www.facebook.com/CateBeauman

First Print Edition: January 2015

ISBN-13: 978-1507503645
ISBN-10: 1507503644

Editor: Invisible Ink Editing, Liam Carnahan
Cover: Demonza
Formatting: Rachelle Ayala

No part of this book may be reproduced, scanned, or distributed in any printed or electronic form without permission. Please do not participate in or encourage piracy of copyrighted materials in violation of the author's rights. Thank you for respecting the hard work of this author.

The characters and events portrayed in this book are a work of fiction or are used fictitiously. Any similarity to real persons, living or dead, is coincidental and not intended by the author.

DEDICATION

To my friend Laura Torres, web designer
extraordinaire.

CHAPTER ONE

Bronx, New York
June 2015

"IT LOOKS LIKE A BAD CASE OF STREP AND A LITTLE dehydration, but Jarrin seems to be doing better already." Reagan winked, smiling at the five-year-old lying in the big bed helping himself to the applesauce the nurse brought in.

"But he's so *swollen*, doctor." The worried mother brushed her fingers through her son's wavy brown hair, sitting close at his side.

"The swelling and fever are part of the body's response to the infection." Reagan rested her hand on Jarrin's mother's shoulder, giving a gentle squeeze of reassurance. "You should see the inflammation start to subside as the Amoxicillin does its job. Jarrin responded well to the IV and his first dose of antibiotics. He's eating and drinking on his own. I want you to follow up with his pediatrician tomorrow, but I feel confident he's ready to go home when he's finished snacking."

"Can I have some more?" the sweet-eyed boy asked as he set down the empty plastic cup.

"Good stuff, huh?"

"Yeah."

Grinning, Reagan grabbed hold of little toes beneath the blanket, giving them a wiggle, thrilled to see the lethargic kiddo who'd cried in his mother's arms only a couple hours ago looking better. "You bet, buddy." She returned her attention to Mrs. Weaver. "We'll get him some more applesauce, and I'll have Kim, your nurse, take care of his discharge."

"Thank you, doctor. Thank you so much for everything you've done."

"You're welcome. Go home and get some sleep, push the fluids and next dose of medicine when Jarrin wakes up, and follow up with his pediatrician first thing tomorrow." She wiggled his toes again. "Make sure you drink lots of water and rest so you can get back to the swimming pool."

"Okay." He nodded as much as his swollen neck would allow.

"Bye." She stood up from her seat at the edge of the mattress and stepped out from behind the curtain, making her way to the nurse's station on achy feet.

Kim glanced up from the computer, her fingers pausing on the keyboard. "Well if it isn't the energizer bunny. What is this, hour fifteen?" The pretty redhead took a pen from the desk and brought it up to her mouth like an imaginary microphone. "Doctor Rosner, how does it feel to know you're mere moments away from ending yet another endless shift?"

Reagan grinned as her friend extended the pretend microphone to her. "I'm too tired to come up with something witty." She chuckled as Kim did. "Was there a full moon or something? I can't remember the last time this place was so *insane*." She walked around to one of the unoccupied computers, yawning as she logged on, clicking boxes with instructions that would help Jarrin's mother get him through the next few hours. "The little guy behind curtain four is requesting another applesauce. He's all set for discharge." She

6

signed off on her last patient, handing over the sheets the printer spit out. "Here you go. Tell Jarrin's mother she can call me at home with any questions or concerns if she has trouble getting ahold of the pediatrician."

"Reagan," Kim said in her warning tone shaking her head, "You're never going to get any sleep if you keep giving every worried parent your private number."

"I don't give it to everyone."

"Practically."

She shrugged. "Mrs. Weaver will rest better knowing I'm just a phone call away. She probably won't even use it."

"Kind of like that creep father who didn't call you non-stop for two weeks?" Kim sent her one of her know-it-all smirks.

She winced, remembering the man who'd been more concerned with scoring a date than remedying his son's flu virus. "That's only happened once. I can't let one moron ruin a good thing for everyone else. Besides, I like following up with our pediatric strep throats and stomach bugs." Too often they dealt with massive traumas that had far less favorable outcomes. Illnesses easily cured by antibiotics, rest, and plenty of fluids were a welcome change. It was satisfying to watch the not-so-sick walk away. "I don't mind easing worried parents' minds. I like knowing Jarrin will be swimming and playing with his friends again by mid-week. Most of our patients aren't so lucky."

"I'm fairly certain you're in the running for sainthood."

Reagan laughed. "I don't think so."

"Get out of here, Mother Teresa, and call me when you get back from the woods."

"Mmm." Her lips curved, and she closed her eyes. "I can already smell the pine."

"A week off and you head for the middle of nowhere. What about the Bahamas or Cancun?"

Reagan shook her head. She didn't want white sand and crystal clear water. She craved to recharge in the shaded quiet of the mountains. "That's what Derek wanted, but my power of persuasion is top notch." She smiled.

"I've never met people more opposite than the two of you, but somehow you make your relationship work."

They *used* to make their relationship work, but the last six months had been rough. She gave Kim a small smile, looking down. "You know what they say about opposites."

"I'll see you when you get back. Don't forget the calamine lotion and bug spray."

She snorted out a laugh. "They're already packed." She turned, making her way to the on-call room, and scrubbed her hands before bee-lining it to the fridge and the sandwich she'd been forced to abandon at three a.m. when the paramedics rang down with four gunshot wounds and two stabbings.

She took a ravenous bite on her way to the table, moaning, rolling her eyes in ecstasy, craving her next sample of cafeteria tuna on wheat. Sitting, she pulled her aching feet from her Danskos and flexed her toes as she slid the elastic from her long brown hair.

Sighing, she absorbed the moment of peace and quiet, perusing yesterday's paper as she struggled to unwind after the grueling, endless night. She flipped pages, pausing when the article on the Appalachia Project caught her attention. The government-run program was struggling to maintain personnel. The organization desperately needed a full-time physician and nurse as the pilot program, which aimed to bring infrastructure to rural areas in the region, limped into its last year.

She glanced at the gorgeous pictures of trees in bloom and pretty waterfalls among the mighty Appalachians. Serenity. "Perfection," she murmured, considering the idea of applying for mere seconds. Then she chuckled—she was a city girl through and through. Seven days in the middle of nowhere was one thing, but an entire year? She yearned for a break from gunshot wounds and stabbings, car accidents and endless traumas of the ER, but a week was plenty to recharge. Perhaps a slower pace was appealing, especially after the night she'd just had, but among the triumphs and tragedies of practicing medicine in an inner city emergency room, she hadn't yet met a situation that had broken her.

She pushed the paper away and took another bite of her sandwich as the beeper on her hip alerted her to an impending patient arrival. She dismissed the familiar tone, shoving a chip in her mouth, reveling in the fact that she didn't have to run down the hall. For the next little while medicine was on the back burner.

She popped a green grape between her lips and took her phone from her bag, noting the new text she'd received moments after she made her mad dash to meet the incoming ambulances. She smiled, realizing the message was from Derek, opened it as the pager still hooked to her scrubs sounded for the second time, and stared at her screen. *We can't see each other anymore. It's over.*

She read the words again in disbelief, pressing her fingers to her lips with the punch of pain. It was over? After a year he was simply finished? Brush off the hands, a two-sentence text, and they were through? A small, incredulous laugh escaped her as she looked at her phone once more.

They'd grown apart since he switched hospitals several weeks ago, making do with quick phone calls before one of them fell asleep, exhausted after a shift. Then she'd gotten the news from the specialist, and he'd distanced himself further.

"You ass," she mumbled, blinking back tears, shoving her phone away. "You're an ass," she said again, frowning when her beeper went off for the third time. "What the crap?" She yanked the piece of plastic from the hem of her pants, scanning through the three calls the staff had received in less than five minutes. The ER was getting slammed. She pulled her white coat from the back of her chair and rushed down the long corridor.

"Reagan, you're still here," Dr. Maxton said, jogging up to her side. "Take ambulance two coming in. Car accident. Seven-year-old female. Vitals are stable. Possible concussion. Peds is tied up with her brother who just came in—massive facial and head trauma."

She nodded. "Sure."

"I've got the gunshot coming in behind it."

"I wasn't kidding when I said the whole night was like this," she warned as the ambulance she was waiting on pulled up. She grabbed gloves on her way out the sliding door, greeting the paramedic, memorizing the vitals he gave her as the little girl with curly black hair and frightened blue eyes was wheeled from the back. "Hi sweetie. What's your name?"

"Mable. I want my mom."

Reagan studied the little girl's pupils, creamy complexion, and bloody lip. "Your mom will come and see you very soon." She took Mable's hand as they reached the examination room and the small team waiting to assist her. "I'm Reagan. I'm going to help take care of you for a little while."

"Okay."

"Does anything hurt?"

"My head."

"Where?"

She pointed to the small gash along her temple as one of the nurses cut away Mable's pink shirt and affixed electrodes to her chest.

Reagan noted the dark bruising cutting across the little girl's trunk from her seatbelt. "Does your tummy feel sick or hurt anywhere?" she asked as she pressed gently around the child's abdomen, searching for signs of internal trauma.

"No. Just my hip."

She glanced at the welt where the buckle had dug into her skin. "I bet it does. Are you dizzy?"

"No." She sniffled, and a tear fell as Kim sent the IV needle into the top of Mable's little hand.

"You're doing great, sweetie," Reagan soothed, swiping a piece of gauze from the table, dabbing at tears. "Have you been to the hospital before?"

Mable tried to shake her head in the neck brace.

Reagan shined a penlight into big blue eyes. "It probably seems kind of scary, but we do some pretty cool stuff here."

"Like what?"

Reagan brushed her hand through the child's hair, quickly scanning Mable's vitals on the monitor to her left. "Well, we take pictures of bones."

"An x-ray?"

She nodded as she examined Mable's legs, feeling for any obvious breaks. "Do you think we could take a picture of your bones? We're going to do something called a CT scan. It doesn't hurt at all, then I'll show you what the inside of your body looks like." She leaned in close, whispering. "I'll even let you take home a disk so you can show your friends."

Mable smiled. "Okay."

"I'm going to go talk to the radiology technologist. He's the photographer. It's kind of busy in here this morning so we might have to wait our turn."

"Will you come back?"

"In just a second. I'll find out when we can get an appointment while my friend Kim bandages the cut on your forehead." She stepped from behind the curtain, picking up a phone. "This is Doctor Rosner in ER. I need a CT scan."

"Take a number."

She smiled. "Curtain ten." She hung up as a frantic woman with blood on her shirt and mascara smearing her cheeks rushed down the hall.

"Mable? Mable?"

"Ma'am, I'm Doctor Rosner. Can I help you?"

"I can't find my daughter. My husband's dead and they won't let me see my son."

Her heart broke for the woman. "I'm Mabel's attending physician. Come with me." Reagan took the mother behind the curtain.

"Mable." The woman broke down in hysterical tears as she clutched her daughter tight. "Oh, thank God you're okay. She's okay? She's all right?" She brushed trembling fingers over Mable's curly hair and the freckles dotting her small nose, then took her daughter's hand in hers.

"She has a bit of a headache and some contusions on her hip from the seatbelt buckle, but I'm not seeing any symptoms of a concussion." She pulled Mable's covers back. "Mable does have some fairly significant bruising along her chest and abdomen here." She examined Mable's stomach region again with several presses of her fingers into soft skin, studying the little girl for any signs of discomfort. "So we're going to do a CT scan to stay on the safe side, but at this point everything looks great."

"My baby's okay."

Dr. Maxton poked his head behind the drape, his eyes grave as they met Reagan's. "Mrs. Totton, I need to speak with you."

Mable's mother stood from the edge of the bed. "Do you have news on my son? Have they told you about Brock?"

"If you could come with me," Dr. Maxton said.

Mrs. Totton swallowed as tears coursed down her cheeks. "I can't leave Mable."

"Mrs. Totton," Reagan took the woman's hand, wishing there was some way to shield the mother from the news she was about to receive. "I'll stay right here with Mable. I'll take good care of her. I promise. We're going to color while we wait for our turn in radiology."

"You'll stay with her?"

She squeezed the woman's hand tighter, knowing deep down that Mrs. Totton already knew her son was dead. "Yes."

"She's my baby."

"And she's just fine. We'll be waiting for you to come back. We'll make a picture for you."

Mrs. Totton walked off with Dr. Maxton. Moments later her muffled wails carried down the hall.

Mable started to cry. "Why is my mom crying? Where did she go?"

Reagan sighed, hugging the frightened child. "She'll be back in a little while, Sweetie. How about we make her something pretty?"

"Okay."

"Let me get what we need." She walked to the

nurse's station as her beeper went off again and several staff members headed toward the sliding doors, awaiting the next ambulance. Regan glanced around the pandemonium while someone in exam area thirteen moaned loudly. She grabbed the stash of coloring books and bucket of crayons and went back behind the curtain, pasting on a smile. "Here we go." She pulled over a table, setting the contents down, reading Mable's vitals again on the monitor. "Do you want to color or draw?"

"Draw."

"Sure." She sat on the edge of the bed. "What should we make?"

"I'm going to make my family and you can draw the Statue of Liberty. That's where we're going today. We left the hotel early to get on the ferry but we got in the crash instead."

"I'm sorry that happened."

"The statue's green but not really. Daddy said the salt in the water made her that way."

"Yes."

Mabel handed her a green crayon. "You can draw with this even though it's not right."

"All right." She smiled, getting to work on the picture as Mable drew four happy faces, all with blue eyes and varying lengths of black hair.

"This is my daddy and mommy and Brock and me."

"Very nice. You're a wonderful artist."

Mable set down her pink crayon mid-stroke. "I don't want to color anymore. I want my mom."

Reagan's brow furrowed as she noted Mable's heart rate accelerating on the monitor and her peaches and cream complexion paling. "Sweetie, what's wrong?"

"My tummy hurts really bad."

Reagan stood, pushing the table away from the bed

and pulled back the covers, noticing the sudden distention where Mable clutched. "Let me look." She pushed on the now hardened abdominal area and the little girl moaned, her eyes rolling back in her head as the automatic cuff on her arm tightened, giving a read off. BP dropping. "Mable? I've got a code!" She hollered. "Curtain ten! Mable?"

The code team rushed in. "What've we got?"

"Internal bleeding. Distended abdomen. Hard to the touch. Vitals are crashing. Intubate her, open her line, and let's get her to OR. Tell them they need two bags of O-negative at the ready. Hang in there, sweetie," she said to Mable, willing her to hold on as they barreled down the long hall through the heavy wooden doors, handing the little girl off to the OR staff waiting for them.

"Reagan." Kim followed her into the next room.

She sat on the bench, sucking in several shaky breaths, trying to steady herself.

Kim sat next to her.

She rushed to her feet. "I need to go in." She let her coat fall to the floor and pulled a surgical gown over her scrubs. "Tie me." She turned her back toward her friend.

"Reagan—"

"I told her mother she was going to be okay. Please tie me."

Kim secured the drape. "There's nothing you can do."

Kim was absolutely right. Mable's fate now rested in Doctor Viner's hands, because she'd made a mistake. "I should've known." She piled her hair on top of her head, securing a disposable hair cover in place.

"Her vitals were stable; her color was good. She was alert, Reagan. You ordered a scan. She was waiting her turn."

Kim's justifications did nothing to relieve the sickening dread weighing heavy in her stomach. "I should've put a rush on it." She slipped a booty over her Dansko and one over her right foot.

"We're slammed, Reagan. We have been for hours. She wasn't going in before the stab wounds and head traumas. You know that."

"We also know how quickly a peds emergency can turn fatal."

"And she wasn't presenting as an emergency." Kim grabbed her arm. "Listen to me."

She shook her head, pulling away, not wanting to hear it. "I can't. I need to be in there." She reached in for a pair of gloves, swore when she realized the box was empty, pulled a fresh container from below, and gloved up. She walked toward the operating suite, stopping short as two nurses came out, their surgical aprons covered in blood. "What are you doing?"

"She's gone. She bled out," Maggie said as she peeled off her saturated clothing, dropping it in the biohazard bin.

Reagan leaned against the wall, shuddering out a breath. "She's gone?"

"Ruptured spleen. Massive hemorrhage. She was loosing blood faster than we could pump it in." Maggie sniffled, wiping at her cheeks. "I hate losing kids. It breaks my heart."

Reagan walked into the OR, staring at the debris and crimson footprints among the puddles of blood littering the floor, swallowing over the ball in her throat as she glanced at the sheet draping the small body. Mable was dead. She'd missed the signs of internal bleeding, and now Mrs. Totton's little girl was dead. She moved to the child's side and eased the cover down, stroking gloved fingers over a pale cheek as tears trailed down her own. "I'm so sorry, sweetie. I'm so sorry I let you down." She settled the drape in place and turned, walking into the hall, pulling off her gloves and hair cover on her way back to the ER.

"Where's Mable?"

Her gaze whipped up to meet Mable's mother farther down the corridor. "Mrs. Totton—"

Mrs. Totton ran forward, gripping Reagan's arms. "Where's Mable?"

She took a deep breath, fighting to keep her emotions in check. How could she tell this woman she'd lost everything? "Mrs. Totton—"

"No." She shook her head adamantly.

Her eyes filled. "Mrs. Totton—"

"Nooooo," she said on a keening wail. "You said she was fine. You said she was okay."

"Mable had an acute rupture—"

"Mable!" Mrs. Totton screamed, collapsing to the floor. "Mable!"

Reagan crouched down at her side. "Mrs. Totton—"

"Get away from me! You said you would take care of her! I trusted you with my baby!"

Two orderlies hurried over, helping up the distraught woman as Doctor Viner came to assist.

"You killed Mable!"

"Let's get her out of here," Doctor V. said. They took Mrs. Totton away, and Reagan turned, crashing into Kim, well aware that Mable's mother was right.

"Here." Kim handed over Reagan's bag. "You did everything you could. We all did."

"I should've insisted on radiology sooner."

"She was in line like the half-dozen other patients waiting."

"I didn't know. I should have."

"Reagan—"

"Her abdomen was soft to the touch." She shook her head, still trying to figure out how she could have been so wrong. "There was no distention or pain, just the bruising."

"Take your bag and go home. Get some sleep and go on your vacation." Kim guided her to the door.

She stopped. "How many ruptured spleens do we deal with? Hundreds? I should've *known*, Kim."

"Go." Kim hugged her and gave her a shove into the bright, sunny morning. "Call me later. I'll see you in a week."

Drowning in a wave of despair, she walked away from the ER she'd practiced in for the last two years more than certain she would never be able to walk back in.

CHAPTER TWO

THE FRAY BLASTED THROUGH THE SPEAKERS OF THE SUV Shane had taken off of Tyson's hands when he officially took over as Head of Security for The Appalachia Project almost two hours ago. He glanced out the driver's side window of the Mitsubishi Pajero as he cruised along the twists and turns of Route Eleven, paying more attention to the scenery than usual. The trees were abundant in varying shades of green, the sky as blue and bright as California's, but it was the lack of civilization and drastic change in the condition of the occasional houses that kept him tuned in. Gone were the large, prettier homes he remembered closer to Lexington. Gone too were shops and restaurants of any sort.

"In three miles, arrive at destination on right," the GPS said.

He looked at the small screen on the dashboard, noting that the next three miles didn't appear to offer anything more than the last hundred had. Muttering a swear, he turned up his music, still trying to shake off the frustration of being there in the first place. He loved his job. He considered himself a team player through and through, but spending three months guarding a pill safe in this godforsaken place when there was so much going on in LA rubbed him the wrong way.

He'd been hoping to snag the month-long assignment in Dubai with the crew filming the new action movie and maybe get his hands on a couple of late-summer premieres, but that wasn't how things had shaken down. Unfortunately, Ethan wanted him in Appalachia.

He zipped around another curve, slowing when he realized he was well over the speed limit, and eased off the gas farther when the sign for Black Bear Gap, population two hundred and twelve, appeared around the next turn. "Good Christ," he said under his breath as he glanced around at houses and buildings long ago boarded up and more than a dozen structures too far gone to repair. He cruised by a one-pump gas station and small grocer that apparently served as the US Post Office and bank as well.

Driving on, he passed a dirt road, then a second and third, knowing his turn was around here somewhere. "Come on, Jill. Don't leave me hanging. What've you got for me?" he said to the GPS, waiting for instructions, but "Jill" stayed stubbornly quiet. "You're speechless too, huh?"

Shaking his head, he flipped a u-turn and pulled into the gas station, stopping by the group of men standing around with cigarettes dangling from their lips, holding cans of soda. He turned off his music and rolled down the window, breathing in a cloud of smoke. "Excuse me. I was wondering if one of you gentlemen could point me toward the clinic."

Six sets of guarded eyes shaded by grimy caps looked him over. "You one of those sons a bitchin' Feds?"

He'd been warned about the local's hostility toward the Appalachia Project and anyone affiliated with it. "Ah, no."

"That sure looks like the vehicle that other fella drives around in, and he's a Fed."

He could only assume the "fella" in question was Tyson. "I don't know what to tell you. I just got off a plane in Lexington. I'm trying to find the clinic."

"I never heard of no clinic," another man said, his mouth full of rotting teeth.

"No clinic around here," another chimed in.

Clearly he wasn't going to get anywhere here. "Got it. Second turn on the right. Thanks, guys." He flipped the Pajero around and accelerated on the empty town road, keeping his window down instead of rolling it back up, forgoing the chill of the air conditioning for the fresh air and heavy scent of pine.

Taking a chance, he took the second right and started up. One mile turned into three, then four as he bumped along the poorly maintained road, following the turns to nowhere. He slowed to a near stop when he caught sight of a little boy and girl running around the corner of a derelict trailer. He swore, taken aback by the chickens roaming about the piles of trash that surrounded the questionable foundation. "Son of a bitch," he said again. Someone lived in there. He'd read the reports and studied the maps and pictures of the area where he would be spending the next twelve weeks, but seeing the conditions in person was surreal. This was poverty at its worst.

Easing off the brake, he continued on, spotting another house and yet another in no better shape than the first. Finally he saw the *Black Bear Gap Clinic* sign and the accompanying log cabin tucked back in the trees. He pulled ahead, studying the pretty structure out of place among the ruins of a once-thriving coal town. To the left of the cabin, he glimpsed a smaller metal building that was more of an oversized shed.

CATE BEAUMAN

Here he was: home sweet home.

Sighing, he parked between a sporty red convertible and another SUV identical to the one he drove. He snatched the keys from the ignition and moved to open the door, pausing when he heard the voices heading his way.

"Please don't leave," the pretty woman in raspberry-colored shorts and a white tank top said as she hurried around the corner of the metal building. "You can't just *go*."

"Oh, yes I can." The blond dressed in snug jeans and a silk shirt picked up her pace as she made her way to the convertible. "I didn't sign up for this."

"Yes you did."

"Forget it." The blond slammed the door and backed out, spewing dirt in her wake as she raced away.

The woman in the shorts closed her blue eyes, pressing a hand to her forehead.

Shane got out. "Rough day?"

She opened her eyes. "You could say that."

He took the four steps separating them and extended his hand. "I'm Shane."

"Reagan." She returned his shake. "You aren't by some chance a miracle replacement nurse the director forgot to tell me about?" She bit her full bottom lip, smiling her hope.

He grinned. "Nah, I'm taking over for Tyson."

"Yeah, I kind of thought so." She blew out a deep puff of air, rustling stray pieces of shiny brown hair falling from the messy pile on top of her head. "I imagine I can't interest you in a crash course in nursing?"

He sucked in a breath through his teeth as he shook his head. "I'm not sure medicine's my thing."

"Yeah," she said again with another small smile.

"I take it you're the Doc."

"Mm, that's me."

She wasn't just pretty—she was gorgeous with her small, slightly tip-tilted nose, straight white teeth, flawless skin, and friendly eyes set in a spectacular face.

"And I take it that was your nurse?" He gestured to the tire tracks.

"For about ten minutes. I guess rural living isn't for everyone."

He glanced around at the trees surrounding them, listening for *any* familiar sounds of civilization. "I think we can safely call this the absolute middle of nowhere."

She smiled fully. "It's a little disconcerting."

"I'm still waiting for the shock to wear off."

She chuckled, looking over her shoulder toward the clinic. "I hate to be rude, but I should probably get back to work."

"Heavy patient load?"

She shook her head. "Not quite."

He recognized what could only be disappointment in her voice.

"The cabin's unlocked. There are plenty of bedrooms to choose from—three others besides mine. See you later." She turned away.

"See ya." He stared after Reagan, sliding his gaze over her firm calves and thighs and excellent butt as she walked off, then pulled his luggage from the back, making his way into the cozy cabin with surprisingly more creature comforts than he'd expected—TV and an Xbox nestled in the entertainment center, a nice kitchen with plenty of fruit in the bowl on the countertop, glossy hardwood floors and pretty rugs. He pushed his sunglasses on top of his head as he noticed the stairs, set down his stuff, and took the steps in twos, nodding his approval at the bookshelves, plush furnishings, and technology area in the loft. He paused by the grouping of windows, studying the decent-sized pond a good hundred yards away, then went back downstairs. He grabbed his luggage before he moved down the hall, taking in the weights and treadmill in the miniature gym, then stuck his head into the area beyond, spotting the small hot tub in a greenhouse-like space. "Nice." He continued on, glancing into vacant bedrooms until he came to the room with several suitcases in it that had yet to be unpacked. Doc's room.

He peeked into the empty space directly across from hers, deciding immediately that this would be his. He set down his bags for the second time, eager to head over to the clinic. He and Reagan had just met, but she was certainly intriguing. What in the hell was a woman who looked like her doing in a place like this? Luckily he had the next several weeks to find out. For the first time since Ethan issued him his new assignment, he actually felt a small stirring of excitement.

~~~~

Reagan smoothed the last of the life-sized sea turtle decals in place and stepped down from the ladder, examining her work. She nodded her approval as she studied smiling jellyfish, dolphins, and schools of brightly colored fish decorating the walls she'd painted a pale blue. The stickers complemented the grinning orca whale examination table in her pediatric room well.

In the two days she'd been in The Gap she'd slept little, spending all but a handful of hours cleaning and slapping color on the walls, organizing, and taking supplies from unopened boxes no one had bothered with in the two years the clinic had been open to the community. Moments after she'd unlocked the door to her new office, it had quickly become apparent that not a single patient had been seen in the twenty-four months the facility had been operational.

She buried another wave of useless anger as she sent a blade through the last box and transferred the small paper gowns to the drawer beneath the exam table. One room down, two to go.

Moving to the next disheveled space, which she'd painted a muted shade of mauve, she got back to her inventory, placing a handful of speculums in a drawer along with the swabs she would need for pap smears. She paused as the newly familiar doubts plaguing her stopped her in her tracks. She picked up the speculum again, turning the instrument encased within the plastic, knowing she would eventually have to use this common tool of her trade. She'd given hundreds of pelvic exams as a resident, then as a board certified physician, but she hadn't touched a patient in the seven weeks since she walked out of the ER.

Her life had come to a standstill, her vacation to the mountains of New Hampshire forgotten while she dealt with a team of lawyers, barely avoiding a malpractice lawsuit. Then she'd done her best to endure the grueling three-week investigation into Mable Totton's death, the final ruling a tragic act of fate—a splenic rupture due to the trauma of the car accident and an already enlarged spleen caused by an undiagnosed case of mononucleosis. In the eyes of her colleagues, Mable's demise was a result of unfortunate circumstances, but she had yet to forgive herself for missing an opportunity to save the seven-year-old's life.

I can't do this anymore. I can't practice medicine.

Take some time, but eventually you'll have to take a leap and jump back in. We've all lost someone, Reagan.

We've all questioned ourselves. The best way to honor that little girl is to get back to doing what you're so damn good at.

She sighed, remembering the words Doctor Viner had used as they sipped coffee after her Medical Board hearing. She'd taken Dr. V's advice, giving herself the time she needed. Now she was jumping back in, hoping to help the people here in The Gap.

"Knock, knock."

She turned, staring into the most boldly green eyes she'd ever seen. The new security guard or bodyguard or whatever the heck he was had been nice to look at with his sunglasses on. Now he was downright delicious—sun-streaked brown hair accentuating the hints of five o' clock shadow along his strong jawline, firm lips, and a killer physique molded like glory in blue jeans and a snug top, adding to his undeniable masculinity, making him ridiculously drool-worthy. "Hi."

"Hey. Nice digs we've got." He gestured toward the cabin.

"It's pretty great. I guess if you're going to ask people to spend several months in a place with no amenities they have to provide something." She put the speculum back and slid the drawer closed.

"It looks like you're busy."

"A little." She swiped at a strand of hair tickling her cheek.

"When you have a minute I'm hoping I can get a quick tour. I'm trying to get a lay of the land so we can figure out how we want to do things."

She frowned. "Do what exactly?"

He stepped farther into the room and leaned against the doorframe, showing off his broad shoulders and bulging biceps beneath the short sleeves of his white tee as he crossed his arms. "I figured you and Tyson had a chance to talk."

"I've been in here pretty much since I arrived Monday. I'm afraid we didn't see much of each other, which reminds me—I forgot to tell you about the order sheet on the kitchen counter. We have to submit our food and supply list to some company in Lexington by tonight. I guess someone brings the stuff down bi-weekly."

"I'll take a look."

She nodded. "So what exactly is it that you and I need to figure out?"

"We'll, you've got a shit-ton of pills locked up in a safe somewhere around here that a lot of folks would love to get their hands on."

"I'm aware of the drug problems here in the area."

"My job is to keep the pharmaceuticals where they belong."

"Okay, but I can't have you compromising my patients' privacy by randomly popping your head in at inconvenient times."

He raised his brow as he glanced around the messy space.

"When I have patients, which I will." And the idea terrified her.

"We're going to have to come up with something."

For forty-eight hours straight she'd been distracted with the chores of preparing her new place. Shane was forcing her to think beyond that, and she wasn't ready. "I need—I'm taking a break." She brushed passed him and stepped outside, sitting on the step in the slowly fading sunlight.

Moments later Shane stood behind her. "Look, Doc, I'm not sure what I just said to get under your skin, but we're going to have to work together here.

Part of my job—the majority of my job—is to waste the next three months of my life guarding a safe full of painkillers."

She looked up, meeting his gaze, trying not to be disappointed in a man she didn't even know. "You don't want to be here."

He shrugged. "I am, so I'll make the best of it."

They both looked toward the road as a branch snapped. Raising her hand, Reagan waved to the man walking by, as she did everyday. He never waved back.

"Friendly folks."

She looked up again. "They don't know me or trust me." But they would eventually. "The 'doctor' who was here before me didn't do his job. It doesn't sound like anyone did. That'll make doing mine harder. If you don't want to be here you should go too."

"Unfortunately that's not an option. I'm not losing my job because I walked away from an obligatory stint in the woods."

She shook her head and let out an exasperated laugh. "No wonder this entire program has been a joke. If everyone's attitude has been as poor as yours, I can't blame the people for staying away." She stood. "I don't want you in my clinic during hours of operation. My goal is to help this community, not drive the families further away. You can come in and count your pills or do whatever you have to when I've left for the night." She closed herself inside and flipped the lock in place, determined to get back to work and make a difference.

CHAPTER THREE

SHANE DUG DEEP, PUFFING HIS WAY THROUGH THE LAST hill on his ten-mile trek on the treadmill. He'd slept like shit, tossing and turning for most of the night. Instead of lying in bed staring at the ceiling, he'd thrown back the covers, pulled on his socks and shoes, and started his workout before the crack of dawn. His arms and pecs still ached from the grueling reps he'd paced himself through, but the mild discomfort of one too many sets was better than focusing on his behavior yesterday.

He winced, remembering Reagan's exasperated words and disapproving eyes as she thoroughly shamed him before locking him out of the clinic. Puffing out another breath, he slowed his pace to a jog, waiting to catch her before she disappeared for the day. He definitely owed her an apology. Reagan had called him out on his shitty attitude, and now he would be forced to eat a little crow. Western Kentucky was his home for the foreseeable future. It was time to stop being a whiny ass and get the hell over it.

He powered off the treadmill as Reagan walked by wearing brown-cuffed cargo capris, white Keds, and a simple fitted white t-shirt. She'd pushed back her hair with a headband, leaving her knockout face unframed. "Doc." Grabbing his towel, he started toward the kitchen, wiping his drenched chest and stomach as he moved her way. "Hey, good morning."

She glanced up as she filled her glass at the sink.

"Good morning." Shutting off the faucet, she picked up her carton of Greek yogurt.

"I made dinner last night, but you never came in. You were out pretty late." He'd waited for her until well after eleven.

"Yeah, I have a lot to do." She started toward the door, grabbing the stack of papers on the table. "Still do. I'm heading over to the mine."

"If you wait a few minutes I'd be happy to come with you." He wiped at the sweat trailing down his forehead.

"I'm all set."

He settled the towel on his shoulder, reading her cues to piss off easily enough. "I guess I'll see you later then."

"Yeah. Bye." She closed the door behind her.

Scratching at his damp hair, he steamed out a breath. "That went well." He rubbed his jaw, listening to the SUV start and drive away. Doc was still frosty, and he couldn't blame her. The Appalachia Project had fallen to shit. The lack of oversight was glaringly obvious. In little more than two years, the small school in town had closed almost before it opened, the dentistry office had been scaled back to a once-a-month walk-in clinic. The only program that was still fully operational, yet dysfunctional, was Doc's place. Clearly she had a big heart and passion for the project's mission. If Reagan was going to go full-throttle, he was going to help...after he showered.

~~~~

Reagan rolled into the last quarter mile of her eight-mile trek, following the directions to the main offices of Corpus Mining Company—at least, she hoped she was following them. During her fifteen-minute drive she'd realized street signs were few and far between the farther she traveled off the beaten path.

Nibbling her lip, she guessed, taking the first available left, and made her way along the bumpy dirt road, smiling her satisfaction when the mining facility came into view. She slowed, studying metal buildings and several tall, sloping structures scattered around the land, realizing they were conveyer belts as she watched the huge machines spew black chunks onto mountain-sized piles of coal.

Returning her attention to her objective, she pulled into a spot next to a white Toyota Tundra and got out, grabbing her stack of flyers. She paused, listening to the warning beeps of trucks backing up and the rattling of the long belts carrying coal to the top. Turning, she moved to what appeared to be the office and stepped in, smiling at the fifty-something receptionist typing on a computer, her nameplate identifying her as Josephine. "Good morning."

Josephine returned her smile. "Mornin', honey."

"I was wondering if Phil McPhee might be available."

"I think he might have a few minutes. Can I tell him your name?"

"Yes. I'm Reagan Rosner, the new physician with the Black Bear Gap Clinic."

The warmth in Josephine's smile dimmed several notches. "Just a minute please." The heavyset woman stood and walked off, giving a quick rap on the door behind her desk, and stepped in. Moments later she reappeared with a thin, balding man dressed in a pale-blue button-down and jeans.

"Can I help you, ma'am?"

Reagan stepped forward, trying another smile. "Mr.

McPhee, I'm Reagan Rosner." She outstretched her hand. "I'm the new doctor at the Black Bear Gap Clinic."

He returned her shake. "What can I do for you, doctor?"

"Well, I know your company employs several members of the Black Bear Gap community. I wanted to come out and introduce myself and pass along these flyers." She handed over the stack she'd made. "I'm hoping we'll be able to work together to help the folks here in The Gap improve their health."

"Ms. Rosner, I'm sure I don't have to be tellin' you people 'round here aren't much for outsiders."

"Yes, I understand. That's why I was hoping—"

"I imagine I should also be tellin' you we here at Corpus Minin' have our own doctor who comes to check up on our men every few months or so."

"Yes—"

"We're a dyin' breed, Ms. Rosner. Kentucky minin's not as strong as it once was. Our company's small— doesn't pay near as much as many of the others—but we take care of our own. We're doin' our best to keep operational for as long as we can."

"That's wonderful. I came today hoping you might be able to help me extend an invitation to your employee's families and let them know I would love to help them manage their health. If your miners need anything in between visits from your own physician—"

"Like I said, we take care of our own." He handed back the papers.

"Yes, but preventative care is—"

"Good day to you. I'm sure you know how to see yourself out."

She wanted to make him realize how important regular medical care was, but nodded instead, knowing that pushing the issue wasn't the right approach. "Yes. Thank you." She opened the door, walking out into a cloud of smoke as three men stood around puffing on cigarettes. She barely stifled a groan of frustration as she took her seat behind the wheel and turned over the ignition, catching sight of Mr. McPhee watching her from the window as she reversed and made her way back toward the clinic.

"He wouldn't even *listen*," she steamed, huffing out a breath. She wasn't foolish enough to think she could change people's minds overnight. Never did she have illusions that the community would flock to her practice right away, but she'd hoped for support from The Gap's biggest employer. Maybe she was an outsider affiliated with a project most of the folks around here didn't trust, but the least Mr. McPhee could have done was give her a chance. She was reaching out, wasn't she? She was nothing like the others who'd headed the program before her—or the man still here.

She turned on the dirt road that would take her back to the cabin, narrowing her eyes as she thought of Shane. It was people like *him* that were making it extremely difficult for her to do her job. She took the last curve to her new home and pulled into her spot next to the other government-issued SUV, got out, and went into the clinic, adjusting the thermostat by a few degrees. Today was going to be *hot*.

She glanced out the window into the bright sunshine, thinking of the small card table she remembered seeing in the storage area. Perhaps setting up a clean water station outside for anyone walking by might not be a bad idea. She set down her stack of flyers, scribbled the latest to-do on her long list, and moved to the last room in need of organizing. She'd gotten a large majority accomplished yesterday evening, working off most of her anger by the time she called it quits sometime after midnight. Shane had pissed her off with his crappy attitude, but he'd also renewed her sense of purpose.

After her nurse tucked tail and left, she'd worried that this whole situation was too much for her to take on alone. Then Shane reminded her that she was the only person the people here could count on, and she'd continued unloading supplies instead of packing her bags, promising herself that she *would* make a difference.

Perhaps she didn't have the staff she needed to assist her, and maybe her confidence was still shaken, but she firmly believed that being in Black Bear Gap was right. Trauma rooms and fast-paced medicine were no longer for her, but *this* was...hopefully. She shook away her doubt as the front door opened.

Shane stepped in wearing carpenter shorts, a blue t-shirt, and flip-flops, the dark color of his shirt masking the magnificence of his spectacular body. He'd looked distractingly amazing standing in the kitchen with trails of sweat dripping down his cut chest and abs. And she hadn't realized he had a tattoo—a sexy crisscross pattern encircling a solid inch of his upper right bicep. "I thought we agreed you wouldn't come in here during office hours."

"I brought you breakfast." He held up a jumbo muffin on a napkin.

"Thanks, but I already ate." She walked into the last of the messy rooms—this one she'd painted a soothing green—hoping Shane would get the hint that she didn't want him around. They lived in the same house, but that was the end of their common ground.

"I think we got off on the wrong foot yesterday." He followed her. "I was an ass."

She dumped cotton balls into the glass jar on the table. "Okay. Thanks."

"Doc." He took her arm, halting her movements as he fought his way around a box, moving closer to her side. "I'm sorry."

She dismissed the tingle of heat where his hand still rested. "I appreciate your apology."

"But you don't accept it."

His gorgeous green eyes held hers as she breathed in his soap. "I think we both have jobs to do and should get to them." She gestured to the stacks of supplies she had yet to put away. "I need to finish this room so I can start hiking tomorrow."

He frowned. "Hiking? Where?"

"Into the hills. I want to introduce myself to the families." If Mr. McPhee wouldn't help her, she'd make things happen herself.

He shook his head. "That doesn't sound like a good idea."

She pulled free of his grip. "There are at least fifty members of the community living in these mountains. Most don't have access to running water and indoor plumbing, let alone cars, which means they aren't receiving regular preventive care."

"Are you going armed?"

"No. I don't think carrying a weapon will send the right message. 'I'll shoot you, then heal you' isn't exactly the tone I'm going for."

"More than one of my team members has been shot at."

She grabbed a package of depressors, dumping them into the next glass container. "I'll wear bright clothes."

"It has nothing to do with hunting and everything to do with the fact that they don't want you here."

"But I am here." She picked up the otoscope, checking the light against her palm, and put it back. "I need to show them that I'm here to help."

"I'll come with you."

She shook her head. "That's definitely not happening."

"Reagan—"

"Shane—"

"I'm in charge of your safety, and I'm telling you this doesn't sound like a good idea."

"No, you're in charge of keeping the drugs out of the wrong hands."

"As head of security, I'm also responsible for everyone on this property. That would include you."

"So far I've avoided any local hostility." She thought of Mr. McPhee's chilly response, dismissing his rude behavior as slightly understandable. "Besides, you've made your thoughts on this project very clear. But more importantly, I can't have non-medical personnel compromising confidentiality," she added for good measure.

He picked up a blood-pressure cuff. "My entire career revolves around confidentiality."

She took the cuff from him, setting it in the basket on the wall. "That may be, but you're not medical personnel."

"So add me to your staff. Teach me how to help you."

She narrowed her eyes, trying to figure his angle. "Why would I do that?"

"You need the help, and I don't have a whole hell of a lot to do."

"I appreciate your offer, but I e-mailed the director of The Project last night. He said he'll send someone out as soon as he can." Which could be weeks or longer.

"It's hard for me to put my money where my mouth is if you won't give me a chance." He leaned his butt against the edge of the examination table and crossed his arms at his chest. "I was a jerk yesterday; I fully admit it. I'm not crazy about being here, but I am, so let me do something worthwhile while I am."

It was hard to argue with the unwavering determination in his eyes. Wasn't she frustrated with Mr. McPhee because he'd written her off before he'd given her the opportunity to try? "Okay. Fine. I can use you in an unofficial medical assistant capacity for the time being."

"All right. I'm not exactly sure what that encompasses, but sign me up."

She nodded. "You can help me clean up this mess and familiarize yourself with where we'll be keeping equipment, but before that I'll need to be confident I can count on you to handle the clerical side of medicine as well as clinical."

"Like?"

"Recording vitals—height, weight, blood pressure, basal temperature, and pulse."

"Show me what to do and I'll do it."

"Come with me." She flipped on the switch in the mauve room she would use primarily for her female patients. "Go ahead and hop up on the table."

He stuffed his hands in his pockets, rocking back on his heels. "I like playing doctor as much as the next guy, but in the interest of full disclosure, I should probably tell you I had a complete examination last month."

She smiled, trying not to be charmed by his easy humor. "Just get on the table."

"You're the boss." He hopped up.

"I'm assuming you know how to weigh someone."

He nodded. "I think I can handle it."

"I think so too. What about height?"

"I'm guessing you're right around five-five."

"Good guess."

"Thanks."

"I'd say you're six foot."

"Correct," he said with a nod of approval.

"But this isn't a carnival game. Do you know how to use the height rod on the scale?"

"I bet I can figure it out."

The height rod certainly wasn't rocket science. "Fine. We'll move on and start with taking an oral temperature."

"I can handle that as well."

"I want to be sure."

He shrugged.

"Luckily we have this great little machine that will take care of almost everything for you." She rolled over the portable vital signs monitor. "You're going to hit this button three times." She pressed the white button. "Then you'll take the temperature probe from the probe well and make sure the machine is showing the code for oral temperature instead of axillary before proceeding."

"ORL" flashed on the small screen.

"Put on a probe cover by sliding this into the box." She demonstrated, fitting a thin plastic barrier over the shiny piece. "Open up."

Shane did as he was asked.

"You'll place this under the tongue in the sublingual pocket and wait for the reading." The machine beeped, and she glanced at the readout. "Ninety-eight point seven."

"That's easy enough."

"You feel comfortable with this procedure?"

He raised his eyebrow. "Yeah."

"Good. Babies will need a rectal reading, which I'll take care of."

"I'll let you."

She smiled, taking his wrist, settling his arm on his thigh, determined to keep her focus on the clinical aspects of her job instead of how good he smelled. "We'll move on to taking a radial pulse."

"I've taken a pulse before."

"Humor me and listen to my instructions anyway." She batted her eyelashes.

He grinned. "Like I said, you're the boss."

She looked down, realizing his smiles didn't leave her unaffected. Clearing her throat, she continued. "For a radial pulse, we're going to use the radial artery, which is located on the thumb-side of your wrist." She settled her index and middle finger against the strong beat beneath his skin. "Count for thirty seconds using the second hand on the clock and multiply by two."

"Will I be able to use a calculator?"

She grinned, shaking her head. "That's not funny."

"I'm pretty sure you're smiling."

Her smile widened. "I shouldn't be. This is serious."

He nodded solemnly. "Vitals are important business."

"Agreed." She turned away, busying herself with writing his numbers down even though it wasn't necessary. She'd sworn herself to an official "man hiatus" after her breakup with Derek, but Shane had the potential to be trouble. She faced him again, finding comfort in the fact that he was her colleague. Never again would she make the mistake of dating someone she worked with. "Um, why don't you show me what you know and we'll move on to blood pressure."

"You got it." He got down.

She took his place on the examination table.

"Let's get a temp on you, Doc." He pushed the button she'd shown him three times, popped the temperature probe into a clean sheath, and slid the instrument under her tongue.

She swallowed in the humming silence, staring into his eyes.

The machine beeped, and he looked at the readout. "Ninety-eight point one."

"Like a pro," she said when he removed the thermometer from her mouth.

"I'm learning from the best." He moved the portable unit out of the way. "Now for your pulse." He took her wrist, resting her forearm on her thigh, then settled his warm fingers against her skin as he looked at the clock. "Sixty-three."

"Great. I—"

He stepped closer, grazing her carotid artery with the rough pads of his fingers as they stared at one another. "I figure I should practice—incase I can't find the pulse in the patient's wrist."

Holy crap, he was beautiful, and charming, and sneaky—definitely a problem. "You, um, you did fine."

"It pays to be thorough."

She swallowed before his eyes left hers to look at the clock.

He frowned. "Hmm."

"What?"

"Much faster." His gaze locked on hers again. "Eighty-four. That's a pretty significant jump. You might want to get that checked out."

Her pulse had been fine before he started touching her. She pulled his hand away. "I'm fine. I just—"

The front door burst open. "Help."

Reagan rushed off the bed and hurried into the waiting area, looking at the woman in ripped jeans and a baggy t-shirt holding a crying little girl in her arms as the child pressed a bloody cloth to the side of her face.

"My daughter's bleedin' real bad."

"Okay." Reagan guided the woman into the pediatric room. "What's your daughter's name?"

"Sue Anne."

"I'm going to have you lay Sue Anne down here on the table and keep the shirt pressed to the wound."

"Okay."

"Can you tell me what happened?"

"She's sayin' she fell on a rock outside the house. Her forehead's cut up somethin' fierce."

"I'm going to take good care of Sue Anne," she reassured, pausing with a jolt as she remembered similar promises she'd made to Mable's mother. Her heart accelerated as images of curly black hair and peaches-and-cream skin turning pale flashed through her mind. "I just need—" she cleared her throat. "I need some gloves." She turned, closing her eyes, doing her best to put away the past. Mable was gone, but Sue Anne needed her now.

"Hey." Shane came up next to her, bumping her arm. "Are you all right?" he murmured.

"Uh, yes." She swallowed, nodding, tensing her body against the need to shake. "Gloves." She yanked a pair from the box. "If you could glove up as well, I may need a hand."

"Sure."

She walked over to the table, steeling herself with a deep breath. "Sue Anne, I'm going to take a look at your forehead, but first I need to ask you a couple of questions."

"Okay." She wiped at her tears.

"Can you tell me how old you are?"

"Seven."

The same age as Mable. "What's your favorite color?"

"Purple."

"Do you feel dizzy?"

She shook her head.

"Do you feel sick to your stomach?"

Sue Anne shook her head again.

"Did she lose consciousness?" Reagan asked Sue Anne's mother.

"No ma'am, but she sure screamed bloody murder."

"That's actually a good thing." She grabbed the otoscope, shining the bright light in Sue Anne's big brown eyes, satisfied with the normal pupil response. "Sue Anne, I'm ready to see if I can help you feel better."

"I don't want ya to."

"I'm not going to touch, just look."

"No." She turned away, heaving out deep breaths. "It hurts."

"Hush now, Sue Anne," the worried mother scolded, patting the girl's leg. "Let the doctor have a look."

Shane crouched down to Sue Anne's level. "You know, this whale table's pretty cool."

Sue Anne studied Shane.

"Doctor Reagan's really gentle. She just gave me a once-over and it didn't hurt at all."

"Jasper Winslow says the Feds is the devil in disguise."

"Sue Anne," her mother hissed.

"That's okay," Reagan reassured. This was the perfect opportunity to show Sue Anne and her mother that Jasper Winslow was wrong. "Sue Anne, I'm going to pull the shirt away from your head. I'll be very careful." She forced her gloves onto her clammy hands and pulled the soiled shirt away from the little girl's head, staring at the blood oozing from the inch-long gash.

You said she was fine. You said she was okay. You killed my baby.

She clenched her jaw, pushing the memories away, concentrating on the ugly wound.

"Can you fix her, Doctor?"

"Definitely. There's a little bruising, so I'm going to press around the laceration and make sure we aren't dealing with anything more than a cut." She pushed gently, making certain there was no movement within the skull.

Sue Anne sucked in a deep breath. "It hurts. It hurts, Mommy."

"I'm sorry, sweetie," Reagan gave the girl an apologetic smile. She felt once more, certain that the bump was benign, and stepped back. "I won't do that anymore."

"I'll tell you what, Sue Anne's a trouper," Shane said, earning a cautious smile from the little girl.

"She's doing great," Reagan agreed. "I'm going to be finished in just a couple more minutes." She tore open an antiseptic packet, wiping away drying blood and dirt that had trailed into Sue Anne's hairline and down along her brow. "How's that?"

"Okay, I guess."

"If I do anything that hurts you tell me."

The child nodded.

She rolled a towel and grabbed a plastic basin. "Sue Anne, I'm going to have you rest your head on this towel just like you would on your pillow at home."

The girl followed her instructions.

"Can you roll to your side for just a minute?"

Sue Ann did as she was asked.

"Great job." Reagan filled a large syringe with saline solution.

Sue Anne's eye grew saucer wide. "What're ya gonna do with that?"

"I'm going to give your cut a bath so we can make sure we get all of the little rocks and germs out of it. I'm not going to poke you with the needle. I promise." She turned her attention to Shane. "Can you hold the basin right here so we can catch all of the water?"

"Sure."

Reagan sprayed the saltwater in a steady stream, removing any remaining gravel embedded in the laceration, making sure to be thorough as Sue Anne blew out several whimpering breaths. "There we go. All cleaned up."

"See? She's pretty gentle." Shane gave Sue Anne a playful poke to the shoulder.

The girl nodded.

"You can lay on your back again, Sue Anne." She dabbed at the wound, drying it. "One more step, but it's a weird one."

"Weird?"

"Very. Sometimes doctors have to sew a cut back together, but I'm going to use glue."

"*Glue?*" Sue Anne's mother asked.

"Yes, it's a special type of adhesive that will allow Sue Anne's wound to heal without much fuss at all. You won't have to come back in the way you would if we used traditional stitches. Glue stitches are great because the barrier keeps infection away."

"I never heard of such a thing."

"It's really pretty amazing." She took the small vile

of purple liquid from the table and squeezed. "All right, are you ready?"

Sue Anne Shook her head.

"You can hold my hand." Shane held his up, and the little girl snatched it. "If you feel scared, even a little, you can squeeze."

"I'm feelin' *real* scared."

"Go ahead and squeeze. Closing your eyes helps too." He slammed his shut, and Sue Anne did the same, peaking from one eye, giggling when Shane did the same.

Reagan smiled. Shane was turning out to be a lifesaver. "I'm going to start. This will be super quick," she said as she gently pushed the skin back together and applied a thin coat of the liquid.

Sue Anne bit down on her lip. "It's warm."

"Squeeze my hand tighter," Shane encouraged.

"I'm almost finished." She applied the next coat. "All right. That's it."

Sue Anne cautiously blinked open her eyes. "I'm all better?"

Reagan smiled. "You're all better." She held out a mirror for the little girl. "What do you think?"

"It's kinda strange...and kinda neat."

"Definitely neat," Shane moved in for a closer inspection. "If I ever need stitches I'm having those."

Sue Anne beamed, looking in the mirror again.

Reagan turned her attention to Sue Anne's mother. "You'll want to keep the wound as dry as possible."

"For how long?"

"Seven days."

"How'm I gonna get her a bath?"

"She can bathe and have her hair washed but the site should stay completely dry until tomorrow right around this time. After that, the adhesive can get wet—

just not soaked—and you won't want to scrub at it."

"I guess that ain't so bad. The things they been sayin' about this place ain't true. Rumor was there's a new doctor."

"That's me."

"I'm thankful for what you done. She was bleedin' a lot more than my home remedy was good for."

Reagan nodded. "Head wounds tend to be pretty messy. I'm going to send you home with some Tylenol. Sue Anne can have a teaspoon every four to six hours if she's complaining of any discomfort. If you notice any reddening, swelling, or pus, I'll want you to come back. Those are all signs of infection." Reagan moved to the closet, taking the trial-sized box of acetaminophen from the shelf. "If Sue Anne starts feeling super sleepy, develops a headache, or you notice her acting different than usual, you should come back too. I'm not particularly worried about a concussion, but sometimes symptoms don't show up right away."

"I don't have no money on me to pay."

"That's okay."

"I'll need to bring you somethin'."

She recognized pride and nodded. "I'd like to check on Sue Anne tomorrow to make sure her wound is healing well."

"I can't be walkin' all the way back down here."

"Would you feel comfortable if I came to you?"

Sue Anne's mother sighed, hesitating. "I guess that would be all right. We don't have nothin' as fancy as this."

"I'm not worried about fancy. My only concern is making sure Sue Anne is healthy." She reached for a baggie of various goodies. "Does Sue Anne have brothers and sisters?"

"Yes. There be four boys and two girls all together."

"I have these if you'd like to take them—they have toothbrushes, toothpaste, a comb, and a few stickers."

Sue Anne beamed. "Can I, Mommy?"

"I imagine so."

Reagan handed off six cheerful baggies she'd stuffed late last night. "So, I'll come see you tomorrow."

"We live about a mile up Redman's Pass."

"I'll find you."

"I'll be thankin' you again, Doctor Reagan. I'll be tellin' people you've got a fine Christian spirit."

"Thank you."

The mother and daughter left and she closed the door behind them, leaning her weight against the window frame as she watched them walk down the road. Sue Anne was one of the lucky ones. She would be back to playing in no time, but even as the girl skipped along the dirt path, Reagan ran through the procedures she'd followed for a simple head wound, afraid she'd overlooked an important step. She gripped the doorknob, her heart thundering, debating whether she should call Sue Anne and her mother back to reexamine the laceration. The wound site had been clean and the frontal bone free of movement, but there was always the chance she'd missed something bigger, something that could cost the happy child her life. She twisted the knob as worry ate at her.

"Congratulations, Doc." Shane pushed a gentle fist against her shoulder. "Looks like you had your first patient."

She smiled, glancing from the window to Shane. "Yes. Thanks for your help."

"No problem." A frown replaced his smile. "What's wrong?"

"Nothing."

He moved to stand next to her, peering out the

glass. "A couple of satisfied customers."

"Yes." But her stomach would more than likely feel unsettled until she saw Sue Anne again tomorrow morning. "I'm going to clean up the mess and get started on the exam room."

"I'll give you a hand."

She nodded. "Thanks."

CHAPTER FOUR

THE FRONT DOOR OPENED, AND SHANE LOOKED UP FROM ESPN's pre-season football highlights as Reagan stepped in. "Hey," he said uncrossing his ankles on the coffee table and sitting up farther on the couch.

She sent him a weary smile as she toed off her Keds. "Hi."

He glanced at the clock, noting her tired eyes. It was almost nine thirty. "Looks like another late one."

She secured the lock on the door. "Yeah, I'm pretty beat, but at least the clinic is officially ready for patients. Thanks again for your help."

"You're welcome. I'm sorry I couldn't do more with the clerical stuff."

"Unfortunately the system requires a log-in. I'll have to assign you one."

"Definitely." He rubbed at his jaw, trying to find a way to delve beyond the small talk. "I made dinner. There's a burger in the fridge and some baked beans."

"That sounds good."

He stood. "I can heat them up for you."

She shook her head, yawning. "That's sweet, but I had a protein bar a couple hours ago."

"Are you sure? It won't take long."

"I'm sure. I think I'm going to head to bed." She yawned again. "I'll see you in the morning."

"Goodnight." He sat back down, frowning as she disappeared down the hall. Doc was working herself hard. He'd stayed with her at the clinic until they put away the last of the boxes, hoping she would knock off for the night when he suggested dinner sometime after seven. But she'd refused, saying she had a computer to update. He'd offered to bring the meal to her, but once again, she turned him down, telling him she didn't have time.

His frown deepened as he tried to figure out his reluctant new principal. She was sweet and patient with injured children, sympathetic to the worries of nervous mothers, but guarded around him. His quick call to Tyson while he sizzled beef on the grill hadn't brought him any closer to solving the mystery. Tyson didn't know anything more about Reagan than he did. He considered reaching out to Ethan. His boss could give him the gorgeous doctor's entire life story, down to her favorite brand of laundry detergent, with a few taps of the computer keys, but what would the fun be in that? He wanted to learn about Reagan from Reagan herself.

A door opened, and second later he heard a faint hum echoing from the exercise room. Recognizing the sound as hot tub jets powering on, he clicked off the television and got to his feet. If Reagan was going for a soak, he had every intention of joining her. She'd accepted his apology earlier today and let him give her a hand, but the air between them wasn't entirely clear. They were going to be living together for the next several weeks, and by the time he left, he hoped to be able to call her a friend.

He walked to his room, stripped down, and pulled on his swim trunks, making his way to the small greenhouse-like area with the faint chlorine smell. Reagan sat among the gentle bubbles in the circular two-person tub, her sexy bikini-clad silhouette highlighted by the single blue light at the bottom of the basin. Her hair was piled on top of her head, her eyes closed while she leaned against the back.

"Looks like we had the same idea," he fibbed.

She opened one eye, then the other, sitting up further.

"Do you mind company?"

"No. Come on in."

He stepped into the warmth, taking the seat opposite her, his leg brushing the smooth skin of hers as he settled in. "This definitely doesn't suck."

"Finding this here was a welcome surprise."

"Can't sleep?"

"No. I'm hoping this will help." She sunk down to her shoulders, resting her head again.

"We spent most of the day together, and I forgot to ask how things went at the mine." He'd noticed the stack of flyers she'd brought with her sitting on her desk on his way out the door.

"Not as good as I'd hoped. Gaining people's trust is going to be a challenge."

He agreed, starting right here with the doctor. "I think you're off to a good start. Sue Anne and her mother left happy enough."

"Hopefully I'll be able to show more people that we're not 'the devil in disguise.'" She made air quotes as she rolled her eyes.

He grinned. "Good old Jasper."

She smiled, shaking her head. "This is a whole different world, a whole new culture."

"It's definitely a big change."

"Mmm," she agreed.

"So why'd you come?"

She shrugged. "Because change can be good. Did you have a chance to look over that medical book I gave you?"

Apparently that was the end of that discussion.

Doc didn't like to talk about herself. "Some of it. It's pretty dry."

"After I get back from my hike tomorrow, we'll work on mastering the blood pressure, which can be kind of tricky."

"I'm already a step ahead of you. I watched a couple of videos on YouTube."

Her eyes widened. "You did?"

"Sure. I have every intention of passing Unofficial Medical Assistant School with flying colors."

She laughed.

He grinned, loving the bold, bright sound. "It's you and me, Doc, against the world."

"That it is, and I don't think that'll be changing anytime soon."

"Oh yeah?"

"I got an e-mail from the director not long after you left. It sounds like it's going to be a while before they get someone else here. Applicants for the nursing position appear to be few and far between."

"I can't imagine why. It's hard to believe someone would want to miss out on all this." He lifted his arm from the water and made a sweeping gesture.

She sent a small rush of water his way. "It's not that bad."

He narrowed his eyes and pursed his lips. "Jury's still out."

"I guess we'll have to see."

"I guess we will."

She sat up. "I should probably get out."

"Yeah?"

"I've got a hike ahead of me tomorrow."

"*We've* got a hike ahead of us," he emphasized as he stood, grabbing a towel, watching water sluice down her sinful body as she gained her feet. "You should really eat if you're going to be burning that kind of energy. I don't want to have to carry you back." He handed over the soft cotton towel.

"Thanks." She hit a button, killing the bubbles. "You said you made burgers?"

"On the grill."

She wrapped the towel around her shoulders. "It probably wouldn't hurt to have one."

"I'll join you."

"Didn't you eat already?"

"Eating's one of my favorite hobbies."

She smiled, shaking her head. "I don't know about you, Shane."

As he smiled back, staring at her in the dim blue light, he knew he was looking forward to more nights like this. He got out, taking her hand as she stepped down. "I guess I'll see you in five."

She nodded. "I'll see you in five."

~~~~

Sweat dripped down Reagan's temples as she sat in the partial shade on the Jacoby's rickety front porch, thankful she'd chosen to wear a tank top with her navy blue hiking shorts. It was barely ten and the temperature was already miserable with the sun boring down and the drowning humidity making it hard to breathe. "Let's take a look here." She focused on Sue Anne, standing in front of her lawn chair, smiling at the little girl despite the wretched heat. She pulled Sue Anne closer, positioning her within the "v" of her legs, pushing the damp blond hair back from her forehead, pleased with the lack of swelling or redness around the clean line of the adhesive. "This looks good." Her shoulders relaxed with the huge sense of relief. "Really good."

"Mmm." Sue Anne moved closer. "You smell real nice."

"Thank you." Shane caught her eye, gesturing to the water bottle in the backpack he carried on one shoulder. His white shirt clung to his tough form, soaked with perspiration. She shook her head subtly, giving her attention to Sue Anne as the little girl reached for her hands, holding them. "Does your cut hurt?"

"No."

"How'd she do last night?" she asked Mrs. Jacoby, who sat on a rusty chair in the same pants and t-shirt she wore yesterday, seemingly far more adapted to the stifling heat.

"Fine. She didn't need none of the Tylenol. She acted like her crazy self—nothin' any stranger than usual."

Reagan grinned. "We'll take it." She squeezed Sue Ann's hands before letting them go to examine the girl's forehead one more time, gently pressing around the injury. "I think you're well on your way to recovery."

Sue Anne's bottom lip tipped down in a pout.

Reagan frowned, her shoulder tensing again. "What's wrong?"

"Mommy says I'm not to be goin' in the creek."

She unclenched her jaw, realizing there were no major problems. "I'm afraid your mommy's right." But the heat was already dangerously oppressive and the shack-like home didn't have air conditioning or any fans she could see through the opened screen door. "Or maybe you can sit with your feet in the water, but you can't get your head wet just yet or I'll have to glue you back together again."

"I think in to your knees sounds like a mighty fine thing." Mrs. Jacoby nodded.

"Even better," Reagan agreed, winking at the little girl.

"I was—" Sue Anne gasped, her face lighting up. "Daddy!" She ran toward the man walking their way, giving him a big hug, Sue Anne's brothers and sister following.

Reagan smiled, recognizing him as the stranger she waved to everyday—the one who never waved back.

Mrs. Jacoby got to her feet. "Byron, this is the doctor who gave Sue Anne a hand."

"Hello." She stood smiling, extending her hand. "I'm, Reagan."

He gave her a nod, returning her shake.

"This is Shane," Reagan added.

"Hey," Shane said, shaking Mr. Jacoby's hand next.

The man nodded again.

"Byron works nights at the mine, and more if they'll have him. Most days he's able to get rides back to the bottom of the road. If not, he stays on for another shift."

Mr. Jacoby had hiked *six* miles one way, Regan thought. "That's quite a walk."

"Brings in the money," he said, brushing his hand across his mouth full of teeth in desperate need of a dentist.

"Yes." She smiled again, sensing an odd tension in the air. "Well, we should be on our way. If you need anything, please don't hesitate to come see us."

"I'm owin' you for the visit."

"We don't charge at the clinic."

"We pay our debts," Mrs. Jacoby said. "How about a chicken?" She took the two steps to the ground from the porch and grabbed one of the birds walking by, holding it upside down by its legs.

"Oh. Well." Reagan looked to Shane for help, unable to see his eyes now that he'd pulled his shades back on. "As much as we'd like to take that off your hands, I don't know that we have a place to keep a chicken."

"We definitely don't have a cage," Shane said, moving to Reagan's side.

Mrs. Jacoby took the animal by the neck, swinging it in three jerking circles, breaking its neck.

Reagan swallowed, stifling a gasp, as Shane muttered, "Jesus."

"This will taste fine for your dinner tonight."

"Uh, yes, it certainly will." Trapped by manners, she reached for the still twitching bird, glancing at Mr. Jacoby watching her as he lit a cigarette.

"Thanks." Shane stepped in front of her, taking the animal, holding it by the leg.

"This really is wonderful." Reagan swiped at stray strands of hair blowing in the stingy breeze. "Really wonderful." She looked at Shane again.

He nodded. "Yeah, definitely."

Growing more uncomfortable by the second, Reagan clasped her hands, clearing her throat. "Mrs. Jacoby, I'm embarrassed to ask, but how exactly do we prepare this?"

"You're gonna need to do some defeatherin'."

"Yes. Right. And how do we do that?"

"Good Lord above. Don't you folks eat?"

"We do but I can honestly say I've never had anything quite this fresh." She slid the dead bird another glance. "If you could just tell me how, I'm sure we'll figure it out."

Mrs. Jacoby took the chicken back. "We'll eat the chicken. Sue Anne," she looked over her shoulder, calling to her daughter as the little girl ran around with her brothers and sister. "Go on and fetch some eggs." She turned back to Shane and Reagan. "I'll send you on with eggs."

Reagan nodded, relieved. "I love eggs."

"From the market I imagine."

"The only kind I've had." She sent Mrs. Jacoby a sheepish smile.

"Then you're in for a treat. Fresh eggs is like a bit of heaven, I believe."

Sue Anne came back with a bucket filled with half-a-dozen eggs.

"Thank Doc Reagan for bein' so kind," Mrs. Jacoby instructed Sue Anne.

"Thank you, Doc Reagan."

"Thank you for the eggs. I can't wait for tomorrow's breakfast." She slid her hand down Sue Anne's hair. "Please come and see me again, but hopefully not for stitches." She winked.

Sue Ann smiled.

"Bye."

"Bye," Mrs. Jacoby and Sue Anne said at the same time.

She and Shane turned, starting down the path they'd followed on the mile hike, disappearing into the blessed shade of the tall trees. She glanced Shane's way several times in the silence. "Well, that was certainly interesting."

He sent her a look as he pulled the water bottle from the pack.

"*Don't* say anything."

He shrugged, used his teeth to open the nozzle, gulped, then handed it over.

"Thanks." She swallowed several refreshing sips of cool water.

"Am I allowed to talk yet?"

She rolled her eyes. "Go ahead."

"Because we're almost too far for me to turn around and trade those eggs for that bird if you've had a change of heart."

She bit her cheek, refusing to smile. "It was a very nice gesture."

"Absolutely."

She grinned, snorting out a laugh. "You have quite a poker face. If it wasn't for your 'Jesus,' I never would've known you were as shocked as I was."

He grinned, grabbing the water bottle from her, spraying her with an icy-cold stream. "You've never had chicken so fresh, huh? I liked that."

She laughed again as he chuckled. "What else was I supposed to say?"

"Hell if I know." He shook his head. "It's not everyday someone hands over a dead bird."

"I think it's safe to say there will never be a dull moment here in The Gap."

"True." He stopped, setting the bag down, pulling off his shirt. "Damn, it's oppressive out here. Right about now I'm craving a cold shower."

She stared at his damp, beautiful muscles, then looked straight ahead. "That makes two of us."

"We could dump a shit-ton of ice cubes in the hot tub and chill out." He wiggled his brows.

"Tempting." *Too* tempting. "But I have to get to work and you have a test."

"Blood pressure one-oh-one." He slid the pack back on his shoulder.

"Absolutely." She smiled at him as they continued on, deciding that Shane might not be so bad after all.

CHAPTER FIVE

"Knock, knock."

Shane looked up at Reagan standing in his doorway, her mouthwatering figure accentuated by black yoga pants and a sky-blue spaghetti-strap top. "Hey." Smiling, he pulled the ear buds from his ears.

"I called you, but I guess you didn't hear me."

"No. I was finishing up a couple of preliminary reports for my boss—big meeting next week."

"Ah. I didn't realize you still did work for your company while you're all the way out here." She took a step into his room.

"Work never stops." He tossed a quick glance toward his bed, glad he took the extra second to pull his covers up and put the pillow back in place when he woke this morning. "There's always something going on."

"I didn't mean to interrupt. I just wanted to tell you dinner's ready."

"Great. I'll be right out."

She took another step toward the small desk he was sitting at, looking at the grouping of picture frames he'd set in the corner—a little piece of home.

"Is this your family?"

He pointed to one picture. "This is my mother, father, sister, her husband, my brother, and his wife." He pointed to another frame his sister had given him for Christmas with two smiling boys and a baby girl posed for the camera. "These are my twin nephews and niece."

She smiled. "They're beautiful."

"They're loud and messy, but we've decided we'll keep them."

Her smile widened. "Your family lives in California?"

He shook his head. "Oregon. About thirty minutes outside of Portland."

"Oh. What about this one?" She tapped the picture taken a couple weeks ago of him, Stone, Sophie, and Abby standing by the arbor on the beach, smiling as the waves crashed behind them. "Those are my friends, Stone, Sophie, and Abby. Stone and I work together."

She leaned in closer, the scent of her shampoo invading his nose as her hair brushed his knuckles. "Is that Abigail Quinn?"

"Yeah."

She gaped at him. "You *know* Abigail Quinn?"

He nodded. "Abby's husband, Jerrod, was my roommate."

She raised her brows. "I have to admit I'm pretty impressed."

He shrugged. "I guess I don't see her the way everyone else does. She's Jerrod's wife and a super nice person. She also happens to be a world-famous clothing designer."

"Wait a minute." She frowned, easing closer yet, picking up the frame. "That's Sophie McCabe. You were the best man at Sophie McCabe's *wedding*?"

He grinned. "Sophie's a friend."

"Who makes insanely awesome jewelry."

"It's pretty nice."

"*Nice*?" She rolled her eyes, shaking her head. "Men."

He smiled, thrilled that she was standing so close,

wanting to know something about his life. They saw each other everyday, walking together into the hills every morning and hanging out in the clinic, but she still kept her distance, rarely speaking of anything but the people of Black Bear Gap, clinical procedures, or ideas that might make community members more comfortable and likely to seek medical care. "I said it's pretty nice."

She rolled her eyes for the second time. "Who are all of these people?" She pointed to the group photo of his coworkers and their spouses and children posed for the shot at Stone and Sophie's cliff-top wedding reception.

"My coworkers and their families."

"They're all stunning. Every one of them."

"Not bad, huh?"

She turned, her face inches from his. "You love them."

He nodded, looking back at the frame as she did. "I'm damn lucky to work with some really great people. "This woman, Wren, she just found out she's pregnant. Abby too, but that's a secret."

"My lips are sealed." She slid her thumb and forefinger across her mouth as if zipping a zipper.

"Stone mentioned he and Sophie were trying, and Sarah and Ethan are on the verge of being parents for the third time." He sat back, stretching. "Basically, it's a baby bonanza back in LA."

"And you're missing it." She smiled sadly as she stood upright again.

He was, but it wasn't so bad now that he and Reagan had found an easier rhythm—morning hikes to introduce themselves to weary community members, afternoons spent endlessly training for the off chance someone might come into the office for medical care.

But no matter how Reagan tried, the people of Black Bear Gap were not receptive to outsiders nosing into their business. "I'll be back soon enough."

"You certainly will. In fact, I believe you can cross off your first official week in The Gap." She leaned her butt against the desk. "So do you want to eat?"

He was hungry, but Reagan couldn't cook for shit. He sucked in a hesitant breath through his teeth. "What's for dinner?"

"Pasta, garlic bread, and a salad."

He closed his laptop and stood. That was a pretty foolproof meal; there wasn't much to mess up. "Sounds good."

"I think I did all right tonight, but I'm not making any promises either."

"It's spaghetti. It can't be that bad."

They walked down the hall to the table. The salad looked fresh and colorful, and the bread perfect and buttery brown. Then he stared at the pasta swimming in a gallon of sauce in the serving dish.

"Not too bad, right?" She snagged her bottom lip between her teeth, looking at him with hope.

"No. Not too bad." He took his chair across from hers and served watery pasta and sauce on her plate, then his own. He rolled thin strands of pasta on his fork and bit into mush.

She sampled her own and winced. "Soggy. Sorry."

"No problem." He ate some more, despite the terrible texture and lack of flavor.

"It's not exactly al dente."

He shook his head. "It's not half-bad soup though."

She grinned.

"I'll grill something tomorrow night." He'd thought of offering to take over the cooking entirely. He was no master chef, but the three meals she'd prepared in the week they'd been living here had been an experience all their own. The fresh eggs she'd attempted to whip into omelets turned into a disaster of flaming cheese and charred vegetables; the sloppy Joe's and fries hadn't turned out much better.

"Sounds good, but you have to admit this is a marginal improvement over the pork chops I made the other night."

He chuckled. "Burnt on the outside, raw in the middle. It takes a special talent to make something quite that bad."

She laughed. "I'm trying."

"I know." He tore a piece of garlic bread and set it on her plate, then placed a huge hunk on his own. "What did you eat before you came to Kentucky?"

"Salads, cafeteria food, takeout. Manhattan makes it easy to survive when you're challenged in the cooking department."

He perked up, surprised she was actually sharing something about herself. "You were in Manhattan?"

She nodded. "I worked in the Bronx but lived on the Upper West side."

"No kidding," he said over the food in his mouth. "Where?"

"Seventy-Eighth Street."

"Huh. Me and my buddies lived on Seventy-Seventh." Had they passed each other on occasion? He immediately dismissed the idea. They couldn't have. Doc's stunning face would've been impossible to forget.

She frowned. "I thought you were in Los Angeles."

"I am. I moved a few months ago. Career change."

"What did you do in Manhattan?

"US Marshall. Fugitive Task Force."

She hummed in her throat. "Sounds exciting."

"I loved it."

"Why'd you give it up?"

He shrugged, thinking of one of his best friend's betrayal. "One of my roommates turned out to be an asshole. I lost my taste for the job and joined Jerrod, Abby's husband, out in LA. It was a good change." He dutifully twirled another bite of pasta. "What about you? Why'd you give up the city?"

Her eyes dulled as she jerked her shoulders and stared down at her plate. "I thought I'd give rural living a try."

He studied her tense movements as she pushed the spaghetti around. There was a story here, but she wasn't sharing. Time for a subject change before she clicked back into clinical mode. "I've gotta ask, Doc. How old are you? You don't look like you're old enough to be out of medical school."

"Maybe I've discovered the fountain of youth." She smirked, chewing a healthy bite of her salad.

He tilted his head, as if considering. "It's possible but doubtful. News like that would've spread."

She smiled. "It's rude to ask a woman her age."

"I've heard that, but I'll risk a faux pas for curiosity's sake."

"Twenty-six."

"You're twenty-six?"

She nodded.

"How the hell are you a doctor?"

She smiled mysteriously. "I got an early start."

"What does that mean?"

"Mmm, I went to college fairly young." She wiped her mouth and set down her napkin.

Frowning, he counted backwards, doing the math. "You had to have been like twelve."

"Pretty much."

His eyes popped wide. "*Twelve*? You went to

college when you should've been in middle school?"

"Basically."

"So you were one of those kid geniuses? Like Doogie?"

"If you want to put a label on it," she answered primly, lifting her water glass.

"What would you call it?"

"I learned quickly."

There was a story here too, yet she didn't seem to want to spill. He narrowed his eyes. "How many languages do you speak?"

"Five."

"Play any musical instruments?"

"Violin and piano. I tried the flute but it wasn't for me."

He huffed out an exasperated laugh. "So you're telling me you went to college at twelve, speak five languages, play two musical instruments, but you can't cook spaghetti?"

She sent him one of her excellent grins. "We all have our talents."

"I'll have to call Sophie and have her send us some recipes. Maybe I can teach you the basics of cooking, since you're teaching me about medicine."

"Sure. I'm willing to give it a try."

"I'm—" There was a knock at the door. He stood, glancing out the windows into the fading dark. So far they'd avoided the backlash other Project members had endured at the hands of disgruntled residents, but there was always a first. "I'll get it."

Reagan got up as he did.

He walked to the front door, keeping her behind him as he opened the door and stared at the teenage girl in jean shorts and a plain white tank top.

"I need—I need the doctor," she said, wiping at her

sweaty brow.

Reagan pushed ahead of him. "I'm Doctor Rosner."

"My sister—she's havin' her baby, but somethin's wrong. It's been a long time. She's gettin' awful tired."

"Let me go to the clinic and get what I'll need." Reagan ran down the stairs toward the building.

"What can I do?" Shane called.

"Get ready to give me a hand."

He swallowed as he looked at the young girl in front of him. Temperatures and blood pressures were one thing; childbirth was a whole different ballgame. "I'll get the keys."

~~~~

"When did Jenny's labor start?" Reagan asked Shirley, turning around from the passenger's seat while Shane maneuvered the SUV up the steep mountain road.

"Her back was hurtin' all day yesterday, then last night when we went to bed, she was cryin' and grabbin' for my hand. Now she's just screamin' a whole lot, but the baby ain't comin'."

"Who's with her now? Your mother?"

"No, ma'am. No one. Jenny gone and got herself knocked up by Terry Staddler from over on the other side of the mountain. We's had a feud with them for years. Mommy said this baby and Jenny ain't welcome to her support. Mommy left for Nan's further up the pass this mornin'. She ain't been back since."

Reagan glanced at Shane as he tossed her a quick look and drove faster, taking the sharp turn in a slight skid. "How old is Jenny?"

"She's fixin' to turn seventeen in October."

Sixteen and completely alone. And they still had a

good half-mile to hike once they made it to the pass. Hopefully the poor girl would be ready to deliver when they got there. "Has she been eating and drinking?"

Shirley shook her head. "I tried givin' her some chips, but she said she didn't want none."

"What about fluids? Has she had water?"

"No."

"Juice, tea, anything?"

"No ma'am. She's been refusin' what I've been tryin' to give her."

Reagan nodded, already certain she and Shane were about to have their hands full. "She has to be dehydrated, which will slow labor. I'll carry my bag. Shane, I want you to bring the oxygen. Shirley, I want you to lead the way—the fastest way."

She nodded. "Yes'm."

Eventually they made it to the pass. Minutes passed like hours as Reagan hurried over rocks and tree roots, the journey all the more difficult in the fading light. The shamble of a house came into view, and long, loud wails carried through the open windows. "Shirley, I'll need fresh water—a cup for Jenny right away and a bowl with a cloth."

"Okay." She ran up the crumbling concrete steps through to the kitchen.

Reagan followed, hurrying into the bedroom off the small living area where the pretty teenager lay on the bed, crying, her heart-shaped face and blond hair soaked in sweat, her oversized t-shirt sagging off one shoulder.

"Good Christ," Shane murmured, stepping up behind Reagan. "Is she all right?"

"She's in pain and scared." She moved to the bed, sitting on the edge. "Jenny."

Jenny made no attempt to acknowledge her;

instead, she clutched at a pillow, screaming with her eyes closed.

"Jenny," Reagan said sternly.

Gasping, moaning, the blue-eyed girl made eye contact.

"Jenny, I'm Reagan. I'm a doctor and I'm here to help you." She settled her hand on the thin girl's stomach, stroking the rock-hard ball. "Your contraction's starting to ebb. I want you to try to breathe in deep and blow out."

Jenny's panicked eyes held Reagan's as she copied Reagan's demonstrated deep, steady breaths.

"Just like that." She nodded, sending Jenny an encouraging smile. "Good job, Jenny. In again and out. Perfect." She brushed a hand through the girl's hair, doing her best to soothe her with a gentle touch for the remainder of the contraction. "Good."

Shirley brought in a cup of water and a small bowl, sloshing liquid over the edges with every step, setting it on the old filing-cabinet-turned-bedside-table. "Here you go."

"Thanks, Shirley." Reagan smiled, ignoring the thundering pound of her heart, knowing all eyes were on her. If she didn't stay calm despite the waves of doubt racing through her mind she would lose the small grip of control she'd gained over the chaotic situation. "Shane, can you ring out the cloth, and we'll cool Jenny off."

"Sure." He set down the bag containing the portable oxygen unit, his knee brushing her leg as he skirted around her in the cramped space. Crouching by the bedside, he rang out the cloth, handing it over.

"Thanks." She fought to keep her hands steady and wiped the cool rag along Jenny's forehead. "How's that?"

She smiled. "Real nice."

"Good." She gave the cloth back to Shane, gesturing for the cup. "Thanks," she murmured when he handed it over. "I want you to drink some of this." She held the plastic up to Jenny's lips.

Jenny shook her head. "I don't want to."

"You need to. Your lips are dry."

Jenny took a sip.

"Good. A little more. Staying hydrated will help us get the baby out faster."

Jenny's eyes grew wide, and she tensed. "Another one. Another one's comin'."

Reagan took the teen's hand, stroking her belly with the other. "I want you to breathe just like we did before." She inhaled deeply and exhaled in example as she had only moments ago. "Yes. Just like that. Just like that, Jenny," she said again. "Keep your hand loose in mine."

Jenny started to whimper. "It hurts so bad."

"I know, honey. I know. Breathe. Breathe."

The contraction ceased, and Jenny sniffled. "I can't do this. I just ain't strong enough."

"Yes, you can. You're doing an excellent job. I'm going to check your progress while Shane gives you more to drink." She stood on not-quite-steady legs, toe to toe with Shane, who got to his feet, trying to move out of her way. "She needs to drink, and we need to keep her calm. She's close. I need for her to be able to listen to my directions."

He nodded. "Got it."

And she knew he did. They'd gotten off to a rocky start, but she trusted wholeheartedly that she and Shane would help Jenny deliver this baby together. "Jenny, I'm going to see how you're doing, and I want to check on the baby too."

Jenny nodded, sipping once, twice, three times, then collapsed back against the pillow as Shane gently wiped her temples with the cloth.

Reagan grabbed gloves and the Doppler, eager to get a heartbeat and an idea of Jenny's progress before the next contraction came. "Jenny, I'm going to examine you. You'll probably feel some cramping." She stuck her fingers inside.

Jenny tensed, squeezing her eyes shut. "It hurts."

"I know that's uncomfortable. Breathe in and out. You're fully dilated." She pulled off her gloves, replacing them with a fresh pair. "Let's hear how baby's doing." She turned on the Doppler, smiling at the strong steady sound of a life waiting to be born. "Wonderful. When you feel the urge to push, I want you to go for it."

"I can't." Jenny shook her head, her parched lips trembling. "I'm scared."

"I think that's pretty normal, but Shane and I are here to help you through this. Do you know what you're having?"

She shook her head, groaning. "Again. Here comes another. I need to push."

"Go ahead. Chin to your chest and push into your bottom."

Jenny followed Reagan's instructions, bearing down.

"Good. Yes, Jenny. That's great. Go ahead and rest."

Shane wiped at the young mother's brow as she lay back.

"I need to push again."

"Good. Go with it. Yes, down in your bottom. Just like that."

"It hurts," Jenny grunted, her body now in control.

"You're doing so well." She rubbed her hand up and

down Jenny's leg. "The baby's head is right here."

"It's burnin'," Jenny cried out.

"I want you to breathe," she said firmly, sensing Jenny starting to lose control again. "Hold Shane's hand and breathe until you're ready to go again. We'll let baby sit here while you rest." Jenny was tiny. The last thing they needed were large tears and a big blood loss.

"You're doing great," Shane encouraged, brushing the hair back from Jenny's forehead.

"I'm going to check on Baby again." Reagan put the Doppler to Jenny's stomach, searching for the fetal heart tones, noting the slight deceleration.

"I need to push."

"Okay. Push. Chin to your chest." The head advanced. "Good girl, Jenny. I can see hair."

"It's burnin'. It's burnin'. Get it out. Get it *out*." Tears streamed down her face.

"You're getting your baby out. Your hard work is paying off, honey."

"I can't do it. I can't." Jenny rested her head on the pillow, sobbing quietly.

"Yes you can."

"I'm tired," she said, breathing hard.

"I know you are. You've been at this a long time. I promise you can take a nice long nap very soon." She put the Doppler to Jenny's stomach as Jenny rested, waiting for the next dip in the baby's heart rate to recover. She made eye contact with Shane. "Let's give Jenny some oxygen. Jenny, I want you to get on your left side for a few minutes."

Shane fiddled with the pump and line exactly as they'd practiced while Shirley helped her sister roll to her side. Shane settled the mask in place, and Jenny pushed.

Reagan listened to the heart tones again, noting

that the baby's heart rate wasn't recovering, despite the new measures. "We need this baby out. Jenny, I want you to really focus and push through the whole contraction."

"I can't," she said, her voice muffled through the mask, her energy fading.

"Yes you can. You need to." She met Shane's gaze, knowing he understood they were quickly moving toward an emergency situation.

"I'm too tired," she panted.

"Jenny, the baby's tired too. We need to get him or her out as soon as we can."

"Come on, Jenny. Let's go. Finish this up," Shane said sternly, giving her shoulder a squeeze of encouragement.

"Listen to the doctor, Jenny," Shirley added.

Jenny nodded, pushing, and the head began to emerge.

"Good. Good," Reagan reassured.

Jenny screamed, groping for Shane's fingers, squeezing his fingertips until they turned red.

"Breathe, Jenny," Reagan said. "The head is out. Go again and we'll have a baby."

Jenny pushed, but baby didn't move.

"Go again. Give it everything you've got."

Jenny bore down, her face red. "I'm tryin'."

Reagan swallowed panic as she stared at the small purple head, knowing the baby should've been born with that push. "Shane, pull the pillows out from under Jenny. Roll her to her back and push her leg to her chest. Shirley, take your sister's other leg and do the same. The baby's shoulder is stuck in the pelvis."

Shane and Shirley moved into action.

"Jenny, keep giving it all you've got."

The girl pushed, and Reagan pulled gently,

attempting to guide the new infant the rest of the way into the world as precious seconds slipped away. The maneuver she'd practiced on her rotation on the delivery ward wasn't working.

"Shane, glove up. I want you to support the baby's head. When I tell Jenny to push, be ready to guide the baby out."

He hesitated for only a second and took her place at the foot of the bed.

Reagan used her body weight to keep Jenny's leg to her chest and pressed down firmly on Jenny's lower abdomen, where the baby's shoulder was held up. "Push, Jenny. Push as hard as you can."

The baby girl was born in a forceful explosion as Jenny screamed.

Reagan rushed in front of Shane, sitting mostly in his lap, not bothering to wait for him to move, and suctioned the infant's mouth and nose, rubbing the lifeless infant. "I need the oxygen." She continued stimulating the baby, waiting for the cry as Shane leaned to the floor.

"Here." Shane handed her the infant-sized mask and she placed it on the tiny face, knowing they were almost out of time.

"Come on, baby. Come on. Shane, keep rubbing her."

He reached around Reagan, his chest pressing to her back as his gloved palms gently jostled the baby while she held the stream of oxygen. More torturous seconds passed in silence.

"Come *on*, baby girl."

Finally the baby let loose a quiet cry.

Reagan's breath shuddered in and out. "Thank God. Thank God. Okay. Okay, baby." She continued to hold the oxygen in place. "Welcome to the world.

Jenny, do you have a name for your little girl?"

"Faith," Jenny mumbled out.

She looked up at Jenny, pale, her eyes closed.

The moment of relief quickly vanished as she noted the amount of blood oozing from the new mother's wounds. "Take Faith," she said to Shane. She secured clips on the umbilical cord, cutting without the usual ceremony of separating two joined lives. "Wrap her up and keep rubbing at her. Jenny's lost a lot of blood."

She lifted herself enough for Shane to move out from under her and focused on the petite teen. "Jenny, I want you to give me a small push so we can deliver this placenta and get you sewed up."

"I can't," she croaked out.

"Just one more push. Good. Shirley, can you get your sister some more water or juice and maybe some crackers? She used a lot of energy today."

"No, ma'am. Mommy's food stamps don't come 'til next week. There ain't nothin' much in the cupboards."

"Okay. Just the water and try to find something sweet."

Shirley left and Reagan immediately began repairing three significant tears, worrying more about the mother than the daughter who had pinked up and was now thankfully fussing.

"We need to get her out of here." She tossed a look at Shane. "I need an ambulance." But an ambulance would take more time than they had. "We at least need to get her to the clinic where I can keep an eye on her." She fought away the utter sense of helplessness in the dirty, remote surroundings. "I'll have to send you down for a backboard, and we'll move her together."

"I'll carry her."

"It's more than a half mile."

"And a hell of a lot faster for us to wrap her up and

go. I can carry her."

There wasn't time to argue. She nodded. "Let's go."

CHAPTER SIX

REAGAN SAT BY JENNY'S SIDE, TAKING HER PULSE IN THE spare bedroom Shane settled her in after their harrowing hike through dark terrain nearly forty minutes ago. She counted off each beat on the second hand of her watch, noting that Jenny's heart rate was strong but still a little fast. She glanced from Jenny's ghostly coloring to the IV line sending saline solution into the teenager's veins, wishing there was more she could do to help. She brushed Jenny's long bangs back from her face, replaying the events of a childbirth gone incredibly wrong. The entire situation had snowballed into a complete disaster. One crisis after another popped up faster than she could handle them, leaving her wondering if she'd been the cause of the problem.

Sighing, she brushed her own hair back, her shoulders heavy with uncertainty. Three months ago she never would have question if she'd done everything right, but now she picked apart every detail. Perhaps if she'd checked Faith's heart rate more frequently or suggested a position change sooner. Maybe perianal massage would have helped with the transition for both mother and baby. If she'd thought things through better, Jenny might not have a third-degree tear.

Jenny opened her eyes, and Reagan smiled, putting away her doubts. There would be plenty of time to rehash them again later. "Hi."

"I'm thirsty," Jenny said, her voice raspy.

"Have a sip." She picked up the glass, holding the

pink straw to Jenny's lips.

"Why am I thirsty if I have this?" She lifted her hand, gesturing to the IV.

"Your throat's dry. There's no reason why you can't drink. If you want I can get you something to eat."

Jenny shook her head.

"If you don't want cereal or a sandwich, I can bring you some broth."

"I'm not hungry."

"You need to have something. The IV will rehydrate you and restore your electrolytes, but food's going to give you the energy you need to recover."

"Maybe later," she said, glancing around the dimly lit room.

"If you're looking for your sister, she wasn't able to come back with us." Reagan wasn't sure how much Jenny remembered of the dicey hike back to the SUV. She'd been in and out of a deep sleep, mostly limp in Shane's arms, while Reagan carried Faith and Shirley guided them by flashlight. Reagan had invited Shirley to the cabin for a meal and to be with Jenny, but Shirley refused, assuring them their mother would skin her alive for calling on the Fed doctor for help in the first place.

"Shirley gave me all the help she can."

Reagan nodded, mystified by Jenny's family dynamics, curious how the sixteen-year-old planned to care for herself and her new baby if Jenny's mother had no intentions of helping her with Faith. She opened her mouth to inquire, staring into weary blue eyes, and changed her mind. There would be time for questions when Jenny was feeling better.

Faith started to fuss, her small, gasping cries carrying down the hallway. "Sounds like Faith's awake."

Jenny picked at her nails, not bothering to respond.

She had yet to see or even ask about her daughter.

"Do you want Shane to bring her in? We had to give her a little formula, but we can try putting her to the breast if you want."

Jenny shook her head. "I'm not ready."

"That's okay. Let me get you some broth. You'll probably be more up to seeing her once you're a little more rested."

Jenny nodded and closed her eyes.

Reagan left the bedroom door slightly ajar and walked to the common area, smiling at Shane sitting on the couch, his ankles crossed on the coffee table as usual, feeding the baby. "Looks like you're a natural."

"She's pretty cute. It's kind of crazy how much she looks like her mom. And this little girl's not afraid to eat, let me just say. We've been home for less than an hour and she's already gulped down an ounce of the formula you gave us." He looked down at Faith. "Don't ever let anyone tell you there's something wrong with a hearty appetite."

She took the cushion next to him, giving Faith a once over as the newborn lay snuggled in the soft blanket they brought down from the study. "She appears to be in good hands." She brushed her finger over Faith's sweet button nose. "Did we have more supplies in the closet?"

"Yeah. Luckily there are a few packages of the newborn diapers. I also grabbed that small bin of clothes I remembered seeing. There's not much, but I threw what there was in the washing machine."

During the chaos of getting Jenny ready for the hike down the mountain, she realized Jenny didn't have any supplies for the baby. They'd made do with one of the diapers in the trial pack she'd added to the welcome bag and swaddled the infant in a clean towel they hadn't used during the birth. "Good. Thank you."

Faith's mouth went slack on the rubber nipple, and Shane lifted her to his shoulder, patting gently, burping her like a pro. "We're going to need more formula before long."

She fixed the blanket, covering Faith's tiny arm. "We'll add it to the supply list, but I'm hoping Jenny will want to try nursing. If she doesn't, we should have enough to get us through until we know what's going on."

"How is Jenny?"

"She's pretty weak and exhausted, but she's stable."

"Do you think we should bring her to the hospital?"

She shook her head. "The nearest facility is more than an hour away. I'll keep her here and make a final decision tomorrow morning. She lost quite a bit of blood, but if she'll eat something and rest for the next few days, she should be okay." She looked toward the hallway where her patient rested, then toward the dark beyond the windows, knowing there was nothing out there for miles. For the first time since she arrived in the mountains, the distance from civilization and help in true emergencies left her with a sickening sense of vulnerability. She alone was responsible for the life-and-death matters of more than two hundred and thirteen people.

"Reagan?" Jenny called.

"Coming." She rushed to her feet, hurrying down the hall, and opened Jenny's door, readying herself for the next catastrophe. "What's wrong?"

"I need to go to the bathroom."

"Okay." She walked to the side of the bed. "Let me help you up. We're going to take it nice and slow."

Jenny sat up and shakily gained her feet.

Reagan wrapped her arm around Jenny's waist,

rolling the IV pole at her side as she assisted Jenny across the hall. "I'm going to give you a peri bottle to use."

"What's that?"

"You'll want to squeeze water over your wounds as you pee so it doesn't sting so much." Reagan helped settle her patient on the toilet and handed over a bottle with tepid water in it. "Start to spray, then pee."

Jenny did as she was told and whimpered. "It hurts. Mommy told me this child is a spawn of the devil himself. I have a mind to believe her."

She blinked, surprised by Jenny's thoughts toward her daughter. "Faith is a beautiful baby girl who has nothing to do with the devil whatsoever. Go ahead and wipe gently—pat the area so you don't get caught up on your stitches—and we'll get you back in bed. I'm going to get you something to eat then I'll bring the baby in so you can see for yourself. I think Shane's half in love already." She helped Jenny stand and start back toward the bedroom.

"I'm feelin' off."

"What does that mean?" Before she could say anything more, Jenny was sagging against her, her eyes rolling back in her head. "Jenny? Damn." She lay the girl on the floor, careful of the IV line, and raised her legs. "Shane, I need help."

Shane hurried down with the baby in his arms. "Shit." He handed over Faith and picked up Jenny.

"Let's get her back in bed." Reagan followed closely, handing off the baby once Jenny was on the mattress.

Jenny came around and started crying. "I feel so weak and tired. I never felt so bad before."

"You're okay, honey," Reagan soothed, feeling the girl's hammering pulse. "You've had a very hard delivery, a nasty wound, and not enough to fuel your body. I want you to close your eyes, and when I bring in some broth, you're going to eat the entire bowl—a few crackers too."

The girl sniffled and nodded.

"Close your eyes." She kissed Jenny's forehead as she tucked her in and started toward the door with Shane.

"Leave the light on," Jenny requested.

"Okay." She closed the door slightly as they stepped into the hall. "I'm going to get her some soup." She headed to the kitchen, afraid she was about to burst into tears herself.

~~~~

Shane stared after Reagan, his brows furrowed in concern as he watched her hurry away. Something was bothering Doc. She'd been amazing throughout the night, dealing with one crisis after another without so much as a blink of an eye, but as she said she was off to make Jenny a simple bowl of soup, he'd sworn he saw a crack in her cool composure.

The last few hours had been downright crazy, but from the moment Shirley knocked on their door, Reagan had been in complete control. Jenny's situation had quickly gone from bad to worse, and before he knew what the hell was happening, he understood two lives were resting in Doc's hands. She'd saved them both, remaining calm under what could only be unbearable pressure.

But now something was off. Reagan was always so sure of herself, her confidence in her craft unshakable, but the flash of defeat in her pretty blue eyes had been unmistakable.

"I'm going to check on our pal," he said to the baby

and brought her to his room, laying her in the center of the queen-sized bed, placing a pillow on both sides of the mattress even though it was highly unlikely the swaddled, sleeping newborn was going anywhere. He looked back at the pretty baby once more and walked down the hall, joining Reagan in the kitchen as she stood with her back to him, resting her forehead against the cupboard and gripping the edges of the counter. "Crazy night around here."

She jumped, glancing over her shoulder, giving him a small smile. "Yeah."

Something was definitely eating at Reagan. He leaned against the fridge, crossing his arms, ready to figure out what it was. "I guess Jenny's going to be down for the count for awhile."

She picked up the can opener, twisting open the can. "Mmm, at least a couple days until she gets some of her energy back." She dumped noodles and broth into a cup and moved to the microwave, putting the mug in to heat for sixty seconds.

"You did a good job tonight, Doc."

She huffed out a barely perceptible breath. "You think so?"

His frown reappeared at the question in her voice. "I *know* so."

"Thanks." The microwave beeped, and she pulled out the steaming cup.

She had yet to turn around. "Are you okay?"

She grabbed a spoon from the drawer. "Yeah, definitely."

He walked over and tugged on her arm, staring into her swimming blue eyes as she looked up at him. "Why do I feel like you're feeding me a line?"

She shrugged.

He slid his palms down the soft skin of her arms,

capturing her hands in his. "Reagan, what's wrong?"

She shook her head. "I guess I'm just coming down from tonight." She blinked, fighting to keep her tears at bay.

"Hey," he said gently. "Come here." He pulled her into a hug.

"I just—everything went so wrong." She sucked in an unsteady breath as she wrapped her arms around his waist.

"And you made it right." He eased back, still holding onto her as he held her gaze. "If you hadn't been there, neither of those girls would be here right now."

She swallowed, looking down. "Jenny lost so much blood. I should've known we had a shoulder dystocia after Faith's head was born. I did so many things wrong." Sighing, she closed her eyes as a tear fell.

He lifted her chin, wiping her cheek with the pad of his thumb. "I'm sorry you feel that way, because I saw a woman in control of a really tough situation. I can honestly say I was scared shitless for a couple of minutes there."

She sniffled. "Really?"

"Damn straight. You did a hell of a job. If I ever give birth I'm definitely calling you."

Her eyes grew wide, and she smiled as he did.

"You were amazing, Reagan."

"Thank you."

"You're welcome." He reluctantly let her go. "So Faith seems to be okay."

She nodded. "She had a rough start, but her Apgar score was more than fine at the five-minute mark."

He didn't know what that was, but Reagan seemed sure, so that was good enough for him. He took her hand again. "Let me fix you a plate of eggs or something. I don't know about you, but I'm starving."

"I should really try to get some food into Jenny. She'll feel better for it."

"She's asleep."

"I need for her to hold the baby." She nibbled her lip as a new wave of worry clouded her eyes. "I'm concerned about her ability to bond with Faith. Her mother told her the baby was part devil. After the delivery, I think she believes it."

"She just had a pretty rough time. Give her a while to catch her breath."

She nodded. "You're right. I just want Jenny and Faith to have the best start possible. They both have so much stacked against them."

"It's going to work out." He squeezed her fingers with his reassurance, even though she was exactly right.

She gave him another small smile. "I know."

Faith started to cry.

"How about you go get our temporary bundle of joy, and I'll cook for you? You can't take care of everyone else if you don't take care of yourself first. We'll get bonding and the rest figured out after."

"Thank you." She surprised him with a quick kiss on the cheek. "You're very sweet."

And he was very attracted to the woman with the remnants of a tear drying on her soft skin. "Scrambled or over easy?"

"Scrambled."

"Coming up."

"I'm looking forward to it." She walked off to get the baby.

He grabbed a pan, watching her walk away. Reagan was letting him help—only because she was vulnerable, but it was a start.

CHAPTER SEVEN

FAITH FUSSED, AND REAGAN'S EYES FLEW OPEN. SHE DARTED glances around in the shadows, wearing pajama shorts and a tank top, realizing she must have dozed off in Shane's bed again. She squinted, her eyes blurry from her lack of sleep, looking at the newborn sandwiched between herself and the man who had quickly become her impromptu co-parent. For two weeks they'd shared the responsibilities of feeding, changing, bathing, and snuggling the infant belonging to the young woman in the room down the hall.

Faith's fussing turned into a lusty cry, and Shane rushed up to sitting.

"I'm coming," he called out.

"She's right here." Reagan couldn't help but smile as she picked up the baby, studying Shane's tired eyes and hair standing up in short spikes. "Go back to sleep. I'll give Faith her bottle."

"That's okay." He yawned hugely. "You got the last one."

They'd both handled the last shift, taking turns walking a fussy baby around the room for more than two hours after midnight. She glanced at the clock with a grimace. Six forty-five. "I'd call us even. I have to get up and get ready."

Groaning, Shane lay back, bare chested and fabulous. "Take the day off. No one's coming anyway." He rolled to his stomach.

"That's the wrong attitude." Although it was

tempting to feed and change Faith and go back to bed, she wasn't getting paid to sleep. "Plus I need to check on Jenny." She smiled at Faith, sliding her palm over the baby's soft head while the pretty girl blinked up at her. "Should we go see how your mommy's doing today?"

"She's fine," Shane mumbled into his pillow. "She doesn't look pale anymore. And she's certainly strong enough to help herself to the food in the fridge and plunk her butt on the couch and watch TV all the damn time."

"Thank you, doctor. I'll be sure to take your thoughts on my patient into consideration." She smiled sarcastically, batting her lashes.

He opened one eye, looking at her. "I know you've got it under control."

But she wondered if she did. Jenny was well enough to spend long stretches of time out of bed, and her wounds were healing well, but she had yet to make an effort where her daughter was concerned. "I don't know what to do about Jenny and Faith," she admitted.

"Bring Jenny the baby and come lay back down. She won't take care of Faith if she doesn't have to."

"But that's the problem." She snuggled Faith closer, her heart aching for the sweet-eyed newborn. "We shouldn't have to force the issue. She should *want* to take care of her baby."

Shane sat up again. "She had a traumatic delivery. Bonding can be difficult for some mothers, especially young mothers after an experience like hers."

Reagan raised her brow.

"What?" He shrugged. "I've been doing some reading."

She looked back at the baby, ignoring the powerful stirrings of attraction for the adorable man sitting among wrinkled sheets. "Did you happen to come up with any pointers on how we can move things in the right direction? I've tried everything I know."

He rubbed at the three days of scruff along his jaw. "We can give her a discharge date."

She scowled. "I'm not kicking Jenny out until I've spoken to her mother."

He scoffed. "Good luck with that."

Her frown deepened. "What does that mean?"

"Doesn't it strike you as strange that Mrs. Hendley hasn't come to see her daughter and new grandchild even once? They've been here for what, fourteen days?"

She sighed. "It *is* pretty surprising. I thought we would've seen her by now, but I guess she's upset with Jenny for her choice in Faith's father."

"And where the hell's he at anyway?"

She shrugged shaking her head. "You're asking questions I can't answer. Jenny isn't exactly an open book."

He yawned again. "I'm just glad we finally got that order of formula and diapers. It's clear Jenny's mother and Faith's father have no intention of giving her a hand." He scooted closer, smiling down at the baby looking up at him. "Hi, beautiful." He kissed Faith's forehead and stroked her cheek. "It's a damn shame everyone in her life seems to have their priorities screwed up."

Reagan made a sound in her throat, watching the way Faith wrapped her little hand around Shane's finger as the baby continued to hold his gaze. Faith didn't appear to be her family's main concern, but she was certainly hers and Shane's. Faith was thriving and forming bonds, but not with the people she should have been. "I'm planning to hike up to the Hendleys this morning and figure out what's going on."

"It sounds like we're going on a walk, huh, Faithy."

Reagan shook her head. "No. I think you should stay here with Jenny and Faith."

He took Faith from her arms, resting the baby against his chest. "Not gonna happen."

"Shane—"

"It might be good for granny to get a look at her and see that she doesn't have horns and a tail." He rubbed his big hand down her tiny back.

She nibbled her lip, considering. "I guess that's not a bad idea."

"Stick with me kid." He winked.

She smiled, rolling her eyes. "I'll make Faith a bottle; although, she doesn't seem all that hungry."

"She just wanted company. Were you lonely, baby girl?" He kissed the top of her head.

Reagan looked away as a rush of butterflies invaded her stomach. There were few things sexier than a gorgeous man with a soft spot for babies. "I'll make her a bottle anyway, then I'm going to shower and check on Jenny."

"Sounds like a plan. I think this little lady here could use a bath herself. Maybe we should wake Jenny and have her give me a hand."

"We don't want to push."

"We need to push some." He set Faith down and pulled on a shirt. "I'll be damned if Jenny's going to sleep in while you and I play mommy and daddy."

"Okay." She nodded and left the room, peeking into Jenny's room, still dark with the blinds closed and curtains drawn. Hopefully today would go well and they could convince grandma to help her daughter with the overwhelming challenges of young motherhood.

She made her way to the kitchen and prepared the bottle, noting the small pile of Faith's supplies soaking in the sink, and started back down the hall, slowing outside Shane's door as his voice carried from his room, strong and smooth in song. He sounded great as he sang Old McDonald. She peaked in as he rested Faith on his thighs, singing about the cow going moo, as her tiny fists moved about. She walked in as he finished.

He looked up. "I think the cow's her favorite."

"You're very good with children."

He shrugged. "I like them. They're cute."

"You'll make a good father someday." She smiled at the baby.

"You're no slouch in the kid department either."

"Thanks." She sat on the edge of the bed, taking Faith's hand in hers, kissing little fingers.

"How many do you want?"

"How many what do I want?"

"Babies."

She jerked her shoulders as her heart crumbled, knowing she would never make children of her own. "I haven't given it much thought."

"Weird question, I guess." He took the bottle from her when Faith started rooting around.

"No, not really."

"'Somedays' don't seem to matter much, because I think it's pretty safe to say we both have our hands full right now."

She smiled. "Yes, we certainly do." But she treasured the chaos of a new baby, fully aware that this would be her only chance to experience what so many took for granted. She stood. "I'm going to go shower."

"We'll have some breakfast, then wake up Jenny. Today she's going to give her daughter a bath."

She nodded. "Okay."

~~~~

Shane adjusted Faith in his arms and settled himself back against his pillows, watching Reagan pull clothes from her drawers across the hall. He studied the woman who was constantly on his mind, trying and failing to figure her out. They'd lived together for more than three weeks and had basically been parents for the last two. More often than not, they woke in the same bed, yet she still refused to let him in, other than the quick moment in the kitchen the night Faith was born.

Doc was passionate about her causes and incredibly kind, but for someone so easygoing and willing to help others, there were too many quick flashes of sadness in her eyes. Behind her pretty smiles and brilliant brain there were wounds, and those small hints of vulnerability were all the more intriguing because she thought no one could see.

Reagan walked into her bathroom, and he looked down, grinning at Faith making sounds in her throat as she gulped down her formula. "Knock it back, champ." He slid his thumb along Faith's tiny knuckles, reminding himself he was getting too attached to the new ladies in his life. Reagan was a constant fascination, and Faith was quickly worming her way into his heart. But in little more than two months he would be leaving them both and heading back to LA.

He brushed his finger along her soft skin, tucking the sweet baby closer, well aware that poor little Faith would more than likely be living in the hills by then. He was craving a full night of sleep and a decent workout—both things he'd done without since their guests arrived—but he wasn't looking forward to watching Faith go, knowing her life would offer her little more than a rundown house and few opportunities.

Her eyes drooped and her mouth went slack.

"Burp check," he murmured, settling her against the cloth he draped on his shoulder, rubbing gently at her back as the shower shut off. "Let's go wake up your mom."

He wanted to get to Jenny before Reagan did. Reagan didn't want to push the teenager too hard, but he was ready to try a little tough love. Jenny had helped herself to their food and TV. She was also willing to sit back and let strangers take care of her baby. Today Jenny was going to start pitching in.

Standing, he walked to the darkened room diagonal to his, giving a quick knock on the doorframe. Not bothering to wait for a response, he entered and opened the curtains. "Time to get up. Faith needs a bath." He turned, looking at the empty bed. "Jenny?" He made his way to the kitchen, certain she was stuffing her face, but she wasn't there. "Jenny?" He peeked his head out the front door, glancing at the empty porch swing, then started back down the hall, knocking on Reagan's bathroom door.

She opened the door a crack, wrapped in a towel, her hair dripping as steam smelling like her shampoo escaped. "What is it?"

"Have you seen Jenny?"

She frowned. "I thought she was in bed."

"Nope."

Reagan opened the door wider and hurried down the hall. "Jenny?"

He followed behind, watching drops of water trail down her spectacular thighs and calves. "I think she's gone."

"She can't be," she tossed over her shoulder as she climbed the steps to the loft.

He raised his brows, waiting for her to accept that Jenny had run off. "I definitely think she is."

She leaned over the above railing looking down at him. "She's gone."

"Yeah."

She came back downstairs. "Hopefully she went home to smooth things out with her mother."

He pressed his lips in a thin line, considering the idea for mere seconds. "Mmm, I'm thinking probably not."

Sighing, she closed her eyes. "Great."

"Ready for that hike?"

"Yes, I guess so. Give me a minute to change."

CHAPTER EIGHT

"WHAT'S THE PLAN IF SHE'S NOT THERE?" SHANE ASKED, wearing navy cargo hiking shorts and a sleeveless white Under Armour top, as he held Faith in the swaddle carrier Reagan had fashioned out of a thin blanket.

"I'm not sure." But she'd been asking herself the same question over the last half hour as they made their way up the path to Jenny's family home.

"Are they even prepared to take care of this baby?"

She skirted around the rocks and stepped over the tree branches jutting from the ground as Shane did the same by her side. "I don't know."

"The house wasn't very clean."

"I remember."

"They didn't have any diapers or a crib."

"I remember that too." Her partner in crime had been inundating her with nonstop questions and comments since they left the cabin.

"Where do kids go to school around here, anyway? And what about college? I doubt they're saving for her education if they don't even have diapers."

Sighing, she tossed him a glance. "Shane—"

"There's nothing *here*."

"Shane," she snapped, stopping and huffing out a breath as she stared at him wearing his navy blue cap backwards with his shades in place. The scruff along his strong jaw accentuated his mouthwatering looks. Faith's sweet little feet dangling from the blanket wrapped around his powerful chest only added to the adorable picture he made. Her heart turned to a puddle of mush, empathizing with the man who had clearly fallen in love with the baby snuggled against him. "I'm sorry I raised my voice, but I don't know what we'll find when we get there or how we're going to handle this entire situation. It's certainly a mess."

"All I'm saying is I think the fact that Granny doesn't give a damn and Jenny ran off should say something."

"It says plenty. Technically Mrs. Hendley's neglecting Jenny, and Jenny abandoned her baby, but we won't get anywhere if I start by bringing that up."

"This whole thing's bullshit."

"Yes it is." She pulled the water bottle from the backpack she carried, handing it over to Shane in the still-pleasant morning temperatures. "We won't leave Faith there unless we both feel one hundred percent comfortable that she's in good hands."

"Then we should turn around right now."

She tipped her sunglasses down, hoping he could see that this wasn't easy for her either. "We can't keep her."

"I know."

"Do you?"

"Of course I do, but it's hard to hand her over when we know what kind of life she's bound to have. We can give her so much more."

She pushed her glasses back in place, giving Shane a sympathetic smile, knowing exactly how he felt. "I've seen more than a few kiddos pass through the ER that I wanted to take home with me, but we're not Faith's parents."

"I don't even *want* kids for a few more years, but this whole situation's a damn shame."

She took back the water bottle. "It certainly is.

Come on." Unable to resist, she wrapped her arm around his waist. "Let's go see what we can do to make it right." But she worried the closer they got to the house. Within minutes, they made it to the clearing and her heart sank. Jenny's family home was in even worse shape in the bold sunlight. Trash and old tires littered the yard, ripped screens covered almost every window, and several planks on the old porch sagged where the roof had caved in. "Ready?"

"Not really."

"I'll go first." She smoothed down her simple white t-shirt and khaki hiking shorts, walked up the crumbling steps, and knocked.

A young, toothless woman with her blond hair twisted back in a braid opened the door. "Yes?"

"Good morning. I'm Reagan Rosner, the new physician at the Black Bear Gap Clinic."

"I ain't got time for this." She started to close the door.

Reagan pressed a hand to the flimsy wood. "I was wondering if Jenny's mother might be here."

"I'm Jenny's mother."

Reagan tried not to gape at the woman, who couldn't be any more than a year or two older than she was herself. "Oh."

"I ain't got time for Feds." She darted glances toward the woods. "I don't want no trouble."

Reagan tossed a look over her shoulder, trying to figure out what Mrs. Hendley was looking at. "I'm not here to cause problems, Mrs. Hendley. I'm hoping Jenny might've come home this morning."

"She ain't been here since you gone and hauled her off to your clinic."

"Yes. She's been staying with me for the last several days. She had a complicated delivery."

"I ain't surprised. That's what happens when you be frettin' with the devil."

"Mrs. Hendley, Jenny's gone and Faith is right here." She gestured toward Shane, with Faith still snuggled in the carrier.

Jenny's mother turned her head away from the child. "I ain't havin' nothin' to do with that baby. I told Jenny as much when she said Terry gone and planted her with his seed. Them Staddlers are pure evil. Jenny gone and got herself in trouble, now she's gonna raise that devil child on her own."

Swallowing, Reagan dug deep, trying hard to find her compassion. "Mrs. Hendley, I can assure you Faith is a very sweet, beautiful baby."

"If that be the case I'm sure she'll be welcome over yonder with them Staddlers."

This was going far worse than she'd expected. "What about Jenny?"

"She can go on to church and make herself right with the Lord. Then she can come back."

"With Faith?"

"No, ma'am."

"Mrs. Hendley, if Jenny isn't willing or able to care for Faith, I'll have no choice but to call social services. As a mandated reporter I'll be forced to involve the State, which would be unfortunate. Technically Jenny's abandoning her child, which can have legal consequences."

Mrs. Hendley glanced from Reagan to Shane. "She don't look abandoned to me. Looks to me like she's got herself a proper mommy and daddy right here. Fancy ones at that."

"We're not Faith's parents. Jenny and Terry are."

"Take her to that no good heathen then."

"What about Jenny?

"Jenny made her bed, now she'll be lyin' in it."

She peeked into the home, spotting Shirley sitting at the kitchen table. "I hate to pry, but how does your husband feel about this entire situation?"

"He don't have much to say, bein' he's locked up and all. The addictive ways of those no-good pills got the better of him. He won't be back 'til next year, earliest. Now good day to you."

Reagan stopped her from closing the door again. "Mrs. Hendley, if you change your mind you're welcome to visit your granddaughter down at the cabin anytime you want."

Jenny's mother's eyes darted to the forest again. "It's a wise soul who heeds a warnin' and knows when to stay away."

She shook her head. "I don't understand."

"For everyone's sake you need to be on your way." Mrs. Hendley shut the door and locked it.

For everyone's sake? What did that mean? Closing her eyes, Reagan turned and stared down at Shane looking up at her. "Well, this was a waste of time."

He shrugged. "I guess it worked out for the best."

"You don't seem too broken up about it."

"Damn straight. There was no way in hell we were leaving Faith here or dropping her off on the other side of the mountain. And what the hell was all of that cryptic crap?"

She shrugged, looking among the trees, slightly spooked as they started back down the path.

"Are you really calling social services?"

She didn't want to. "By law I have to. We have an abandoned child in our care."

"But she's being cared for. I'll take care of her."

"Shane—"

"We're not sending her off to get lost in the

system."

The idea of watching social services take Faith away didn't sit any better with her than it did Shane. "We'll wait a few days and see if Jenny reappears."

He nodded. "I can live with that."

She touched his arm, stopping him from walking on. "I don't want her to go any more than you do." She adjusted Faith's sunhat as she spoke. "I love her as much as you do."

"I know."

"I just wanted to be sure."

"We're on the same page here, Doc."

They always seemed to be. She smiled, and they made their way back to the SUV, the trip far less eventful in the light of day. Reagan helped free Faith from the wrap and got in the backseat, holding the baby. "We're going to have to remedy this situation immediately. I can't even believe we're driving without a car seat."

"I'll take care of it as soon as we get home." He drove the mile and a half at a snail's pace and eased into the drive.

Reagan came to attention, spotting the young boy and his mother sitting on the steps by the clinic.

"Looks like a potential new patient."

"Maybe." She assessed rosy cheeks as the little boy rested his head on his mother's lap. "He certainly looks feverish."

Shane got out, taking the baby as Reagan closed the back door.

The woman stood, holding the little boy's hand. "Are you the doctor?"

"Yes. I'm Reagan."

"Jodi."

Reagan crouched in front of the little guy with

brown hair and freckles, his brown eyes glassy. "It looks like someone's not feeling very well."

"Josiah here's got himself some mighty ear pain. My home remedies ain't doin' nothin' for it." She looked over her shoulder. "We wouldn't of come otherwise."

She stood. "I'm glad you did. I'm here to help." She tried a friendly smile.

"Bess Jacoby said you sewed up Sue Anne."

"I did." She looked at Shane.

"I've got Faith. Go help your patient."

"Thanks." She returned her attention to Jodi and Josiah as Shane walked toward the cabin. "Should we go see what's going on with Josiah's ear?"

Jodi hesitated. "I don't have no money on me."

"We don't turn anyone away here at the clinic."

"We got insurance, but the car ain't workin' and the doctor ain't due back to the mine for a few more weeks."

"It sounds like you've come to the right place." Reagan unlocked the clinic door and flipped on the lights. "Come on in. Josiah, my ocean friends in the pediatric room are going to give me a hand in helping you feel better today."

Josiah glanced at Reagan, then his mother.

Jodi looked over her shoulder again as she stepped inside.

Reagan cast her eyes toward the trees as she'd done at the Hendleys, realizing that the people of The Gap weren't just weary of The Project; they were afraid. But of what? She closed the door and led the mother and son to the cheerful examination room, hoping to put another family at ease and show them that she was here to help not harm.

~~~~

"I ordered the car seat and one of those portable cribs," Shane said to Sophie as he held the phone with his shoulder and slid the washcloth over Faith's legs in the kitchen sink he'd turned into a temporary tub.

"Sarah and Alexa said they would send some of the girls' baby clothes out."

"That would be great. We appreciate any help we can get." Reagan said she would wait a few days before she called in the social workers, but he had every intention of dragging out the inevitable for as long as possible. On more than one occasion he'd heard Austin speak of Hailey's experience in foster care. He intended to keep the sweet baby girl out of the system for as long as he could.

"Sarah and Alexa both thought three-to-six-months sizes would be the best."

"Sure. She's growing like a weed. Reagan weighed her yesterday. She's up half a pound." It was still hard to believe that the little lady relaxing in the warm water weighed less than a gallon of milk.

"You sound like you're more than half in love."

He smiled. "What can I say? She's cute."

"What about the doctor? You sound a little smitten there too."

He huffed out a laugh, surprised Sophie had caught on. "What can I say? She's cute too. Hell, she's gorgeous," he amended.

"What does she think about you?"

He pressed his lips together as he raised his brows. "Well, the jury's still out on that one."

"If she's as smart as you say she is, she'll come around."

"She's pretty guarded.

"I'll be rooting for you."

He grinned. "Thanks."

"So, how's Faith's mother doing?"

He blew out a long breath. "She took off this morning."

Sophie gasped. "Oh my gosh. I can't even imagine."

"She's young, overwhelmed, and not getting any support at home. I'm hoping she just needs a couple of days to decompress." But he wondered if Jenny had any intention of coming back for her daughter. During her two-week stay in the cabin, Jenny had changed Faith once and fed her twice, and that was only because Reagan had sat with her, encouraging and praising her the entire time.

"That sounds tough."

"It's not easy. There aren't any resources here like there are in LA."

"Stone told me you're staying in a pretty small place."

He chuckled. "'Small' is a bit of an exaggeration. There's a gas station and minimart five miles down the road."

"Wow."

"It's definitely different."

"But it sounds like you're handling it."

He was playing full-time dad to a child that didn't belong to him and part-time medical assistant to a doctor who was more than capable of handling the office on her own. "I'm hanging in here."

"Oh, I have a customer. I'll send the recipes when I get home and coordinate with Sara and Alexa on the clothes."

"Thanks, Sophie."

"Of course."

"Oh, hey. Congratulations again. You and Stone are going to be awesome parents."

"Thank you."

He smiled from the unmistakable joy in her voice. "Bye."

"Bye, Shane."

He grabbed the phone and set it down. "Time to get out. You're starting to look like a raisin." Faith fussed as he lifted her from the water and tucked her in the towel he'd unfolded on the counter at his side. "I know you hate this part, but I actually got the bottle ready first this time." He popped it in her eager mouth, and her crying stopped. If he happened to see Reagan do that the other day when she bathed Faith... He was learning.

"Come on, Pretty Girl. Let's get you dressed before you pee on me. Then we're taking a nap. Don't feel like I'll be put out if you decide to sleep for three or four hours." He paused, looking out the window as a woman he hadn't seen before walked out of the clinic, with Reagan waving behind her. "All right." He nodded his approval. "Looks like Doc's officially in business."

He moved to his room, securing Faith in her diaper as the baby cried her discontent. "We're almost finished." He wrapped her in her blanket, tucking her in his arm as he settled himself against the pillows, giving her back the bottle.

The front door opened and closed. "Shane?"

"Down here."

Reagan hurried in, her eyes full of excitement. "How are things going?"

"Good. Faith is clean, eating, and will hopefully be sleeping in the next couple of minutes."

"I can take a turn. I know I've been gone for awhile."

He shook his head. "We're fine. Looks like you've had a run today."

She smiled. "Two patients—one ear infection and a

strep throat."

"Good stuff."

She nodded, sitting on the edge of the mattress. "That's not the best part. I was talking with Jodi, Josiah's mother, about her gardens—trying to break the ice a little. She was telling me how she grows some of the best corn around but constantly has trouble with her beans. Apparently, Sue Anne's family seems to have the opposite issue." She swiped her hair behind her ear. "Anyway, while Jodi was talking, I got this idea. I was thinking we could organize an evening where families can get together here at the clinic and swap fruits and vegetables for a bigger variety of healthful foods—kind of like a farmer's market. We can offer some simple snacks and drinks, and I'm hoping I might be able to throw in a few nutrition facts while we're at it. There are so many kiddos with bad teeth. They're drinking too much soda."

"Sounds like you've got a plan. Go get 'em, tiger." He liked seeing her like this—her eyes bright, her hands punctuating certain words as they spilled from her mouth, caught up in her own enthusiasm.

"I will." Her smile dimmed as she touched Faith's toes peeking out from the blanket. "But I don't know how many people will come."

"So you won't have standing-room only on your first try."

She licked her lips. "They're afraid."

He frowned. "Who?"

"The people here. They're frightened by either me or the clinic."

"Why do you say that?"

She shrugged. "I don't know. That was the sense I got when I spoke with Jenny's mother and then again with Jodi."

CATE BEAUMAN

He remembered Mrs. Hendley's weird spewings about heeding warnings and staying away, but she also seemed like a bit of a whack job. "I don't know, Doc. When I look at you 'intimidating' isn't exactly the first word that comes to mind."

"Maybe not to you, but they were certainly uneasy. Maybe I'm trying to make sense of an unusual situation, but I don't think so. Both women kept looking toward the trees, like they were being watched or something." She shuddered. "It gave me the willies."

"We'll keep an eye on the situation, but things have been pretty low key so far."

She nodded. "I just really want this to work. I can help this town if they'll let me."

He took her hand, lacing their fingers. "You're an amazing woman. Eventually they'll figure that out."

She smiled. "Thank you."

"Give them time."

She nodded, breaking their connection, touching Faith's toes again. "Any word from Jenny?"

He shook his head. "But I talked to Sophie. Sarah and Alexa are going to send out some of their daughters' baby clothes. And I ordered a couple things from Amazon." Closer to two dozen, but Reagan didn't need to know that. "I'm not sure how the hell they'll get them here, but they're on the way."

"Shane."

He shook his head again, not wanting to hear her tell him that Faith's time here was limited. "I know. She's not staying forever, but while she is here, we're going to give her everything we can."

She rested her hand on his arm. "You're a good man."

He shrugged. "This is the right thing to do."

"Yes, it is." She stood. "Are you and Faith good for

awhile?"

"Definitely. We're about to catch some Z's."

"I'm going to head back to the clinic. Call me if you need anything."

"Will do."

"Have a good nap, sweetheart." She leaned down, the scent of her shampoo invading his nose, as she kissed the baby's forehead.

"I imagine you don't have one of those for me."

She lifted her head, her face an inch from his, and smiled. "No."

"Didn't think so." He closed his eyes and rested his head against the pillow, wanting to pull her mouth to his. "We'll see you after work. I'm grilling chicken."

"Can't wait. Bye."

"See ya." He settled Faith in the center of the bed, more than happy to turn it off for a while.

CHAPTER NINE

REAGAN CROUCHED ON THE SCARRED TILE FLOOR OF BLACK Bear Gap's minimart and post office, securing Faith in the new car seat Shane had wrestled from the box. She'd been waiting for a good ten minutes while he loaded up several more items into the SUV. Instead of taking their usual morning hike, they'd traveled into town when Mini, the town's postmistress, called up to the cabin to let them know their stuff had arrived. Reagan had been expecting a car seat, crib, and maybe a small package of clothing from Shane's friends, not most of Amazon's warehouse jammed into the trunk of the Pajero.

"I think that's everything." Shane walked back inside, looking casual and delicious in gray athletic shorts and a simple black t-shirt.

"Who's walking back to the house, you or me?" She smiled up at him then looked down, checking the straps cocooning the baby in her seat once more.

"I know it looks like a lot." He shrugged. "I wanted to make sure we covered all the bases."

She chuckled, rolling her eyes. "I think you did— and then some." She picked up the carrier. "Cutie Pie here is ready whenever we are—"

"Howdy, Doc Reagan," a heavy-set woman with long salt and pepper hair said as she walked by, holding a basket loaded down with chips, soda, and packaged cupcakes.

Reagan tried not to wince as she perused the

unhealthy options, pasting on a smile instead. Usually people avoided her and Shane. If this woman was seeking her out, she would run with it. "Good morning."

"I've heard of your curin' ways and saw the flyers about the food swap tonight at your clinic."

Word had traveled throughout the hills over the last week, but not without effort. She, Shane, and the baby had hiked far and wide, spreading the word and hanging flyers on every available telephone pole she could find, enticing members of the community with a full-fledged cookout instead of simple snacks. Rumors of more than ten families potentially attending left her giddy. "Yes, I hope you'll join us." She held out her free hand. "Reagan Rosner."

"Daisy Dooley. I ain't got much more to offer up than some green beans."

"That's fine. I'm sure someone will happily take them off your hands."

"I might stop up now that the truck is runnin' again."

"Please do."

Daisy stepped closer, peering into the car seat. "That be Jenny's girl?"

"Uh, yes. This is Faith."

"She's a right pretty thing. It's a darn shame her mamma took off."

"Yes." She nodded, swallowing uncomfortably. She didn't like speaking of her patients; although, confidentiality didn't appear to be a big concern up here in The Gap. Neighbors seemed to know all there was to know about the people in the next house over and mountain beyond. "I'm sure she'll be back."

"That feud between the Staddlers and Hendleys been goin' on for decades at least."

She wanted to ask what the feud was about but nodded instead. "I see."

"It's a real Christian thing for you and your husband to take Faith in."

"Oh, uh—" She looked at Shane grinning, but then a black-haired, stocky man walking into the store caught her attention with his incessant coughing. Her brow furrowed, watching him stop and rest against the wall. "Excuse me. I think I should go check on that man."

"He'll be fine soon enough. That'd be Henry, my husband. He's been coughin' off and on for years."

Henry didn't sound good at all and looked even worse. "Is Henry taking anything for his cold?" Although his coloring and wheezing alerted her to bigger problems than just a simple virus.

"No, ma'am. He's not one to fret."

"I would be happy to listen to his lungs if you and Henry want to stop by the clinic."

"He'll be all right. If you mine all your life, you cough." She shrugged.

"Your husband's a miner?"

"Was. Been retired 'bout five years now. "

Henry stood and started their way. "You ready, Daisy?"

"I'm talkin' to the new doctor 'bout Jenny's runnin' off."

Reagan smiled at Henry, wanting to change the subject. If Jenny thought she and Shane were gossiping about her she would never come back. "Hello, Mr. Henry. I'm Reagan."

He nodded. "Nice meetin' ya."

"I heard your cough. If you'd like to come to the clinic, I would love to see if we can take care of that for you." She noted his struggle for each breath and his blue-tinged fingernails.

"I ain't needin' no fool medicine."

The instinct to argue was tempting, but the people of this town were still feeling her out. Pushing would only take her back a step. "If you change your mind, I'm happy to help."

Henry started coughing again, bending at the knees with the effort.

Shane pulled the carrier away from Reagan, turning Faith farther away. "Faith and I will be waiting in the car."

She nodded. "I hope we'll see you tonight," she said to Daisy, knowing there wasn't much else she could do.

"You just might." Daisy smiled, seemingly oblivious to her husband's health issues.

"Great." She smiled back and walked outside, her smile dimming as she settled herself in the front seat, securing her safety belt.

"That guy was coughing all over the place."

"That guy is very sick."

"Hopefully he didn't give the baby anything."

Reagan shook her head. "Henry's not contagious. Whatever he has Faith isn't going to catch. His oxygen saturation is dangerously poor." She looked toward the door as the couple walked out of the store, Daisy with her bag of goodies and Henry puffing a cigarette to life.

Shane raised an eyebrow her way.

She narrowed her eyes, scoffing. "Try to have some compassion."

He shook his head. "I don't get it. If you're coughing like that, why the hell would you want to go and fill your lungs with smoke?"

"Addictions are a powerful thing."

"I guess." He turned over the engine.

"If you've never had one it's hard to understand.

Since we haven't, we're in no place to judge."

He moved to put the SUV into gear, pausing with his hand on the gearshift. "I'm not trying to be insensitive. It just seems like common sense to me. You're looking at this clinically."

"I'm pretty sure that's my job."

He shrugged. "Maybe he would be able to breathe if he stopped."

"It would help, but I doubt it will solve the problem."

He frowned. "Are you thinking it's cancer or something?"

"I can't say definitively, but it's serious nonetheless."

"Hopefully he'll change his mind and come in."

"Hopefully." She looked at Henry struggling into the driver's side, then glanced back at the mirror Shane had attached to the headrest in front of Faith's car seat, looking at the sleeping baby. "We should go. Ms. Lindy's coming in at ten so I can examine her knee."

He reversed and pulled onto the road. "Another one. I think it's safe to say the morning hikes are paying off. What's this, four patients in the last week?"

She smiled. "Three." But she wouldn't be happy until she had a full patient load. Everyone in this area needed regular medical attention. There were bound to be more Henry's scattered all over the mountain. She tossed a glance over her shoulder at the beat-up pickup driving in the opposite direction. "I don't understand why they won't let me help."

"They're coming—slow and steady."

"Yeah." But Henry didn't have time for slow and steady. He needed help now.

~~~~

Shane turned over dozens of hot dogs and flipped just as many hamburgers on the grill, surrounded by the families that showed up for Reagan's food swap. Fewer people came than she'd expected, but the event appeared to be a success nonetheless. The evening sky was clear, and the late summer temperatures tolerable. The people of The Gap had exchanged corn and beans, huckleberries and wild grapes, among many other fruits and vegetables. And he'd overheard Reagan talking with two of the women about incorporating homemade jams and smoked meats next week, along with other fresh produce.

He zeroed in on The Gap's new physician, watching her rub her hand up and down Faith's back in the sling as she stood among a small group of women and children. She'd dressed casually in jean shorts and a black tank top, but she'd also added a hint of makeup, which she never did. Doc always looked good, but this evening she was smoking hot. He returned his attention to the food on the grill, checking the temperature on the burgers, and slid them onto the platter. "Hot dogs and hamburgers are ready," he called, setting them on the dining room table he and Reagan had dragged outside.

Several kids came running as he tuned in to the familiar, non-stop hacking coming from under the shade tree a few feet away. He glanced Henry's way, watching the crotchety fifty-something fight his way out of the lawn chair he sat in seconds after arriving over an hour ago. Shane grabbed a bottled water and walked over to the man. "Can I bring you a hot dog or hamburger?"

"I'll help myself just fine, thank you."

The water was for Henry, but Shane twisted off the cap and drank, knowing he would refuse. "You got it.

There's potato salad and coleslaw—a whole bunch of other stuff too."

"Thank you kindly." Henry coughed again, gasping and hacking, then sat back down.

Shane frowned, noting the blood on Henry's fingers before he wiped the bright red smear on his overalls. "How about some water?"

"Moonshine does me good," he wheezed.

"Right." Shane nodded. "If you'll excuse me." He strolled over to Reagan. "Ladies," he interrupted the group with a big smile, rubbing his hands down Reagan's soft arms as he walked up behind her. "Hot dogs and hamburgers are ready if any of you would like to help yourselves." He tugged her gently back against his chest, moving his head close to her ear. "Henry's coughing up blood."

Her gaze whipped up to his. "What?"

"Henry had blood on his fingers after his latest coughing fit."

They both looked in his direction as he tried to stand again and fell over in his chair.

"Shit," Shane muttered and hurried over. "Are you all right?" he asked, helping the man back into his seat with the assistance of a couple of the other men.

"Just lost my balance is all."

Reagan rushed over. "Take Faith," she said to Shane.

Shane lifted the sleeping baby from the pack, and Reagan bent down at Henry's side. "Mr. Henry, I'm hoping I might be able to get a listen to those lungs."

"I'm feelin' just fine."

"I can go get my stethoscope—"

"I won't have no woman listenin' to nothin' of mine." He struggled to his feet. "Takin' on a man's job far as I'm concerned." He started toward the beat-up pickup.

"Doc Reagan." Daisy took her wrist as concern clouded her eyes. "I'm sorry."

"Don't worry about it." She gave Daisy a small smile and eased her away from the crowd gathered around. "Ms. Daisy, I would really like to help Mr. Henry. He needs an examination and x-ray, which I can do right here in the office."

"I appreciate your concern, but Henry saw Doc Hargus just a couple months ago."

She blinked. "A couple months ago?"

Daisy nodded. "Late June, it was. Gave him a clean bill of health."

"But his cough—"

"Just mighty allergies, Doc Hargus says."

Her brow furrowed. "Doctor Hargus said Henry's cough is a result of allergies?"

"Sure did. Gave us some prescription cure, but Henry ain't much for medicine."

Her frown deepened, and she licked her lips. "Doctor Hargus is the physician from the mine?"

"Yes, ma'am. Been there close to ten years I'm thinkin'."

Shane studied Reagan as she pressed her lips firm, humming in her throat as she nodded. Doc's sexy brain was working overtime.

"Ms. Daisy, I would really love to see him. We might be able to get Mr. Henry some oxygen treatments ordered up and sent right to your home."

"Doc Hargus will be back next month."

Henry coughed again, leaning against the truck, fighting for his breath.

"I'd hate Mr. Henry to go a whole month without a little relief. I can see him tomorrow. We might be able to get that cough under control."

Daisy sighed. "He's a proud man, Doc Reagan. Mighty proud."

Reagan smiled sympathetically. "Some people prefer male doctors. I completely understand, but I also think he's in need of a little care."

Shane stared at the beautiful woman standing inches away, admiring her, *wanting* her. Henry had insulted her and maybe even embarrassed her in front of the very people she was trying to win over, but she wasn't able to let him walk away without trying to help.

"I'll try to send him on back tomorrow."

"I hope you'll come along too."

She nodded. "We'll be in if I can make him see what's right."

"You're welcome any time. I'd be happy to send my notes on to Doctor Hargus if that will make Mr. Henry more comfortable."

"You're real kind, Doc Reagan. Real kind."

"Thank you."

Daisy walked to where her husband waited as Reagan met Shane's gaze.

"What?" He closed the distance between them.

She tossed a look over her shoulder and moved even closer, standing toe to toe. "Something's not right. Daisy must've misunderstood Doctor Hargus's diagnosis."

"The allergies?"

"Yes." She swiped her hair back. "I'm not a pulmonologist by any means. Emergency medicine's my specialty, but I can tell you without a doubt Henry doesn't have allergies. He's coughing up blood for heaven's sake."

"Daisy probably got something mixed up."

She nodded.

He studied her troubled eyes. "But you don't think

114

so."

"I don't know." She jerked her shoulders. "I don't know what I think, but I'm certainly concerned."

"Hopefully he'll come tomorrow and you can get it figured out."

"Hopefully." She sighed, stroking her finger over Faith's cheek. "I'm going to go mingle. I'd like to see if we can win over a few more community members before everyone decides to leave."

He glanced around at men and women conversing and kids playing or helping themselves to the cookies and brownies on the table. "Things are going great."

"Yeah," she said on another deep sigh, taking a step away.

"Hey Doc?" He snagged her hand.

She stopped. "Yes?"

"You'll always be a winner in my book." He winked, hoping to make her smile, grinning when she did. "Everything's going to work out."

She nodded.

"I'll dress up a couple of burgers for us."

"Sounds good." She sent him another smile. "Thanks."

"You got it." Reagan was trying her hardest to show these people they could trust her. The least he could do was make her a sandwich and provide a little comic relief.

CHAPTER TEN

"OKAY, MR. HENRY." REAGAN HELPED HER RELUCTANT patient free himself from the lead shield she'd wrapped around his waist. "You can put your shirt back on and sit with Daisy in the examination room. I'm going to look at the images we just took and hopefully have some answers for you in just a few minutes." Although she was fairly certain she knew what was wrong with Henry as she listened to his wheezing inhales and exhales while he pulled his t-shirt over his head.

"Allergies is what I got."

"I'm sure I'll only be a couple of minutes," she repeated, keeping her friendly smile pasted in place. The last hour had been pure *hell*. Coaxing Henry into answering her questions and convincing him to actually follow her to the tiny lead-lined room at the back of clinic had taken plenty of Daisy's prodding and a small act of God. "I appreciate your patience with all of this."

"Missin' my game shows is what I'm doing," he grumbled and walked out.

Sighing, she closed her eyes and rested her head against the doorframe, taking a moment before she removed her weighted apron and rolled the portable x-ray machine into the corner of the small space. She'd met more than her fair share of difficult patients over the past several years, but Henry was in a class all his own. He'd tested her patience, constantly arguing with her and questioning every inquiry she made. And he'd dished out more than a few sexist comments, but whether Henry liked it or not, he needed her help.

She moved down the hall to her office, sitting at her desk, uploading the images she'd just taken onto her laptop. Her brow furrowed as she studied the front-to-back view, switched to the lateral image, then back to the original. "Yikes," she whispered, zooming in on the huge mass of fibroids present in both of Henry's lungs. "Damn." She shook her head. Henry was in worse shape than she originally thought.

She clicked open another window, looking at similar images she'd pulled up on the Mayo Clinic's website at two this morning while she fed Faith her bottle and researched different lung diseases. Henry had all of the symptoms of pneumoconiosis. The x-rays appeared to confirm her suspicions.

She knocked over the box of pills at her elbow and her frown deepened as she picked up the over-the-counter pack of antihistamines and the bronchodilator Doctor Hargus had prescribed. None of this made any sense. She'd been certain Daisy had misinterpreted Doctor Hargus's diagnosis, but Daisy was exactly right, and the items she held in her hands were even more confusing. Henry Dooley didn't have asthma or allergies; he was dying. How had the mine's physician missed such a glaringly obvious advanced disease? Henry assured her Doctor Hargus had taken x-rays two months ago, yet the very sick man in the next room had been ill for far longer than sixty days. From the reading she'd done this morning, he would have had Progressive Massive Fibrosis for years.

Standing, hoping for more answers, she picked up her computer, bringing it with her to the sage-green examination room she'd used for the limited testing she was able to do here in the office. "Knock, knock."

A quiet argument ceased as she opened the door, sending Daisy and Henry a small smile, watching Daisy take her husband's hand.

"What's he got, Doc Reagan? What's wrong with Henry?"

She rolled the stool closer to the couple and sat down, dreading the news she was about to share. Licking her lips, she clasped her hands on top of her laptop. "I did quite a bit of reading last night about some of Henry's symptoms, the chronic cough and shortness of breath, which led me down a couple of different paths and a starting point for our appointment today. After completing some of the simple tests we did here this afternoon, along with the chest x-rays, I believe Henry has a condition called pneumoconiosis."

"I never heard of no such thing," Henry grumbled.

"Perhaps you've heard the term 'black lung disease.'"

Henry rushed to his feet, wheezing. "I ain't got no black lung."

Her heart went out to the miserable man as she recognized the fear in his eyes. "Mr. Henry, I'm concerned you do."

"I won't be hearin' none more about this."

"Henry, sit down," Daisy demanded, her voice quaking.

"Don't you be talkin' to me like that, Daisy. I won't be havin' no woman raisin' her tone to me."

"Please sit, Henry," Daisy tried again.

He sat on a huff that turned into a long, nasty coughing spell.

"Mr. Henry." Reagan handed Daisy a tissue and rubbed the pale woman's arm as she spoke. "There are two forms of pneumoconiosis—simple and a more serious form known as progressive massive fibrosis. I believe you have progressive massive fibrosis."

"Dear baby Jesus." Daisy's voice broke. "What can we do to fix it?"

"At this time there's no cure, but we can treat Mr. Henry's symptoms."

"Why didn't Doc Hargus tell us about this? Why'd he say allergies?" Daisy demanded, then blew her nose.

She shook her head. "I'm not sure. There may've been a mix up with the x-rays, or perhaps Mr. Henry's got lost. Mr. Henry, you're sure you had an x-ray in June?"

Henry narrowed his eyes. "I ain't stupid, girl."

"Of course you're not. I'm planning to give Doctor Hargus a call later this afternoon, and I'd like to send you to a specialist in Lexington."

"That be more'n two hours away," he barked.

She nodded. "But I think Doctor Jacobson will be a good resource for you and Ms. Daisy. I looked into our options and he seems to be the best. He's a very well-respected specialist in Kentucky. He has the highest rating out of all of the physicians in the area. He'll be able to perform the pulmonary functions tests I'm not equipped to handle here."

"If you didn't perform the tests then you ain't able to say one way or the other."

"I'm certainly not a pulmonologist, Mr. Henry, and I hope you'll get a second opinion, but your symptoms and thirty years in the mining profession are pointing me in this direction. Let me show you what I mean." She rolled closer to the husband and wife and opened her laptop. "This image on the left is Mr. Henry's lungs. Do you see these large white masses?" She pointed to the cobweb-like scatters. "This is scar tissue making it hard for Mr. Henry to breathe. This picture here on the right is that of another patient with a confirmed case of advanced black lung disease."

Daisy expelled a long breath. "They look the same."

Reagan nodded. "I'm afraid so."

"There ain't never been no one diagnosed in The Gap." Henry crossed his arms. "Corpus Minin's got one of the best safety records in the state. Worked for them my whole life. They take care of their men."

"Again, Mr. Henry, I want you to get the second opinion. I would be happy to call Doctor Jacobson for you and schedule an appointment. In the meantime, I'll send home a tank of oxygen and a mask that should help with some of the dizziness and confusion, which I believe is due to your low oxygen saturation. You won't be able to smoke though."

"Keep your oxygen," Henry spat. "I need my smokes."

Her heart went out to the man. First a devastating diagnosis, now the idea of having to give up his cigarettes. "Your symptoms will be easier to manage if you can cut down or quit smoking altogether."

He shook his head. "Black lung's a killer. If it's got me, it's got me, but I ain't givin' up my smokes."

"Will you go to the appointment in Lexington if I set it up?"

"No, ma'am, I won't."

"Yes, he will. He'll go, Doc Reagan, and we'll be takin' the oxygen."

"Now, Daisy—"

"We'll be takin' the appointment and the oxygen."

"I'm afraid I can't give you the oxygen if Mr. Henry's going to keep smoking. It's extremely dangerous."

"He won't be smokin' none, I'll promise you that, Doc Reagan. We'll take the oxygen."

She nodded. "I'll get the equipment and show you how to use it, then I'll make a few calls and get back to you with a date for an appointment." And hopefully a few explanations from Doctor Hargus.

"Thank you."

"You're welcome." She walked from the room for the equipment, not missing Henry's nasty glare on her way out.

~~~~

Shane strummed his guitar, playing the chords of Collective Soul's *World I Know* as he gently rocked the porch swing. He breathed in the fresh mountain air, perfectly content with Reagan at his side, her knee resting against his thigh as she sat cross-legged, holding Faith, while crickets sang their deafening chorus. Lamplight filtered though the screen door, casting Reagan's gorgeous face in shadows as she spoke.

"I've been researching since the moment Henry and Daisy left, and I'm not finding anything." She absently swiped at long strands of her silky brown hair blowing in the warm breeze. "I can't seem to find much of anything on cases of progressive massive fibrosis here in Eastern Kentucky."

Reagan had been late to arrive home from the clinic and quiet during dinner, clearly preoccupied by her thoughts. He'd finally pried her away from her computer half an hour ago, shamelessly using Faith as an excuse to entice her outside for a rock on the swing, like they did almost every night. "Maybe it's not the black lung thing."

"It is," she insisted.

"Easy, killer."

She winced. "Sorry. I'm just frustrated." She sighed, sliding gentle fingers down Faith's arm. "Doctor Jacobson pretty much said it wasn't either—more clinically, of course, but he was definitely dismissing my diagnosis. He hasn't even seen Henry yet and he's written him off."

"I'm sure he'll change his mind after Henry's appointment."

She shook her head. "I don't know. He spoke to me as if progressive massive fibrosis is some sort of myth, especially after I told him Henry's been employed by Corpus Mining his entire career."

"What does that have to do with anything?"

"Apparently Corpus Mining has one of the best safety records in the US. They have for years, or so I'm told, but regardless of that fact, Henry *still* has every symptom I've been able to track down, and his x-rays speak for themselves."

"Well there you go. You can't argue with an x-ray."

"I guess." She sighed again. "I put in a call to Doctor Hargus over at the mine, but he hasn't gotten back to me yet. I want a look at Henry's June x-rays and any others that might be on file. I just don't understand how he came up with allergies. Henry's lungs are full of fibroids."

He'd never seen Reagan this riled up. From what she said, Henry was in for a rough ride, but there was something more going on here. "You're a good doctor, Reagan. If you're this sure it's pneumo...whatever the hell you said, then it is.

"I'm just not—I like facts and data." She swiped at her hair for the umpteenth time. "It's hard to paint a complete picture without all of the information."

"I have no doubt you'll find it. Hopefully the oxygen will keep Henry comfortable until he can get to his appointment."

"Daisy said it was helping a bit when I called to check on them a while ago."

"That's good. You're doing what you can."

"Which isn't enough." She nibbled her lip, frowning as she stared off into the trees.

He'd hoped the balmy air and starlight might help her decompress, but that didn't appear to be the case. Maybe he needed to try something else. "If Cute Stuff here sleeps for a couple hours, I want to teach you to cook."

Reagan closed her eyes with a small groan.

He raised his brows. That wasn't exactly the reaction he'd been hoping for. "Or not."

"I'm sorry." She laid her hand on his arm. "I'm tired and a little grumpy."

"Grumpy? Nah. Keyed up?" He took his hand off the strings of the guitar and demonstrated an inch with his thumb and index finger. "Maybe a bit."

"Sorry," she repeated.

"No problem."

"How about a rain check on the cooking?"

"You've got it." He picked another song and started playing Pharrell Williams' Happy.

Her eyes widened seconds before her face warmed with a grin, then she chuckled.

He grinned back, thrilled to finally see that big smile of hers, and kept going.

Faith cooed, moving her arms in the light blanket.

Reagan looked down. "I think she likes it."

Shane played on and Faith cooed again, kicking her legs.

Reagan laughed and Shane stopped, scooting closer against Reagan's side, smiling down at the baby girl staring up at them. "Is that your new favorite, Faithy?"

He touched Faith's fist, and she grabbed hold of his finger. "And I thought you liked Old McDonald." He pressed a kiss to the baby's forehead, completely in love, and looked up at Reagan. "She likes pop music already. I think we're in trouble."

"We might—" Something rustled among the trees.

Shane set down the guitar and rushed to his feet when a branch snapped, much closer this time. Animal or enemy? "I'm armed," he bluffed.

"Don't shoot." Jenny stepped out of the woods in jean shorts and an oversized Bud Light t-shirt.

"Jenny." Reagan stood.

Jenny walked forward, standing in the beam of the porch light, her long blond hair tied back. "I—I'm back."

He studied the pretty teen's shy eyes and nervous gestures, wanting her to walk into the woods and disappear again. Faith was thriving under his and Reagan's care, and Reagan hadn't brought up social services since their hike back from the Hendley's home a week and a half ago. He wanted to make sure everything stayed exactly the way it was.

"I uh, I came for Faith."

Reagan turned the baby slightly, as if shielding her. "We're glad you're back, but we're not just going to hand her over."

She licked her lips. "Faith—Faith's my child."

"Who you abandoned," Shane added.

"Shane," Reagan warned, tossing him a hot look.

"I know I did Faith wrong, but I'm ready to take her on and make things right."

The crickets continued their songs, filling the tense silence while Jenny stared down at the ground.

"Um, why don't we go inside and figure out what's going on," Reagan suggested. "We would love to hear your plans." She looked at Shane.

Holding her gaze, he nodded. "I'll throw a couple of snacks together, and you can tell us what's going on."

Jenny hesitated, clutching her hands together, and walked up the steps.

"Come on in." Reagan opened the screen door, letting Jenny in before her and turned, facing him. "You might be upset with her, but she needs to feel supported."

He steamed out a long breath, trying to figure out how Reagan was able to be constantly compassionate. "I'll try my best, but she's not walking out of here with this baby." He slid his hand through Faith's soft hair.

"Of course she's not. I'm not going to let that happen any more than you are."

He glanced in at the teen slumped in the kitchen chair, her arms crossed at her chest, surprised by the stirrings of sympathy for her. Rubbing at his jaw, he sighed again. "Okay. Let's see what she's got."

"Supportive," Reagan reminded and stepped inside, smiling. "Jenny, we're so glad to have you back."

Jenny peeked up from under her lashes.

"You want something to eat or drink?" he said, mirroring Jenny's crossed arms, unsure of how to proceed.

"No." She shook her head. "I know you two're mad at me."

"We're not mad," Reagan assured. "We just hope you'll tell us what's going on so we can help you *and* Faith."

"I didn't do her right when I left." She kept sneaking glances at the baby.

"Do you want to hold her?"

Jenny nodded. "She's gotten so big."

Reagan settled Faith in her mother's arms. "She's

growing quickly."

Jenny stroked Faith's cheek. "She's so pretty."

"She looks just like you," Reagan said.

And she did. Faith was Jenny's mirror image—plump lips, a cute nose, sweeping eyebrows, and big exotic eyes set in a heart-shaped face. When Jenny and her daughter grew up, they were going to be stunners.

"She's just as sweet as she is beautiful." Reagan slid her finger along Faith's little hand as she took a hesitant step back.

Shane studied Reagan, noting the worry in her eyes despite her smiles and kind words, and he rested his hands on her shoulders, squeezing gently, realizing she didn't like this anymore than he did.

She looked back and sent him a silent thank you, surprising him when she leaned against him, resting her head on his chest.

Jenny pressed her nose to the top of Faith's head. "She smells real nice."

"Faith is definitely a water baby. She likes her baths."

"You took good care of her." Jenny swallowed. "I don't know why I left. I guess I wasn't thinkin' straight."

Reagan stepped away from him and sat down next to Jenny. "You're here now."

He took the seat next to hers.

"I heard maybe you might be wantin' to keep Faith for your own." She looked at Reagan.

Reagan shook her head. "We want what's best for Faith, but I'm not her mother."

Doc was good with the gentle understanding, but he wanted answers. "Did your mother say you can come home?"

Jenny shook her head. "Me and Terry's gonna get jobs in Lexington."

"You and Faith's father are back together?" Reagan asked.

"Yes, ma'am."

"Is Terry here?" Shane looked toward the dark beyond the screen door.

Jenny shook her head. "He didn't want to come."

"His baby's just about a month old. Doesn't he want to see his own kid?"

Jenny jerked her shoulders, staring down at her daughter.

"Where are you and Terry planning to work?" Reagan steered them back on point, grinding her heel into Shane's toes.

Son of a *bitch*, that hurt. He yanked his foot away, frowning at her as she sent him a not-so-friendly smile before Jenny looked up at them.

"We'll find somethin' I figure."

"What about school?" he asked, prepared if Reagan tried to make another underhanded move.

She shrugged again. "I'll be gettin' my GED."

"What about food, formula, diapers, a place to stay?" he grilled. Reagan wanted him to be supportive, but they also needed to be realistic.

She met his eyes. "I don't know."

"Jenny, why don't you and Faith plan on staying here for a few days while we work this out?" Reagan offered.

"Terry'll be waitin' on me to bring Faith to him."

"You guys will be living with his family?" Shane asked.

She shook her head. "They aren't wantin' nothin' to do with Faith neither."

He looked at the beautiful baby, trying to understand how two families could cast off a child over some dumbass feud. "So where are you two staying?"

"At an abandoned huntin' place half mile east of here."

The idea of Jenny taking Faith away to God knows where sickened his stomach. Jenny wasn't ready to raise a baby. She was a child herself. "It doesn't make much sense to leave a place where there's food and a bed for you and your daughter."

Jenny darted him another look.

"We would love to have you." Reagan smiled.

"I guess maybe for a couple days."

Reagan rested a hand on Jenny's shoulder. "If you really want to raise Faith in Lexington, I can help you get in touch with resources that can help."

Jenny nodded. "I've had time to do some thinkin'. I want to take care of Faith. I want to do her right."

Shane glanced from Jenny to the baby, not liking this whole thing, but Jenny was here. That was a start. "I'll move Faith's crib into your room."

"Thank you."

He gave her a nod and walked down the hall, struggling with the idea that the baby and Reagan wouldn't be sleeping with him tonight. He'd gotten used to having them both in his bed.

Chapter Eleven

Reagan sat at the small desk in her room, scanning yet another document she'd downloaded, finding nothing more than the basic information she'd read time and again. Stretching her neck muscles, she rubbed at her eyes, trying to banish her growing sense of frustration.

Since diagnosing Henry two days ago, she'd read every article in every journal she could get her hands on, hungry to be as knowledgeable about progressive massive fibrosis as she was about the conditions she dealt with on a regular basis in the ER. She was well versed in bullet wounds and broken bones, stitches and strep throat, but complicated lung disease was out of her league. Her job in the trauma room was to stabilize and ship her patients off to the specialists who would serve their needs best, but here in the mountains she was all things to over two hundred people, and she needed help.

She'd reached out to Doctor Jacobson, and he laughed at her, shaking her already broken confidence. He'd argued the absurdity of an almost nonexistent disease among the hill of Eastern Kentucky and the mine's great safety record, certain Henry didn't have black lung. But she was positive he did. Undoubtedly, Doctor Jacobson was the Pulmonologist, but she had actually examined the patient.

Desperate to quell her own insecurities, she'd spent the three hours since dinner scouring the internet and most of her day at the clinic banging her head against the wall, making phone call after phone call, trying to track down any one of the three doctors who'd treated the five confirmed cases of black lung diagnosed here in Eastern Kentucky over the last fifteen years.

By closing time, she'd discovered two of the physicians were deceased and the other had retired. That man, Doctor Heinz Schlibenburg, was exactly the person she had every intention of contacting...as soon as she could find him. Doctor Schlibenburg, one of the world's most revered pulmonologists and a top expert in pneumoconiosis, had apparently dropped off the face of the Earth. He'd quit his practice, no longer attended lectures or collaborated on new research, but he certainly lived somewhere.

She typed the doctor's name into another search engine, frowning when Faith's fussing in the next room caught her attention. She opened the first document, trying to ignore Faith's cries growing louder. Nibbling her lip, she forced herself to stay put and focus on her job, but it was a struggle listening to the baby cry when she knew exactly what to do to make Faith stop.

During the two days Jenny had been back, she and Shane had done their best to give the new mother her space, offering to help on occasion or gently guiding when Jenny appeared to need a hand, but for the most part they'd let her be. Eventually Jenny and the baby would leave. She needed to see for herself that Faith would be okay.

Faith's short, gasping cries grew louder yet, and Reagan got to her feet, unable to stand the baby's demands for comfort for another second. She walked next door, watching Jenny pace with her child, wearing the shorts Reagan had unearthed from the small pile of clothing donations at the clinic.

"Hush now, Faith. Hush now," Jenny said, bouncing the baby gently.

"Knock, knock."

Jenny turned. "She won't quit her fussin'."

"This tends to be her fussy time of night." Reagan smiled encouragingly. "She usually quiets down with a rock on the swing, or sometimes she'll settle with the lullabies Shane downloaded on his phone. I'm sure he'll let us borrow it."

Jenny shook her head. "I don't want Faith gettin' used to fancy stuff. She ain't gonna have nothin' fancy when we move to Lexington."

Reagan stepped farther into the room, noting Jenny's defensive tone. The teenager had been on guard for forty-eight hours straight, saying little and staying mostly in the loft or her bedroom. Jenny clearly didn't trust her or Shane, which wasn't doing Faith any good. Taking a chance, Reagan sat on the bed. "Would you like me to take her for a couple of minutes?"

Jenny shrugged. "I've a mind she won't quit for you neither."

"I'm here to help if you want."

Jenny handed Faith over.

"Shh," Reagan soothed close to Faith's ear as she stroked her fingers along the baby's back. "You're all right, sweet girl."

Faith's crying turned to whimpers.

"There you go." She settled Faith on her lap, smiling down at the baby while she rubbed her tiny tummy. "That's a little better, huh?"

Jenny plopped herself into the chair next to the bed. "She don't like me."

"Yes she does." She continued rubbing Faith's stomach.

"She don't cry for you or Shane. Just me."

"She cries for us as well. Don't you, Faithy?"

Jenny picked up one of the baby's rattles, fiddling with the toy. "Faith thinks you're her mommy."

Faith probably did. She and Shane had been caring for her from the moment she took her first breath, but Reagan shook her head anyway. "Babies pick up on emotion. Right now you're frustrated. I'm feeling a little more calm."

Faith passed gas.

Reagan wrinkled her nose. "Plus she appears to be gassy. Rubbing her tummy like this helps move the trapped air in the right direction."

Jenny huffed, setting the toy down. "I don't know nothin' about raisin' babies like you do."

"You're learning." She leaned in closer, whispering conspiratorially. "And I don't know either. I read or guess, just like you're doing."

Jenny smiled, her first smile since she'd been here.

Encouraged by the small chink she made in Jenny's armor, Reagan scooted closer to the chair. "The most important thing is you're trying."

"It don't seem like much."

"Sure it does."

Jenny shook her head, staring down at the floor. "I ran off. I'm a stranger to my own baby."

She placed her hand on Jenny's arm. "You won't be for long. Before you know it, she'll forget all about me and Shane." And the idea hurt her heart.

Jenny licked her lips and looked at Reagan. "I'm feelin' nervous about headin' off to Lexington. Terry's wantin' to get married."

She nodded, suppressing a wince. The last thing Jenny needed was marriage on top of everything else. "There's no rush for you and Faith to leave."

"We can't be stayin' forever."

She glanced at the GED booklet Shane told her he found on one of the bookshelves in the study. "There's nothing wrong with staying while you prepare for your future." She gestured to the book.

"We can't stay that long. I ain't smart like you. It'll be a while yet before I'm ready for my GED."

She ached for the beautiful young woman with such a hopeless path—a sixteen-year-old mother with poor self-esteem and few chances to strive for more than what she already had. "You're smart, Jenny. I have little doubt in my mind about that. You just haven't had a lot of opportunity. There's a big difference. I can help you prepare for the exam—or Shane."

She stood, pacing restlessly. "He don't like me."

"Yes, he does." Although he certainly didn't do much to show it. "He's very attached to Faith." She grabbed Jenny's arm, pulling her down to the bed next to her. "We both want what's best for you and your baby, and I think the best thing is making sure you have an education."

Jenny rolled her eyes. "That's what the teachers say."

She held back a sigh. Jenny was so young. "They're right. There's a huge freedom in knowing I can move anywhere in the world and support myself."

She laughed humorlessly. "I ain't gonna be no doctor."

"You can be anything you want to be." She lifted Faith, settling her in her arms now that she was calm. "You've got your whole life ahead of you."

"And a baby to raise."

"I work with several single mothers in the city."

Some of the hopelessness left Jenny's eyes. "You do?"

She nodded. "Absolutely. There are single parents

all over the place. You're young, but that doesn't have to hold you back. If you want something bad enough, you can do anything." She looked down at the baby finally drifting off. "You'll be a great role model for your daughter."

"I guess."

"It looks like Cute Stuff's ready for bed." She stroked her finger down the baby's soft cheek, missing the time they usually spent together. "If you want to take the pre-test in the booklet Shane gave you I can help you prepare for the test."

"I probably won't do so good."

"I bet you'll surprise yourself."

"Okay."

She smiled, surprised and relieved that they might be getting somewhere. If Jenny got her GED, trade school could be an option. "Great. We can look at your results tonight or tomorrow before I go to work." She stood and settled Faith in her crib. "Night, Faithy." Kissing her finger, she touched the baby's nose.

"Do you like it? Bein' a doctor?"

She turned, facing Jenny again. "Yes. I love it. Practicing medicine's a huge responsibility, but I can't imagine doing anything else."

"Sometimes I think maybe I might want to be a nurse or somethin'."

Her excitement grew. There were all kinds of programs she could help Jenny get into. "Nursing's a great profession. You would certainly be able to provide a comfortable living for you and Faith."

"Terry says I should be stayin' home raisin' babies."

She bit her tongue instead of vocalizing her thoughts on Terry's archaic sense of women's rolls in the twenty-first century. "Is that what you want?"

She shook her head.

"There's nothing wrong with being a stay-at-home mom, but there's nothing wrong with being a career mom either." She leaned against the desk. "I would love to have you come over to the clinic sometime and see what medicine is all about." She didn't miss the spark of intrigue. "We can look into Certified Nursing Assistant programs. You could always work your way up to an LPN then an RN if you do a good job. A lot of facilities will pay for training."

Jenny grabbed the pencil off the pad of paper full of doodles. "I guess I could take the pretest now."

Reagan grinned. "Take your time and let me know when you're finished, and we'll figure out the rest."

"Okay."

Reagan stood and started back to her room, changing her direction when she heard the faint strumming of Shane's guitar.

~~~~

Shane glanced up when the screen door opened. His fingers faltered on the guitar strings as he stared at Doc silhouetted in the light shining from the house. He trailed his gaze up her snug jeans and pale pink bow-back tank, taking in every inch of her sinful body. She looked good. Damn good. "Hey."

She smiled, stepping outside "Hey."

"I see you've finally pulled yourself away from the computer." He'd peeked in her room over an hour ago, inviting her to come out for one of their evening chats. She'd answered him with some absent mumble, and he'd realized she was still on the hunt for information. Reagan had sunk her teeth into black lung, and she wasn't letting go. "How's the research going?"

She sat next to him on the swing, smelling as

amazing as she looked. "Not well. I can't seem to find any real data on the black lung cases I tracked down here in the state, but I did find two of the three doctors who treated the patients."

He raised his eyebrows, trying to figure out how that constituted a bad start. "That sounds like a pretty good day to me."

She wrinkled her nose as she shook her head. "They're both deceased."

He sucked in a breath through his teeth. "Being dead definitely puts a wrench in things."

"Exactly." She chuckled. "Don't do that."

He smiled. "What?"

"Make me laugh when I'm totally frustrated."

He grinned. "I always thought that was the perfect time *to* laugh. I like seeing you smile."

"I don't want to smile right now. I need to stay in the zone and focus." She made straight lines with her hands, gesturing tunnel vision.

He fiddled with the guitar strings, quietly playing the first few chords of Kansas's Dust in the Wind. "You have to be miserable to stay focused?"

"No, but I feel pretty miserable right now." She sighed, resting her head against the seat. "I guess that's why I came out here."

"Because you're unhappy?"

"Because you're good for me." She sat up straight, her eyes growing wide as her gaze whipped to his. "I mean you always know what to say...to make me feel better...and to put things into perspective."

He bit his cheek, struggling not to smile at the look of absolute horror on her face. He *was* good for her. It was a damn good feeling to know she recognized that, even if reluctantly. He would let her off the hook and let her admission slide...for now. "Maybe the dearly departed doctors have a colleague or someone who could help you out."

"Yeah." She cleared her throat. "Maybe. But I'm on the hunt for the third physician. From what I've been able to find, he was about to publish some sort of article on progressive massive fibrosis a few years ago, but he retired instead."

"Why?"

"I don't know." She expelled a long breath. "I can't seem to nail down anything, hence the frustration."

"I can imagine. I take it you haven't heard back from the mine's doctor."

"No. I called again today, but I got his voicemail." Her shoulders relaxed, and she crossed her legs as she usually did, resting her knee against his thigh. "I just want to be able to help Henry."

"You are."

She shook her head. "Handing over oxygen isn't enough."

"Reagan, he's dying."

"And his family's entitled to compensation. He needs a confirmed case of progressive massive fibrosis to receive the benefits he and Daisy deserve."

Doc was a hell of a woman. Henry had been a bastard, fighting her tooth and nail, and she refused to give up on helping him. "It's going to work out. Henry will see Doctor Jacobson in a couple of weeks, and he'll confirm the black lung thing. You'll find your vanishing retired expert, learn all you want to know, and all will be right with the world."

"I hope so."

"Have a little faith, Doc."

She smiled. "So I should probably tell you your plan worked."

He frowned. "What plan?"

"Giving Jenny the GED booklet."

"Whoa, subject change."

She grinned. "Yes, subject change. Jenny's taking the pre-test right now."

He raised his brows. "No kidding. How'd you talk her into that?"

She tilted her head, frowning this time. "Why do you think I talked her into anything?"

"Because she gave me a go-to-hell look when I handed it to her this afternoon."

"Ah. Gotta love teenage rebellion." She chuckled. "Jenny's young and smarter than she realizes. She hasn't been exposed to the opportunities you and I have."

"That's because there aren't any—not here, anyway."

She gave a decisive nod. "Exactly. That's the problem for the families here in The Gap. That was the entire point of the Appalachia Project—to give the people here a chance." She brushed at her hair as the breeze blew. "Jenny's interested in nursing. I was thinking you could keep an eye on Faith a couple days this week so she can come in and see what working in a doctor's office is all about."

And she was already back at it—Reagan to the rescue. "Yeah, sure."

"We can help her, Shane. We can help her give Faith a chance."

"She's trying. We have to give her that."

"I think she'll try harder if we continue to encourage her. Her confidence is shaken—her self-esteem is poor."

"Parenting the parent."

She nodded. "Definitely."

He studied the beautiful woman with the big heart

sitting in the shadows. "How do you do it—overlook everyone's flaws and give them what they need?"

She shrugged.

"Jenny and I are still trying to feel each other out, and you're already over the fact that she up and left her kid."

She jerked her shoulder for the second time. "She made a mistake. She's trying to fix it. Not everyone gets that chance."

He set down his guitar, sensing another one of Reagan's untold stories. "I imagine we all have a few moments in our lives we wish we could take back."

She didn't say anything as she stared ahead.

"I got drunk after my junior prom and puked all over my date while I was trying to smooth talk her into bed.

She laughed. "I guess that didn't go as planned."

He shook his head. "Not so much."

The porch was silent again, except for the crickets singing their songs among the trees. He wanted her to share something, to offer up something of hers for free, but the quiet stretched out for a minute then two then three. "So what about you? What moment do you wish you could take back?"

"I can't think of anything off the top of my head."

He raised his brow as she avoided his gaze. "Nothing in twenty-six years?"

"I answered a question wrong on my MCATS. I had my heart set on a perfect score, but I kind of freaked and blanked."

MCATS. More medical stuff. "Sounds tough."

"My parents were very disappointed—after all their hard work..."

He swallowed frustration. "I've noticed you don't have much to say about yourself, Doctor Rosner."

"There's not much to talk about. What you see is what you get."

He narrowed his eyes, pressing his lips firm as if speculating. "Mmm, I'm not sure I agree. You're gorgeous, dedicated, not to mention really damn smart. Then there's all of these little facets that I find fascinating."

She stood on a quiet huff, walking to the edge of the porch.

"What?"

She turned, crossing her arms, leaning back against the railing. "Answer me a question."

He sat where he was, staring at her in the halo of moonlight. "Sure."

"I've always wanted to know why physicalities rate first with men. Why are looks more important than intelligence?"

He stood, certain this had nothing to do with physicalities and everything to do with her reluctance to get personal. "I like beautiful women. I'd be a liar if I said otherwise."

Shaking her head, she turned away.

He stopped in front of her, shoving his hands in his pockets. "But I prefer the whole package."

She turned back. "Which is?"

"Brains and beauty."

"But beauty comes first."

He considered, wanting to be completely honest. "Not necessarily."

"When you listed off some of my qualities—in your opinion—you spoke of physical appeal first, then dedication and my brain."

He stepped closer. "I think you're stunningly hot." He brushed her hair back from her temple. "Your body could easily be on any number of billboards or featured in sexy magazines."

She laughed humorlessly and stepped away.

He caught her by the elbow and blocked her way with his body, trapping her against the pole. "But then there are all of these mysterious pieces that fascinate the hell out of me." He touched her cheek. "And they have nothing to do with your looks."

She pressed her hand to his chest. "Shane—"

"I'm attracted to you. I have been since the second I laid eyes on you, but now I know you—or what you'll let me know of you, and I'm completely intrigued."

"What am I supposed to do with that?"

He could keep talking or he could do what he'd been wanting to for weeks. Holding her gaze, he trailed his fingers up her neck, pausing on her hammering pulse, then brushed his thumb over her full bottom lip as her trembling breath heated his skin. "Kiss me back."

She gripped his wrist. "I can't," she whispered.

He moved in despite her weak protest, capturing her lips slowly, feeling her slight give of response. Easing back, he caressed her jaw. "Reagan—"

Shaking her head, she clutched his other wrist, her breathing growing ragged. "I can't," she whispered again.

He took her hands, settling them at her sides on the rail under his, pushing their bodies closer. "Why don't I believe you?"

She laced their fingers. "I don't know."

Eyes locked, chests heaving, he knew she was lying to them both and came back for more, tenderly coaxing her into following his lead as he cradled her face, tugging and teasing her bottom lip.

Moaning, she surrendered, opening to welcome the slide of his tongue, and his heart kicked into high gear, his fingers diving into her soft hair. He deepened the kiss, intensifying their embrace, hungry for her sweet taste.

She slid her palms up his arms, molding his triceps, clinging, meeting him demand for demand as he wrapped her up tight.

And just as quickly, she froze and pushed back. "We can't—I'm not doing this."

Her mouth was swollen from his, her eyes hot with desire, and just like that, it was over. "Why?"

"I—I'm on a break."

He shook his head, trying to catch up. "A break?"

Swallowing, she nodded. "I'm taking time off from men."

He raised his brows. "You're taking time off?"

She nodded again, her breathing still unsteady. "Yes."

"For how long?"

"Indefinitely."

He stepped back, rubbing at his chin, doing his best to shake off Reagan's curve ball. "Huh. For a few seconds there it kind of felt like the break was over."

She shook her head. "It's not."

"I—"

"Reagan." Jenny stood in the screen door. "I finished."

She sidestepped further away from Shane, licking her lips and smoothing her hair. "Finished?"

"The pre-test."

"Yes. The pre-test," she said almost desperately. "I'm going to go help Jenny."

He held her gaze, silently promising her this wasn't over. "Sure."

"Goodnight." She walked inside.

"Night." He crossed his arms, leaning back against the beam, watching her walk away. So Doc was on hiatus. He flashed back to the way she'd wrapped her gorgeous body around him, whimpering as she clung. "The hell with that." Reagan assured him her "man break" wasn't over, but he had every intention of proving her wrong—every chance he got.

CHAPTER TWELVE

THE HOUSE WAS STILL QUIET WHEN REAGAN GLANCED OVER her shoulder toward the bedrooms and snuck out the front door, fully aware that rising an hour earlier than usual was a blatant attempt to avoid any possible run-ins with Shane.

Closing the door quietly, she walked down the dirt path and let herself into the clinic, flipping on the lights before she sat at her desk and powered up her laptop, eager to get to work after a restless night of sleep. She typed Doctor Schlibenburg's name into Google, sighing when Shane's voice echoed through her mind for the umpteenth time. *Kiss me back.*

Groaning, she shut her eyes, resting her head against the soft fabric of her chair. She'd done little but think of Shane since he'd cornered her on the porch last night. When she joined him on the swing, she'd wanted light conversation and to share the exciting new Jenny development. Never *ever* had she planned to make out with Shane Harper.

She narrowed her eyes, recalling how she'd ended up in the predicament in the first place. First, she'd foolishly slipped up and told him he was good for her, then he'd used her admission against her. Shane was a sneaky one, maneuvering with his humor and charm, listening to the things she had to say all the while waiting for the perfect opportunity to strike with words and simple touches that made her pulse pound—as it did now simply remembering. And he could *kiss*. She'd melted under the teasing pressure of his lips, caught up in the clever slides of his tongue and enticing nips of his teeth, recklessly following him wherever he led.

She rubbed at her temple, fully aware that she'd faltered—big time. But one mistake—a mistake she wouldn't make again—could easily be overlooked. Her hiatus was not in jeopardy. Her goal of avoiding the opposite sex on any sort of romantic plane would stay firmly intact, because complications with men— especially men who looked, tasted, and felt like Shane—were nothing she had time for—or wanted.

Sitting up straight, she readied a pen and pad of paper, determined to get back to work and forget the whole thing, and muttered a swear when the front door opened.

"Mornin'," Jenny stepped inside, her hair damp and dripping, wearing one of the two pairs of shorts she owned and the Bud Light t-shirt she'd arrived in the night she came back.

Reagan smiled. "Good morning."

Jenny fiddled with her fingers as she rocked back on her heels. "Uh, Faith's havin' her bottle with Shane. He said I should come on over."

"Of course." She stood, hoping to ease Jenny's nerves. "Come on in and..." Her thoughts vanished and her stomach betrayed her with a rush of tingles as Shane walked up the steps, looking begrudgingly sinful in one of his snug exercise tops and jeans, holding Faith in his arms.

"Looks like you made it," he said to Jenny. "Hey, Doc. We missed you this morning." He held her stare, as he closed the door behind him.

"Uh, yes. I had some stuff to do." Even as she fumbled for an excuse, she knew he didn't believe her. She tore her gaze from his, flicking a glimpse at his lips and rock-hard arms, well aware of exactly how they felt wrapped around her, holding her tight. Clearing her throat, she leaned her butt against the desk. "Is there something you need?"

"Nah. I just thought we'd come by for a quick visit. Faith wanted to wish her mommy good luck."

Jenny smiled, taking the baby's hand. "Mommy's gonna learn all about nursin' so she can take care of you right." She turned her attention to Reagan. "I wasn't sure how long you'd be wantin' me to stay."

She hadn't been expecting Jenny this early, but she wasn't going to turn her away. She had every intention of capitalizing on Jenny's enthusiasm and running with it. "Probably for an hour or so. Today we'll get familiar with some of the equipment, and I can show you how to take and record some basic vital signs."

"Doc's great with vitals," Shane said.

Reagan swallowed, rubbing at her heart accelerating in her chest, remembering Shane's fingers sliding along the skin of her neck—exactly his intention, she had no doubt. "We should probably get started."

"We'll see you later." Shane waved Faith's hand. "Good luck, Mommy," he said in a foolish girl voice.

Jenny laughed, and Reagan smiled despite herself.

The door closed behind him, and she wiped her damp palms on her jeans, not quite steady—which she was also certain Shane had intended. Definitely sneaky. Drop by with the pretenses of a casual morning greeting, get her all stirred up and make her remember—not that she'd forgotten—and then just leave. "I'm so glad you decided to come in."

"I want to get to learnin'."

She beamed. "That's excellent."

Jenny walked over to the white coat hanging on the

hook in the office area, fingering Reagan's monogramed name. "You got your own coat."

"Yes. My friends gave that to me as a gift when I finished medical school—for my residency." An idea struck her as Jenny continued to admire the stitching. "I actually have something for you."

"You do?"

She nodded, walking to the supply closet, unlocking one of the doors. "I imagine you'll need smalls." She took out two pairs of blue scrubs and handed them over. "When you come in for your training, I'll want you to wear these."

Jenny's eyes filled with excitement. "I need—you want me wearin' these?"

"Definitely. This is very much an internship. By the time we're finished here you'll not only be ready to pass your GED with flying colors, but you'll also be ready to kick butt in a CNA program."

"I don't want to be a CNA."

Her stomach sank a little. She could help Jenny go as far as she wanted in the medical field. She had enough of a name behind her to cement Jenny's future if her eager new student was willing to work hard. "You don't?"

Jenny shook her head. "I want to be a LPN. I was lookin' at the computer in the study last night after you went to bed. I can make more money bein' a LPN. Then maybe when Faith is old enough for grade school, I'll start schoolin' to be a RN."

She *loved* that Jenny had goals and a plan. "Okay. We can make that happen if that's what you really want."

"I do. I'm supposed to be meetin' Terry tonight. I'm tellin' him I ain't marryin' him right now."

Reagan nodded, treading lightly. "I think that's a

CATE BEAUMAN

good choice for you and Faith."

She played with the string on her new pants. "He's gonna be mad."

"How mad?"

"Pretty mad." She emphasized her words with wide eyes.

"Are you afraid he'll hurt you?"

She shook her head. "Terry ain't like that, but he won't be wantin' to hear about me workin' to support myself."

She saw her opening to ask more about Faith's father without appearing as if she was prying. She and Shane knew nothing about him. She leaned against the exam room doorway, wanting to keep their conversation casual. "So, how old is Terry?"

"Eighteen."

"Oh. So he's in high school—a senior?"

"No. He dropped out Sophomore year. He's been talkin' about the GED, but I'm thinkin' he don't really have a mind to take it."

"He works then?" she prodded.

"He did." Jenny sat in one of the waiting room chairs, seemingly relaxed. "At the mine, but he got himself fired for being late too many times."

Reagan stifled a sigh. Terry was going absolutely nowhere, and if Jenny stayed with him, neither would she. "I see."

"That's why we gotta go to Lexington, because there's no other jobs around here. Although I'm not feelin' quite as excited about movin' now that I get to do my internship."

And thank God for that. She walked over to Jenny, taking the chair next to her, more determined than ever to help. "If Terry truly cares for you, he'll support your choices. I'm proud of you. Your decision to pursue

148

your education and get a good job will give you a chance to give Faith everything you want for her." She took her hand, squeezing gently. "And yourself."

"I want to be a good mommy."

"You already are."

She shook her head. "I wanna be better."

"Then you will be. You're welcome to the books Shane ordered in on parenting and infant care, and you know you can use the internet as well."

She nodded. "But I—" Jenny let loose a long sigh. "The other night when I came back, I stood in the woods for a long time watchin' you and Shane on the porch while he was playin' the guitar, and you were holdin' Faith. He's so handsome and you're so pretty. You two were talkin' and laughin' and lovin' on Faith like a cozy picture in a magazine. I wanted nothin' more than to be in your picture."

Her eyes filled as she stared at Jenny. The sweet, beautiful girl in front of her was lonely and desperate for a connection. She wanted a place to belong. Reagan thought of her own childhood, empathizing with Jenny entirely. "You know, I bet if someone were to look in our window tonight, they would see a similar picture— a mommy and her baby girl and their friends, sitting at the dinner table, laughing and sharing the events of their day over a hot meal."

Jenny blinked at her own tears. "That sounds mighty nice."

She nodded. "It sure does." She hugged Jenny, holding on, smiling when their new house member wrapped her arms around her.

Jenny drew away, wiping at her cheek. "I'm gettin' all messy."

"That's a girl's prerogative." She winked, and Jenny chuckled. "What do you say I show you around here and we'll start with a lesson on measuring height and weight accurately."

The front door opened again.

Reagan turned, expecting to see Shane, but a tired-eyed woman no more than twenty stepped into the waiting room, hugely pregnant. Reagan stood. "Good morning."

The woman gave a quick nod. "I was—I was wonderin' if I might be able to get an appointment." She crossed her arms at her chest.

"Sure." Reagan smiled, sensing the woman's discomfort. "Come on in. I'm Reagan."

"Uh, Mary Jo."

"Is the appointment for you, Mary Jo?"

"Yes. I, um, I've been having some pains."

"Why don't you come with me and we'll see if we can figure out what's going on." She held up a finger to Jenny to tell her to wait, then led Mary Jo to the mauve exam room and closed the door. "Go ahead and have a seat in the chair or on the exam table, wherever you feel most comfortable." Reagan sat on the rolling stool as Mary Jo took the chair. "How far along are you?"

"Right around thirty-six weeks."

"You're getting close." She wiggled her brows. "You must be excited."

Mary Jo gave her a small smile. "Yes."

"Do you know what you're having?"

She shook her head.

"A surprise. Is this your first pregnancy?"

"Yes, ma'am."

"Can you describe the pain you're having?"

"It ain't a pain so much as this tightenin' in my belly."

"Tightening." She nodded. "Mary Jo, I would like to give you a quick exam."

"Yes, ma'am."

"Come on up." She helped Mary Jo settle on the table and felt around the soft mound, locating the baby's butt. "He or she is head down." She felt around again, certain that everything appeared normal, and was rewarded with a solid kick to her palm. "I guess the baby's had enough of that."

Mary Jo nodded. "Yes, ma'am."

Mary Jo was a tough nut to crack. Her discomfort with being there was more than apparent. "I'm not feeling anything concerning." She grabbed the Doppler. "Let's go ahead and have a quick listen."

Mary Jo nodded again.

Reagan squirted a small glob of gel on Mary Jo's abdomen and turned on the machine, smiling when the heartbeat filled the room. "Perfect." She wiped away the mess and helped Mary Jo sit up. "Does the tightening hurt?"

"No, ma'am. I'd say it's more troublin' than anythin' else. My belly gets hard, and there's pressure."

"Does the sensation come regularly?"

She shook her head. "Just now and again."

"Well, it sounds like you're having Braxton Hicks contractions."

"Contractions?" Mary Jo's eyes widened.

"Practice contractions, which are nothing to worry about. Your body's getting ready for the big day."

Mary Jo puffed out a breath that could only be relief. "I thought maybe somethin' was wrong."

She shook her head. "You've got a head down baby with an excellent heartbeat."

"Thank you."

"You're welcome. If your contractions become regular and there's pain, I'll want you to come back or visit your regular doctor. Your due date is right around the corner, but we like to see babies make it as close to forty weeks as possible."

"Yes, ma'am." Mary Jo's eyes darted to the door as they had several times over the last few minutes.

Clearly her new patient was in a rush to be on her way. "Is there anything else I can help you with?"

"No, ma'am."

"I hope if you have any other questions or concerns you'll stop in or give me a call." She handed over one of the flyers Mr. McPhee had refused when she brought them to the mine. "Oh, wait." She opened the closet door and held out one of the new baby welcome bags she kept on hand. "Here you go. You can take one of these too. There's some pamphlets for you, a few diapers, a bib, and a storybook for your baby."

"Thank you."

Reagan opened the door, and they walked into the waiting area. "Good luck and congratulations."

"Thank you," Mary Jo said again, starting toward the door, but then she stopped, turning back. "Doctor, Daisy's sayin' you diagnosed Henry with black lung."

She was about to give her newly familiar speech on confidentiality, but ignored the technicality, sensing Mary Jo was here for more than Braxton Hicks. "Yes, I did."

"You's is sure it's black lung?"

"X-rays and the tests I'm able to perform here in the office are leading me to believe Henry has progressive massive fibrosis."

"You's is sure?"

She nodded. "I feel very comfortable with the diagnosis."

"Daisy's sayin' Henry's goin' to see some specialist in Lexington."

"Yes. Doctor Jacobson."

"Henry's got himself oxygen."

She nodded again, trying to figure out where Mary Jo was going with her questions and statements. "He does."

"My husband, Jed, he's coughin' all the time, real bad like Henry. I'm hopin' you can give him the tests. Jed's wantin' to wait for Doc Hargus, but that's sure a time until he'll be back, and Henry seems more comfortable."

"How old is Jed?"

"Twenty-two."

Twenty-two years old and he sounded like Henry? "How long has Jed been mining?"

"Mmm, about four and a half years now."

Advanced lung disease after four years in the mine? There had to be another explanation for Jed's symptoms. "I can certainly see him. When would he like to come in?"

"He ain't wantin' to, but he's got himself the cough, and he's weezin' somethin' fierce at night. It keeps me up."

"Is this a new cough?"

"Fairly—probably over the past year it's gotten much worse. His energy level's real bad. Doc Hargus calls it bronchitis, but the prescription cure he hands out ain't done nothin' for it."

"Bronchitis?" She hadn't even examined Jed yet, but that didn't sound right.

"Yes, ma'am."

She walked into her office, looking at her appointment book. "Do you think he might be able to come in at ten?"

"We can make it."

"I'll write down his name."

"Daisy's tellin' folks you're real kind."

153

"Daisy's a lovely woman."

"We'll be in at ten."

"I'll look forward to seeing you."

Mary Jo nodded, then looked at Jenny. "Jenny, I been hearin' you was back."

Reagan walked to the teen, sliding an arm around her shoulder as she heard the hint of disapproval. "She certainly is." She pulled her closer against her. "Patients will be seeing a lot of Jenny around here. She's my new intern."

"Intern?"

Reagan nodded as Jenny sent her a thankful glance. "Jenny's training for nursing school."

Mary Jo's brows rose. "Nursin' school?"

"Absolutely." She smiled. "I'm proud to have Jenny here with me."

Mary Jo looked from Reagan to Jenny and back. "We'll be seein' you at ten."

"I'll look forward to meeting Jed."

The door closed behind Mary Jo.

Jenny dislodged herself from Reagan's hold. "You was nice to say that. Folks around here aren't takin' too kindly to me these days."

"They'll come around."

"Probably not. I ran off. Now I'm stayin' with Feds."

She clenched her jaw, detesting the word *Feds.* "Can I ask why the community doesn't like The Project?"

She shrugged. "I can't say really. It's not like you're a mean person or nothin', but Pastor warned us of the Feds' evil ways when word came that the clinic and all the rest was movin' in."

"Evil ways?" She led Jenny toward the scale for their first lesson.

"You know, interferin'. Comin' into the mountains

with lies and propaganda."

She shook her head. "I don't think I understand."

"Feds is liars. Feds say they came to help, but they're a distrustful bunch here to stir up trouble and take away our jobs."

Frowning, she set the weights back to zero. "How are we taking away your jobs?"

She shrugged. "Pastor McPhee says Feds think coal is dirty energy. Feds will do and say anything they can to shut minin' down for good."

She paused with her hand on the height rod. "Pastor McPhee? The owner of Corpus Mining?"

"No. Well, sorta," Jenny corrected. "Phil McPhee runs the mine operations. Bill, his brother, runs our church."

"Oh." Regan nodded, pressing a hand to her suddenly queasy stomach, understanding for the first time that something was definitely off. "I guess we should probably get to work."

"I'm ready."

~~~~

"Who's that pretty girl?" Shane said to Faith, sitting next to her on the floor as she lay on the quilt, staring up at the toy mirror he dangled in front of her. "Who's that *smart* girl?" he added, remembering his conversation with Reagan on the porch mere hours ago. He'd thought of little else since she walked away; hell, she was constantly on his mind, but what she said and how she responded to his kiss had kept his brain busy well into the night.

Her sexy moans and the way her silky tongue had eagerly sought his own filled his thoughts even now. Clearly she was interested in more than just their moonlight talks. And she was *definitely* avoiding him: sneaking out before everyone was awake, then trying to get rid of him when he strolled into the clinic this morning.

Apparently Reagan had mistakenly thought he was going to let her off the hook easy. Not even close. "Doc's keeping her distance." Grinning at the idea, he picked up Faith. "You know what that means, don't you?"

Faith cooed as her little fists moved about.

"Exactly. Reagan's running scared." He touched his finger to Faith's nose and chin. "But I'm going to catch her."

Faith cooed again.

"I agree completely. She doesn't have a chance."

The front door opened, and Jenny rushed in. "I'm runnin' late. I'm sorry. Let me wash my hands and I'll take Faith off your hands."

"Take your time. We're fine." He had reports to finish for Ethan but nothing that couldn't wait.

Jenny dashed passed them, turned on the sink, hurrying in seconds later to crouch down next to the baby. "Hello, Faith." She slid her hand along the baby's cheek. "Mommy's home."

"How'd it go?"

She shrugged. "Fine."

He glanced over at the blue scrubs she'd set on the table, admiring the woman in the building next door even more. Reagan had let Jenny's disappearing act slide and was moving forward, trying to give her a shot at a future. He needed to do the same. "Looks like you have some fancy new threads."

She looked to where he gestured. "I guess."

"I was thinking about making a snack. Do you want something?"

"No, I'm all right."

"You sure? I make a mean chips and salsa—or we could do nachos."

Faith made one of her sweet little sounds.

"Wait. What?" He lifted Faith to his ear. "Nachos?" He pulled her away, nodding to the baby. "You got it champ." He looked at Jenny. "Faith says nachos."

Jenny smiled. "I do like corn chips."

"I'll get us some." He handed Faith to her mother. As he got to his feet, Faith started crying, and Jenny's easy smile vanished. "I think she might be ready for a snack too," he added.

"I'll get it." Jenny stood, bringing Faith with her to the kitchen.

He grabbed the chips from the cupboard and shredded cheese and salsa from the fridge, noting that the baby seemed to be a sore spot between him and their semi-permanent houseguest. "So, Reagan told me you were working on the GED pre-test last night."

She shrugged as she measured out formula, holding Faith in her other arm.

He dumped chips onto a plate and heaped on the cheese. "How'd you do?"

"Fine."

"Great." He popped the food in the microwave, hitting the button for thirty seconds. "When do you think you'll be ready for the test?"

"I ain't sure. Reagan's gonna help me with some of the math and grammar sections."

And here was his opportunity to help Reagan give Jenny her chance. "I can give you a hand."

"Reagan's gonna do it. She says she's real good with Algebra."

He doubted there was little Reagan couldn't do—except cook. "If you change your mind, I'm pretty good

157

at Algebra too. Solving for 'x' or 'y' can actually be kind of fun."

Jenny looked at him as if that was doubtful.

"You sure you don't want to give it a try? We'll snack, explore the wonders of high school math, bond."

She grinned. "Maybe I could surprise Reagan with my learnin'."

"Sounds like a plan. I can feed Ms. Fussy if you want to grab your book."

Her smile disappeared. "I can take care of Faith on my own."

Definitely a sore spot. "I agree. You're doing great. I'll gorge myself on cheesy chips while she knocks back her bottle. Let me know when you're ready."

She glanced at the floor, peeked up at him, and nodded.

He grabbed the food from the microwave, remembering the salsa, and sat at the table, biting into a crunchy piece of pure heaven.

"Here it is." Jenny came out with the book, taking the seat at his side. She opened to the page she had bookmarked. "Reagan thought I should start with this here."

He leaned closer to her side. "Quadratic and linear equations."

"They don't make much sense to me."

He grabbed another chip, offering Jenny the plate, pleased when she took one. "You've come to the right place." He picked up the pencil and explained the wonders of Algebra while Jenny fed the baby.

CHAPTER THIRTEEN

REAGAN SAT IN FRONT OF HER LAPTOP, LOOKING AT THE series of x-rays she'd taken earlier in the day—front and lateral images of Buck Ely's lungs, full of fibroids. Sighing, she pushed her hands through her hair, overwhelmed by the results she kept finding. Since Henry's diagnosing three weeks ago, she'd confirmed three more cases of progressive massive fibrosis. "Unbelievable," she mumbled, rechecking her data, sure this couldn't be right. Four men out of four were gravely ill, and one of those patients was a twenty-two-year-old man with a baby due any day.

"The last patient just headed out," Shane said from the doorway.

"Huh?" She glanced up, her gaze trailing up his jeans and white Ethan Cooke Security t-shirt.

"The patient you had in exam room one. She left."

"Great. Thanks."

He stepped into her cubicle-sized office, coming up behind her and leaned down, looking at the images on her screen as she did. "Another one?"

"Yes." She turned her head, realizing his face was mere inches from her own, and scooted her chair to the right. During the days since her...error in judgment, she'd managed to avoid alone time with Shane—until now. Between Jenny's lessons, her ongoing research, and the slight uptick in patients, as well as helping with Faith, avoiding a moment like this had been fairly easy. They'd worked together everyday in the clinic, on

159

occasion side by side, and he had been nothing but professional—not to mention a lifesaver. Shane and Jenny had quickly become invaluable members of her team. "We've got a huge problem here. Something's very wrong."

"It's pretty insane."

"It's more than that. Four men, Shane. Four men right here in The Gap are dying, and their doctor never picked up on it." She shook her head in disbelief. "I need to put a call in to Doctor Jacobson and let him know I'm sending another patient his way." She rested her elbows on her desk, sighing as she rubbed at her temples.

Shane crouched down next to her. "What's going on, Doc?"

"'I'm overwhelmed," she admitted, and it felt good to say so. She missed talking to him. "Between this," She pointed to the x-rays on her screen, "major tooth decay, rampant diabetes, not to mention the three cases of early-stage heart disease. And that's just this *week*." She closed her eyes, squeezing at the painful tension in the back of her neck. "The need is so great."

He took her hand. "And you're helping."

She shook her head. "I don't know."

"I do." He laced their fingers. "What'd'ya say we go home, and I'll cook for you."

She studied his big, warm hand swallowing hers. "I really need to transcribe my notes from today."

"They'll be here tomorrow." He slid his thumb along the sensitive skin of her wrist. "You need a break. You've been going hard for days on end. A night off will do you some good."

Shane cooking and the thought of a long conversation where she could actually share her thoughts and feelings sounded like heaven, which made her want to pull free of his gentle grip. She was too comfortable with the man staring into her eyes, despite her mistake—and that worried her. "I probably shouldn't."

"One night, Doc."

It *was* just one night. It wouldn't hurt to recharge her batteries a little. She gave in to what he offered and what she desperately needed. "I guess the notes could wait."

"Good call." He stood, pulling her to her feet, not bothering to drop her hands or move when her breasts brushed his hard chest.

"Shane."

"Yeah?"

"Take a couple of steps back."

"Will you swing with me tonight?"

Another thing she missed. "Will you keep your lips to yourself?"

He smiled. "If you want me to."

"I definitely do."

He shook his head, frowning. "You definitely *want* me to kiss you?"

She smiled. "You know that's not what I—" The front door opened, and she shoved him away.

"Doc Reagan."

Reagan rushed around Shane, recognizing Daisy's voice raised in alarm, and hurried into the waiting room. "Ms. Daisy."

"Doc Reagan—"

"Is everything all right?"

"Yes. We just got back from Lexington."

"Oh, great. How did the appointment go?"

"You's was wrong," Henry accused, his chest heaving from the first stair. "You's was *wrong*."

"Hush, Henry," Daisy scolded.

Confused, Reagan guided Daisy further into the room. "Come on in and tell me what's going on."

"We saw Doc Jacobson. He ran all the tests, and he's sayin' Henry don't have black lung. He's got himself COPD."

"COPD?"

Daisy nodded. "Yes."

"I won't be listenin' to no women doctors no more," Henry spewed as he climbed the last step, struggling for his breath. "You's put me in my death bed, foolish girl."

"Hey." Shane stepped up to her side.

"It's okay," she murmured. "Mr. Henry, I don't think you—"

"Women ain't paid to think," he spat, pointing his finger as he glared. "Here you been tellin' all these men they got black lung. They be riskin' their jobs for nothin'."

"Mr. Henry—"

"Three family men may be outta jobs 'cause you're more trouble than you're worth."

"That's enough," Shane warned, his green eyes going hot.

She shook her head, stepping in front of Shane, worrying far less about Henry's insults than Doctor Jacobson's diagnosis. "Mr. Henry, I don't know what to say. I was sure—"

"I got nothin' more to be sayin' to you, girl."

"Doc Reagan." Daisy took her arm. "I'm sure you did your best, but Henry's not dyin'. He's gonna get better. We'll be seein' Doc Jacobson from now on. Good day to you."

The door closed behind Daisy, and Reagan stood where she was, trying to swallow over the ball of emotion. She was wrong. She shook her head. But she wasn't. Henry had progressive massive fibrosis.

"Reagan—"

"Go ahead on home." She moved back to her office, taking her seat, pulling up four sets of x-rays on her screen. "You and Jenny should eat without me."

"Doc—" He rested his hands on her shoulders.

She shrugged him away. "I need to look this over."

"Reagan—"

She blinked, desperate to keep her tears at bay. "Please just leave me alone."

He sighed. "If that's what you want."

"It is."

"Okay." He walked to the door, hesitated, then left.

She closed her eyes and rested her face in her hands as her breath rushed in and out too quickly. She was wrong—again. She'd been positive of her diagnosis in all four cases. They were identical. "How can this be?" With a trembling finger, she clicked on the mouse, zooming in on the cobweb-like matter crowding Henry's right lung, sure this couldn't be right, but she'd made a mistake like this before. She'd been certain of Mabel's condition too.

You killed my baby!

The words echoed through her head like a nightmare, and she rushed to her feet with the surge of panic. "No. No," she whispered, sitting again, needing to get to the bottom of where she'd gone so wrong.

~~~~

Shane sat across from Jenny at the table, glancing out the window toward the clinic, waiting for Reagan to come home. He'd held off dinner for as long as possible, hoping she would join them, but thirty minutes turned into forty-five, and Jenny had wandered into the kitchen, foraging through the fridge, declaring herself half starved.

Reluctantly, he'd plated up the meatloaf and potatoes, debating whether he should go check on Doc, but he'd taken his seat instead, knowing she needed her space.

Chewing another bite, he hardly noticed the delicious flavors of the new recipe Sophie sent along as his gaze wandered toward the clinic again, remembering the devastated look on Reagan's face when that bastard Henry told her she was wrong. She'd been upset, as upset as he'd ever seen her, and there wasn't much he could do to help, mostly because Reagan wouldn't let him. He forked up more meat and potatoes, catching Jenny's eye, sending her an absent smile.

She glanced over her shoulder toward the clinic. "Reagan usually ain't—isn't," she corrected, "this late."

"She said she had some stuff to do."

"Why're you lookin' out the window every five seconds then?"

"Why are you so nosy?" he said without heat.

She smiled. "I'm just curious."

"How'd you do with the math problems we discussed this morning?"

"Okay, I think. I'm hopin' you'll look 'em over."

During the couple of weeks since their first study session, Jenny had become more relaxed. She actively sought him out for help with her studies or when she needed a hand with Faith. "I can do that after we finish up here." He scooped up a bite of the potatoes she'd made. "These are really good by the way."

She smiled again. "I'm a pretty good cook." The phone rang. "I'll get it." She dropped her fork and dashed off like any teenager would. Jenny was a mother, a student, and Reagan's unofficial intern, but she was still very much a child. Now that she was here and they seemed to be finding their way, he was glad she'd come back. He lifted his water glass and set it down as the front door opened.

Reagan walked in, toeing off her shoes, her long hair curtaining her face.

"We kept a plate warm for you."

She glanced up, her face pale and drawn, her eyes weary. "I'm not hungry."

"Terry's wantin' me to meet—" Jenny stopped short, frowning. "Reagan, you're not lookin' so good."

"I'm fine." She forced a smile. "I'm a little tired after the last few days."

"We fixed you a plate—meatloaf. I made the potatoes. And there's green beans."

"That sounds wonderful, but I think I'll save it for my lunch tomorrow. I'm going to bed." She walked off, her strained smile vanishing as she passed Shane's chair.

Jenny sat back down, her brow furrowed. "What's wrong with her? I never seen her look like that before."

"I think she's stressed out and tired." And he had every intention of checking on her in a minute. "What were you saying about Terry?"

"He wants me to meet him."

Jenny had gone off to visit Terry twice since she'd been back. Reagan had warned Shane to tread lightly where Faith's father was concerned, but that didn't mean he couldn't ask questions. "Why doesn't he ever come to the cabin?"

She shrugged as she swallowed her bite. "He's intimidated, I guess."

"Doesn't he want to see his daughter?"

"He's wantin' me to bring her with me one of these

times."

"What do you guys do?"

"Talk and stuff."

It was the "and stuff" he was worried about. "Are you two having sex?"

Her eyes grew huge. "Shane," she drew out in a mortified tone as her cheeks burned bright.

"Jenny," he repeated back the same way. "I just don't want you doing anything you're going to regret."

"No. We ain't havin' sex." She huffed out a breath and rolled her eyes. "He wants to, but after birthin' Faith I'm not ready."

"Good. I hope you'll talk to Reagan or even me if you decide you are."

"I'm not fixin' to make more babies anytime soon, and I'm not gettin' married neither. I got plans. In fact, I've been wantin' you to tell me about Los Angeles."

"You want to go to LA?"

She shrugged. "I know I don't want to stay here. You'll be leavin' before long, and Reagan won't stay forever."

The idea of having Jenny and Faith close by wasn't bad. "Tell you what, I'll keep an eye on Ms. Fussy while you go see Terry. When you get back, I'll show you the area where I work and live via the wonderful world of Google Maps."

She beamed. "Okay."

When she left for the next couple hours, he wanted her thinking about her future—and Faith's. If she was looking forward to a fresh start, she would be less easily persuaded by a boy thinking about his dick.

"I'm going to go check on Reagan before Faith wakes up," he said. "Be careful."

"Yes, daddy." She blinked, smirking.

"I'm not your daddy. I'm your friend."

"You're right." She smiled as she took a huge bite of her meal.

"See you when you get back." He walked down the hall and knocked on Reagan's door.

She didn't answer.

"Reagan." He twisted the knob and stepped into the dark.

"I'm trying to sleep."

He closed the door behind him, squinting, waiting for his eyes to adjust. "I wanted to make sure you're okay."

"I'm fine."

He sat on the edge of the bed next to her. "I don't know, Doc. For some reason I'm just not buying it." He turned on the bedside lamp, the pale light accentuating her pallid color.

She groaned. "Shane, go away." Rolling to her other side, she put the pillow over her head.

He stood, looking down at her wearing the jeans and black shirt she'd had on at the clinic. "If that's what you want."

"I do," she said, her voice muffled.

Instead of leaving, he lay on top of her, pulling her pillow away.

She expelled a surprised breath. "What are you *doing*?"

"Squishing you."

"Get up."

He adjusted his weight, settling himself mostly on his forearms. "Mmm, I don't think I can do that."

"I can't breathe."

"Oh. Sorry." He tugged on her shoulder, rolling her to her back so they lay face to face. "There we go."

She smiled. "Get off."

"You don't seem to want to talk to me, so I'm afraid

I've had to switch to more persuasive tactics."

"Bully tactics."

He smiled. "Maybe."

She shoved at his chest. "I want to go to sleep."

He pressed his lips firm, furrowing his brow. "I just don't see you getting a whole lot of rest." He played with her hair, his fingers brushing her cheek with each slide of his hand as he stared in her eyes. "What's swirling around in that brain of yours?"

"Henry."

"Henry's a crotchety asshole. He was way out of line."

She shook her head. "I misdiagnosed him."

"Mistakes happen."

Scowling, she huffed and pushed at him again.

Wrong approach. "Everyone makes mistakes, Reagan."

"I'm a doctor. I can't afford them." She swallowed. "I was so sure he had complicated black lung. His symptoms are textbook. The x-rays are spot on too." She closed her eyes as they filled, and her lips trembled.

"Hey." He gripped her jaw, giving a gentle shake. "You're a damn good doctor. Look at everything you've done for the people here over the past few weeks."

"And four are misdiagnosed."

"*One* is misdiagnosed. Just because Henry doesn't have it doesn't mean the others don't."

Tears fell from the sides of her eyes as she breathed in a quaking breath. "I don't want any of them to have it, but they're all presenting with the same symptoms. Everything's exactly the same. I just don't understand how Doctor Jacobson came to his conclusion. Their x-rays don't favor that opinion."

He wiped his thumb along her damp skin, hating that she was taking this so hard. "So talk to him."

"I sent him an e-mail and left a voice mail. He hasn't gotten back to me yet."

"So the guy's stupid."

She chuckled and he smiled.

"One 'oops' isn't make or break."

The flash of fun vanished from her eyes. "Sometimes."

"But not this time."

"It's more than an 'oops' if three men lose their jobs and this town starts believing the pastor."

He frowned. "You lost me."

She sighed another shaky breath. "Jenny told me the pastor told everyone that the only reason we're here is to cause trouble and help the government shut down the mines."

"That doesn't even make any sense. Why the hell would he say that?"

"Because they're old fashioned and afraid of progress, I imagine. Education and good health brings new opportunities. Mr. McPhee made it very clear that this community takes care of their own when I tried to drop off my flyers."

He went back to playing with her hair, wrapping long locks of soft brown around his fingers. "Sounds like brainwashing to me."

"Yeah—a little."

"But church has nothing to do with their jobs."

"No, but black lung does."

"Henry couldn't work anymore, even if he wanted to."

"Yes, but the others can—at least for now."

"So there you go."

She shook her head. "It's not that simple. If a miner is diagnosed with progressive massive fibrosis, they're entitled to compensation. If they have the simple form of black lung or some other less debilitating condition, they receive nothing. Statistically most miners won't even get their symptoms checked, because they don't want their companies finding out."

"Why?"

"Because if something is found the company might find a way to get rid of them. A miner with lung problems is a liability. You and I both know The Gap is tiny. Everyone knows Jed, Buck, and Travis came in to see me for an examination and that their x-rays were positive for something. Now they have no choice but to go and see Doctor Jacobson and hope for a complicated black lung diagnosis. If he comes up with something other than progressive massive fibrosis they'll more than likely be out of work and have no compensation to fall back on."

Henry's rabid spewings made a little more sense now. "That's on McPhee. You did your job. You have nothing to feel bad about."

She sighed. "I guess."

"Take the night off, Doc, and look at this with fresh eyes tomorrow." Unable to resist, he touched his lips to hers, staring into her eyes as he drew back and moved in again, studying her as she studied him.

She halted him with her hands on his shoulders. "Shane—"

"I know. You're on a break." And he would respect that tonight when she was raw and her defenses down. "How about dinner? You've been running around for hours."

Her shoulders relaxed. "It smells great, but I'm not hungry."

"Sophie sent along another batch of recipes. Try a little for me?"

She nodded. "A little."

"How about a walk in the morning? We haven't done one of those in a long time." And he missed their time together. She'd made herself scarce, keeping herself busy with work, Jenny, and the baby. "Or what if we give the rowboat a try?"

"The rowboat?"

"Yeah, the rowboat that's been sitting in the pond down there that no one's touched." He smiled, liking the idea more and more. "It'll be fun. Some of the leaves are starting to change."

"If you promise to keep your lips to yourself."

He sucked in a deep breath, encouraged that she was worried enough to ask for conditions. "I hate to make promises I don't want to keep, but I think I can make that happen."

She smiled. "Then I'd love to try out the boat."

Faith started to fuss in the next room. "That's my cue."

"Where's Jenny?"

"She went to meet Terry."

She frowned. "I definitely don't like this Terry."

"That makes two of us, but she says she's not having sex."

"At least that's something."

Faith's cries grew louder. "I'll feed Faith. You feed yourself."

"Okay."

He got up and pulled her to her feet, regretting that they couldn't stay just the way they were, lying cozy in her bed. "See you in a few." He turned to leave.

She grabbed his hand. "Shane. Wait."

He faced her. "Yeah?"

"Thank you."

He squeezed her fingers. "You've got it."

Chapter Fourteen

Shane tied his hiking boots and stood, pushing his black cap onto his head with the bill facing backwards. He snagged the backpack he'd stuffed with a water bottle and snacks, and moved to Reagan's door across the hall, knocking.

"Yeah, come in."

He stepped in, stopping short, staring at Reagan's hair piled in a messy knot on top of her head, still wearing the tank top and cotton short shorts she typically wore for pajamas as she sat among dozens of papers scattered all over her bed. "Damn, Reagan. What are you doing?"

"Work," she said, not bothering to look up from her laptop as she typed.

He pushed some of the mess away and sat next to her, reading the e-mail she was composing.

Dr. Jacobson,

I'm e-mailing my request for a meeting in your Lexington office. I've reexamined Henry Dooley's results and cannot, in good conscience, write off his symptoms as chronic obstructive pulmonary disease. Through steadfast research and hours of x-ray reexamination, I find it impossible to agree with your diagnosis. As you know, the past few weeks have brought to light three more patients presenting with identical symptoms and results. Please contact me at your earliest convenience so that we may further discuss this matter.

Dr. Reagan Rosner

She hit "send," and he captured her jaw in his hand, easing her face in his direction. Dark circles colored the skin below her eyes. "Doc, have you slept?"

"No. I stayed up searching for Doctor Schlibenburg."

"Did you find him?"

She shook her head. "But I sent out several e-mails to other area physicians. I need a third opinion. I want Doctor Schlibenburg's, but until I track him down, someone else's will have to do."

She was driving herself crazy. "What about this stuff?" He gestured to the folders and papers.

"I looked over all the charts I transcribed during the past few weeks."

"*All* of them?"

She nodded pulling free of his grip. "Every single one." She crawled off the mattress, stacking papers. "The diagnoses are right. Blood sugars were within diabetic ranges, the symptoms of early-stage heart disease appear to hold true, the research I continue to gather supports progressive massive fibrosis in all four of the cases I've screened."

He studied her movements, which were growing more frantic with every paper she gathered. Doc was rattled. "Reagan, Doctor Jacobson disagreed with Henry's diagnosis. That doesn't mean the rest are wrong."

"Henry's isn't wrong either," she snapped and closed her eyes, sighing. "Sorry."

"Don't worry about it." After a decent dinner, good conversation, and an hour-long snuggle with Faith, he'd thought Reagan was in a better place when she headed off to bed last night. Apparently not. He stood, settling his hands on her arms, rubbing her soft skin. "This is really getting to you."

"There are men depending on me to get this right. They're counting on accurate decisions that afford them the best medical care I can provide."

"You're extremely good at what you do."

She shook her head, pulling away. "Mistakes aren't acceptable—ever. In this profession you don't always get another chance. When an ambulance rolls up with someone in the back, their family members are counting on me to make the right calls. They're trusting me to heal and send their babies home with them."

He drew his brows together. What in the hell was she talking about? "Last time I checked we don't have an ambulance in The Gap, so you can check that concern off your list. And the men you're treating definitely aren't babies."

Whirling away, she huffed out a long breath, pressing her face into her hands.

"Hey." He tugged her around, pulling on her wrists until she looked at him. "Why are you letting this eat at you?"

"I let them down."

"No, you haven't." He cupped her cheeks in his hands. "You absolutely haven't."

"They came to me because they're suffering. They came because they have the same symptoms as Henry, which I assured them all was black lung. They have families to support, Shane."

"That's McPhee's problem," he reminded her.

She shook her head. "It's just as much mine." She dropped her gaze. "I don't want to talk about this. Let's just go for a boat ride."

He stroked her soft skin with his thumbs. "You need to get some sleep."

"I'm fine."

He shook his head. "You're definitely not fine, Doc. You're exhausted. Let me tuck you in for awhile."

"I really am okay. She gave him a small smile, resting her hands on top of his. "I worked in one of the busiest trauma centers in the city. I'm used to running low on sleep."

He wanted to take care of the woman who felt the need to take care of everyone else. "But you don't have to today." He kissed her forehead. "I'll wake you up with time to shower. I'll even bring you breakfast in bed."

She hesitated on a small groan. "That sounds great, but sleeping now will only be torture when I have to open my eyes in less than three hours. I'll catch an early night tonight. I'm fine," she added, hugging him.

He wasn't convinced by her reassurances, but wrapped his arms around her, nodding anyway. "Okay."

"Give me a minute to get dressed and we'll—"

"We're almost out of milk," Jenny came to the door, holding up the gallon. "There's not enough for a bowl of cereal."

"So have eggs," he said.

"Fine," she huffed.

He studied the teen's hot, miserable eyes holding his, trying to figure out why she was getting so worked up over a stupid gallon of milk. "We'll go into town and get more later."

"Later," she huffed again and stormed off.

Reagan met his gaze. "What was *that*?"

He jerked a shoulder. "Hell if I know. She's had her panties in a twist since she got up. She didn't have

175

much to say when she got home last night either."

"I'll go check on her."

"I think you should do yourself a favor and let her cool off."

A cupboard door slammed, and she nodded. "I'll talk to her first thing when we get back. Maybe we should offer to take Faith."

He wanted a morning alone with her. Now that Faith and Jenny were here and the clinic fairly busy, they barely had any one-on-one time the way they used to. "Faith's still asleep." Another cupboard slammed. "Although she won't be if Jenny keeps that up."

"She and Terry might've had a fight."

"We'll figure it out when we get back."

She hesitated. "All right. I'll get dressed."

He glanced down at her pretty breasts in the thin cotton top and her shapely legs in tiny shorts, wishing they were staying right here. "I'll be waiting."

Thirty minutes later, he was pushing the paddles through the water in a steady rhythm, bringing them closer to the middle of the large pond while birdsong played through the trees and branches snapped occasionally in the woods. He glanced at Reagan, her sunglasses shading her eyes in the morning sunshine as she leaned back, resting her elbows on the back of the boat, looking around. "Not bad, huh?"

"It's perfect." She smiled. "I didn't realize how much I needed this."

He smiled back, noting the hint of color in her cheeks and her relaxed posture. "I'm still trying to figure out why this is the first time we've gotten around to doing this."

"Things have been pretty bonkers; plus, babies and bodies of surprisingly deep water don't exactly mix—especially without a life jacket."

"True." He stopped rowing, letting the boat drift, and glimpsed at his watch. "It looks like we have about fifteen more minutes before we need to head back—unless you want to blow off work for the day."

"Tempting," she said on a sigh. "But I can't."

He slid his gaze over her, enjoying her sinful legs in jean shorts and the way her gray Harvard sweatshirt leant her a sexy collegiate appeal. "So keep going?" He wanted to draw out every second of their time.

"For a little while."

"You've got it."

She nibbled her bottom lip. "Although maybe we should head back. Jenny was pretty upset."

"She's fine." He moved them back toward the middle of the water, cementing her decision.

"She didn't seem fine."

He shrugged. "She's a teenage girl. My sister acted like that all the time. One second she was laughing and the next she was in tears. Her teen years were rough on all of us."

She grinned. "I'm so sorry you had to go through that. I'm sure it was a cakewalk for her."

He chuckled. "She got through it, and so will Jenny."

"I just want to be sure we really try and understand her. I think that's important for someone her age."

He read between the lines. "Who didn't understand you?"

She met his gaze through the amber tint of her lenses. "This isn't about me."

"It never is," he said with a small hint of annoyance coloring his words. She talked freely about the clinic and her problems there, but even after all of their weeks together, she still wasn't willing to give him anything else.

"I'm talking about Jenny."

"Yeah, I know."

She sat up, her posture no longer relaxed. "What do you want to know, Shane?"

"Only what you want to tell me."

"There's not much to say."

He shrugged, paddling back to shore. Apparently their easy morning together was over.

"Fine. You want the story of my life, I'll give you the abridged version. I started talking in full sentences at one, could read at a sixth-grade level by three. At the ripe age of four, my parents put me in school. I had the finest tutors and instructors Chicago had to offer for hours on end every single day, because nothing but the best would do for Doctor Derek Rosner's brilliant daughter." She swallowed, her eyes hot. "Did you want to know that I had few friends, never got to just be a little girl who went to sleepovers or played at the park, and that my parents were far more interested in fostering my brain, obsessively molding me into who they needed to be? I left for college at twelve—didn't even get a say in where I went. Luckily by the time I was in medical school, I'd finally grown up enough to look like everyone else, instead of the freak genius kid sitting in classes among adults. I found a group of friends, ditched the nanny who lived with me, and started calling my own shots. That's my story. You've got it."

He stared at the miserable woman holding his gaze. "Sounds tough."

She jerked her shoulders. "It's over now."

"But it still hurts."

She frowned, as if considering. "I think it makes me mad more than anything. That's why I don't talk about it."

Anger was a balm for old wounds. "Did you follow their dreams or your own?"

"Mine. I was supposed to choose a residency at the Mayo Clinic where my father did his, but I went to the Bronx instead."

He nodded. "Good. How long did it take them to get over it?"

"I'll let you know when they do."

He winced. "Ouch. Do you talk to them?"

She shook her head. "I haven't seen or heard from them since my first year of medical school."

"So what's that? Ten years?"

"Pretty much."

His family was so close. His parents had supported all of his major decisions. "I'm sorry."

"It doesn't matter."

"Sure it does. They were foolish not to see who you are."

She looked down. "Thank you."

Several strong strides brought them back to the sandy bottom. He stood, stepping to the boggy edge, helping her out.

She tried to pull away, but he stopped her. "Thank you for telling me your story."

She gave him a small smile. "Like I said, there wasn't much to say."

He shook his head. "There was plenty. And I admire you more for it."

She sent him another small smile. "Your parents must be proud to know they've raised such a kind, honorable man."

"I've heard rumors I'm their favorite."

She grinned. "I'm sure you are."

"Come on." He kept her hand in his as they started along the faint path, just able to make out the tip of the cabin's roof through the overgrowth. "We'll have to do this again."

"Yeah. Definitely." She slowed then stopped. "What's that?"

"What?"

She pointed east. "That building."

He caught sight of the corner of the wooden structure. "I don't know. Want to check it out?"

"Sure."

They walked a good fifty yards, stopping in the small clearing by the tiny shack that reminded him of an ice-fishing hut.

"This couldn't be a house." Reagan dropped his hand, moving closer. "It's much too small, but it's in fairly decent shape." She picked her way through the underbrush toward the door. "Maybe a hunting cabin?" She peeked in the one and only window. "There's a table and some sort of heating unit." She stepped back, rattling something.

He recognized the sound as metal, his gaze following the rusted chain. "Stop!" he said as he lunged forward, hooking his arm around her waist, yanking her up before her foot found its way into the trap. Losing his balance, he fell backwards, landing so she fell on top of him.

She stared down at him, her eyes huge. "What are you—what was that?"

"A bear trap."

She swallowed "Oh." She pressed her palm to her chest, taking a deep breath, and stood, lending him her hand. "I guess this is a hunting cabin."

Studying the structure, he shook his head as he gained his feet. "I bet this is an old moonshining place."

"How did you know about the trap?"

He brushed off his shorts. "We apprehended more

180

than a few fugitives in the woods when I was still on Taskforce. We kept our eyes out for that kind of stuff all the time."

She nodded.

He walked closer to the rusted metal, picked up a sturdy stick, and activated the trigger. The wood broke in half as the dangerous teeth snapped around it. "People get serious when they don't want other's messing in their business."

"I guess so."

"Come on." He turned away and took her hand. "Let's go home."

She nodded, gripping his fingers as they walked back through the forest.

~~~~

Reagan's heart still galloped as she rinsed the conditioner from her hair, thinking of her close call with the bear trap. She and Shane had been home a good half-hour, yet she shuddered again, remembering the slam of rusty teeth snapping the thick branch in half as if it were nothing. That would have been her leg if Shane hadn't stepped in to save the day.

Her semi-relaxing morning had quickly turned dangerous with the frightening reminder that she was very much an outsider in this odd mountain town. *People get serious when they don't want other's messing in their business.* She chuckled humorlessly as she shut off the water, drawing unfortunate parallels between Shane's statement and her own situation at the clinic. She was here to help, and no one was happy about it.

Shaking her head, she wrapped herself in a towel and stepped into her bedroom, gasping when she spotted Jenny sitting on her bed. "Oh, you scared me."

CATE BEAUMAN

"Sorry." Jenny's shoulders sagged in the casual pink t-shirt Reagan had given her from her own stash of clothes.

"That's okay." She sat next to her. "Did Faith keep you up last night?"

"No more'n usual."

She heard Faith cry at two and Jenny get a bottle, but the house had been quiet otherwise.

"You seem upset. Do you want to talk about it?"

"Nothin's wrong," she said, her voice quaking.

"Are you sure?"

"Yup." A tear fell down her cheek.

She scooted closer to the teenager, tucking a lock of long blond hair behind Jenny's ear. "Jenny, what's going on?"

She jerked her shoulders. "Nothin'."

"Where's Faith?"

"She's sleepin'." Her lips trembled.

She took Jenny's hand. "You can tell me."

"I made a mistake."

"Okay."

She looked at Reagan with shattered eyes. "You're gonna be mad."

She gave her a sympathetic smile. "I'm sure I won't."

"Shane's gonna be mad."

"I'm sure he won't." But she was starting to understand where this was going.

"I had sex with Terry."

She pressed her lips together, absorbing the wave of frustrated disappointment. "All-the-way sex?"

She nodded.

"But you're still healing."

"It hurt some."

"Did he use a condom?"

182

Jenny started crying. "No."

Reagan stifled a sigh. "Did he pull out?"

"He said he was gonna but he spewed his seed in me instead."

She hugged the girl and closed her eyes as Jenny sobbed. "It's too soon for us to do a pregnancy test."

Jenny cried harder. "I don't want no more babies. Raisin' Faith's hard enough."

She drew Jenny away. "Why did you do it, honey?"

"He's mad at me for stayin' here and workin' with you on my schoolin', and because I said I won't marry him."

She plucked a tissue from the box and wiped Jenny's tears. "You're making good choices for you and Faith."

"I sure didn't last night."

She shook her head. "No. Not exactly." She caught another tear. "You don't have to make Terry feel better by participating in stuff that doesn't feel right for you."

"I don't want to see him."

"Then you don't have to." Now they just had to cross their fingers they wouldn't be dealing with another pregnancy.

"I'm not seein' him no more. I'm thinkin' he wants me to be pregnant so I'll give up bein' foolish." She rolled her eyes.

She had a feeling Jenny was exactly right. "School is *not* foolish. Providing a future for you and Faith is exactly the right thing to do, Jenny."

"I know." She wiped at her cheeks.

"I wanted to run an idea—" Shane stopped in the doorway, frowning. "What's wrong?"

Jenny looked at Reagan, her eyes pleading for privacy.

"Girl stuff." Reagan hugged Jenny again. "If you

want to talk you know where I am."

Jenny gripped her tight, sucking in a shuddering breath. "I'm so lucky you've taken me and Faith in."

She ran her hand down Jenny's hair. "And nothing's changed. You're going to keep studying and start your nursing program."

She nodded.

Reagan kissed her cheek and handed over a fresh tissue. "Put on your scrubs and we'll go to work."

"Okay." She walked out, looking at the floor instead of Shane.

Shane stepped in and closed the door, taking the spot Jenny had vacated. "What's up?"

She took a deep breath, dreading the conversation they were about to have. Jenny had the men in her life pegged well: Terry was trying to hold her back, and Shane was going to be mad. "She's struggling with a decision she made."

He narrowed his eyes. "She slept with him."

She held his gaze instead of answering.

"That little bastard." He rushed to his feet.

She grabbed his arm before he could take a step. "Sit down."

"Reagan—"

"Don't you dare say anything to her," she said in a hissing whisper. "She'll think I told you."

"You didn't have to. I can put two and two together easily enough." Closing his eyes, he shook his head.

"They didn't use protection."

His eyes flew open, and he collapsed back against the mattress. "Son of a bitch."

"We'll give her a test as soon as possible."

"And if it's positive?"

"We'll figure it out."

He scrubbed his hands over his face. "Parenting

sucks sometimes."

She smiled sadly. Parenting *did* suck sometimes, but this would be as close to the experience as she would ever get. "It's the hardest job on the planet—or so I've heard."

"Without a doubt."

She stood, reaching for her robe, realizing she'd forgotten she was only wearing her towel. She slid the mid-thigh-length material over her arms, belting the fabric in place.

Shane rubbed at his jaw. "I'm changing the subject."

"Okay."

He sat up. "I have an idea I want to run by you."

"Sure." She sat next to him.

"How would you feel if I gave Ethan the name of that doctor you're trying to track down?"

She frowned. "Why would you do that?"

"Because my boss is a freaking computer genius. If Schlibenburg's out there, Ethan will find him."

For the first time in days she felt a stirring of hope. "Really?"

"I'd bet my career on it."

"Sure. This is great." She stood, hurrying to her desk, and wrote down his name. "There's all kinds of information about his work online, but then it just stops. Ethan won't have any trouble tracking him down until he gets to the last five years." She walked back, handing over the paper.

He took the paper from her. "I'll see what he can do."

"I really appreciate this."

"No problem." He frowned, sliding a gentle finger over the half-dollar-sized bruise on her lower thigh. "You got banged up this morning."

She swallowed, absorbing the rush of heat from his touch. "It's fine." She stepped back, holding his gaze.

"How are you doing after our little adventure?"

"Okay. I'm a little shaken up. I never thanked you for helping me out."

He shrugged. "No big deal."

"If you hadn't grabbed me, it would've been a whole lot worse."

He winced. "I don't even want to think about it."

"We should probably tell Jenny to stay away from that place. There could be more traps."

"I'll let you handle it." He stood. "I need a few minutes to digest Jenny's latest development."

"Okay."

"I'm going to work out before she heads off to work."

"Have fun."

"I'll talk to Ethan." He gestured to the paper in his hand.

She nodded. "Thanks."

He walked out, and she hurried over to her computer, checking her e-mail, noting that Doctor Jacobson had yet to respond to her request for a meeting. None of the other half-dozen physicians she'd contacted had e-mailed her back either. If Ethan could find Doctor Schlibenburg, she might be able to bypass Doctor Jacobson altogether.

CHAPTER FIFTEEN

REAGAN SLID A DISINFECTING WIPE OVER ONE OF THE plastic chairs lining the wall in the waiting area while Jenny did the same on the opposite side of the room, still sniffling. She pulled a tissue from the box on the small table stacked with magazines, tapped Jenny's shoulder, and handed it over, smiling sympathetically. "Here you go."

"Thanks." She blew her nose. "I can't seem to quit cryin'. I'm feelin' so *mad* at myself."

"Sweetie, you made a mistake."

"A big mistake."

"We've all made them."

"I let you down. And Shane." Her lips wobbled.

She shook her head, leading Jenny to one of the dry seats, crouching in front of her. "You're being awfully hard on yourself. Shane and I were young once. I can *promise* you we both did things we aren't particularly proud of."

"I don't want more babies right now." She sucked in several shuddering breaths. "I won't be able to do nursin' if I'm tryin' to feed two mouths and my own."

She took Jenny's hands. "You'll be able to do your nursing, Jenny—one way or the other. Forty weeks is a long time to get plenty accomplished if that's the way things work out. Either way, I'm not going to let you go through this alone. No matter what, I'm not walking away from you and Faith."

She nodded and sniffled some more. "I never met

someone as kind as you."

Reagan hugged her tight. "You're an amazing person. I want you to remember that." She drew away. "Now go in the bathroom, wash your face, and get out here so you can do your first height, weight, and temperature check on a patient."

Her red-rimmed eyes grew huge. "On a patient? Other than you and Shane?"

"You bet." She wanted to cheer Jenny up, but more, she wanted to show her she was ready and capable of this next step. "I'll be standing right next to you the whole time."

"Okay." Jenny hurried off to the bathroom and closed the door.

Sighing, she stood and glanced at the clock, frowning as she realized their first patient of the day was fifteen minutes late. "Hurry and press a cold cloth to your eyes. Eunice should be here any second."

"I'm comin'." Jenny opened the door, wiping water droplets from her pretty complexion. "Do I look better?"

She studied Jenny's pink nose and her slightly swollen eyes. "You're on your way."

"Good." She tossed away her napkin. "I put out the stuff for Eunice's pap smear, but she might not be comin'."

Reagan peeked her head into the mauve examination room, giving the small table of supplies a visual once over, making certain Jenny hadn't overlooked anything she would need for the well-woman appointment. "Why wouldn't she be coming?"

Jenny rubbed at her arms as she pressed her lips together, her discomfort obvious.

"Jenny, why wouldn't Eunice be coming?"

"Well, Terry was tellin' me about Henry. Word's

travelin' fast through The Gap about him not havin' black lung. They're sayin' the others probably don't have it neither and that your interferin' ways are costin' people jobs."

Reagan turned away, straightening the cheaply framed picture of meadow flowers. "I see."

"I didn't want to tell you." Jenny hurried around to face her, gripping her arm. "You're a good doctor, Reagan. You saved me and Faith. You're helpin' lots of folks around here who need it."

"I can't help them if they won't come in."

"Maybe Eunice is just runnin' behind like you suspect."

"Maybe." But it was doubtful. She glanced at the clock again. "Go ahead and put the well-woman kit away. You can take the rest of the day off."

Jenny shook her head. "I don't want to leave you. What if you get busy?"

Her second appointment was late as well. "I'll call you if I get in over my head."

Jenny hesitated, then nodded. "I'll come right over if you need me."

Someone walked up the front steps. "Hold that thought." She smiled at Jenny, wiggling her brows, more than a little relieved that the rumors swirling around Henry's case weren't ruining the progress she'd worked so hard to achieve. "I guess Eunice *was* just running behind." Her smile faded and her stomach sank when Shane walked through the door wearing jeans and a black t-shirt, holding Faith.

"Hey."

"Hey," she and Jenny said at the same time.

Shane tilted his head, his brow raised in question. "What's wrong?"

"Eunice didn't show up for her appointment, and it

don't look like Carrie's bringin' her girl in for a check-up either."

Shane looked at Reagan, holding her gaze. "Huh."

"Huh" certainly said it all. Shane knew as well as she did that they were back to square one with the people of Black Bear Gap.

"I was gonna take vitals on my first real patient." Jenny shrugged, but the disappointment in her voice was unmistakable.

"You'll just have to catch the next one," he said.

Reagan met Shane's gaze again as she exhaled a long breath, struggling to hold back her tears. She should have expected this to happen the moment Henry came in here insulting her and telling her she was wrong. Why hadn't she prepared herself for the town to close rank? The hours and effort she and Shane had put into this place didn't matter. They would always be the outsiders. In the minds of the people, she and the man staring at her were part of some government conspiracy sent to eliminate jobs. No amount of kindness was going to change that. But Jenny still needed a chance to learn. Swallowing her disappointment, she forced a smile. "Shane's right. You'll have to catch the next one, but we can practice on him in the meantime."

"Again?" Jenny rolled her eyes.

"I'm sure Shane would love to help us out."

"Yeah. Definitely."

"Great. Today we're going to learn how to do a blood draw."

He frowned. "Wait a minute. What?"

Jenny's eyes brightened. "This is great. I read about a venipuncture procedure in that book you gave me, but I never saw a blood draw done in real life."

"Perfect. We'll do a full panel and send it off to the

lab. When the results come back, I'll show you how to read them."

"Aw, Doc, I'm not a big fan of needles." He looked at her with such dismay she struggled to hold back a smile.

"It'll just take a second. Hand Faith over to Jenny, and have a seat in the lab chair while I grab the stuff I'll need."

He muttered a curse as he followed her into the next room and sat down. "How the hell did I get myself roped into this one?"

"I think you should know you're scoring major brownie points." She gathered her supplies, bringing them over to the table.

He perked up. "What kind of brownie points?"

"The feel-good kind—that deep down tingle of satisfaction that comes from knowing you're furthering an eager student's education."

He blinked at her, clearly unamused.

She grinned, winking. "This won't hurt a bit. Peds used to call me up to their wing all the time to start IVs. They say I have the magic touch."

"I guess we'll see."

"I really do appreciate this, Shane." Jenny stood close by, rubbing Faith's back as the baby slept in her arms.

"I think I should at least get a batch of chocolate chip cookies out of the deal. From *you*," he emphasized, pointing to Jenny.

"Okay. I'll bake you up a treat."

"Now we're talking."

"All right. Down to business." Reagan went to the sink, washing her hands. "Jenny, if Shane were a real patient, the first thing you would do is ask him his name and birthdate to make sure you're drawing tests for the right person. Since the workup we're doing today commonly accompanies most physicals, you'll also want to confirm that your patient has fasted for the appropriate amount of time—typically twelve hours."

"Well, I didn't fast, so we should probably save this lesson for another day." Shane moved to stand.

Reagan halted his movements with a hand to the chest. "Brownie points have been awarded, Mr. Harper, but your cool points are quickly dwindling."

He sat back, clenching his jaw, steaming out a breath through his nose.

She pulled on gloves. "We glove up and look for a vein. Shane's pretty easy. He's muscular and has low body fat, so they're easy to spot." She slid her finger along a couple of her options. "We'll take this one here." She grabbed the blue band. "We'll tie the tourniquet." She secured the elastic in place. "Shane, go ahead and pump your hand."

He did as he was asked, accentuating his veins further.

"If our patient didn't have veins we could easily see, we would palpate the antecubital fossa and locate the median cubital vein here." She demonstrated, tapping the skin of his inner elbow, then grabbed an alcohol packet. "I'm going to clean the area with this alcohol pad before making my stick." She looked at Jenny. "Why would I want to do that?"

"To keep pathogens from enterin' his bloodstream, which can lead to infection or contaminate your sample."

She beamed at her student. "Excellent." She grabbed the needle. "I'm going to grasp Shane's arm firmly and place my thumb about two inches below the puncture site and pull his skin taught. Slight poke," she said to Shane as she pushed the evacuator tube onto the needle. Within seconds, blood filled the vial. "Go ahead and relax your hand," she said as she pulled off the tourniquet. "We'll take three vials for a full workup." She filled two more. "We need to give the blood a gentle mix with this side-to-side motion." She showed Jenny, then put the glass down as she picked up a piece of gauze. "Put this over the site and apply pressure as you remove the needle. You'll then want to engage the safety device like this and toss your syringe in the sharps box." When she finished, she took Shane's hand, settling his fingers on the gauze. "We'll have our patient continue to apply pressure, then we'll tape the gauze in place like so." She studied Shane as he looked at his arm. "How are you feeling?"

"Not bad. You do have a pretty gentle touch, Doc."

She smiled. "Thanks. Make sure you leave the gauze on for a good half hour." She directed her attention to Jenny. "So what do you think?"

Jenny nibbled her lip. "I'm gonna need lots of practice."

"Blood draws are pretty intimidating at first, but we'll have you practice on an orange for awhile until you're comfortable." She picked up the tubes. "I need to make up a couple of labels for these, then we can take them down to Mini for a rush to the lab."

"When will we get the results? Jenny asked, adjusting Faith in her arms.

"Typically within forty-eight hours. I'll be right back." She walked to her office and sat down, typing up Shane's name, birthdate, and the codes the lab would need. She hit print when the e-mail from Doctor Jacobson caught her eye. "Finally." She clicked open the message, reading his response.

193

Doctor Rosner,

Thank you for your e-mail and request for a meeting, but I don't see the need to waste each other's time. It is my professional opinion, as Henry Dooley's doctor and as one of the state's leading pulmonologists, that he does indeed have chronic obstructive pulmonary disease. Although I appreciate your concern, it is not needed or warranted. I spoke with the Dooley family this morning, and they have informed me you are no longer their physician of record in this matter, which would make further contact not only unethical but illegal.

Thank you,

Doctor Steven Jacobson

"You bastard." She read the condescending paragraph again and slammed her laptop closed. "You son of a bitch." She clenched her fists as her chest heaved and her heart pounded with the surge of molten anger. She turned her head and jumped when she noticed Jenny standing in the doorway.

"You're *pissed*, huh?"

"Yes, I guess you could say that." Clearing her throat, she peeled off the stickers that had just finished printing and stuck them to the vials of blood, trying to regain her composure as her pulse pounded in her head. "Why don't you go get Faith ready for a trip to town? I'll be right there."

Jenny nodded and walked out the front door with the baby.

She stood, walking to the window, gripping the sill and stared out at the endless acres of trees, trying to remember the last time she'd felt so damn mad.

"Do you want me to stick around for a while?" Shane asked from the doorway.

She shook her head.

"Two missed appointments doesn't mean the whole day's a wash."

She closed her eyes, resting her head against the glass. "I think we both know no one will be stepping foot in here again anytime soon."

"They'll come back, Reagan. Just give them time."

She pressed her lips firm. "Right."

"I gave Ethan that doctor's name."

"I appreciate it." She turned and grabbed the vials of blood, taking them back to the small lab area. Standing around staring out the window wasn't going to solve anything. "You can go on home."

"Why don't you come with me?"

"I have stuff to do." She cushioned the tubes of glass in bubble wrap and set them in a biohazard cooler, filling the container with ice.

"Like?"

"Going into town." She walked toward the door and stepped out, waiting for Shane to follow, and locked up. "Jenny, Faith, and I are going to drop this off with Mini and get a couple gallons of milk."

"I can handle that for you."

"No," she said too sharply. She didn't want Shane to handle anything for her. She just needed to get *away* from here.

"I think I should come too."

"I don't need you to come." She fell into step beside him as they made their way down the short path to the cabin.

"I'd like to anyway."

She stopped. "Why?"

"Because things are a little different than they were

the last time you and Jenny went down. Things seem to be a little tense around here." He gestured to the clinic. "Last time the community wasn't real happy, the school burnt down."

She sighed a long breath. "You talked to Jenny."

"We had a couple of spare seconds in the lab. Her conversation with Terry might've come up."

She absorbed another wave of humiliation. "So stay here and guard the office."

"I don't give a damn about the office." He took her hand. "But I do care about you and the girls."

"Fine. We'll all hop in the SUV and have a fun family adventure."

"Don't get pissy with me, Doc. I'm not the bad guy here."

And he wasn't. "You're right. I'm taking my frustrations out on you, and I'm sorry."

"I don't mind being a punching bag, but at least give me a heads up as to why. There's more going on here than Henry."

She stared down at the dirt path, blinking back tears. "Doctor Jacobson sent me an e-mail."

"And?"

"He stands by his diagnosis. He made it very clear he's the specialist and Henry's case is no longer my business."

"He's an asshole."

She smiled, then chuckled at Shane's blunt opinion, surprised that she could laugh. "Yes."

He smiled back. "So let's get out of here for a while. We could pack up the ladies, throw the drugs into a duffel bag, and head to Lexington for a night."

The idea of escaping, even for one night, was very appealing. "Don't tempt me."

"I'll go transfer everything out of the safe right

now."

She wanted to go—badly. "I can't." She shook her head with regret. "What if someone needs help?"

He rocked back on his heels and puffed out a breath. "I've gotta give it to you, Doc, you're dedicated, even when they don't deserve it."

"I see it as responsible."

"And dedicated." He captured her jaw. "Let's get a gallon of milk. And we need to pick up chocolate chips. Jenny owes me cookies."

She lifted his arm, examining his bandage. "You were a good sport today."

"I really hate needles." He winced.

"So how'd you end up with a tattoo?"

"I was incredibly drunk."

She rolled her eyes.

"One of my roommates, Gavin, got shot in the back—an apprehension gone wrong. He almost died. When we figured out he was going to make it, Jerrod, me, and a couple of our other buddies went out, had about five too many beers, and woke up with matching tattoos on our arms."

Grinning, she pressed his knuckles to her cheek. "You're a good guy, putting your discomfort aside for Jenny."

"I don't know about that. I kinda just didn't want to look like a weenie."

She laughed.

He grinned. "And I get my favorite cookie out of the deal, so it's not so bad."

Somewhere along the way, Shane had become a vital part of her existence in this odd, desolate place. "How about we go one better and plan on an early dinner tonight, junk food, and maybe a board game?"

He sucked in a deep breath. "Sounds pretty

intense."

She laughed again. "It's what we've got."

"True." He took her hand. "Let's go to town."

~~~~

Reagan steered around a sharp turn as Shane's eclectic mix of music played through the SUV speakers. She avoided another jut in the dirt road, sending Shane closer to her side with the movement.

"I'll fill up the tank," he said.

"I can get the milk if you want." Jenny leaned forward from the back seat, using the rearview mirror to slick her lips with cheap gloss.

Shane frowned, turning to look at her. "What are you getting all dressed up for?"

"We're goin' into *town*. It's been a long time since I've been down to the market."

"We went last week," Reagan reminded her with a grin.

"Like I said—a long time."

"We need to get you out more." Shaking his head, Shane turned back, his eyes full of fun.

Reagan smiled, savoring the normalcy Jenny and Shane brought to her life. She needed this simple ride with the people who had become her little family. "Jenny, if you grab the milk, I'll get the mail and drop off the blood samples."

"Sounds like a plan to me."

She pulled up to the pump for Shane and got out, waiting for Jenny to finagle Faith's car seat from the base. "Don't forget the chocolate chips," she said as she open the market door for Jenny to step in before her. "Good morning, Hazel." She smiled at the clerk behind the counter.

Hazel turned away instead of greeting her, busying herself with the packages of cigarettes.

Reagan exchanged a glance with Jenny and walked to the mail window as Jenny moved to the coolers of milk. "Good morning, Mini. I've got a lab drop off." She handed over the small cooler.

"I'll get your mail." Mini barely met Reagan's eyes as she spoke.

The friendly small talk she'd grown used to over the past few weeks was glaringly absent. "Thank you."

Mini came back moments later with a bundle. "Here you go."

"I appreciate it." Struggling to keep her smile in place, she turned, gasping when she bumped into one of the men who typically stood out front. "Oh, excuse me." She tried to move around him, but he stepped in her way. "Excuse me," she said again.

"You Feds ain't nothin' but trouble."

She breathed in putrid smoker's breath as his face loomed inches above hers. "If you would please move—"

"Get out of her way, Obediah," Jenny said, moving toward her.

"Shut up, Jenny," he warned, pointing his finger. "I ain't finished with what I've got to say to the good doctor here."

Shane pulled open the door, taking his wallet from his pocket, pausing as he looked from Reagan to the man, Jenny, and back. "Is there a problem?"

"The problem's you," Obediah spat. "You Feds is liars and kidnappers." He gestured to Jenny. "You done nothin' but interfere and ruin our lives since you came."

Shane set a fifty on the counter. "Hazel, I'm sure this will cover our gas and groceries."

Hazel took the money and turned away.

"Let's go," he said to Reagan and Jenny.

"Bad things happen to no-good Feds," Obediah said as they walked out.

Reagan swallowed, glancing at Shane as they made it to the SUV. She took the passenger's seat, staring at the group of men looking their way as Shane helped Jenny settle Faith in the base.

"Let's get out of here." Shane turned over the ignition and took a right onto the main road. The ride was faster than usual—and silent—as the vehicle climbed farther into the hills and Reagan's mind raced. Within minutes, Shane pulled into the drive and Reagan got out, walking up the steps to the cabin. She let herself in, hurrying down to her room.

Closing herself inside, she leaned against the door and crossed her arms at her chest as she took several deep breaths, fighting back tears. Everything was ruined, her credibility shot, but that wasn't the worst part. Jenny and Faith had been lumped into Fed status along with her and Shane. *Bad things happen to no-good Feds.* What would've happened if Shane hadn't insisted on coming to town with them today? She sniffled, worrying about the potential danger she'd brought to the young mother and her baby.

A knock sounded at the door. "Reagan?"

"Um." She moved away from the door and wiped at her cheeks. "This isn't a good time."

He opened the door anyway. "Are you okay?"

She nodded. "Yeah. Fine." She walked to her desk, avoiding eye contact, fiddling with the edge of Henry's x-ray films. "Can—can we talk later?"

"We could, but then I wouldn't be able to tell you Ethan just called."

She whirled around. "He found him? He found Doctor Schlibenburg?"

"I told you he would. It's just his number—a cellphone registered to his daughter. Ethan's still trying to pinpoint his address."

She took the number he handed her and closed her eyes, fighting another wave of emotion. "I don't—I don't know how to thank you."

He pulled her into a hug, running his hand down her hair. "You could stop trying to be so brave all the time and just cry for a change. I bet you'll feel better afterwards."

She held on to him, shaking her head. "I avoid crying at all costs. It gives me a headache."

He eased her away enough to look into her eyes. "Did that man put his hands on you?"

"No."

"I'm sorry I wasn't there to head that off from the beginning."

"It's okay. None of us knew that was going to happen." She swallowed. "I'm going to Lexington tomorrow. I'm meeting with Doctor Jacobson."

"Does he know you're coming?"

She shook her head.

"What about Doctor S.?"

"I'm going to call him, but I'm going to see Doctor Jacobson too. He's going to explain to me Henry's diagnosis, whether Henry's my patient or not."

"Do you think that's the right move?"

"It's the only one I have left. He's telling me one thing and my gut's telling me another."

"Then I guess you've gotta do what you've gotta do."

She touched his cheek, treasuring his support, wondering what she would do without him. She'd never had anyone in her life quite like him. No one understood her the way he did. "Thank you." She kissed him, chastely. "You're the best."

"Go ahead and make your call. I'll throw together some sort of lunch."

"Okay."

He closed the door behind him, and she hurried to her bedside phone, dialing Doctor Schlibenburg's number, listening to it ring a dozen times. Pressing her lips together, she hung up, refusing to be discouraged. She would try again later, but for now she was going to help Shane make lunch. By tomorrow afternoon, she would have answers.

CHAPTER SIXTEEN

REAGAN SAT IN DOCTOR JACOBSON'S OFFICE PARKING LOT, tapping her fingers impatiently against the steering wheel and staring at the digital clock. She'd only been waiting fifteen minutes in her parking spot close to the front door, but she'd been up since four, running through what she planned to say in anticipation of a more productive conversation and in-depth explanation of Henry's diagnosis. Doctor Jacobson wouldn't find it quite so easy to be rude and evasive without the shield of his computer. Face to face interactions were best whenever possible, and she intended to have one.

Nine 'o clock finally arrived, and she got out of the Pajero, grabbing her laptop case, making her way up the walk, her black pumps echoing on the pavement with her quick strides. She paused by the front door, giving herself a once-over in the reflection of the glass, and stepped inside the upscale waiting area, wearing a charcoal-gray pencil skirt and fitted white sleeveless blouse. For an extra boost of confidence, she'd taken the time to curl the ends of her hair and apply her full arsenal of makeup. More than ready to begin, she stopped in front of the receptionist's window.

The pretty black-haired woman slid the glass to the side. "Good morning."

Reagan smiled. "Good morning. I need to speak with Doctor Jacobson please."

"What time's your appointment, ma'am?" She

began to type.

"I don't have one."

Her fingers paused on the keyboard as she looked at Reagan. "I'm sorry. You'll have to—"

"If you would please tell Doctor Jacobson that Doctor Reagan Rosner is here to see him, I'm sure he'll make an exception."

"Ma'am—"

"I'm not leaving until I talk to him." She smiled pleasantly again as the woman eyed her.

"Just a minute please." She slid the partition closed and picked up her phone. Moments later, a tall, well-built blond man opened the office door.

"Doctor Rosner?"

"Doctor Jacobson." She held out her hand. "It's nice to finally meet you."

He returned her shake. "Why don't you come on back?"

"Thank you."

He walked her to his office, shutting the door behind her. "Have a seat."

She sat down, studying his handsome features, noting the lack of a wedding ring on his finger. "Thank you for meeting with me on such short notice."

He settled himself behind his desk. "I thought we agreed we wouldn't meet."

"No. You decided that, but I'm afraid I need answers."

He steepled his fingers. "I'm afraid there's not much I can do for you."

She crossed her legs, folding her hands in her lap, doing her best to give off the pretense of calm. "You can help me understand your diagnosis."

He shook his head. "My hands are tied."

Her eyes sharpened on his. "Consider this a

professional courtesy."

He sighed. "All right. When I saw Mr. Dooley, we performed several pulmonary functions tests, and I reexamined the x-rays you sent along via e-mail versus the images our radiology department took here.

"Can I see your x-rays?"

"I don't have them on hand."

"I'd be happy to wait while you get them."

He sat back in his chair. "Doctor Rosner—"

"That's fine. I brought the series I took with me." She pulled the sheets from her bag, stood, and moved to the window, putting the image up to the light. "I'm looking at fibroids—dozens filling Mr. Dooley's lungs, especially the upper right lobe here." She pointed to the large white spots.

"I see a classic case of chronic obstructive pulmonary disease."

Her gaze whipped to his, shocked that he was still willing to say so. "With all due respect, Doctor Jacobson, I don't agree. Correct me if I'm wrong, but if Mr. Dooley was afflicted with COPD, wouldn't we be seeing infective changes in association with a background of hyperinflation, a flattened hemidiaphragm, and less prominent lung markings?"

"Doctor Rosner, I'm very comfortable with my diagnosis."

Her temper started to heat with his flippant answers. "Frankly, Doctor, I'm not. I've examined this image time and again, comparing it to both COPD and complicated black lung. This is classic progressive massive fibrosis."

"I could see how you might come to that conclusion. Your films are grainy and subpar."

Clenching her jaw, she looked from him to the perfectly good picture. "The images I've taken are certainly of good quality."

"Doctor Rosner, we could go round and round all day, but I just don't have the time. I won't be reversing my diagnosis."

She moved back to her bag, putting her films away. They weren't getting anywhere here. "I will be speaking with the Dooleys again, and I will be urging them to seek a third opinion."

He shrugged. "As you have every right to, but let me remind you that you're a general practitioner. I'm the lung specialist."

She wouldn't waste her time explaining her specialization in Emergency Medicine. "And typically I would respect that—"

"Doctor Rosner, I'm not telling you how to do your job, nor am I questioning your decisions. I would appreciate the same courtesy."

Pompous ass. "This isn't about ego or hurt feelings."

He raised his brow.

Apparently Doctor Jacobson was more than fine with being rude, even face to face. "This is about someone's *life*. I'll be suggesting a third opinion. Should I discover any more cases of black lung, I won't be passing them on to you." She grabbed her bag. "Enjoy your day, Doctor." She closed the door behind her and walked out, shaking with fury.

She took her seat behind the wheel, steaming for most of the two-hour ride home. Never had she met a man so full of himself. Doctor Jacobson wouldn't even listen to what she had to say. He was so impressed with his own credentials that he was blind to the facts staring him right in his smug face. The jerk of a doctor was certain Henry didn't have progressive massive fibrosis. He didn't actually take the time to defend his opinion, but that was fine, because every fiber of her being told her Henry did.

She passed the Black Bear Gap gas station and minimart, glancing toward the men standing around smoking their cigarettes and drinking their soda, and punched the gas, more determined than ever to get to the bottom of this mess. The town didn't believe her, Doctor Jacobson had written her off, and none of the other physicians she'd reached out to would call her back—including Doctor Hargus at the mine. But all that was fine too, because she wasn't backing down. The families here needed her whether they knew it or not, and she finally had Doctor Schlibenburg's number, which she intended to call again.

She pulled into the parking lot next to Shane's vehicle, slammed her door, and hurried inside, relieved that he and Jenny were up in the loft. Now wasn't the time for a chat.

"Reagan?" Shane peered over the banister.

"Later," she called over her shoulder, making a bee-line to her room. Closing her door, she set her laptop case on her bed and picked up the number she'd tried more than a dozen times yesterday. Dialing, she started pacing, waiting through the first three rings, then four. "Come on," she whispered. "Please pick up."

"Hello?" came a voice on the other end. A man's voice, with a subtle German accent.

She stopped dead, her eyes widening. "Uh, yes. Is this Doctor Heinz Schlibenburg?"

"Who's asking, please?"

"This is Doctor Reagan Rosner. I'm a physician working with the Appalachia Project in Black Bear Gap, Kentucky." She moved to the window, staring out. "I've been researching advanced pneumoconiosis. I saw your name mentioned—"

"How did you get this number?"

"I found it," she fibbed.

"I'm retired," he interrupted.

"Yes. I know." She turned, realizing Shane was standing in her doorway. "I'm hoping we might be able to meet. I believe I have four cases of progressive massive fibrosis right here in the community—"

"I can't help you," he interjected.

Her shoulders grew heavy as she realized the biggest name in pulmonology—the man she'd been counting on to back her up—was turning her down. "Please, Dr. Schlibenburg. I've had one doctor tell me I'm wrong. The half dozen others I've contacted won't even call me back." She held Shane's stare as she spoke.

"There is nothing I can do."

She swallowed and turned away again. "I'm desperate enough to beg, Doctor, if that's what it takes. You're my last hope."

"I don't—"

"Please, Doctor." She pressed her lips together, closing her eyes.

Dr. Schlibenburg sighed in her ear. "I can meet with you tomorrow for *one* hour. One o' clock."

She blinked her eyes open. "Okay. Yes. Yes. I'll take any information you can give me. Where can we meet?"

"Wait a minute, Doc," Shane whispered, stepping closer.

She shook her head, ignoring him as she moved to her desk, picking up a pen.

"I'm close to Berea. Call this number when you reach the town and I will give you directions to my home. Come alone."

"Yes. I'll call when I arrive." The phone line went dead, and she frowned. "Hello?" She shrugged and put the receiver back in the jack.

208

Shane grabbed her elbow, turning her around. "Reagan, what are you doing?

"Finding answers."

"I thought that's what the Doctor Jacobson thing was about today."

She shrugged. "He's not interested in cooperating."

"Why?"

"Why?" She laughed humorlessly, pressing her fingers to her temple. "Isn't that the million-dollar question? *Why* did Dr. Jacobson completely blow me off yet again? *Why* can't I find another doctor who will look at my x-rays?" She started pacing for the second time as her frustration grew. "*Why* is Eastern Kentucky the *only* Appalachian region with extremely low reports of a disease that regularly runs rampant in coal mining communities?"

He shook his head. "I don't know."

"Neither do I, but Doctor Shlibenburg does. Or I think so, anyway—at least I hope. I'm meeting him tomorrow."

"Yeah, I heard that. What about Jenny and Faith?"

She frowned. "What about them?"

"Are we bringing them with us?"

"Where?"

"To the meeting."

She steamed out a long breath, her patience already shot as she and Shane played twenty questions. "Meeting?"

"Tomorrow. With Doctor S."

"I'm going by myself."

He shook his head. "No, you're not. I don't like this—any of it."

"That's the only way he'll speak to me."

"I'm not letting you go off to meet with some guy you don't even know."

"He's a colleague who not only had billing as top pulmonologist in the country but also lived and worked in this region for forty years. Besides, you gave me his number."

"For a *phone* call."

"This isn't your choice; it's mine. I need these answers, Shane. I *need* them."

He shoved his hands in his pockets as his eyes grew dark with temper. "You're chasing after something that sounds like trouble."

"What's that supposed to mean?"

"It means you need to let this go."

She expelled an exasperated breath. "Let it *go*?"

"Yes. Has it ever occurred to you that there may be more to this than what you see? Why is it that no one else wants to touch it?"

"I have no idea, but one thing's for sure, my practice is ruined." She rushed up to stand in front of him. "All the people we've helped won't come back because they think I'm wrong."

"That's their choice. You're a good doctor. If they can't deal with one mistake—"

"I didn't make a mistake. Henry has black lung and so do at least three other men. I'm sure of it."

"Damn, Reagan." Jamming his hand through his hair he walked away, then back. "You're driving yourself *crazy* over some nasty bastard who's more hung up on the fact that you're a woman than the fact that his bad habits are killing him." He grabbed her arms, holding her by the biceps. "You need to come to terms with the fact that Henry sucked on one too many cancer sticks. He's got COPD. You made a mistake. You're wrong. Move on."

She blinked with the slap of his words, his lack of faith in her as painful as any fist. "Get out."

210

"Reagan—"

"Get *out*."

Clenching his jaw, he held her gaze and left her alone.

~~~~

Shane lay in bed, staring at the sliver of moonlight cutting across his ceiling in the dark. He glanced at the bedside clock as he'd done several times throughout the night, watching the early-morning hours tick by. Sighing, he rolled to his side, trying to get comfortable, then rolled to the other, fought with his sheets twisted around his leg, and sat up. "Damn it," he muttered, punching his pillow into a ball, then settled his hands behind his head as he thought of Reagan.

They hadn't spoken since they argued. Hell, she hadn't come out of her room since she demanded he get out. Wincing, he remembered the flash of hurt in her eyes when he basically told her to get over herself and move on. "Idiot," he murmured, chastising himself for handling the situation so badly. He hadn't exactly been Mr. Cool during their brief shouting match, but it bothered him that Reagan wouldn't let this whole black lung thing go. One physician was telling her she wasn't seeing what she was sure she did, and several more wouldn't touch the cases she wanted them to take on. Now she was meeting with Doctor What's-His-Face alone at some secret location, and Henry didn't even want her help. Something definitely didn't feel right.

Clenching his jaw, he closed his eyes and opened them when he heard the loud bang outside. Seconds later, tires squealed and men shouted. Shane rushed to his feet and yanked on his shorts. He hurried to the closet and grabbed his gun, shoved a magazine into the clip, and wrenched open his door, swearing when Reagan plowed into his chest.

She stifled a scream, gripping his biceps as he caught her around the waist, turning with her and taking the brunt of their collision as they crashed into the wall.

"There's someone outside," she said on a trembling whisper, her eyes huge with terror.

"I know. Call the cops." Not that the police would do him much good. Kentucky State Troopers were a rarity in Black Bear Gap; their nearest hub was a good twenty minutes away. "Stay in here with Jenny and the baby." He let her go and started down the hall.

"Wait." She grabbed his hand. "What are you doing? Where are you going?"

"To figure out what the hell's going on." He turned again, eager to be on his way, certain the clinic was going up in flames. When people were unhappy around here, things caught on fire.

She tugged on him again before he'd taken two steps. "Don't go out there."

"Reagan, I have to. Stay with Jenny and Faith." He hurried down the darkened hall to the side door they rarely used and peeked out the curtain over the glass. The coast appeared clear as he stepped outside, listening and scanning his surrounding with every step he took, his weapon gripped in both hands, aimed forward and ready to fire. He moved closer to the clinic, relieved to see the building still intact, but noted the black scrawl covering sections of the metal. Turning, he startled when he spotted Reagan standing on the porch in the light pouring from the open front door. "Jesus. That's a good way to get yourself shot."

"Sorry. That's why I waited up here." She ran to him in her tiny shorts and thin cotton spaghetti strap top, her feet bare. "I thought you would want this." She handed over the sturdy police-issue flashlight.

"You should've waited for me to come back inside."

"We both heard them leave." She crossed her arms in the chilly air.

"Next time wait anyway." He turned on the flashlight, shining the beam on the walls of the building.

GET OUT. FEDS AINT WELCOME. QUACK. SLUT. TRADER.

He moved toward the front door, assessing the damage. "A couple more good kicks and they would've had this." He looked at Reagan as she shook her head and turned away. "Where are you going?"

"Inside. I've seen enough."

Sighing, he followed. This definitely couldn't be easy for her. "I'll call it in."

"I already did." She nibbled her lip as she looked up at him. "She's not safe here with us."

"I'm assuming you're talking about Jenny and their attempt at spelling 'traitor.'"

She stopped, frowning. "How can you make a joke at a time like this?"

"I'm not. There's nothing funny going on around here, Doc." Luckily the vandals had kept their warning to spray paint and minor destruction, but he still needed to call Ethan and figure out how they were going to proceed with this latest development.

Reagan walked inside with him following directly behind. Before he could blink, Jenny came bursting out of her room with Faith in her arms.

"I was so scared. I thought somethin' happened to you two. You guys were out there for so long."

They'd been gone less than ten minutes, but he wrapped his arm around her as Reagan did the same, sandwiching Jenny and the baby between them. "It's okay." He kissed the top of Faith's head, holding Reagan's gaze. "We're okay. Everything's all right." But it wasn't. The peaceful days in The Gap were clearly over.

CHAPTER SEVENTEEN

REAGAN DROVE ALONG ROUTE TWENTY-ONE, HALF-listening to the music on Shane's MP3 player instead of the country music on the radio. She yawned despite the catchy beat pouring through the SUV's speakers and the brilliant sunny day, shook her head in an attempt to banish the exhaustion hazing her brain, and yawned again. "Crap," she said, rolling down the window to let in the mild temperatures and fresh air instead of the air conditioning.

Two mostly sleepless nights were starting to take their toll. By the time the police made it to the clinic, snapped their photos of the destruction, took Shane's statement, and helped him secure plywood over the clinic's damaged doorway, it had been after two. Convincing Jenny it was safe to go back to bed had been another feat until Shane offered up his room to the entire crew. An hour after Kentucky State Troopers left the cabin, they finally went to bed. For the sake of Jenny's comfort, three adults and one infant roughed it on a queen-sized mattress with her and Shane squished, almost falling off their prospective edges, while Jenny and Faith slept deeply until sunrise.

Her gaze met Shane's more than once throughout the wee hours of the morning as she listened to the creaks and cracks of the settling cabin and occasional rush of wind among the trees. His bold green eyes held hers, unreadable in the shadowy light shining in from the hallway, while tension hung thick in the room.

Their argument earlier in the day had been overshadowed by the events of the evening, but not forgotten. He'd hurt her with his callous words and indifference. He'd shrugged off her problems as if they were nothing, as if potentially misdiagnosing not one but *four* patients was no big deal. Shane expected her to turn her head and look the other way, but that wasn't who she was or how she worked. Shane was worried there might be more to the entire situation than what they were seeing, but that mattered little to her. This wouldn't be the first time she'd stepped on toes or pushed back to get the right results. She was a healer. She couldn't and wouldn't let the matter go until she knew for sure Henry and the others were getting the best course of treatment for a proper diagnosis.

Doctor Jacobson had hinted her concerns were nothing more than egocentric; Shane had basically done the same, but it wasn't true. If she was honest with herself—and there was no other way to be—she could admit that this entire situation shook her to her core, fueling her self-doubt further and making her question everything about herself professionally. But at the end of the day, this was about four men—probably more—in need of help.

Shortly after she'd kicked Shane out of her room yesterday, she got back to work, losing herself in her research. Instead of focusing on black lung itself, she moved to the cause—coal dust. After hours of digging, she'd come across several of Corpus Mining's older safety records, noting the facility did indeed have an excellent track record—impeccable even. So where did her patients contract their disease?

"In one mile, arrive at destination on left," the GPS told her as she guided the Pajero around another sharp curve, sighing when she passed a neighborhood and gas station. "Civilization." Twice in two days she had the opportunity to be out and about. Yesterday she'd been too focused on her meeting with Doctor Jacobson to enjoy her proximity to an actual store, but today was a different story.

She glanced left and right, smiling when she spotted a full-sized grocer, then the strip mall. She peeked at her watch, tempted to stop in and find something special to bring home for everyone, but it was twelve thirty and she had no idea where Doctor Schlibenburg's home was.

"Later," she promised herself as she pulled into the gas station and parked, dialing the number she called yesterday. The line rang four times, then five, and she nibbled her lip. What if he'd changed his mind and didn't answer?

"Hello?"

She sighed a quiet breath of relief. "Dr. Schlibenburg, this is Reagan Rosner. I've made it to Berea."

"You're early."

"Yes. I didn't want to be late. I'm not exactly sure where you live. If you give me your address, I can punch it into my GPS. I'm at the Gas-n-Go on Third Street."

"Are you alone?"

She frowned as she tried to ignore the wave of discomfort, remembering Jenny's fears about the mystery man she was meeting being some sort of nut job. "Yes."

"Did you tell anyone you were coming?"

Her brows drew further together in the uncomfortable silence, debating whether or not to be truthful. Saying yes might prompt him to cancel their appointment, but if he was a whacko, she wanted him to be aware that someone knew where she was. "Yes. The man in charge of security for The Appalachia Project knows I'm here. He's a former US Marshal—Fugitive Task Force. He hunted and apprehended criminals for several years," she added for good measure. "He won't tell anyone, Doctor Schlibenburg," she said when the line stayed quiet.

"Follow Route Twenty-One west for seven miles. Turn left on Corville Road."

"I have a GPS," she reminded him.

"I will give you the directions myself."

Reagan scrambled for a pen and grabbed the gas receipt Shane left in the console, scribbling down the directions. "Route Twenty-One, seven miles. Left on Corville."

"Travel one mile," he continued. "Take another left on Dean's Pike and the next immediate left for three miles, where I will wait for you."

"Okay. Thank you."

Dr. Schlibenburg hung up, and she pulled the phone away from her ear, blowing out a long breath at the abrupt end to their call. If this man wasn't well respected and known for his brilliant research, she might have listened to Jenny's pleadings to stay home and paid more attention to Shane's long, disapproving looks at the breakfast table.

Dismissing Jenny and Shane's concerns as paranoia, she eased back into traffic, following the directions she'd been given. Minutes later she turned on the road that had to be Doctor Shlibenburg's driveway, seeing that the dirt path twisted off into the trees far beyond. Glancing around, she realized there wasn't another house anywhere to be seen. She put her hand on the gearshift knob, half intending to reverse, when the laptop case full of charts in need of answers caught her attention. "Stop being a baby," she murmured and picked up her phone, dialing the cabin.

"Hello?" Shane's deep voice answered.

"Hey. I just wanted to let you know I made it. I thought you might want the directions."

"If you're calling to give them to me I should probably write them down."

She pressed her lips together, reading his snarky tone loud and clear. They hadn't said much to each other since their quick conversation in the dark by the vandalized clinic. "Never mind." She moved to end their call.

"Wait. Doc."

She put the phone back to her ear. "What?"

"Give me the directions."

"Route Twenty-One to Berea. West for seven miles after the Gas-n-Go. Take a left on Corville. After a mile, take another left on Dean's Pike, then the immediate right and travel three miles."

"Got it. He gave you an hour?"

"Yes."

"I want to hear from you by two-fifteen or I'm calling the cops and sending them your way."

Knowing Shane would be watching the clock comforted her. "I'm sure I won't need them, but thanks. I should go."

"Bye."

"Bye." She ended the call and took her foot off the brake, more relaxed now that Shane knew where she would be. Her phone rang again, and she stopped. "Hello?"

"You're out in the middle of nowhere."

She looked around at the wall of trees as thick here as they were at the clinic. "Tell me about it."

"This isn't a good idea, Doc."

She didn't want to argue again. "I have to do this. It's only an hour."

"I'm sure I don't have to remind you to keep your keys in easy reach. And a solid knee to the balls would give you plenty of time to run."

She smiled. "I'll keep that in mind, but Dr. Schlibenburg is in his sixties, and I'm running late."

"There's always time for general safety tips."

Faith cooed in the background.

"Oh, Faith says an elbow to the nose works well too."

Helpless to his charm, she grinned, despite wanting to hold on to her hurt feelings. "Tell her I said thanks."

"Take care of yourself, Doc."

"I'll call you in an hour and fifteen—okay, probably a little longer than that, but sometime in that ballpark."

"See ya."

"Bye." She started on her way, shaking her head and chuckling, well aware that it was getting harder to resist the man handing out tidbits of self-defense advice. Shane's easy humor had once again defused a touchy situation. Her smile disappeared, knowing his time here in Kentucky was quickly coming to an end. In just a couple weeks he would be heading back to LA. But now wasn't the time to worry about that.

She pulled around the circular drive and stopped in front of the large two-story house painted a dark chocolate brown with black shutters. Interesting color choice.

Leaning over to the floor of the passenger's seat, she gathered her bag and purse, sliding her phone in the front pocket where she could easily grab it should the need arise. She righted herself, gasping and jumping when the tall, thin man with short, spiky white hair and wire-rimmed glasses appeared by the driver's side door. Smiling, she stepped out in another professional outfit—tailored navy blue slacks, matching heels, and a white spaghetti-strap top. "Doctor Schlibenburg, I'm Reagan Rosner."

He took her hand for a quick shake. "Doctor Rosner. Please come."

Her smiled dimmed as he turned and started toward the front door.

"Your home is lovely—very secluded, peaceful." She followed him up the steps and through the door where he proceeded to twist three locks into place. "And secure." She swallowed, trying to smile again.

He glanced at his watch. "Time is wasting."

"Yes."

He moved to the spacious living room where the curtains were drawn. "Sit, please. Tell me what it is you need exactly."

She studied the man who had been revered as one of the best pulmonologists in the US as he sat on the cushion next to her, his discomfort apparent with each shove of his hand through his hair while his eyes darted from one concealed window to the next. "I um—I brought along the files I'm hoping you might be able to look at." She pulled out the films.

Dr. Schlibenburg snatched the first image from her, holding it up to the lamp as he turned it on. "Progressive massive fibrosis."

She blinked at his rapid-fire answer. "What?"

"This patient has an advanced case of progressive massive fibrosis."

Her eyes watered with his confirmation. She wasn't wrong. Coming here and seeking answers had been exactly right. "Are you—are you sure?"

"Yes. The right lung is full of fibroids. The left is

quite bad as well. The diagnosis is unmistakable. Your patient will soon suffer the effects of heart failure if he hasn't already."

"Okay." She pulled out the next x-ray. "What about this one?"

He held it up. "Yes. Not as severe, but it will be in time."

"Yes," she repeated, closing her eyes. *Finally.* After all the research and time, she would get the help she needed.

"The more white we see the more fibroids." He pointed to the thick circles among the cobweb-like structures filling the lung cavity. "He also has classic tissue shrinkage, indicating a worsening condition."

"That x-ray belongs to a twenty-two-year-old man."

Doctor Schlibenburg's gaze whipped to hers before he gave his attention back to the film. "Give me the next."

She presented Doctor Schlibenburg with another film and another until all four patients' images had been studied and discussed.

"Definitive black lung, different extremes, but progressive massive fibrosis all the same." He turned off the lamp, sending the room into shadows as he handed back the last film. "Your findings are correct, Doctor Rosner."

"So what should I do? The pulmonologist I've referred all four of these men to has diagnosed that first patient—the only one of the four he's seen so far—with chronic obstructive pulmonary disease."

"Yes."

"But he has complicated black lung."

"Yes."

She shook her head. Why wasn't he surprised? Why wasn't he concerned? "Dr. Schlibenburg, I don't understand."

"Is your patient a smoker?"

"Yes. He was," she corrected. "Until a few weeks ago. All of the men are—two packs a day, a couple even three."

"For how long?"

She looked at her notes. "Henry started smoking when he was twelve, so forty years. The other patients vary from five to twenty years."

"Forty years of smoking. Twenty years underground in the mines."

"A recipe for bad lungs," she said.

"Smoking is the primary risk factor of chronic obstructive pulmonary disease."

"Yes. Eighty percent of COPD deaths are due to smoking."

"These are high numbers."

"They are," she agreed.

He nodded.

She waited for him to expand on his statements. "Doctor Schlibenburg, I feel like we're speaking in riddles. These men have black lung, not COPD. I've been doing research into the mine—"

He made a loud, strangling sound in his throat as he stood.

She stared at him as he paced around. Perhaps she'd solved the mystery to the doctor's sudden retirement. He'd clearly lost his mind. "Doctor Schlibenburg—"

"These days the mines are more rock than coal."

She nodded. "Coal is growing scarcer. Machines are grinding into the rock to get to the coal seams and are releasing silica into the air."

"Silica dust is more dangerous than coal dust. It's an accelerative factor when lung disease is already present." He picked up a glass vase on the side table and set it back down with a snap, moved to the bookshelf and did the same with an angel knickknack. "It exacerbates poor conditions."

"Which doesn't make any sense. All four patients have spent their entire career with this one mine. Corpus Mining has an exemplary record, and has for years."

He hurried to the picture on the wall, straightening the already straight frame.

She tucked the hair that escaped her updo behind her ear, struggling to concentrate on their odd conversation while he scurried about the room. "I uh, I discovered the name of the physician on staff at the mine while Mr. McPhee Senior ran the company and for the next few months after his death—Doctor Paul Pattel—"

He puffed out a loud breath, making her jump.

"Do you know him?"

"I did."

"Doctor Hargus, the mine's current doctor, won't return my calls. I was thinking of reaching out to Doctor Pattel—"

The mantel clock struck two. He whirled, facing her. "Time is up."

"But I still need answers."

"I've given them to you. Your patients have advanced black lung."

"That's only a small part of my problem. None of the pulmonologists I've spoken to will look at the x-rays."

"Black lung is not a popular diagnosis."

"But it *is* their diagnosis. These men need care. Their families are entitled to compensation."

Dr. Schlibenburg looked from the mantle clock to

his watch. "Time is up, Doctor Rosner."

"I'm asking for your help. You can help me, Doctor Schlibenburg. You're well versed in pneumoconiosis. There are rumors you were going to publish some sort of article—"

"Not everyone wants to hear what I have to say."

"I do."

"It's time for your departure." His voice sharpened.

She gathered her items as he became more agitated, leaving the x-rays behind, hoping he might reconsider. "I need your help. These men need your help."

"There is nothing I can do."

She stood and walked hurriedly to the door as he dragged her forward by the arm. "Please." She yanked away from his hold. "The article you were going to release, it was about progressive massive fibrosis."

"It's after two." He unlocked the door.

"Can I get a copy? Maybe the information would—"

"No," his voice rose again in a quick bark.

"It would stay between us. Your knowledge—"

"I can do nothing more for you, Doctor Rosner. I've already done too much."

"You've given me nothing. I have valid diagnoses but can't do anything with them."

"Goodbye, Doctor Rosner." He twisted the locks, grabbed her by the elbow, and shoved her outside.

She stumbled forward, catching herself on the railing before she fell. Staring at the closed door, she glared as her heart pounded, more shaken than she cared to admit. Her cell phone rang on the way down the steps, and she stifled a small scream. Walking to the SUV, she pressed "talk." "Hello."

"You're still in one piece."

She started the vehicle and followed the circular

drive, spotting Doctor Schlibenburg watching her from the corner of one of his drawn curtains. "I am. I'm on my way back now."

"How'd it go?"

She shook her head, trying to make sense of whatever that was. "Not well."

"Doctor Jacobson was right."

Shane's assumptions irritated her. "No, he wasn't."

"So it is black lung?"

"Yes." She accelerated, a good ten miles per hour over the speed limit when she hit the main road, wanting to distance herself from the odd man.

"But your meeting didn't go well?"

"Not particularly."

"You lost me, Doc."

She huffed out a breath. "It's complicated. I should go. I'll be home in an hour." She passed the stores she no longer cared to stop at and picked up speed even more as she left the center of town.

"See you when you get here."

"Bye." She hung up and tossed the phone in the front seat, following the road mindlessly for miles as she attempted to understand what she couldn't explain to Shane. Her patients had progressive massive fibrosis, but there wasn't a damn thing she could do about it. Doctor Jacobson refused to acknowledge the findings, and no one else would touch it, including the biggest name in pulmonology. Her patients had worked or currently worked in a mine with an exemplary health and safety record, yet a twenty-two-year-old had a disease that shouldn't have showed up in his lungs for years to come, if at all.

She steamed out a frustrated breath, looking toward Henry and Daisy's simple ranch-style home as she entered Black Bear Gap town limits, trying to figure out where to go from here. There were certainly physicians in other parts of the country she could contact. She could call someone in Manhattan in less than five minutes, but her colleagues and friends didn't specialize in black lung, nor was the distance conducive to Henry or the others from a treatment standpoint. She needed someone close, and she needed them fast.

Glancing in her rearview mirror, she frowned when she noticed the black car that had been behind her for much of her trip back from Berea. Paranoid after last night, she took a quick right, pulling into the gas station, watching the vehicle continue on. Gripping the steering wheel tight, she closed her eyes and rested her head against the seat. "Get a grip," she murmured as she opened her eyes and looked around at the group of men standing around, staring at her. The town hated her. They'd shown her as much by painting her office with insults and destroying the clinic's front door, but spray paint and minor damage were a long way from her delusions of being followed.

She slid her hair back behind her ear and moved forward again, taking the road to the clinic. Minutes later, she pulled up in front of the cabin, relaxing her shoulders, knowing Shane was inside. A glimpse of civilization had been great, but it was good to be home.

~~~~

"They certainly got our attention," Shane said to Ethan as he paced about the living room, bringing Faith's half-empty bottle Jenny left on the coffee table to the sink.

"Sounds like it.

He dumped the leftover formula down the drain and set the nipple in the small bowl of soapy water.

"Overall the incident was pretty benign—no real threats and minor damage—nothing a little paint and new door won't fix."

"That's good, because I'm going to have to call the director and let him know you've seen some activity."

"Yeah, sure. I figured as much." He grabbed the rattles and stuffed elephant off the counter and put them in the basket where they kept Faith's toys.

"He'll want to know how we're handling it."

"At this point, I think we should just keep doing what we're doing. We'll keep the porch lights on throughout the night and get a better lock for the doors. If things continue to heat up, we'll change tactics, but last night wasn't anywhere near as bad as some of the other shit that went on around here when The Project first began. Nothing caught on fire."

Ethan chuckled humorlessly. "Well, I guess that's something."

He straightened Jenny's schoolbooks and grabbed the empty water glass from the side table. "I'll take it."

"You said a couple of the 'messages' were aimed at Jenny. Are you thinking she's the target?"

"No, I think this is about Doc and her diagnoses, which might be right after all." He glanced at his watch, as he had several times since she got in her SUV this morning and left. Reagan was due home in less than thirty minutes. He wouldn't be able to relax until she walked through the door.

"I don't get it. What's the problem then?"

"They think she's wrong. Reagan referred her patients to some lung specialist in Lexington, Doctor Jacobson. Apparently, Jacobson told one of the guys he has something else—COPD. Now everyone in The Gap is in an uproar because a bad diagnosis messes with job security and access to compensation." He shook his head. "Honestly, I don't know what the hell's going on. She went to meet with some colleague in Berea—a former bigwig pulmonologist. She said she wasn't wrong when we spoke on the phone right before I called you, but she didn't say much else. I'll get the scoop when she gets back."

"Should I be thinking about sending in backup?"

"No. Right now I'm all set. I can handle a few assholes spray-painting the clinic. If things change you'll definitely be the first to know."

"I want to start implementing more frequent updates so we can begin transitioning Chase over to the assignment. A couple more weeks and you're out of there."

"Yeah." He wanted to stay more than he wanted to leave, but as he looked around the living room he'd just tidied and pulled a burp cloth from his shoulder, he knew it was time to go. "I'll—" He caught a movement out of the corner of his eye and glanced out the window as Terry grabbed Jenny's arms and yanked her toward him. "You little fucker."

"What?"

"I need to call you back." He hung up and rushed outside. "Hey!"

Terry dropped Jenny's arms like a hot potato and stepped back.

"What's going on out here?" He walked to Jenny's side in bare feet. "Are you okay?"

She nodded, rubbing at her biceps.

"This ain't got nothin' to do with you, Fed." Terry stepped closer to him, dressed in jeans and an old Rolling Stones t-shirt.

"When you've got your hands on Jenny it does."

Terry advanced again, coming almost toe to toe. "Mind your own fuckin' business."

"Terry, stop. Go on home," Jenny pleaded as Shane raised his eyebrows, getting his first good look at the pimple-faced teen with brown eyes, black hair, and a decent build.

"I think you should follow Jenny's advice and walk into those woods and not come back."

"You tryin' to keep me away from my girl and baby? They're *my* family, Fed."

The little prick hadn't asked to see his daughter once, which was just fine with him. "I'm trying to prevent a call to the cops and an arrest for domestic violence."

A stirring of fear flickered in his eyes. "I didn't hit Jenny."

"You put your hands on her during a disagreement. I see your handprints right there." He gestured to the red marks on her arms. "Which I better not ever see again."

"What ya gonna do about it, Fed?"

It was tempting to kick the kid's ass and wipe that smirk off his face, but Terry wasn't worth the trouble it was bound to cause. "Jenny, I think we should probably go in."

"Okay," she said quietly, meeting his eyes quickly then looked at the ground.

"Keep your hands off my girl, prick."

"Keep your feet off federal property." He started to turn away, and Terry grabbed his arm.

"You think you scare me?" His eyes glinted as his breath heaved. "You think 'cause you're a Fed you're better'n me?" He pushed Shane.

"Stop it!" Jenny shouted.

Enough was enough. Shane rushed forward, yanking Terry up by the collar. "Get the hell out of here and don't come back." He shoved Terry to the ground, sending the kid sprawling, and walked up the steps with Jenny. "Next time I'll call the cops." He closed the door as Terry gained his feet and carried on with his rant and Jenny burst into tears. Clenching his jaw, he rubbed at the back of his neck. Women's tears didn't bother him, but that didn't mean he knew what to say in this situation. "Are you okay?"

"Yes." She sucked in a shaky breath. "He's been gettin' so mad lately."

He wanted to point out the obvious and tell her to stay away from the little asshole, but he remembered Reagan's request that they try their best to understand Jenny. "I'll get you something to drink. Go sit down." He walked to the kitchen, filling a glass with filtered water, trying to figure out how he should handle this, wishing more than ever Reagan were home. Sighing, he went to where she sat sniffling in the corner of the couch. "Here."

She looked up with red eyes. "Thanks."

He snagged the box of tissues on the coffee table and sat next to her.

"I don't want Terry bein' Faith's father." She cried harder, pressing a tissue to her eyes. "He don't— doesn't," she corrected, "want anything to do with her."

"Good."

She blinked, looking at him in surprise. "Why would you say that?"

"Because Faith deserves better, and so do you. You're a smart, beautiful young woman. You have ambition and an amazing little girl. Someday some guy—a guy who deserves you—is going to scoop you two up and never look back."

"You think?" She wiped at her cheeks.

"I *know*." He snagged the glass of water she hadn't touched and drank.

"What about you?"

"What about me?" He drank again.

"I was thinkin' maybe you might want me."

He swallowed and choked. "What?" he croaked out in between his fits of coughing.

"You're hot. I mean your face and body looks like one of them movie stars. You've got yourself a good job and a house out in Los Angeles. You could be Faith's daddy."

He coughed again. "Jenny, I'm twenty-eight."

She shrugged. "My daddy's lots older than Mommy."

"Jenny, we're friends," he added when their twelve-year age gap didn't appear to be a problem.

"You don't want Faith?"

He set down the glass. "I love Faith very much."

She stared down at the floor. "You don't want me." Hurt tinged her words.

He scrubbed at his jaw, fighting the urge to swear. "Jenny, I love that you're staying here with me and Reagan. We both love helping you with the baby. You're working hard to change your life. I admire the hell out of you, but I also think of you as my little sister."

Her gaze flew to his. "Little sister?"

"Yeah."

A fresh batch of tears coursed down her cheeks. "I think that's about the worst thing you've ever said to me, Shane." She rushed to her feet and ran to her room.

"Son of a bitch," he muttered, closing his eyes and resting his head against the cushion. The doorknob twisted and he opened his eyes as Reagan walked in. Thank *God*. "Hey."

"Hi." She slid off her heels. "Where's Jenny and Faith?"

He trailed his gaze up her tailored slacks and fitted shirt, both of which accentuated her sexy body. "In their room."

"Oh." She breezed past him and down the hall.

He sat where he was a moment longer, got up, and followed. "Where'd you go?" He pushed open her door she'd closed halfway and paused mid-step, staring as she stood in her white lacy bra and pants. Goddamn, she was gorgeous.

"I'm changing."

"Yeah, I see that. Sorry." He turned away, facing his own room, swallowing a big ball of lust. "Were you ah—were you planning on telling me about today?"

"There's not much to say. You can turn around."

He faced her and walked in, struggling with another punch of longing. She'd put on her sinful short shorts and clingy white tank top that drove him *crazy*. "I thought you said Doctor Schlibenburg said it was black lung."

"He did." She moved to the dresser and took off her earrings.

He sat on the edge of her bed. "That's a pretty big deal."

"Yeah." She reached behind her neck, fighting with the clasp on her necklace.

He stood, stepping up behind her. "Let me do it."

She dropped her hands, looking into his eyes in the mirror. "Thanks."

"I thought you would be more excited now that you have your confirmed diagnoses." He glanced down at the stubborn clasp.

"Me too. Thanks," she said when he handed her the necklace. "Doctor Schlibenburg has no intention of backing me up. In fact, when my hour was up, he shoved me out the door—literally."

He frowned, pulling the pins from the fancy twist in her hair, watching her silky brown strands fall past her shoulders, breathing in the scent of her shampoo. "The guy pushed you?"

"After he dragged me to the door."

He slid his fingers through soft, glossy locks, holding her gaze in the glass.

She sighed, closing her eyes. "That feels good."

"Good." He massaged her scalp, watching her shoulders relax.

She let loose another deep breath.

"I'm sorry things didn't go the way you were hoping."

"Me too." She backed up against him as he continued to work his magic.

"I'm also sorry about yesterday."

"All's forgiven."

He slid her hair to one side and brought his mouth to her neck.

Her eyes flew open.

He pressed his lips to her skin for a second time, then a third, as goosebumps puckered her arms and she fisted her hands at her sides.

"Shane."

"I know. You're on a break."

"Exactly."

He wrapped his arms around her waist. "What about a break from your break?" He trailed his hands up her sides, waiting for her to tell him to stop, and snagged the tip of her ear with his teeth as he cupped her firm breasts.

She bit her bottom lip as her nipples went taut against his palms. "Shane, I really—"

He turned her to face him. "Should," he finished for her, capturing her face in his hands. "You really should." He kissed her deeply, savagely, groaning.

She moaned, clutching at the loops on his jeans then sent her hands up his stomach, around to his back, and into his hair, pulling him closer.

Finally. God, finally. He gripped her hips and lifted her, sitting her on the nearby desk, yanking her forward and grinding them fire to fire.

She whimpered, wrapping her legs around him, clinging as tongues tangled and her fingers made their way under his shirt.

"Let me lock the door," he whispered, nipping at her chin as Faith started crying.

She shook her head, panting, her cheeks rosy and her eyes dark with need. "No."

"Reagan." He eased back.

"I'm sorry. I'm not trying to be a tease. I just—I don't know. I'm sorry," she repeated and got to her feet.

It was tempting to pull her back to him and make her forget about her break, but he moved, letting her have her space. If he and Reagan were going to end up in bed, she was going to be his partner without any regrets. Clenching his jaw, he rubbed at his chin. "So what are you going to do about the black lung thing?"

"Nice segue." She huffed out a breath, pressing her fingers to her temple.

He shrugged. "I'm game for picking up where we just left off."

"That's okay." She swallowed. "The answer to your question is: I don't know what I'm going to do."

He crossed his arms at his chest, physically aching to touch her again. "I should probably tell you Terry was here this afternoon. He had his hands on Jenny."

She raised her brows. "Do you need help burying his body?"

He smiled. "He was looking for a fight. He pushed

me, so I shoved him to the ground and told him not to come back or he'll be dealing with the cops next time."

"Okay. Are you all right?"

"Yeah. Definitely, but there's more."

"I can't wait to hear it."

"Jenny doesn't want Terry to be Faith's father."

"Wise girl."

"She thought I might be a better solution."

Her eyes grew wide. "*What?*"

"She thought maybe I could do the whole dad thing. I make good money, have a house in LA, and of course a muscular build."

Reagan sat on the bed and collapsed back, covering her face as she groaned. "Have we stepped into some insane alternate universe?"

He leaned against the wall instead of following her to the mattress. "I'm thinking maybe."

"What did you say to her?"

"That you and I want to help her with Faith, and that I think of her as a little sister."

"That'll sting but it will also pass." She sat up again. "It sounds like you handled it well."

"She ran to her room crying, so maybe not."

"I'll talk to her."

He nodded. "I need to call my boss back."

"What did he have to say?"

"Not a whole lot other than he's going to talk to the director about the vandalism, and he wants me to start easing Chase into his new assignment."

"Your replacement."

He nodded as he stared at Reagan, not loving the idea of being replaced.

She bit her lip, darted a glance to the floor, and met his gaze. "I guess I'll go talk to Jenny."

"Okay."

She walked off, leaving him alone in her room. In just a couple more weeks Reagan would be dealing with this insane alternate universe on her own, and it didn't sit well with him.

~~~~

"I followed her to Berea and back."

"What was she doing in Berea?"

"I'm not sure. She pulled into a gas station, made a phone call, then took off a few minutes later. She went down a couple of isolated roads, so I kept my distance, then stopped following altogether. She was gone about an hour. I'm heading back that way now. I'll have details for you within the next few hours."

"Keep me up to date."

"I will." He hung up as he merged on Route Twenty-One, ready to find out what Doctor Rosner had been up to this afternoon.

CHAPTER EIGHTEEN

"IF YOU LOOK HERE, YOU'LL SEE SHANE'S NON-FASTING glucose levels are well within normal range," Reagan said as she and Jenny sat next to each other in the office, going over the results of Shane's blood draw.

Jenny nodded. "He seems to be smack-dab in the middle of all the ranges we've seen."

"He's very healthy."

"What about this one?" Jenny lifted another sheet.

"This is an STD panel."

Jenny's eyes widened. "Like in Sexually Transmitted Diseases?"

"Like yes." She smiled. "Sex is part of medicine, and I'm pretty sure Shane's had it a few times before."

Jenny blushed as she stared at the paper.

It was moments like this when she remembered just how young Jenny was. She had a baby, yet the idea of Shane taking a woman to bed made her blush. Reagan flashed back to the moment Shane held her gaze in the mirror and slid his hands over her breasts. A quick wave of tingles whirled through her stomach with the memory, and she cleared her throat. "Go ahead and read off the results for me."

"Mmm, well, it looks like he's negative for HIV, syphilis, and hepatitis A, B, and C."

"Good—"

Jenny's stomach growled, and she winced as she pressed her hand to her abdomen. "Sorry. I didn't have much of a lunch today."

"We're pretty much finished here. Go on home and get yourself something to eat. I have a couple more things to do, then I'll be over myself."

"Okay." She stood, putting the chair back against the wall. "Thanks for showin' me how to read the results. I definitely think I'm gonna have an advantage over other nursin' students."

She smiled with the rush of pride for the young woman who'd come so far over the last few weeks. "I agree. You're my prize student. You're picking up the information quickly."

Jenny smiled back. "I think maybe that's 'cause I've got good teachers." Her stomach growled again. "I'm gonna go see Faithy and have a snack."

"I'll be home soon." She watched Jenny leave and walk up the path, nodding her satisfaction that Jenny was filling out the jeans she'd given her a bit more. Jenny had put on a little weight since she moved in—a healthy five pounds the teenager had needed. She waited for Jenny to climb the steps to the cabin and got back to work, filing Shane's test results, then glanced at her appointment book, sighing as she crossed off the five names of the patients who'd failed to show up today.

Getting back to the task she'd begun long before Jenny had come in, she picked up the phone and dialed yet another number she'd jotted down, this time in Nashville, Tennessee. Throughout the afternoon, she'd officially exhausted every pulmonology option in the state of Kentucky and had even tried a few of the doctors over the border in Virginia and West Virginia. Since Doctor Jacobson's misdiagnosis, she had reached out to more than twenty reputable physicians, and not one would answer her plea for help. It was time to move on to the next closest state.

"Good afternoon, Doctor Yancey's Office."

"Yes, good afternoon. This is Doctor Regan Rosner up in Black Bear Gap, Kentucky. I was wondering if I might be able to leave a message on Doctor Yancey's voicemail.

"He's in between patients. I can patch you through to his line."

"That would be great. Thank you." She tapped her pen against the desk, listening to the canned music.

"This is Doctor Yancey."

"Doctor Yancey, this is Reagan Rosner up in Black Bear Gap, Kentucky. I'm the physician on staff working with the Appalachia Project."

"Yes, hello."

"Hi. I imagine you don't have a lot of time, so I'll cut right to the chase. I have four cases of progressive massive fibrosis on my hands. I'm looking for someone to glance at my x-rays and verify my diagnoses."

"Mmm. I'd love to give you a hand, but my time's pretty tight right now."

"Oh." She sighed at yet another excuse.

"But I could look them over in a couple of weeks, although it'll probably be closer to three."

She sat up further in her chair with the first stirrings of hope. "You can?"

"Like I said, it won't be right away. I'm getting married Saturday—in fact my rehearsal dinner's tomorrow night. My new wife and I are leaving for Bora Bora Saturday for two weeks."

She'd been chasing her own tail for *days* getting nowhere. What was a couple of weeks if she might finally get the backup she needed? "No. That's fine." She pressed a hand to her forehead. "I can't tell you how much I appreciate this. I would like to send along several chest x-rays and medical histories for each of my patients. I have one patient who's quite ill. I'll mark his as the priority."

"Sure. I'll get to them as soon as I can."

"Thank you, Doctor Yancey."

"I should probably put it out there that I'm not particularly well versed in black lung. I'll have to study up."

"That's okay. I'll attach the research I've gathered. I'm just so thankful you're willing to take a look."

"Not getting much help up there?"

"No. None, in fact."

"Huh. I need to go. I'll call with my findings."

"Thank you again, and congratulations."

"Thanks. I'm happy to help."

"Great. Bye." She hung up, biting her bottom lip, grinning, laughing as she spun around once in her chair. "*Yes!*" She turned back to her computer, composed an e-mail, and attached several files, marking Henry's as urgent, smiling as she sent them off.

Encouraged for the first time in too long, she grabbed her laptop, turned off the lights in each of the rooms, did a visual check of the closet where the drugs were held, and was ready to call it a day. She was actually going to get some help. Doctor Yancey had a name behind him too—not anywhere near as big as Doctor Schlibenburg's, but she would take what she could get. Her phone rang, and she went back to her office. "Black Bear Gap Clinic. This is Doctor Rosner."

Someone breathed heavily on the other end.

She frowned. "Hello?"

The line went dead, and she shook her head. "Okay then." She moved toward the door, pausing when the phone rang again. Seconds passed while she debated whether or not she should let it go, but then she rushed into her office, picking it up. "Black Bear Gap Clinic. This is Doctor Rosner."

"Doctor Rosner, this is Cliff Yancey."

Her brow furrowed. "Yes."

"I just scanned the notes you sent along with the file you marked a priority."

"Yes," she repeated, certain he was going to tell her he couldn't help her after all.

"I'm very concerned with this patient's x-rays, especially his right lung. The upper lobe is in terrible shape. He has to be working very hard for every breath."

"I'm afraid he is. I know he's using oxygen."

"I'm worried about heart failure."

She nibbled her lip. "If I can convince my patient to come see you, would you be willing to take on his case? I would be happy to manage his care locally with your advice."

There was a long pause.

"I know you're getting married—"

"I am, but the other problem is I'm booked for the next several months—"

"Henry doesn't have several months."

"No, he doesn't. His condition has progressed far past anything I can do. At this point the goal would be keeping him comfortable. He doesn't have much time, maybe a couple of months at the most, and that's being optimistic."

"But his family would receive compensation if we can document black lung. I'm meeting a lot of resistance with the specialists in the area."

Doctor Yancey sighed. "I can squeeze him in tomorrow."

"Tomorrow? When?"

"First thing in the morning."

She winced. "Okay. I need to speak to him, but I'll accept the appointment on his behalf and call you back with a definitive answer."

"I'll plan on seeing him at eight."

"I'll go talk to him now."

"Let me know about tomorrow."

"I will." She hung up and walked outside, securing the two heavy-duty locks on the new metal door Shane had installed late yesterday afternoon. Ignoring the graffiti still displayed all over the building, she walked quickly up the path and steps, hurrying into the house. "I'm going into town," she said to Shane as he sat on the couch with his laptop on his legs and phone at his ear.

"I'll call you back," he said to someone and disconnected. "What's going on?"

"I found a pulmonologist who's willing to diagnose Henry with progressive massive fibrosis—or he will be after he's done a bit more research. Henry will have to go see him in Nashville."

"Nashville? Isn't that like five hours away?"

"Four and a half." She snagged the keys from the bowl on the entryway table. "I'll be back."

"Whoa, wait a minute, Doc." He set his laptop on the cushion and stood, looking tasty in jeans and a sleeveless black top. "I don't think you should be going anywhere by yourself."

"I don't see a whole lot of choice. I don't want you leaving Jenny and the baby."

"I wasn't planning on it. We can bring them with us."

She shook her head. "I don't know how long I'll be." She tuned into Jenny talking to Faith in the bathroom. "And it sounds like Faith's in the bathtub."

"She spit up—big time. I'll tell Jenny to hurry."

She shook her head for the second time, sniffing the spicy scent in the air. "It smells like dinner's ready."

"It will be in about five minutes. I made chili."

"You two go ahead and eat without me. I'll bring my phone." She held up her cell phone.

"Doc—"

"I need to go." She hurried back outside, not wanting to waste any more time debating the issue. If Henry and Daisy were going to get to Nashville for the appointment they would have to leave now. She got in the SUV, driving down the road faster than was technically safe, following the twists and turns she knew well. She made it to town in record time, breezing by the general store and gas station, pulling into Henry and Daisy's drive, relieved to see their beat-up pickup parked by the small ranch-style home. She walked to the door and knocked.

Daisy answered wearing a long lime-green dress. "Doc Reagan."

She smiled. "Hi, Ms. Daisy. I'm hoping I might be able to speak with you for a couple of minutes."

"Yes." She opened the door wider. "Come in."

"Thank you." She stepped into the simple room decorated with several crosses, noticing Henry snoozing in his La-Z-Boy while the TV blared with the excitement of a game show.

Daisy shut off the television. "Henry, Doc Reagan's here."

"Huh?" He blinked open his eyes. "What?"

"Doc Reagan."

Reagan smiled at him, noting the slight blue tinge to his lips and his swollen feet, despite the portable oxygen unit at his side. "Hi, Mr. Henry."

"What are ya doin' here?"

"I wanted to stop in for a visit." She smiled again.

"How's the oxygen helping you?"

"I don't need no oxygen," he grumbled then coughed. "Gave up my smokes, didn't I?"

"Doc Reagan, can I offer you sweet tea?"

"No, thank you. May I sit?"

"Yes. Please."

She waited for the woman to join her on the lumpy couch. "Ms. Daisy, Mr. Henry, I came by because I've been thinking about you quite a bit."

"That's real kind of you." Daisy took her hand.

She gave plump fingers a gentle squeeze, pleased that they were off to a good start. "I haven't been able to stop thinking about how sorry I am that I'm not able to help you and Mr. Henry with his care."

"He's doin' some better. Ain't you, Henry?"

He grumbled his agreement.

Reagan studied the man again, watching his struggle for every breath. "I'm glad to hear it." She cleared her throat, understanding that this was going to be as difficult as she'd anticipated. Daisy wasn't willing to accept that Henry wouldn't be improving. "Ms. Daisy, Mr. Henry, I've spent some time over the last few days talking with a few of my colleagues— friends," she added, wanting to keep the conversation as informal as possible. "I was sharing my concerns about some of my neighbors here in The Gap."

"We don't need none of your concern, girl," Henry spat.

"I have a friend who would like to visit with Mr. Henry," she went on, ignoring Henry's comment. "In fact he would love to see Mr. Henry tomorrow."

"Tomorrow?" Daisy asked.

She nodded. "Doctor Yancey's down in Nashville—"

"*Nashville?*" Daisy gaped. "Doc Reagan, that'd be

almost five hours away."

"I ain't goin' down to Nashville," Henry barked and coughed.

"It is a long drive, but I'm hoping you might reconsider. I can help out with gas and a hotel. I'd be happy to treat you and Mr. Henry to a nice dinner and breakfast."

"That's real Christian of you."

She nodded, slightly encouraged. "I've studied Mr. Henry's x-rays dozens of times. I'm certain your diagnosis should be progressive massive fibrosis," she addressed Henry. "Doctor Yancey agrees." Or he would.

"Get on out of my house, girl." He pointed to the door.

"That's enough now, Henry." Daisy looked at Reagan. "Now Doc, we ain't goin' through this again. We're seein' Doctor Jacobson. We have ourselves another appointment next week."

"Ms. Daisy." She took the woman's hand again. "I'm very worried."

"There's no need. Henry's feelin' fine."

"Ms. Daisy, I think Mr. Henry needs to be seen sooner. I'm noticing some edema."

"Edema?" Daisy blinked, looking at Henry. "What's that?"

"Edema is water retention. See how puffy Mr. Henry's feet are becoming? Doctor Jacobson really should look at that."

"I guess I could put in a call—"

"You don't need to be puttin' in no calls, Daisy. It's time for you to be leavin', girl. Comin' by to stir up trouble's what you're after." He coughed, tried to stand, and fell back.

Reagan rushed to her feet. "Mr. Henry—"

"You're makin' him upset, Doc Reagan."

"Yes. Okay." At this point she was doing more harm than good. "Please make the call, Ms. Daisy."

"It don't sound like he's wantin' me to. Henry's care is none of your never mind, Doc Reagan," Daisy's voice grew stern as she got to her feet. "We're in good hands with Doctor Jacobson."

She blinked back tears of frustration as she watched the man struggle to breathe.

"It's time for you to be on your way."

"I'll see myself out." She glanced back at Henry and walked out, shutting the door, leaning against it, sucking in several shaky breaths of her own. Why wouldn't they *listen* to her? How could Daisy insist her husband was fine when he absolutely wasn't? With nothing more she could do, she walked back to the SUV and got in, searching for the paper she wrote Doctor Yancey's number on, and dialed.

"Doctor Yancey's Office."

"Yes, this is Doctor Reagan Rosner. Can you please put me through to Doctor Yancey's voicemail."

"One moment, please."

"Thank you."

She backed up while the canned music played in her ear and started toward the cabin.

"You've reached Cliff Yancey. Please leave your message and I'll get back to you."

"Doctor Yancey, this is Reagan Rosner in Kentucky. I uh—" She swallowed, afraid she would break down. "I've spoken with my patient." She swallowed again, struggling to speak over the ball of emotion caught in her throat. "He's going to pass on the appointment at this time. Thank you very much for your help." She hung up, sniffled, wiping at her cheeks as she took the last curve and pulled into her spot in the driveway. Resting her forehead on the steering wheel, she closed her eyes, fighting to steady herself, before she opened her door and went inside.

The warm, delicious scent of chili and cornbread filled her nose while lullabies and cooing filled the air as Faith stared at the mobile dangling above her bouncy seat. Reagan gave Jenny a small smile when the teen glanced up from her studies. "Hi."

"Hi. I thought I would get back to it. I'm thinkin' I might be close to ready. I'm gonna take the practice test tomorrow."

Her smile warmed. "That's wonderful." She moved over to the bouncy seat set in the center of the big table. "Hi, Faithy."

Faith smiled at her, and her heart melted. "Oh, come see me." She took the baby out of the seat, snuggling her, breathing in the scent of baby powder, kissing her forehead. "Mmm, this is just what I needed." She closed her eyes and pressed her cheek to the baby's. "You're so soft and sweet. I love you, baby girl Faith." She opened her eyes and looked at Shane standing in the kitchen.

"How'd it go?"

"About as well as I should have expected. He and Daisy don't want to hear anything I have to say." Her voice wavered, and she cleared her throat as she adjusted Faith in her arms, giving the baby an over-the-shoulder view. "How are things around here?" She gestured to Jenny, wanting a change of subject.

"Okay."

She nodded. "Good. Faith's going to come hang out with me for a while." She moved down the hall to her room, settling the baby in the center of her bed while she took off her work clothes and slid on a pair of sweatpants and a simple black t-shirt. Lying down on her side next to the baby, she played with the infant's tiny fingers and toes. "You're getting so big." She picked up the book she'd been reading to the baby before she left for the clinic this morning. "Should we continue with our story?" She adjusted them so they snuggled against her pillow, holding the cloth book close enough to help Faith grab hold of the crinkly sensory piece. "You like that butterfly? Do you like purple, Faith?"

Faith cooed.

She chuckled. "It's your favorite?"

Faith cooed longer and louder, kicking her legs.

"Your *very* favorite? It's a pretty great color."

"Knock, knock." Shane stood in the doorway. "I saved you some dinner."

"Thank you." She settled Faith in the center of the bed again while the baby yanked and tugged at the fabric. "Cutie Pie and I are reading."

He stepped farther in. "Good book?"

"She seems to like it."

He sat down, taking her chin in his hand. "You look sad."

She shrugged. "I can't help someone who doesn't want it."

"No you can't."

Faith tucked herself and rolled to her stomach.

Reagan's eyes widened as Shane's did. "Did you see that? Has she done that before?"

"Not for me."

Reagan beamed, picking up the baby. "Faithy, you just rolled. Yes you did."

Shane laughed, sliding closer, his arm brushing hers as he grinned at the baby. "Who's our big girl?"

Faith smiled at him, cooing.

He kissed her little hands. "Are you my big girl?"

"What's goin' on in here?" Jenny came to the door.

"Faith rolled," Reagan said. "It was probably an

accident. It's a little early for her to be doing that, but we'll celebrate anyway."

Jenny smiled sadly.

Reagan settled Faith in her lap. "What's wrong?"

She jerked her shoulders. "I guess I'm just lookin' at the three of you sittin' there on the bed, and I'm seein' a perfect little family. Sometimes I find myself thinkin' you two should be her mommy and daddy."

Shane stood. "But we're not." He took Faith from Reagan. "She's got a great mom right here." He handed the baby to Jenny. "Faith loves her mom."

Faith clutched at Jenny's index finger she offered. "I guess she does."

Reagan stood. "Of course she does, sweetie. You're an excellent mother. I'm very proud of you." She hugged the teenager.

Jenny hugged her back. "I find myself wishin' you were my momma. Your children are gonna be mighty lucky to have you the way me and Faith are."

Her smile dimmed with Jenny's unintentionally hurtful words. "Thank you. I think I might go help myself to the meal Shane saved."

"I'm gonna give Faith her bottle and put her down to bed. Oh." She stopped and turned. "I was helpin' Shane put the food order together for the next couple of weeks. Do you want anything special?"

"I can't think of anything."

"Shane was gonna ask the new guy that's comin' what he'll be wantin'."

She looked at Shane, then Jenny, as they were all reminded again that Shane was running out of time here in The Gap. She sent him a smile despite the newly familiar sinking sensation in her stomach every time the subject came up. "It looks like you and I will have to start taking turns in the kitchen."

Jenny wrinkled her nose. "I'll cook."

She chuckled. "Maybe Chase cooks."

She and Jenny both looked at Shane.

He shook his head. "I have no idea. I'll e-mail him tonight and see what he wants and ask him about his kitchen abilities. I can't imagine they're any worse than yours." He bumped Reagan's arm with his elbow.

She smiled again, but she didn't want to think of another man living in the cabin. "So harsh."

"Sometimes the truth hurts." He winked as he delivered another insult.

"Well then, by all means, let me sample some of your *excellent* cuisine, Mr. Harper."

"Definitely. Come on." He held out his arm and she hooked hers through his, walking with him down the hall to the kitchen.

CHAPTER NINETEEN

REAGAN WALKED THROUGH THE FRONT DOOR INTO THE dark, toeing off her shoes in the blue glow of the TV.

Shane and Jenny looked over their shoulders from their seats on the couch while the action flick played. "Hey." He hit pause. "Welcome home, stranger."

She sighed, glad to be finished for the night. "Thanks. Don't stop your movie on my account. I have some stuff to do. Go ahead and enjoy." She started down the hall as gunfire sprayed through the speakers in the living room once again.

"Hey." Shane followed, looking relaxed and comfortable in black sweatpants and one of his white Ethan Cooke Security t-shirts. "Why don't you change your clothes and come take a load off?"

She couldn't *wait* to get out of her jeans and sweater and pull on a pair of her own sweatpants. "Mmm, maybe in a few minutes. I want to wrap up a couple of things first."

He snagged her by the elbow. "Doc, it's eight thirty and you're just getting home."

"I came home for dinner, which was really good by the way." She pulled the hair tie from her hair, letting her long locks fall free.

"And left again right after dish duty. You're working too much." He leaned his shoulder against the wall and put his hands in his pockets.

"The bi-annual inventory isn't going to do itself."

"I told you I would help."

"And I appreciate it, but I should be finished up tomorrow." Both he and Jenny had offered her a hand more than once, but counting cotton swabs and chux pads for the director's spreadsheets kept her busy. "Tell you what—give me half an hour and I'll be down."

"The movie will be over by then. How about we plan on dinner and a movie tomorrow? Me and Jenny are going to try our hand at that pizza recipe Sophie sent me the other day."

Homemade pizza and a movie with her two favorite people. She beamed. "That sounds great. I could make cookies or something for dessert."

He tossed her a pained look. "How about you pick the flick and leave the rest to us."

She chuckled. "Fine."

He smiled. "I guess I'll see you in the morning."

"Goodnight." She watched him walk down the hall, sliding an appreciative glance over his spectacular backside, then turned and went into her room, changing out of her work clothes into her comfy pajamas after another long, tedious day. Sitting at her desk, she opened her laptop, glancing at Henry's x-ray, which she'd been looking at earlier in the afternoon, and flipped to her e-mail, sighing her disappointment when there was nothing new in her inbox.

It had been a week since she and Doctor Yancey spoke. She realized he was on his honeymoon, but Henry was running out of time. She thought of her disastrous impromptu meeting with the Dooleys and Henry's increasingly poor health. Over the last several days she'd struggled with the helpless frustration of waiting for a concurring second opinion if she had any chance of standing up to Doctor Jacobson on Henry and Daisy's behalf.

Standing, she spotted Doctor Schlibenburg's

number peaking from the pages of her handwritten notes, hesitated, then picked up the phone. Doctor Yancey was helping her with her patients, but she wanted Doctor Schlibenburg's unpublished article. Clearly he had something important to say. Maybe if they spoke on the phone a few times, he would see he could trust her. Dialing, she waited through several rings.

"Hello?"

She frowned when a woman answered. "Hello, is Dr. Schlibenburg there?"

"May I ask who's calling?"

"This is Reagan Rosner. I'm hoping I might be able to speak with him."

"I'm afraid that's not possible."

"Oh, okay." She rubbed at the tension settling in the back of her neck with yet another setback. "Would you please pass on a message? I wanted to thank him for meeting with me—"

"Ms. Rosner, this is Doctor Schlibenburg's daughter. My father passed away."

Her hand fell to her side. "*What*?"

"My father died last week."

"Oh my God. I'm so sorry."

"Thank you," she said, her voice wavering. "How did you know my father?"

"He was consulting with me on one of my patient's diagnosis. I'm a physician with The Appalachia Project in Black Bear Gap."

"My father didn't practice anymore." She sniffled.

"It was a professional favor." She pressed her fingers to her temple, struggling with disbelief. "I'm really so sorry," she said again. "I can only express my sincerest condolences. Your father was a very nice man." She shrugged helplessly, unsure of what else to say.

"Thank you."

"If there's anything I can do, please let me know."

"That's very kind. Goodbye, Doctor Rosner."

"Bye." She hung up and sat down on her bed, pressing a hand to her stomach. Doctor Schlibenburg was *dead*. How could that be? Had he been in some sort of accident or succumbed to a fall? Surely it wasn't his health. His mental state had been questionable, but he'd seemed in good physical condition when they met. But now he was gone. Her blood ran hot then cold with the unexpected tragedy. Shaken, she walked to the bathroom, pulled off her clothes, and stepped in a steamy shower, hoping to get warm.

~~~~

Shane lay in bed reading the reports Ethan had sent him, briefing him on his next assignment. In a week he would be on his way back to California, then off to Madrid for two weeks before he returned to his regular duties in Los Angeles again.

His door opened a crack. "Shane?"

"Yeah?" He sat up. "Come on in."

Reagan walked in wrapped in her robe, her hair dripping, her face pale as she leaned back against the door, closing it with the weight of her body.

He pushed his covers back and stood. "What's wrong?"

"Doctor Schlibenburg's dead."

Of all the things he'd been expecting her to say, that wasn't one of them. "*What*?"

"He's dead."

"How? What happened?"

She shook her head. "I don't know exactly. His

daughter answered his phone when I called tonight. She was understandably upset. I didn't want to ask. She said he passed away last week."

"Did he seem sick when you met him?"

"*No.* He was a little strange and very keyed up, but he didn't appear ill. Perhaps he fell, or maybe he had a heart attack." She swiped at her wet hair, breathing in a shaky breath as she walked to where he stood. "Regardless, it's a terrible tragedy, and I'm a horrible person."

He frowned at the sudden change in their conversation. "No you're not. Why would you say that?"

"A man's dead—someone's father—and all I can think about is how I won't be able to convince him to help me."

He took her hand. "Come sit down and talk to me."

She shook her head. "I don't want to talk about it. I don't want to think about Henry or black lung, graffiti or Doctor Schlibenburg." She let loose another shaky breath as a tear fell. "I don't want to think at all."

"Okay."

Staring into his eyes, she stepped closer, crowding his space, walking him back to the bed.

He gripped her arms, stopping when his legs connected with the mattress. "Reagan, what are you doing?"

She slid her hands beneath his t-shirt, trailing her palms up his stomach and chest. "I don't want to talk." She stood on her tiptoes and pressed her lips to his. "I'm so sick of thinking," she said on a whisper.

He gave into lust over reason, following her lead, opening his mouth to the teasing darts of her tongue. "Reagan." He eased back as another tear slid down her cheeks. "Stop. Reagan."

She shook her head and shoved him, knocking him

off balance, sending him backwards.

"Shit."

She crawled on top of him, straddling him at the waist. "Don't you want me, Shane?" She tugged up his shirt, torturing him with hungry, open-mouthed kisses along his stomach and pecs. Her breath heated his skin as she went to work on his neck.

He closed his eyes, gripping her shoulders. "Christ, yes I want you. You know I do, but you're upset."

"So make me forget." She nipped at his jaw, holding his gaze, combing her fingers through his hair.

"I uh—" He pulled at her robe and dropped his hands in defense. "I don't think this is a good idea," he tried again breathlessly.

She sat up abruptly, tracing the ridges of his six-pack. "I know what I'm doing. I know what I want: I want you."

He stared into her hot blue eyes as she bit her bottom lip, daring him to send her away. Rearing up to sitting, he touched his lips to hers.

"I need you," she whispered, cupping his face. "I need you."

He pushed the hair back from her temple. "I'm right here." Their mouths collided, and he yanked at the tie on her robe, sliding the cotton from her shoulders, down her arms, staring at her magnificent breasts and tiny waist. "God, you're gorgeous."

She pulled at the hem of his shirt, freeing him from his top.

He ran his hands up her smooth thighs and hips and clutched at her ass, capturing her mouth. "If this isn't working for you, Doc, tell me now."

"Take me."

Groaning, he devoured her, feasting on her sweet flavor, staring into her eyes, letting his fingers wander over the soft skin of her arms and waist while he nipped at her jaw and neck, pausing to meet her gaze again before moving to her collarbone, then her breasts, bathing the soft, sensitive peaks with moist kisses.

She moaned, gripping his shoulders, grinding herself against his erection through the barrier of his sweatpants with each sinuous rock of her hips.

"God, Reagan," he murmured, taking her hand, kissing her palm, her wrist.

"Shane." She went after his neck, then his ear, tugging with her teeth. She played with the hem of his pants, helping him awkwardly from his remaining clothes. "Take me faster."

She was destroying him with her demands. He captured her mouth again as she gripped him in her hand. "I don't have any condoms," he realized in horror.

"It's okay," she murmured against his mouth, rising up, taking him in.

"Reagan," he groaned, clutching at her hips as she sunk him deeper into her hot, wet fire.

Gasping, she hooked her arms around his neck. "It's okay."

Seduced beyond reason, he wrapped his arms around her waist, pulling her as close as they could get, arrowing himself deeper, moving to the rhythm she set.

"Oh, God. Oh, God," she shuddered out, stiffening, tipping her head as she bowed back, calling out quietly.

He lay back against the pillows, gripping her hips, pumping frantically, watching her eyes widen with stunned pleasure as she tensed again, calling his name.

Before she could recover, he tugged her down, chest to chest, and rolled, pinning her beneath him. He wanted her under him when he finished them both off.

"Shane. Shane," she whimpered against his lips as her eyes held his.

He pushed her hands to her sides, clasping their fingers, and tortured them both with long, slow thrusts, drawing out the ending.

Her breathing grew unsteady for the third time and her fingers squeezed around his as he kissed her, feeling himself build as she did.

He waited for the pulsing rhythm of her climax to entice him over and exploded on a loud groan, pushing himself deeper, filling her. He puffed hot torrents of air against her damp neck, lying still as her fingers went lax against his. Easing back, he looked into her eyes. "This was an amazing and unexpected end to the evening. How you doing down there?"

She smiled. "Great. Very relaxed."

"I aim to please."

She wiggled her brows. "I appreciate it."

He chuckled before his smile faded. "I take it you're on birth control."

"Something like that."

His shoulders tensed with her non-answer. "What does that mean, exactly?"

"It means you don't have to worry. I'm disease free. So are you. Jenny and I studied your blood workups—"

"Reagan, are we covered here or not?"

"We're covered, ace." She tapped his cheek with her hand. "I can't get pregnant, so go ahead and take it easy."

Her statement was an unexpected blow. "You can't have kids? Are you sure?"

"Pretty positive. Over the past couple of years I've had several ovarian cysts and some pretty damaging scaring."

He slid his fingers along her temple, sad for her,

seeing the way she was with Faith. "I'm sorry."

"I mourned pretty hard after the specialist told me. I guess I still am, but I'm slowly coming to terms with the fact that I won't be making babies."

"When did you find out?"

"About two months before I came here. The man I was seeing fairly seriously couldn't handle it, so he broke things off."

Her hiatus now made perfect sense. "Good for me; stupid of him."

She smiled.

"He didn't deserve you, Reagan."

She shrugged. "Most men want a family—or at least eventually."

"There's more than one way to make a family."

She smiled again, tracing his ear.

He didn't know what else to say, so he kissed her instead, deeply, tenderly, wanting to vanish the sadness that had crept into her eyes. "So what should we do now?"

She moved her hands to stroke the back of his neck. "I should have you pull out so I can put my robe back on and go to my room."

He shook his head. Reagan had come to scratch an itch, but she wasn't going to walk away so easily. "I want to lay with you for a while."

"I'm restless."

"And tired." He touched his fingers to the dark circles marring her pretty skin. He pulled himself free of her and tugged her against him. "Lay here with me for a couple of minutes."

She yawned. "For a few minutes." She relaxed in the crook of his shoulder.

He stroked his hand down her arm for several minutes, watching her slowly drift off to sleep. He twisted off the lamp and snuggled closer, closing his eyes, looking forward to laying here with Reagan the way he'd wanted to for weeks.

CHAPTER TWENTY

REAGAN OPENED HER EYES AND LOOKED AT SHANE STILL sleeping as the sun peeked in around the edges of the curtains, wincing as she glanced at the clock. She never intended to stay with him through the night. Heck, she'd never planned to walk into his room and rip off his clothes, but she had, and now she would have to deal with the consequences of her reckless behavior.

Her gaze trailed over his messy hair, beautiful face, and equally spectacular body, half covered by the sheets. She studied his sexy tattoo encircling his bicep, ignoring the kick of her pulse rate, fisting her hand on her stomach as she yearned to touch him.

Taking Shane to bed was a mistake; there was no doubt about it. Wanting him again when she shouldn't, could only lead to disaster. But she *did* want him, *craved* him, which sent up a shrill of alarm bells in her heart. He was leaving. In six days Shane would go back to Los Angeles, and she would stay here.

Last night had been unexpected, their startlingly deep connection unanticipated. And now it was over. She had inventory to take, and Shane had bags to pack and details to see to before his departure. Biting her bottom lip, she grabbed hold of his wrist, lifting his arm draped around her waist, and inched herself away from his warm body.

Free of him, she sat up, sighing her relief when he didn't stir. Leaving before he woke was better. Later they would have to talk, but for now she needed to go.

She stood, walking to her robe that had fallen near his side of the bed, and gasped when powerful arms wrapped around her waist.

"Going somewhere?" he asked next to her ear.

"You scared me." She turned, staring into sleepy green eyes. "I didn't hear you get up." She smiled, waiting for him to release her. "I have to shower and get ready for work."

He shook his head. "I think the patients of Black Bear Gap can wait their turn."

"I really have to—"

"Lay down with me." He lifted her off her feet and collapsed to the bed, trapping her beneath him.

"Shane—"

He kissed her temples, her chin, her lips.

"Mmm." She closed her eyes, getting lost, wrapping her arms around him, then opened her eyes just as quickly when he settled himself more truly between her legs, fully aroused. "Shane," she whispered. "We can't do this." Even as she spoke she spread her legs wider, tilting her hips, inviting him to enter.

"I definitely think we can." He pushed himself inside, sucking in a deep breath as she clutched at his shoulders, whimpering with the flash of heat.

"We should hurry," she gasped as he thrust, staring into his eyes.

"How about we just see where we end up." He nuzzled her neck. "But I have to admit, Doc, you've got me pretty stirred up."

She slid her hands down his back and grabbed at his ass. If she was going to be foolish and sin a second time, she planned to sin well. "Then take me for a ride."

His eyes changed, the green going dark and dangerous. "You want a ride?"

Her stomach clutched with a swarm of flutters, the

intensity of his stare promising to take her to sinful places. "Mmhm."

"You've got it."

She grinned, eager, ready as he devoured her mouth, rolling with her over the mattress. He sat up, settling her on top of him so she took him in deeper as she wrapped her legs around his waist, but by no means was she in charge as he gripped her hips, sending her to the brink with his hurried rhythm.

"Shane," she gasped. "Shane."

"More," he said against her mouth, kissing her brainless. "More, Reagan." He laid them back against the sheets, rolling her to her stomach, and entered her from behind. She cried out, clutching the headboard as he reached down, teasing her into a frenzy with skillful fingers while he nipped at her shoulder with his teeth. She screamed into the pillow, orgasming with a power she'd never experienced.

"God, more Reagan. I want to see you." He turned her, shoving himself deep, pumping while flesh slapped against flesh.

She bowed back, flying over the edge again, realizing the loud, throaty purrs were coming from her. He gyrated faster, harder, and jerked, throwing his head back and let himself go, collapsing forward, his ragged breathing filling her ear. "Holy shit."

"Mmm," she agreed, too drained to do anything but stare at the ceiling while she waited for her heart rate to settle. Never *ever* had she been so expertly ravaged. "That, Mr. Harper, was incredibly impressive."

He looked up, grinning, his face sheened in sweat as he tossed the sheet over them. "If you're going to do something, you might as well do it right."

"That felt pretty right."

They both chuckled.

His smile vanished as he traced his thumb along her bottom lip. "So did last night when we did things a little differently."

"There's nothing wrong with variety." She tried to play it light even though it worried her that the tenderness of hours before hadn't been lost on him. She swallowed. "I should get in the shower."

"In a minute." He kissed her long and deep, sending her emotions into a mess of confusion.

"Shane," Jenny called from the hallway.

His head whipped up. "Yeah?"

She opened the door. "Do you know where Reagan—" Her eyes grew wide as they darted from Shane's to Reagan's. "Sorry." She stepped out and shut the door.

"Damn." Shane closed his eyes.

"I didn't lock the door. I never planned to..." She scrambled out from under him, wrapping herself in her robe. "I'll go talk to her." She hurried from the room, rushing to the commotion in the kitchen. "Jenny."

Jenny tossed a not-so-friendly look over her shoulder. "I can't talk. I need to make Faith's bottle before she wakes up."

"Jenny." She touched Jenny's rigid arm. "I'm sorry."

Jenny whirled. "I didn't know you two were sleepin' together."

She slid her hand through her hair. "Jenny—"

"Do you love him?"

She pressed her lips together, realizing she had no idea exactly what she felt. "It's complicated."

Jenny huffed out a breath and turned back to the process of mixing powder and water.

"I care for Shane very much. He's a special man. I'm sorry if we surprised you. I never meant for any of this to happen. *Believe* me."

"Me findin' out?"

She leaned back against the counter. "Any of it." She rested her face in her hands, realized they smelled like Shane, and dropped them. "None of this was supposed to happen."

"Don't cry or nothin', Reagan." Jenny's voice gentled. "I'm not that mad. I guess maybe I'm just a little surprised even though I shouldn't be, now that I think about it. You two are always touchin' each other and lookin' at each other."

Sighing, she closed her eyes, resting the back of her head against the cupboard. "I guess I never noticed."

"Is he good at it?"

Her eyes flew open as she stood straight. "*Jenny*."

She grinned. "I'm just curious. Shane looks like he'd be *real* good at it."

She glanced toward the hallway, shook her head, and leaned in close. "He's amazing." She fanned her hand in front of her face, and she and Jenny laughed. She pulled the girl into a hug. "I'm sorry if this hurt your feelings in any way."

Jenny hugged her back. "I thought I liked him like you do, but then I realized maybe I think of him more like a brother—kinda like how he thinks of me like a sister."

"Okay." She kissed Jenny's cheek. "I think that's good."

"So what are you gonna do? He's leavin'."

"I'm going to let him go and get on with his life."

Jenny frowned. "But—"

"He lives in Los Angeles and I don't." She kissed Jenny's other cheek, reminding them both of the facts, whether she liked them or not. "I need to take a shower. We can talk about whatever it was you wanted in a few minutes."

"I just wanted to tell you I started my period."

"You did?"

She nodded.

Reagan wrapped her up in another hug. "Thank *goodness*." She eased away. "No more sex."

Jenny shook her head. "No more sex."

"But if you decide you want to—"

"I don't. I don't want any more babies. I've got a life to make for me and Faithy."

"I'm so proud of you." She ran her hand down Jenny's long hair. "You've come such a long way."

She smiled. "Thank you."

Shane's phone rang as Reagan stepped away. "I'm going to shower. Tonight's pizza and a movie, right?"

"Right."

"I can't wait." Crisis averted, Reagan started back down the hall, slowing when she heard Shane's voice.

"I'll only be in town for a day or two. Ethan's sending me to Madrid for a couple of weeks, then I'll be back. Yeah. Definitely. Sounds fun." He chuckled. "A boring dinner with your new boss, then we'll go hang out at Smitty's. I'll write it down. It has been awhile. Okay. Bye, Amber."

Frowning, Reagan swallowed, absorbing the rush of hurt. Sex with her then plans for a date with another woman before the sheets had a chance to cool. She lifted her chin, determined to shake off the sense of betrayal. She and Shane had blown off some sexual tension, nothing more. No big deal. She stepped back in his room, pasting on a smile. "I talked to Jenny. Everything's fine. And she's not pregnant."

He set down his phone. "That's great."

"Yeah. Great." She took a step in retreat as she glanced at the mess they'd made of his bed. "I'm going to shower and head to the clinic."

"I'll be there soon."

"No," she said too sharply. She cleared her throat. "You don't have to." She slid the hair back behind her ear. "I'm almost finished with inventory." She tightened the belt on her robe. "I'm sure you have a lot to do to get ready to go home."

"Reagan—"

"I don't want you coming in today." She turned and walked into her room, shut the door, and locked it, leaning against the wood. She and Shane had a little fun, now it was over.

~~~~

Shane peeked in Reagan's empty room as he walked down the hall after his shower. He glanced at Jenny sitting on the couch holding Faith while she read a magazine, and he kept moving toward the kitchen for a cup of coffee.

Jenny set down her reading material and followed. "Mornin'."

He poured a mug full of coffee, trying to bury the residual awkwardness of Jenny finding him and Reagan in bed. "Morning. Did Reagan leave?"

"Yeah. She was out of here pretty quickly." She leaned her hip against the counter.

He nodded, sipping the hot brew. Reagan had been in a hurry to shake him loose pretty much since he pulled himself free of her last night. "Listen—"

"If this is about you and Reagan doin' it, we don't have to talk about it. I'm cool with the whole thing."

He raised his brow and drank deep. "I'm glad I have your blessing."

She adjusted Faith in her arms as the baby's eyes drooped. "You don't have to be grumpy about it. I'm actually kinda glad. It's nice that she has you. Reagan's so strong. I want to be just like her someday."

"She's pretty great," he agreed.

"She's sad though sometimes. I don't think most people notice, but she is."

He paused with the mug halfway to his mouth, surprised Jenny had picked up on the emotions Reagan fought so hard to hide.

"She's such a nice person," Jenny went on. "But a lot of times I think she might be kinda lonely too. I guess I always thought women who were as beautiful and smart as Reagan didn't have problems, which is silly because she does. I guess maybe she might have even more because she expects so much of herself."

He made a sound in his throat, seeing Reagan through Jenny's perspective.

"I'm just glad me, Reagan, and Faith've got each other. She's always tryin' to make sure everythin's all right for everybody else, and I think maybe you try to make sure everythin's all right for her. I promise I'll take care of her after you leave." She walked away.

He stood where he was, struggling with the sickening weight of guilt. He was leaving, going back to his life, but Reagan and Jenny were stuck here—Reagan trapped by her obligations and Jenny by her circumstances. He walked out to where Jenny sat, flipping through the same magazine while Faith slept in her arms. "What are you reading about?"

"Oh, this ain't—*isn't* school stuff. I'm readin' up on fashion. I figure when I turn eighteen Faith and me'll be leavin' and I'll be wantin' to know how to dress so I don't look like I'm so poor."

He studied one of the trendy outfits Jenny stared at, then looked at the pretty young woman wearing the baggy clothes Reagan had given her. "You like fashion?"

"Sure. I mean what girl doesn't?"

"What about jewelry?"

She looked at him as if he were a fool. "Does a bear poo in the woods?"

He chuckled. "You've got a birthday coming up. The big one-seven."

"Yeah. It's the day after you leave. Reagan said she's gonna take me and Faith to Lexington. We're gonna shop and stay in some fancy hotel."

"Sounds fun." And he was going to miss it.

She nodded as she smiled. "I'm pretty much countin' down the days. I've never had much of a birthday, so this one's gonna be pretty special."

"Sounds like it." He drained the last drop from his cup. "I have some work to do before I head over to the clinic."

"Oh, Reagan wanted me to remind you that she don't—doesn't need you."

He rubbed at his stomach as Jenny's words hit home. Reagan didn't need him. "I guess I'll go get to those errands then."

"'Kay."

CHAPTER TWENTY-ONE

REAGAN SAT IN HER OFFICE TAKING NOTES WHILE SHE watched her third how-to video on baking the perfect birthday cake. Jenny's birthday was just around the corner and there wasn't a bakery in town to save the day. She watched the cheery woman pour the batter in the pan and seconds later, through the magic of time lapse, pull the perfectly golden cake from the oven. Wincing, she shook her head, remembering the unfortunate incident involving flames and the need for her kitchen sink hose the last time she attempted to bake anything.

The clinic door opened, and she slammed her laptop closed when Shane stepped inside wearing relaxed fit jeans and a black zip-up hoodie, his snug top beneath accentuating his broad shoulders and chest.

"Hey."

"Hi." She licked her lips, sliding her legal pad beneath a book on her desk. "I finished the inventory a little while ago. I really don't need you today."

"Yeah, I got the message the first two times you and Jenny told me." He leaned against the doorframe, crossing his arms at his chest. "I wanted to talk to you about Jenny."

"Sure." She steepled her fingers on the desk, trying to appear casual while frantic gasps and moans echoed in her head as she remembered the way his powerful body dominated hers. "What's up?"

"It's her birthday next week."

"Yeah. I was just planning out some stuff for her."

"I want to do something for her before I leave."

"Oh, okay. Sure."

"I've ordered her some stuff. I'm having it overnighted, so it should be here in two or three days." He smiled as she did. "I was thinking we could do a cake and maybe some presents Wednesday night."

"But you leave Thursday morning. That sounds a little hectic."

"I'll make it work."

She shrugged. "Sure. We'll have a party Wednesday then."

He moved closer, sitting on the edge of her desk. "What's up, Reagan?"

She reached for her water, scooting a couple inches away as their legs touched. "What do you mean?"

"I have this hunch you're not only avoiding me but regretting last night."

She sighed, looking at the straw in her water bottle instead of him. "Last night shouldn't have happened."

"And this morning?"

She stood, walking to the file cabinet, too restless to be still. "That was a mistake too."

"A mistake?" Now he stood. "How can you say that?"

She pressed a hand to her stomach as it started to ache. "We never should've ended up in bed. It's my fault. I initiated the whole thing. I take full responsibility."

"I'll take half of it. I'm pretty sure I was your willing partner—just as you were mine."

She met his stare. "There's no need to make a big deal out of one night. We had sex. It's over."

"Bullshit. We have something—a connection. We have since the beginning."

She didn't *want* to have a connection with Shane. What good did it do either of them when they lived on opposite sides of the country? "You're good in bed. I had a nice time—"

He snagged her wrist, yanking her against him. "Don't do that."

She pressed her hands to his chest as he wrapped his arms around her waist. "Shane—"

He held her tighter. "Last night wasn't about fun."

She needed it to be. "Yes."

He shook his head.

"Okay. Fine. Clearly we're attracted to one another, but that's just pheromones and chemical reactions—simple science."

"No." He rubbed his lips against hers. "The way you looked into my eyes, the way you kissed me, that had nothing to do with science. You said you needed me, and I needed you right back." He nibbled her bottom lip, following his sexy assault with a slide of his tongue until her breath shuddered out and she gripped his jacket. "What we have is more than a chemical reaction." He captured her mouth, leaving her helpless to do anything but answer his edgy demands. He eased back, tugging on her lip. "We have more."

She pulled away, running her trembling hand through her hair. "I can't do this—"

A vehicle honked several times and screeched to a halt outside.

She and Shane rushed to the window. "It's Ms. Daisy." She dashed out the door with Shane following behind.

"Doc Reagan." Daisy stumbled out of the driver's side, her cheeks tear streaked. "It's Henry. He's not wakin' up."

Reagan looked through the windshield at the man

slumped in his seat. "Help me get him out," she said to Shane.

Jenny came running outside with Faith. "What's wrong?"

"Get me the AED and intubation kit," Reagan said as she and Shane dragged Henry out of his seat, laying him on the ground, assessing his graying color and purple lips. She got to her knees, ignoring the bite of gravel through her jeans as she pressed her fingers to his neck, searching for a pulse. "No pulse. Call nine-one-one," she said to Shane.

Shane grabbed the resuscitation equipment from Jenny as she hurried back. "Call nine-one-one," he told her.

"Tell them we have a cardiac arrest," Reagan hollered, pulling at Henry's shirt as Jenny ran back inside.

Shane crouched down and tore the white t-shirt, exposing Henry's chest and stomach.

"Start CPR," she said to Shane as she opened the AED case, pulling the stickers off the shock pads, securing one to Henry's upper left chest and the other to his right side before the machine could tell her what to do. She connected the plug to the machine as Shane finished his first set of compressions. "Stand back," she said after Shane gave Henry two good breaths, waiting for the first electrical charge.

The machine jolted the lifeless man then alerted it was safe for them to touch him.

"Continue CPR." She yanked off her cardigan, settling the soft wool under the back of Henry's neck, opening his airway further, then pulled on gloves and prepared the endotracheal tube, sending the catheter home within seconds with the aid of her laryngoscope and blade. She removed the stylet, inflated the endotracheal balloon, and secured the tube with tape before the AED alerted them to stand back again.

Moments later they were given the all clear and she bagged him, giving Henry quick breaths. "Switch on the next count." She took Shane's place, taking over compressions, pushing deep into Henry's sternum in a rhythm she knew well while Shane supplied his air.

"They're on their way," Jenny said as she rushed over. "There's an ambulance that just left a call over in Rock Creek. It's comin' here."

"Stay back," Reagan said as the machine instructed her to stop CPR while it analyzed Henry's non-existent vitals and delivered another shock.

Henry didn't respond.

"Come on, Henry." She started compressions again, trying her best to tune out Daisy's pleadings to save her husband as she fought to revive a man on a dirt driveway in the middle of nowhere. The machine charged, shocked, and she did her compressions again, bringing Henry back for mere seconds, twice, and lost him just as quickly. For twelve more minutes she and Shane followed the same procedure, switching off, even when she knew there was little to no chance Henry was still with them.

"Reagan."

She glanced up at Shane.

"It's over, Reagan."

She shook her head as Daisy prayed desperately for God to give Doc Reagan the strength and knowledge to make Henry live again. "Not yet. Not until the ambulance gets here." The sirens echoed off the mountains and the lights flashed as the vehicle pulled up. Paramedics rushed over.

"No pulse or respirations for twelve minutes," she told the first responders as they swarmed in with their equipment.

"Let's get an IV—"

"No," Daisy said quietly. "No more. My Henry's had enough. He's gone to be with our Lord and Savior."

Reagan looked up at Daisy's tear-streaked face. "Are you sure, Ms. Daisy?"

She nodded.

Reagan looked at her watch. "Time of death: four eighteen."

Daisy sobbed quietly while Jenny held her close with one arm as the paramedics put Henry on the stretcher and covered him with a white sheet.

Reagan stood on shaky legs, walking over to the woman. "I'm so sorry, Ms. Daisy."

"He was doin' better, Doc Reagan. He wanted to go to the market. When we was gettin' back in the truck he said he wasn't feelin' so good and slumped over."

She took Daisy's hand, pressing it to her cheek. "His heart was very weak. Will you come into the cabin? We can call your family."

She shook her head. "I'm goin' to follow the ambulance to the hospital. I'll have my children meet me there."

"Would you like me to come with you?"

Daisy wiped her eyes. "I think that might be nice."

"Let me get my purse. Why don't you let me drive? We can take the SUV."

"That would be fine."

"Okay." She kissed the woman's cheek.

Shane followed her into the house. "I'll pack up the girls and we'll meet you at the hospital."

She shook her head. "This is something I should do on my own. Jenny and Faith will be in the way."

"I don't think it's a good idea for you to be going off by yourself."

She faced him. "Shane, the poor woman just watched her husband die. I'll be with her until her family arrives."

"Which is what I'm worried about. Henry's family hasn't exactly been nice."

"I'm the least of their worries at this point."

"I want you to call me on your way home."

She looked at the gorgeous man with concern radiating in his eyes, wanting nothing more than to stop time so she could step into his arms and let him soothe away her raw grief. Because she needed him, she took another mental step back. "I might be late."

"Call me anyway." He took off his hoodie and settled it around her shoulders.

"Thanks." She grabbed her purse, putting her phone in the front pocket. "I'll be fine."

He snagged her hand. "Doc."

She pulled away. "I need to go. I need to make sure Daisy agrees to an autopsy so she receives the money she's entitled to." She held his unreadable gaze, then hurried out the door, kissing Jenny's cheek, then Faith's before she got in the Pajero. As she drove away, she breathed in Shane's scent wafting from his jacket.

~~~~

Shane walked to the window, looking out into the dark toward the driveway, as he'd done several times over the last two hours. Reagan had been gone since the ambulance rolled away sometime after four thirty. It was well after nine, and she had yet to make contact or answer the message he left on her phone.

He glanced at his watch, steaming out a breath as he reached for his cell phone, shoving it away again when headlights cut across the windows. Moments later Reagan walked inside still wearing his jacket. Clenching his jaw, he leaned against the wall, jamming his hands in his pockets. "You didn't call me."

She toed off one shoe, then the other.

"I said you didn't call me."

"Yeah, I heard you the first time." She set down her purse, sighing wearily, closing her eyes for the briefest of moments before opening them again to meet his gaze. "What?"

"If you're going to be heading off on your own, I need to know what's going on. I need details."

"You had them. I was with Daisy." She walked toward the hallway.

He blocked her path. "I asked you to call on your way home."

"If I thought there was a need, I would have."

She was exhausted, her eyes troubled and sad. He wanted her to talk to him the way she usually did. The fact that she was doing her best to avoid him pissed him off. "Look, Doc, our jobs work pretty much the same way. Preventing problems before they begin is a hell of a lot easier than trying to fix them later. Next time I ask you to call, do it."

Her eyes widened then narrowed. "Excuse me?"

"You heard me."

Shaking her head, she huffed out a breath as she pressed her fingers to her temples. "You know what? I'm not doing this. I'm tired. I'm going to bed." She attempted to skirt around him.

He blocked her way again. "What's going on with you? I thought we fixed things."

"My patient passed away this afternoon. I've been with his grieving widow and family for much of the evening. Believe it or not, our roll in the sheets didn't really cross my mind." She walked away. "And there was nothing to fix," she tossed over her shoulder. "I made my thoughts on our situation perfectly clear."

If she thought he was going to let her walk away after that, she was foolishly mistaken. "Hold up."

She moved faster, fanning the flames of his anger.

"Wait, dammit."

She whirled. "What? What do you want from me, Shane?"

"I want to know why you've checked out on me."

"Checked out on you? I didn't check out on you."

"Bullshit. Thirty seconds after I came in you, you were ready to toss back the covers and make your way to your own bed."

She let loose a humorless laugh. "Oh, I get it. This is about your ego. Am I supposed to be falling all over you?"

"Don't go there. You know that's not what—"

"You keep talking about the way we are when we're together, about connections, but what the hell good do they do us, Shane? You're leaving. By this time next week you won't even be here anymore. We had sex. Big deal. Nothing's changed." She shoved past him. "Absolutely nothing's changed." She slammed her door and twisted the lock in place.

He walked to her door, resting his head on the wood, knowing as much as she did that everything had changed.

CHAPTER TWENTY-TWO

SHANE WALKED DOWN THE HALL, FRESHLY SHOWERED AND shaved, wearing jeans and a long-sleeved t-shirt. He sniffed the air as he got closer to the kitchen, recognizing the scent of the bran muffins Reagan ate almost every morning. If he was lucky, he would catch her before she headed out for the day.

He quickened his pace, certain he was about to miss her, and stopped in the common room, surprised to see her sitting at the table with a cup of tea in her hand, reading some medical magazine. She paused with the mug halfway to her lips and set it back down as their eyes met.

"Hey." He tried a small smile.

"Hey." She closed her magazine.

He shoved is hands in his pockets and rocked back on his heels in the uncomfortable quiet. "I was—"

"I have stuff to do," she mumbled as she gained her feet and grabbed her laptop case leaning against her chair.

"Reagan—"

"Later." She walked up the stairs to the loft and disappeared.

"Great." Sighing, he moved to the coffeepot for his morning cup, set down the pot, and shook his head, regretting last night's argument as much now as he did then. Their "conversation" hadn't exactly gone as planned, so today he would have to try again. Reagan had been wrong about many of the things she'd said, but on one point she'd been perfectly right: He was leaving.

She'd assured him their relationship hadn't changed, but they both knew their night together had intensified an already strong bond, whether she wanted to admit it or not. But he *was* heading back to LA in just a few days, which made their complicated situation nearly impossible. When it came down to it, there were few plausible solutions where he and Reagan were concerned, short of Reagan ditching the clinic and abandoning Jenny and Faith, which would never happen, or him giving up his job and staying here in The Gap, which was just as ludicrous. At the end of the day, he and Reagan didn't work as a couple. Their careers pulled them in different directions, keeping them a continent apart.

He pressed his hands to the counter, clenching his jaw. Despite the obstacles standing in their way, he didn't know how he was going to let her go. When he and Doc first met, he'd hoped to be able to call her a friend by the time he left, but he and Reagan were so much more.

Steaming out a breath, he poured his coffee and reached for his phone as it started ringing. He frowned at Ethan's number on his screen, noting the time. It was barely seven in Los Angeles. "Hello?"

"Hey, Shane. It's Ethan."

"What's up?"

"We have some problems in Madrid. I'm pulling you from Kentucky. I need you back here tomorrow."

"*Tomorrow?*"

"Yeah. Chase is flying out this afternoon. He'll meet you at the airport in the morning before your flight."

He shoved a hand through his hair as he glanced from Faith's basket of toys to Jenny's schoolbooks scattered across the coffee table to Reagan's half-empty teacup she'd abandoned. "I wasn't planning on heading out early. There's no way around this?"

"Not really. Cally decided she wants to throw in a couple more concert stops. Jackson's on his way overseas right now to check out the venues. Her management team is releasing the dates today."

He jammed his hand through his hair again. "Well fuck, man."

"I thought you'd be happy about this."

A couple of days after he'd arrived in Black Bear Gap he would have jumped at the chance to make a quick exit, but that was before Reagan, Jenny, and Faith walked into his life. "I guess I just wasn't expecting it. What time's my flight?"

"Ten fifteen."

What the hell was he supposed to do? He couldn't exactly say no. This was how his job worked—here today, gone tomorrow. He rubbed at the back of his neck. "Okay. I'll stop by the office when I get back."

"Chase will call when he lands in Lexington. You guys can figure out how you want to handle things with Reagan and her kids."

Her kids. But Jenny and Faith weren't just Reagan's. Somewhere along the way he and the woman upstairs had become parents to a sixteen-year-old girl and her infant daughter. "I'll wait for his call." He hung up and closed his eyes, loathing the idea of leaving.

"Shane?"

He turned as Jenny walked his way. "Yeah."

"Did Reagan go to the clinic already?"

"No. She's in the study."

"Okay, I—" She frowned. "What's wrong?"

"I uh, I'm leaving tomorrow."

"Tomorrow?" Jenny gaped. "I thought you were

stayin' until Thursday."

He sighed. "Change of plans."

Her eyes watered, and she blinked. "Are you leavin' 'cause you and Reagan are fightin'?"

"No."

"She had a long day yesterday." She swallowed when her voice shook. "It's gotta be hard watchin' someone die no matter how hard you try to save them."

"Jenny." He rested his hand on her shoulder. "I'm not leaving because of Reagan. I have to go to Madrid earlier than expected."

"Oh." She stepped back from his touch, crossing her arms. "I guess I'm probably never gonna see you again, huh?"

Her sad eyes tore at his heart. "Sure you will." But he didn't know when.

She shook her head. "I'll be lucky if I actually get out of The Gap. I don't think I'll be headin' to Los Angeles anytime soon."

He closed the distance between them, settling his hands on both of her shoulders, looking into her eyes. "I'll see you again, Jenny."

Doubt clouded her eyes, but she nodded. "I should probably get some studyin' in before Faith wakes up. She didn't sleep good last night."

"I'm going to talk to Reagan."

"I'm guessin' she won't be seein' you again either."

"Jenny—"

"I have to study." She hurried off, leaving him to stare after her.

"Son of a bitch." This wasn't how he wanted to say goodbye. He was supposed to have more time to iron things out with Reagan and make sure Jenny and Faith were settled. Rolling his tense neck, he walked upstairs where Reagan sat curled up on the couch with her laptop in her lap. She was so pretty in her yoga pants and a sweatshirt with her hair pulled up in a ponytail "Doc."

She looked his way, her eyes shadowed and guarded. "This isn't a good time."

"I need to talk to you."

She shook her head. "Not now."

"I have to—"

The clinic line rang. "Hold on." She picked up. "Black Bear Gap Clinic, this is Doctor—" She frowned. "What's wrong?" Her eyes grew wide as she stood. "*What*?" She pressed her fingers to her temple as she turned away. "I'm so sorry, Daisy." She moved to the window, her hand tensing on the frame. "No, of course I didn't. You and I agreed together that Mr. Henry should have an autopsy so you and your family can be compensated fairly, but as his spouse, you are the only person who can request cremation." She rested her forehead against the glass. "I don't want you to apologize. I'm going to come down to the house and we're going to get this figured out. You're welcome." She hung up and turned, her shoulders looking more burdened than before.

"What's going on?"

"There've been a few complications with Henry. I need to go see Daisy. I'll be at her house. If my plans change I'll let you know."

"Thanks."

She nodded and started passed him.

"Reagan."

She glanced over her shoulder.

"When you get back we need to talk."

She nodded and left him upstairs. Seconds later the door closed and the SUV started down the road.

"Dammit." They were going to have to do better

than this. They were running out of time.

~~~~

    Reagan sat in the SUV, gripping the steering wheel as she stared at the cabin, trying to find the energy to get out of the driver's seat and go inside. The last forty-eight hours had been unbearably draining, leaving her exhausted and mildly headachy. First Doctor Schlibenburg's shocking death, then her night with Shane and the fallout after, and now Henry.

    She sighed a weary breath, resting her forehead against the backs of her hands, still struggling to believe that the funeral home had cremated him. Somehow paperwork had gotten mixed up, and instead of performing the autopsy she'd ordered, Henry had been turned into ash before his wife and family had a chance to say their final goodbyes.

    Shaking her head, she got out of the Pajero and grabbed the huge box addressed to Shane from the backseat. She slammed the door with her hip, riding a swift rush of anger. The coroner's error not only robbed Daisy of her ability to grieve but also cost the widow the compensation she had a right to.

    She walked up the steps, still high on her fury. Procedures had been overlooked. *Huge* mistakes made. Now that Henry was gone, there would never be proof of his disease except for the x-rays Doctor Jacobson refused to admit were black lung. The ugly idea that Henry's expedited trip to the crematorium wasn't an accident at all crossed her mind more than a few times while she played phone tag with the hospital and director of the funeral home. The very thought seemed as preposterous as it did feasible. Now if only she could run her theory by Shane, but they weren't exactly on the best of terms.

Taking a final steeling breath, she fought with the box and doorknob and stepped inside to the scent of some sort of heavenly baked good.

"Good. You're home." Jenny came barreling down the hall with Faith crying in her arms.

She set down the box. "What's the matter?"

"Faith's been fussin' all day."

"Let me wash up." She went into the kitchen and scrubbed her hands, noting the two circular cake pans on the cooling rack by the oven. Shrugging, she dried off as Faith cried harder. "What's the matter, Ms. Faith?" She took the baby from Jenny. "What's got you feeling so sad?"

"She's been off all mornin'. I'm startin' to worry."

Reagan pressed her cheek to the baby's forehead as she sat on the couch. "She's not feverish, so that's good. How did she do with her bottles?"

Jenny sat next to her. "She sucked on the nipple some, but then she pulled away."

Reagan laid Faith in her lap, looking the baby over, feeling for swollen glands. "We'll check her ears and make sure she doesn't have an infection starting."

Faith let out an all-out wail, and Reagan saw the small bump on her lower gum. "Oh, poor baby girl."

"What?" Jenny scooted closer.

"Sweetie, Faith's teething." She lowered Faith's bottom lip. "See?"

Jenny winced. "Her gums'r lookin' real red."

"They're irritated and sore." She lifted Faith, hugging her, kissing the baby's forehead. "Oh, honey."

"What should we do?"

"Wash up the teething rings Shane bought and throw them in the freezer. In the meantime we can give her a clean finger." Reagan demonstrated, pushing gently on the baby's gums.

Faith wailed her protest then settled, whimpering and biting down.

"Maybe that feels pretty good after all, huh?" Reagan kissed her again. "How did you get big enough for teething rings?"

Shane walked into the living room. "You're back."

She looked up, dismissing the flutters in her stomach as their eyes met. He was too handsome for his own good. "Yes."

"I really need to talk to you."

"I need to talk to you too." She wouldn't be able to settle until she discussed her new thoughts on Henry.

"Okay."

"Um, Faithy and me'll go take care of the teethers so we can get her feelin' better," Jenny said.

Shane's brow furrowed. "What's wrong with Faith?"

"She's gettin' her first tooth."

His brow creased even deeper. "She is? Isn't she too young?"

"Reagan says she's gettin' a tooth, and her gums are lookin' awful sore." She took the baby, walking off with her finger in the Faith's mouth the way Reagan showed her.

Shane shook his head. "Wasn't she just born yesterday?"

She tried her best to ignore her soft spot for Shane's adoration for Faith. "Kids grow."

"Too fast apparently." He sent her a small smile. "Can you come with me for a minute?"

"Sure. Your box came in." She stood, gesturing toward the entryway.

He followed her gaze. "Good."

She reluctantly followed him to his room, not looking forward to the conversation they were about to have. He would undoubtedly want to pick apart their latest disagreement and discuss how their night together had meant far more than either of them... She stopped short in his doorway, staring at the mess and half-packed suitcases on his bed, her heart sinking as her gaze met his. "You're leaving."

"Yeah." He took her hand, tugging her further into the room and shut the door. "I have to go to Madrid earlier than expected. Cally Carlyle added more concert dates to her tour."

Cally Carlyle, one of pop music's biggest names— and Shane was her bodyguard. The punch of reality reminded her that he didn't belong here in The Gap. "Oh. When?"

"I leave for LA tomorrow."

She slid several strands of hair behind her ear, absorbing the next blow. "Oh."

He squeezed her fingers he still held. "I want to have Jenny's party tonight. I baked her a cake."

She swallowed. "Okay. Sure."

"I'm going to finish up most of my packing, then I'll make dinner."

Why did she feel like she was going to cry? All along she'd known this was coming. "I can, uh—I can help."

"It's supposed to be a party, not a punishment."

She smiled as he did. "It's a good thing your package was at the post office."

"Thanks for picking it up."

She nodded, glancing at his bags.

"I don't want to leave with the way things are between us."

Did it really matter? He would go back to his life and she would stay here. "It's fine."

"No, it's not." He took her other hand as he stepped

closer. "I'm sorry for pushing you last night when you'd clearly had a long day."

She shrugged. "I apologize for my short temper." But she couldn't apologize for what she'd said. Everything was true. Whatever this was between them didn't do either of them any good. She pulled away, reaching for the doorknob. "I'll let you get back to packing."

"Is everything okay with Daisy?"

It was far from it, but he had enough to worry about. The Gap and its problems were no longer his. Her issues and ideas about Henry's cremation were her own. "Yes, just a mix up."

"Didn't you want to talk to me about something?"

"No. It's no big deal—nothing I can't handle." Over the last several weeks she'd gotten used to Shane's support. For eleven weeks, she'd had someone to lean on, but those days were over. He would go, and the next man would come, followed by two more after that. She would never have with them what she had with Shane. "I guess I'll see you in awhile."

He nodded and she left, walking to her own room, pausing and pressing her lips firm as the echo of Shane zipping a suitcase carried into the hall.

CHAPTER TWENTY-THREE

"*HAPPY BIRTHDAY TO YOU,*" SHANE AND REAGAN SANG IN unison as Shane set Jenny's pink-and-white-frosted cake in front of her at the table. "Go ahead and blow out the candles."

"After you make a wish." Reagan smiled, placing her free hand on Jenny's shoulder while she held Faith in her other arm.

Jenny glanced up, smiling before she closed her eyes and blew out the seventeen candles he and Reagan had struggled to light.

"Did you make a wish?" Reagan wanted to know.

"Of course."

"Awesome. Now cake or presents?" Shane asked, wiggling his brows, rubbing his hands together, impatient for Jenny to open her gifts.

Reagan laughed, rolling her eyes. "You're like a kid on Christmas, and they're not even your presents."

He grinned. "Hey, this is exciting stuff. So, cake or presents?" he asked again, turning up the wattage on his smile.

Jenny darted a glance from the semi-sorry looking cake he'd decorated to the small pile of gifts. "Um, gifts."

"Good choice. The cake isn't going anywhere." He handed over the card from Reagan.

Jenny smiled and opened it. "Aw, Reagan." She unfolded the paper inside and her eyes grew huge. "I get to get my hair done by a *real* hairstylist? And have a massage when we go to Lexington?"

Reagan nodded. "And a manicure and pedicure."

"I'm actually goin' to a *spa*." Jenny rushed up and wrapped her arms around Reagan, careful not to disturb the sleeping baby. "I've never had a gift so nice. Thank you."

Regan hugged her back and kissed her cheek. "You're welcome. I can't think of anyone who deserves a day of pampering more. You've been working so hard."

Shane stared at the two women and pretty baby girl who'd become such an important part of his life, hating that this was their last night together.

"Next." He picked up the large box he'd rifled through before dinner and set it on the chair next to Jenny. "It's not wrapped super fancy, but I think you're going to like it."

Jenny tore at the mailing box he'd retaped, folding back the flaps, and gaped. "This thing's *full*." She pulled out several pretty frosted silver boxes with McCabe Jewelry's insignia on them. "Oh my heavens." She opened assorted earring, necklace, and bracelet sets, gasping each time. "I have *jewelry*. *Designer* jewelry from Rodeo Drive."

"There's more." He gestured to the box.

She dove back in, tossing tissue paper aside, squealing as she pulled out a huge bag of cosmetics and hair stuff, trendy tops and sweaters, shorts, skirts, designer jeans, shoes, boots and belts, all from Abby's *Escape* line. "I've got like ten new outfits here."

"Probably more," Reagan said. "You can mix and match everything."

"I just hope everythin' fits, but I'm wearin' it even if it doesn't." She slid her hand down one of the creamy cashmere sweaters.

"It'll fit. Abby guarantees it. I sent her a picture of you. She and her pals picked out all the stuff you'll need."

Jenny squealed again, jumping up and down as she threw herself into Shane's arms. "This is the best birthday ever. *Ever*."

It hurt his heart to know he would more than likely miss her future ones. He hugged her back, leaning down and resting his chin on top of her head as his gaze met Reagan's. "That's what we wanted."

She eased away. "Thank you, Shane."

"I have one more thing." He pulled the sheet he'd folded into his back pocket.

"What is it?"

"Read it and find out."

She opened the paper, scanning the words. "It's plane tickets for me and Faith."

"It's a credit. I want you and Faith to come see me out in Los Angeles."

Her eyes watered. "You want us to come visit?"

"Absolutely." He hugged her again. "And after you use those tickets, we'll get you both another. Just because I'm leaving doesn't mean we won't see each other again." He kissed her forehead and glanced at Reagan as she cuddled Faith closer, blinking rapidly.

"Thank you." Jenny wiped at the tear falling down her cheek. "I sure do love you and Reagan to pieces. You've been so good to me and Faith."

What could he possibly say when Jenny and Faith had been just as good for him? "How about some cake?"

Faith opened her eyes and started fussing.

"Well, it looks like someone's awake," Reagan said quietly, wiggling her arm in a soothing, rocking motion. "Go ahead and have your cake. I'll give her a bottle. Hopefully she'll fall right back to sleep."

"I'll take her." Jenny took Faith from Reagan. "In fact I'm probably gonna give Faith her bottle and go to bed myself. It's pretty late."

He raised his eyebrow. Jenny was a night owl. "It's nine o'clock."

She glanced at the floor, then toward Reagan, before she looked at him. "I didn't get much sleep with Faith's teethin'."

He nodded, understanding that Jenny was bowing out of the rest of the evening. "Good night then."

Reagan frowned. "What about your cake?"

"I'll eat it for breakfast." She flashed Shane a quick grin, grabbed a bottle she'd readied for the baby, and started down the hall. "Thanks for everythin', guys. I've never had anythin' so special." Moments later her bedroom door closed, and Faith stopped crying.

"Well, so much for her party." Reagan started gathering unused dishes. "But I think it's safe to say she likes her stuff."

He picked up the glasses still out from their dinner. "Sophie and Abby are the best."

"You have great friends." She put away the plates.

"I do."

"I'm sure it'll be nice to get home."

"It'll be nice seeing everyone." He put the dirty cups in the dishwasher. "I'm looking forward to being back in civilization, but I'm going to miss you and the girls."

She turned away, restacking the napkins already perfectly in place. "We'll miss you too."

"I have something for you."

She glanced over her shoulder. "I don't need anything."

"I have it anyway." He closed the dishwasher and

took her hand. "Let's go see."

She walked with him to his room, hesitating in the doorway.

"Come on in." He handed her a small box similar to the ones Jenny had opened.

"What's this?"

"I guess you'll have to open it and find out."

Swallowing, she held his gaze.

"Open it, Reagan." He held his breath as she pulled off the lid, revealing sapphires twisted among delicate sterling silver ropes, forming a simple bracelet.

"Shane, this is *beautiful*."

His shoulders relaxed and he smiled, certain she liked it. "I asked Sophie to design it for me. She wanted me to describe you—even though I talk about you all the time—so she could get a feel for the piece." He took the jewelry from the soft padding and fastened it on her wrist. "I told her you have the most amazing blue eyes and an incredibly kind heart. I also told her you're smart and beautiful and probably the strongest woman I know."

Her eyes grew misty in the dim moonlight pouring in through the windows.

He traced his fingers along her jaw. "She thinks you sound pretty special." He played his thumb over her bottom lip. "I absolutely agree."

"Shane—"

He touched his lips to hers. "Stay with me tonight," he whispered.

She blinked, eyes still watery. "I can't," she trembled out.

He kissed her again, cupping her face. "Stay with me, Reagan. One last night."

She gripped his wrists, staring at him, finally bringing her mouth to his.

He closed his eyes with the rush of relief, wrapping his arms around her, easing her back against the door as he shut and locked it. Clasping their fingers, he pulled her hands above her head, savoring her taste and the slides of her tongue meeting his, neither of them in any hurry.

Minutes slipped by before he slid his palms down her waist and hips, unzipping the simple black skirt she'd changed into for Jenny's party.

She unsnapped his jeans as he cupped her ass and pushed her forward, rubbing her against him, relishing her small, throaty moans. He flicked the front clasp on her bra, taking off the undergarment as he peeled off her sweater next, letting them fall. He wandered back to her pretty black panties, tugging at the elastic edges until they too fell to the floor.

She lifted his shirt over his head, sending it to join her clothing; his pants and boxers came next, more pieces joining the heap.

He picked her up, and she wrapped her arms around the back of his neck as they lay on the mattress. Their mouths collided again in a long, lazy dance, and then he moved down, feathering kisses over her neck, collarbone, breasts, making a trail to her belly button.

Pausing, he met her eyes and kept going, stopping between her legs. He laved his tongue where sensitive flesh and thigh met, growing hungrier, eager to give pleasure as she whimpered and played with his hair.

He dipped his fingers inside her wet warmth, pulled them out to slide against delicate skin, plunged and rubbed in a slow, gentle rhythm until her stomach muscles trembled with her rapid intake of breath. He took her hands in his, waited for their eyes to meet, and finally tasted her, sucking, teasing as her thighs tightened and her hips rocked in time with his tongue.

"Oh, God. Oh, God, Shane," she whispered on a quiet moan. "Shane," she called louder, gripping his fingers, arching her back. He sent her over slowly, drawing out her orgasm with delicate pressure.

Gasping, she lay still, breathing deep as he made his way back up, kissing dewy skin, and she opened her arms to him. He settled himself and entered her, both of them groaning as he sunk deep.

She touched his cheek, smiling as they moved together.

He smiled back, kissed her chin, then took her lips, kissing her until her breathing changed and her hands tensed against his waist. He watched her, holding her gaze as desire flashed in her eyes. "Come with me," she whispered in the height of passion, and he followed her, filling her.

~~~~

Reagan stroked her fingers up and down Shane's damp back, closing her eyes as her heart stuttered when he kissed her neck. Here they were again, in his bed, the connection he spoke of undeniable as they held each other close. Perhaps she should have said no when he asked her to stay. She was definitely foolish for hanging on when their situation was so hopeless, but she wanted this last night as much as he did.

He lifted his head, looking into her eyes, smiling as he brushed the hair back from her forehead. "Thanks for staying tonight."

She smiled back, wanting desperately to keep the mood light as she memorized the way his green eyes held hers as his body covered her. She'd shared more, experienced more with the man above her in three months than she had with anyone else in her twenty-six years of living. Tonight he'd gifted her a gorgeous bracelet and pretty words. He'd given her pleasure and true intimacy. Tomorrow morning he would be gone. "Thanks for having me."

He kissed her again and pulled away abruptly. "I can't do this. I'm not leaving. I'm calling Ethan. He needs to send someone else to Madrid."

Her gaze darted to the pictures on his desk he had yet to pack, the symbols of the life waiting for him back in California. She wanted him to stay but knew he needed to go. He'd given his time to Black Bear Gap. Now it was time for him to move on. Their ending would come eventually—if not tomorrow, then some other month in the near future when Ethan called him back from Kentucky. It was better to go their separate ways now before their feelings grew deeper. "No."

He frowned. "I want to stay here with you and the girls."

"There's nothing here for you."

"*You're* here."

She wouldn't be responsible for holding him back. She shook her head. "You have a job to do in Madrid."

"I don't want to leave you here."

"This is where I belong." New York was no longer her home. She couldn't go back to the hospital or her old life. Deep down she'd known since the moment of Mable's death. Until she found her new place, she needed to be here. "Jenny and Faith need me."

"You're going to stay until she's eighteen?"

"I still have nine months left on my contract. After that—" She shrugged. "We'll see. I promised Jenny I wouldn't leave her and Faith. I'm not going anywhere until I know I can take them with me."

"That sounds like a lot to take on."

She shrugged again. "I can handle a lot."

"I don't doubt it." He pressed his lips to her jaw. "What about coming to Los Angeles? I could help you find a place. I could help you with Jenny and the baby."

He meant what he said now, but when he got home to his life, Kentucky would be a thing of the past. He already had a woman waiting for him. "My home's in New York," she lied.

"I don't want to say goodbye."

"So we won't. You'll get on your plane tomorrow and the girls and I will get in the SUV. You'll do your job in Madrid and Los Angeles and wherever else Ethan Cooke Security takes you, and Jenny, Faith, and I will make plans to move on with our lives." It sounded so simple, as if watching him walk away wouldn't break her heart.

He kissed her. "It doesn't have to be this way."

She needed it to be—clean breaks were always better. "Yes it does."

"But it's not that way right now."

"No, it's not."

He entered her again, clasped their fingers, and took them both to places where goodbyes and shattered hearts were forgotten.

CHAPTER TWENTY-FOUR

SHANE CARRIED FAITH THROUGH BLUE GRASS AIRPORT AS he, Reagan, and Jenny approached the security terminals where he and Chase had arranged to meet. He glanced at Reagan by his side as she handed Jenny another tissue, loathing that their previous night together was the last they would share. They'd slept little, lying wrapped in each other's arms, talking and making love until his alarm reminded them both he had a plane to catch. He looked her way again, catching her eye, sending her a small smile before he spotted Chase by the diner. Reluctantly, he raised his hand in greeting, knowing this was it. "There's Chase."

"He's *really* cute," Jenny said, blowing her nose.

Shane slid her a baleful look.

"I'm just sayin'." She smiled, her eyes red and her nose pink.

He studied his well-built coworker and friend, certain Chase would be playing a starring role in several of Jenny's teenage dreams. "Let's just be clear that Chase is eye candy and nothing more. He's the same age as me."

"Got it, Dad." She rolled her eyes.

Chase gave them a nod and started their way, his gray eyes and expression serious, as usual. "Hey, Shane." He held out his hand.

Shane accepted his greeting. "Hey." He adjusted Faith in his arm. "Chase, this is Faith, Reagan, and Jenny."

Reagan shook Chase's hand. "Hi, Chase. Thanks for coming out to join us in Kentucky."

"Are you gonna be Reagan's new medical assistant?" Jenny asked.

Shane adjusted Faith again, trying to ignore the twist of resentment at being replaced.

Chase looked from Shane to Reagan. "Uh, I don't think so."

"I don't think I'll be needing an assistant anytime soon, other than Jenny, of course." She placed her hand on Jenny's shoulder.

Shane handed over the Pajero keys to Chase, glancing at Reagan as she looked down. "I guess it's about time for me to hit the road."

Jenny's lips wobbled again. "I sure hope you'll be ready to see me and Faith sooner rather than later." She walked up to him, wrapping her arms around him.

He hugged her back, kissing her cheek. "Any time you want. I mean it." He held her jaw in his hand. "You stay away from Terry and concentrate on yourself and Faith."

She nodded.

He slipped his hand in his pocket, pulling out five hundred dollars. "This is for you and the baby. If you need something, get it. If you run low, let me know."

She shook her head as she took a step back. "I can't take that."

"Yes, you can—I want you to. Faith's growing fast. She needs clothes and diapers and formula. Pick her out a couple of new books for me."

Jenny hugged him again, her shoulders trembling as she sucked in several shaky breaths. "I love you, Shane."

He clenched his jaw, certain this was the hardest thing he'd ever done. "I love you too." He stepped away from her, needing the space, and smiled at the baby staring up at him. She'd grown so much since he, Jenny, and Reagan fought to bring her into the world. By the time he saw her again she would probably be crawling and have no idea who he was. "Goodbye, Ms. Faith. You take care of your mom and Reagan. They'll need someone to keep them out of trouble." He kissed her forehead, breathing in her baby powder scent, and handed her over to Jenny.

"No goodbyes," Reagan said, her voice thick as he stepped up to her.

"No goodbyes." He cupped her face in his hands, stroking her cheeks with his thumbs. "Call me if you need anything."

She gripped his wrists. "I will."

"Anything, Reagan."

She nodded. "Okay."

He captured her lips longer than he meant to, hanging on as she clung to him. "Take care."

"You too."

He stepped away, leaving his heart behind, and shook Chase's hand, knowing the only thing that made going even slightly bearable was that Chase was a good man and things in The Gap had settled down again. "Take good care of them."

"I will."

Jenny started to cry, and Reagan took Faith, wrapping her arm around Jenny's waist, murmuring something close to her ear.

Jenny nodded.

He glanced at his watch, aware that he'd waited as long as he could. He pulled his boarding pass and license free. "See you around."

Reagan smiled. "See you."

He walked to the TSA agent, handing over his

items, walking past the point of no return, and looked back as Reagan, Jenny, and Faith stood as a unit while Chase waited off to the side. He paused, noting the tear sliding down Reagan's cheek.

"Damn it," he murmured, stepping their way, ready to throw away his career. But he stopped when Reagan gave a quick shake of her head. Sighing, he lifted his hand in a final wave, turned, and walked away from the three most important people in his life.

~~~~

Reagan sat in the passenger's seat, staring out the window as the familiar landscape of Black Bear Gap came into view. She glanced at the dashboard clock, then toward the partly cloudy skies. Shane was in the air by now, his destination home.

Sighing quietly, she looked to the bold reds, yellows, and oranges of fall trees in their glory and rundown buildings, no longer wanting to be here without him. She'd come to Eastern Kentucky to start over and help the people in this tiny town, but nothing had turned out the way she'd planned. In three short months she'd alienated an entire community and fallen in love with a man who left her behind. She pressed her hand to her aching heart, certain she would never quite be whole again.

"There's not much here."

She looked at Chase, giving him a small smile. "No. The gas station and market are pretty much it."

He slowed, leaning closer to the windshield as he turned his head from side to side, his gaze darting around, taking everything in. "I saw the pictures and maps, but actually being here... This place is pretty desolate."

"It's a bit of a shock."

He raised his brows. "It's definitely different from LA."

"Mmm," she agreed, studying the man who would spend the next three months with her and the girls. He was certainly gorgeous with his dark brown hair, square jaw covered in a close-shaven boxed beard that looked more like five 'o clock shadow than scruff, firm lips, and long, straight nose. His build was equally as tough as Shane's, but their eyes were different. Where Shane exuded fun and friendliness, Chase seemed guarded and intense. "But time passes surprisingly quick. You'll be back in California before you know it."

He nodded, sending her a knowing look, then chuckled as he glanced in the rearview mirror. "Jenny's out cold."

She peeked over her shoulder, smiling her first genuine smile as she stared at Jenny's mouth hanging open and her face still blotchy from a morning of crying. "Yeah, Faith's teething. Neither of them are getting a lot of sleep."

"She's pretty young."

"She is. She'll be seventeen in a couple more days, but she's a great mother." She trailed her gaze over the pretty blond and her baby. Shane was gone; the people in The Gap hated her, but the two girls resting soundly needed her. They were counting on her strength. She sat up straighter, smiling again. For the first time since Shane turned their worlds upside down with the news of his early departure, her sense of purpose was renewed. "I'm incredibly proud of her."

He nodded as he started up the dirt road to the cabin, following the twists and turns. "So Shane's been keeping me filled in on the happenings around here. It sounds like things got pretty eventful."

She shrugged, thinking of Henry's accidental cremation and her lack of resolution with his and the other men's cases. Things were still fairly eventful—for her anyway. "I guess it depends on how you look at it. I don't have any patients to speak of, and the one I was trying to help just died, so it should be quiet."

Chase turned the last corner, slowing for the cop car parked in the driveway. "What's this?"

She frowned. "I don't know."

He pulled into the spot next to the police vehicle. "Maybe there's a little more excitement than we thought."

"Maybe." She opened her door and got out as an officer stepped from the vehicle, dressed in slacks and a button-down.

"Doctor Rosner?"

She nodded. "Yes. I'm Reagan Rosner."

He closed the distance between them, offering his hand. "I'm Detective Joseph Reedy."

She accepted his greeting. "It's nice to meet you...I think."

The detective smiled. "I have a few questions for you."

Her brow furrowed again. "Is this about Henry?"

"No, ma'am. Doctor Heinz Schlibenburg."

Her frowned deepened. "Doctor Schlibenburg?"

"Yes." He looked toward Chase.

"Chase Rider, Head of Security for the Appalachia Project," he said as he shook the detective's hand.

"Nice to meet you." He gave his attention back to Reagan. "Doctor Rosner, can we go inside?"

"Yes. Please. Right this way."

Jenny got out, yawning and holding Faith's carrier. "Is everythin' okay?"

She nodded. "Everything's fine." Even though it

clearly wasn't. "Go ahead and lay back down for a while. You still look tired."

"Okay."

Reagan led the way up the steps to the house, letting Jenny in, then the officer and Chase. She shut the door, waiting for Jenny to close herself and the baby in their room. "Can I offer you water or coffee, Detective?"

"No, thank you."

"Chase, I'm not sure what you want to do..." She wanted to be finished with the pleasantries and hostess duties and figure out what in the world was going on. What did a detective have to do with Doctor Schlibenburg?

"I'll stay here if you don't mind."

"Sure."

They sat on the couch as the detective took the chair.

She smiled at the detective even as her stomach churned. "Detective, I'm afraid I'm a little confused by your visit."

"Doctor Rosner, I'm here because we're investigating the murder of Heinz Schlibenburg."

She gripped the edge of the couch as the detective's words sunk in. "I don't—I didn't realize—*murder*?" She shook her head. "His daughter told me he'd passed away, but I had no idea he was *murdered*."

"I'm sorry to bring you such terrible news. Were you and the doctor close?"

"No. We just recently met."

"Doctor Rosner, Effie Schlibenburg, the doctor's daughter, shared your name with us. She said you told her you and her father had been in contact. I'm hoping you might be able to help me piece together Doctor Schlibenburg's last days."

"Yes. Of course. I'll do my best. When *was* his last day, exactly? Effie only said he had died."

"We're keeping the case quiet until we have more facts."

"Why?" Chase asked.

"We don't believe the community is in any danger."

"So Doctor Schlibenburg was targeted?" she wanted to know—and understand how something like this could have happened.

"There's a possibility, but back to your original question, Doctor Rosner. The coroner estimates the doctor expired late October sixth or in the early hours of the seventh."

She swallowed bile. "I met with Doctor Schlibenburg on the sixth."

"Maybe we should stop right here," Chase said, holding up a halting hand. "I think we should contact an attorney before you say anything more."

She shook her head. "I didn't hurt Doctor Schlibenburg." She looked to the Detective, her eyes going wide. "I didn't harm Doctor Schlibenburg, Detective."

"Let me put you both at ease. You're not a suspect at this time. We're simply trying to nail down his last day."

"I want to help." She pressed her fingers to her temple, willing away the stirrings of a nasty headache. "May I ask what happened to him?"

"I'm afraid we're not disclosing the details at this time."

She nodded. "I just can't believe this."

"I can only imagine how difficult this is." He pulled out his notebook. "You said you met with Doctor Schlibenburg on the sixth."

"Yes." She laced together her icy fingers in her lap.

"At his residence?"

"Yes. We had a one o' clock meeting."

"What time did you arrive?"

"Just before one—probably twelve fifty-five."

"What time did you leave?"

"Right after two."

"What was your meeting about?"

"He was consulting with me on one of my patient's diagnosis—four patients, actually."

"If you can, go back through the details of your conversation. Perhaps he said something that might be helpful to us now."

She didn't think the jumbled question-and-answer session with the late doctor would help the detective but nodded anyway. "Sure. I've been practicing medicine in The Gap for the last three months. The people here are slow to trust outsiders. Eventually community members started coming around for wellness checkups. Over the course of a few weeks, I ended up with four patients presenting with identical symptoms and similar x-rays. I was certain they had a lung disease called progressive massive fibrosis. It's a complicated form of black lung."

The detective nodded as he jotted down notes.

"I sent my findings off to a specialist in Lexington who didn't agree with my diagnosis."

"His or her name please."

"Doctor Steven Jacobson."

He wrote again.

"After contacting other specialists in the area without results, I started doing research on the internet and came across Doctor Schlibenburg's name. I called him and asked if he would be willing to meet with me, which he was, albeit very reluctantly."

"Can you expand on that?"

"He agreed after a bit of begging." She smiled sheepishly. "Doctor Schlibenburg was one of the top pulmonologists in the US—if not the best—when he was still practicing. I was eager for his opinion. Perhaps you saw the films I left with him."

Detective Reedy made a sound in his throat as he jotted down another note.

"Anyway, he agreed to an hour-long meeting at his home. He wouldn't give me his address over the phone." She frowned with the memory. "He asked me to call when I got to Berea. From there he told me how to get to his house."

"Was anyone else there when you arrived?"

"No. He didn't strike me as a man who had many guests."

"Why would you say that?"

"He kept his curtains closed and he had three locks on the door. He didn't like me being there. He watched the clock like a hawk. When my time was up, he kicked me out."

The detective's pen paused against the paper. "Kicked you out?"

"Yes. He dragged me to the door and shoved me outside. I almost fell down his stairs."

"You had a physical altercation?" The detective scribbled on his pad.

"No. I made him upset when I asked if he would share an article he was rumored to have written."

"What was the article about?"

She shrugged, shaking her head. "I'm not exactly sure, but I can only presume black lung."

The detective frowned. "Why did that upset him?"

"I'm not sure on that either. But he refused. I pushed a little, and that's when he got agitated. He was nervous the entire time I was there."

"So you asked him for an article—subject unknown—and he got pissed?"

She shook her head. "Not pissed, just more distressed than he already was. He said people didn't want to hear what he had to say, but I assured him I did."

"What did he say exactly?"

"He said 'Not everyone wants to hear what I have to say.' My belief is his article is an in-depth look at the disease. Doctor Schlibenburg dedicated many years of his life to progressive massive fibrosis. I have men here in this community with that very diagnosis. I'm a big believer that knowledge is power. If Doctor Schlibenburg's findings could help me, I wanted them."

"How would you describe the doctor?"

"He was a bit strange—very paranoid."

"Do you believe he suffered from a mental illness?"

"I'm not a psychiatrist, but if I were still practicing in the ER and he were to come in, I certainly would've called in the psychiatric department for an evaluation. I remember thinking he must have retired because he'd lost his mind." She rubbed at her arms, remembering the isolation of the area and her discomfort with being there. "Honestly, I was relieved when I started heading home; although, I did hope to meet with him again, which is why I left the films—I wanted to appeal to his conscience and remind him four men needed his help."

"Aren't the films your records?"

"Typically films are discarded. I keep all images backed up on my computer."

The detective nodded.

"My goal was to show him over time that he could trust me. I called to follow up and thank him for our meeting the night I got his daughter on the phone."

"And when was that?"

"Monday." Was it really only three nights ago that she'd sought out Shane for comfort?

"And on the sixth when you left, did you notice any vehicles or anyone lurking around?"

She flashed back to the moment when she'd thought she was being followed and immediately dismissed it. A car had driven behind her for an undetermined amount of time, then kept going when she turned into the gas station. "No."

"This has been very helpful, Doctor."

"I'm glad I could answer your questions."

He nodded. "If I have any more I'll get back to you."

"Please do."

The detective stood. "Thank you for your time," he said to both Chase and Reagan.

Chase gave a quick nod, and she walked Detective Reedy to the porch.

"Bye, Doctor Rosner."

"Goodbye." She stepped back inside and closed the door, gripping the knob with a clammy hand as her gaze met Chase's. "I'm going to head to the clinic."

"Do you need me to come?"

"No. Shane usually stayed here with Jenny and Faith."

"Is there anything I can do to help with the Doctor Schlibenburg situation?"

She shook her head, desperately wishing Shane was still here. "No, thank you."

"I'm going to get settled in then."

"Sure." She walked outside, crossing her arms across her chest in the cool air, watching the detective drive away with fallen leaves swirling behind his car. She pressed her lips together, knowing the officer would be back. The sickening feeling in her stomach made her certain Doctor Schlibenburg's death was connected to their consultation—the same sickening feeling that also made her positive Henry's cremation was an attempt to hide the truth about black lung.

Chapter Twenty-Five

REAGAN SAT AT THE SCARRED TABLE IN THE TINY SATELLITE library ten miles west of Black Bear Gap. Rock Creek was no bigger than The Gap, but the town did boast a diner open on the weekends and the region's elementary school, not to mention the library that was about the same size as her galley kitchen back in Manhattan.

She closed yet another book she hadn't found helpful and picked up the next option the librarian had suggested, hoping for more luck than she'd had so far. For almost two hours she'd poured through the short stack at her side, searching through periodicals and other local documents pertaining to the area's mining history. It was worth a shot, since nothing else seemed to be panning out.

Doctor Schlibenburg was dead, Henry had been turned into dust, and a twenty-two-year-old man had a condition no one his age should have. Four years working underground was not long enough to develop the type of progression he had in his disease, especially in a mine with an impeccable safety record. Too many variables weren't adding up, and she had every intention of getting to the bottom of it.

Yesterday's search through the Mine Safety and Health Administration's website brought her no closer to discovering the data she sought. For a time she'd thought she struck gold when she found several documents on Corpus Mining, but her excitement waned when she realized all of the records were dated prior to 2005—the same reading she'd done the night before her visit with Doctor Schlibenburg. Not long after that, the well of information simply dried up. MSHA had nothing available on the corporation for the last decade. By the time she closed up the clinic for the afternoon, she'd exhausted her search, having no choice but to send off an e-mail to the local district office asking for help when she'd hoped to keep her quest for answers a secret. She had yet to hear back.

Sighing, she closed another book, struggling with her constant sense of frustration, and picked up the last hardback, flipping through the pages. She sat up straight, coming to attention when she found a chapter dedicated to Corpus Mining. She held her place with her right hand and flipped back to the copyright page, noting the book had been published just shy of twenty years ago. Finding her spot again, she devoured the words, stopping on every picture.

She studied "Senior McPhee" as Rand McPhee, head of Corpus Mining Corporation, had affectionately been called, standing next to his sons two decades younger than they were now. She turned to the next page, finding a photograph of Doctor Paul Pattell. He appeared jovial and kind, the caption stating, "He's the best darn doc a miner could ask for."

She read of the men who were happy to work for Corpus Mining, men of strong Appalachian pride. There were photos of Black Bear Gap in its prime. Once upon a time, the town had been pretty and charming. The rundown buildings had been lovingly kept, and the presently abandoned streets were full with the bustle of small-town living. She shut the book and walked up to the front desk, smiling at the sweet older woman sitting behind it.

"Did you find what you was lookin' for?"

"I did." At least she was off to a better start than yesterday. "You wouldn't happen to have anymore books like this one, would you?"

The woman tipped the volume' s spine her way. "I sure don't."

"That's okay. Thank you so much for helping me today."

"You're welcome, honey. It's not often we get youngin's as pretty as you interested in minin'."

She smiled again. "That's very kind." She opened the book to some of the pictures. "The Gap is so different now."

"Yes, Ma'am. Used to be a fine place—a fine place indeed. Then things changed after Senior died."

"Senior McPhee?"

"Mmhmm," she confirmed, nodding.

"What changed?"

"Corpus ain't what it was. Coal minin's a dyin' venture."

"That's what I've heard."

"Gotta get what you can from deep under the ground."

She hummed her agreement as she turned to the page where Doctor Pattell smiled. "He seems very nice. He has a kind smile."

"A saint he was. Saw to my Mathias 'til the day he passed of the cancer."

"The doctor passed of cancer?"

"No, ma'am. My Mathias."

Her spirits lifted slightly with the hope of contacting a potentially great resource.

"Doc died of carbon monoxide. They say it was a suicide."

"Suicide?" She glanced back at the man—another

closed door she wouldn't be able to open.

"Now his wife'll tell ya different. She insisted 'til the day the Lord took her that Doc didn't do himself away."

Interesting. "What do you think?"

"It's hard ta say. I can't think of no one who'd want to do him harm, and fact is Doc seemed a happy man—a dotin' granddaddy he certainly was, and devoted to Edna sure enough."

"Well that's a shame."

"It is indeed—maybe even more shameful than the heathen they got themselves in The Gap. The sins of that woman doctor be mighty. Causin' trouble, spreadin' lies, doin' the devil's work."

Reagan closed the book with a snap, making certain to keep her smile in place. Apparently she was well known even ten miles out of town. "Thank you again for your time."

"You come see me again now and I'll tell ya a few good stories."

"I'll do that." She went back to the table, gathered her laptop and purse, and walked out the door with a polite wave for the woman who had no idea she'd conversed with the heathen herself. She settled behind the wheel and made her way back to town, rehashing her conversation with the librarian. Doctor Pattell had killed himself despite his devotion to his family and his widow's insistence that he hadn't, Corpus Mining "wasn't what it was," and she had men sick with a disease that by all intents and purposes shouldn't exist in a facility as exceptionally run as the one up the road. Why did her shoulders feel heavier now than they had when she walked into Rock Creek Library earlier this afternoon?

She entered Black Bear Gap's town limits and turned into the market parking lot. Getting out close to the entrance, she passed through the plume of cigarette smoke, ignoring the grumbles from the men standing around as she stepped inside. "Hello, Hazel," she tried, knowing the cashier wouldn't answer and went to the mail window. "Good afternoon, Mini."

"Afternoon, Doc Reagan."

Reagan glanced over her shoulder, adjusting her stance, forever watchful for another ambush. This time Shane wasn't here to keep disgruntled community members in check.

"Here you are, Doc Reagan."

"Thank you." She took the stack and quickly headed home, still needing to pack for tomorrow's trip to Lexington. She pulled into the drive, then grabbed the mail and her laptop case, running through her list of to-dos as she walked inside. Toeing off her shoes, she smiled at Chase sitting on the couch with his phone at his ear.

He sent her a wave.

She mouthed *Jenny* and he pointed to her room. Nodding, she took the stairs to the study and made herself comfy on the loveseat, wanting to check her e-mail one last time while the house was still reasonably quiet before she dedicated the rest of her day to the girls.

Jenny had been mopey since she woke from her nap yesterday. Reagan tried distracting the melancholy teenager with popcorn and a funny movie. They even took turns painting each other's nails with a couple of the new polishes Jenny received from Abigail Quinn, but nothing cheered her up. By the time they called it a night, she had a bed-full of guests. She, Jenny, and Faith bunked in her room, which worked just fine for her. The girls' company had been a comfort, chasing away the loneliness of their first night at home without

Shane.

She opened her laptop and glanced at the time—three twenty. It was lunchtime in California. Was Shane eating with his buddies? Did he think of her as she thought of him? She shook her head as her stomach pitched and her heart ached. For stretches of time she'd done a good job of putting him to the back of her mind, but he consumed every second otherwise. Shane had officially been gone for more than twenty-four hours. She'd made it through her first full day without him. Pressing her lips together, she sighed. One day down, only an entire lifetime to go, but hopefully each day would get a little easier.

Her e-mail dinged, alerting her to a new message. Welcoming the distraction, she clicked on the few short sentences from the regional Mine Safety and Health Administration field office.

Doctor Rosner,

Thank you for your e-mail. I looked into your inquiry, and I'm afraid the information you seek on Corpus Mining Corporation has been misplaced. As soon as I'm able to track down the records you're requesting, I'll be sure to send them on the way.

Sincerely,

Markus Starks
Supervisor

"You've got to be *kidding* me." How had ten years of safety records been misplaced? Groaning, she flopped back against the cushion and closed her eyes. One step forward, eight hundred steps back. "Enough.

Enough of this for today." She shut the lid on her laptop and gave a quick search through the mail, pausing when she spotted the pink envelope addressed to her. Tearing it open, she frowned as she pulled out a slim strip of white paper with a URL printed on it. "What's this?" she murmured, looking at the envelope and postmark seal. "Canada."

She opened her laptop again and punched in the web address, hesitating with her finger hovering above "enter," wondering if this was someone's attempt at infecting her software with some sort of virus. She glanced at the postmark again and hit the button anyway. Within seconds, several hyperlinks popped up. She selected the first one, staring in disbelief at the documents filling her screen—the information she'd been searching for: Corpus Mining's Safety records for 2013. She exed out of the document and opened another link, then another, realizing the ten-year paper trail was right here. She located 2014's and blinked. "Oh my God," she whispered, her heart pounding as she scanned sheet after sheet, noting *several* infractions for unsatisfactory dust levels as well as numerous on-the-job injuries, some of which were labeled "significant to substantial."

"High negligence," she mumbled as she read, yet Corpus Mining had all of their air violations reversed after the company submitted new samples proving their dust readings were within normal ranges. Surprisingly, the company was still in good standing with the Mine Safety and Health Administration and OSHA, even though they had numerous blights on a once outstanding record.

She sat back against the cushion again, rubbing at her shoulders. She'd stumbled onto seriously damaging information that now made her four former patients' diagnoses make perfect sense.

She glanced toward the stack of mail, noticing a baby-blue envelope much like the pink she'd just opened and tore at the top, pulling out another white strip, this one covered with...part of a sentence?

...face several struggles not only in their place of employment but also within their daily lives, their condition making the most common tasks unmanageable.

She searched the remaining pile of mostly junk mail and closed her laptop when Jenny and Faith started up the steps.

"You're home," Jenny said as she took the last stair.

Reagan stood, pocketing the mysterious piece of paper. "I am."

"I meant to study while you were gone, but I guess I fell asleep instead."

"Then you must have needed the rest." She took a still-sleepy Faith from Jenny. "Hi, sweet girl." She kissed the baby's forehead as she snuggled her close. "Did you and your mommy have a nice nap?"

Faith rested her cheek against Reagan's chest.

Reagan wrapped her arm around Jenny's shoulder. "How are you doing this afternoon?"

Jenny shrugged. "Okay, I guess."

"Have you packed yet?"

She shook her head. "I've never been to any fancy places, so I don't know what to bring."

"We should probably figure it out."

Jenny smiled. "I guess we should."

"Come on." She gestured with her head. "Let's go get you packed up for our first official girl's weekend," she said as they started downstairs.

"I am pretty excited."

"Me too." She found what she'd been looking for; the answers were finally coming, but black lung would have to wait for a couple of days. She was as ready as Jenny to get out of this town for a while. Their trip to Lexington would be good for both of them.

~~~~

"The detective was out to see her yesterday. She's been asking questions about the mine," he said as he stared through his binoculars, watching the doctor put clothes in a suitcase.

"I guess you should keep a real careful eye on her then."

He tightened his focus on her beautiful face as she smiled at the blonde. "She's back at the cabin now. It looks like she's getting ready to go somewhere."

"I want to know where."

"You'll be the first." He hung up, more than happy to keep watch over the lovely Doctor Rosner.

CHAPTER TWENTY-SIX

REAGAN CARRIED FAITH IN THE FRONT PACK AS SHE PERUSED another selection of warm tops for Jenny. Abigail Quinn had gotten Jenny's wardrobe off to an excellent start, but it never hurt for her to have a few more options. Chilly fall temperatures had rolled in with a vengeance. Gone were the cool starts to the mornings and mild afternoons. Winter was making its way south, and they were going to be ready, especially when Reagan had three hours to kill and their hotel room was so close to an actual mall.

She adjusted the bags she held on her arm, full with various sizes of sleepers, cute outfits, and socks for the baby, stopping when the pretty pink cable-knit crop sweater caught her eye. She ran her hand over the soft cashmere and picked it up, grabbing an adorable pointelle sweater in a cream color as well, imagining Jenny's slim build filling out both pieces nicely.

Faith stirred in the carrier, and Reagan rubbed her hand up and down the baby's back as she carried the small pile of new clothes toward the registers. She paused when she spotted a navy blue sweater in the men's section that would look perfect on Shane. Sighing, she shook her head and kept going, forcing a smile for the cashier when she set her stuff on the counter.

"Good afternoon."

"Hi." She pulled out her credit card and swayed as Faith started to fuss.

"I just love babies." The sales associate grinned, leaning closer to Faith. "Your daughter's beautiful."

She forced another smile, not bothering to correct the woman's natural assumption. "Thank you."

"How old?"

"Just about twelve weeks."

"Aw. They grow fast," she said as she rang up the items and folded them into a bag.

"They sure do."

Faith settled and closed her eyes again.

"That'll be one hundred and fifty dollars and thirty-eight cents."

Reagan handed over her credit card, then signed her slip.

"Come again."

"Thanks." She started back through the store, making her way toward the mall, looking again at the sweater that reminded her of Shane as her phone rang. Fighting with the bags, she finally reached into her purse. "Hello?"

"This is so *amazin'*! I think I might've died and gone to heaven."

She smiled, infected by Jenny's giddy pleasure. "So you're having fun?"

"*Yes*. They keep callin' me Ms. Hendley, and they gave me lemon water and a couple of fancy chocolates on a pretty plate to eat while I wait for my hair to process. I'm usin' their *guest* phone."

She laughed. "I'm glad you're having a good time."

"It's the best. First the massage, then my nails—I got a French manicure on my fingernails and on my toenails to match."

"I can't wait to see." She started toward the exit.

"I watched the lady real carefully. When we get home I wanna try and do one on you."

322

"Sure." She liked having another girl around. It was fun playing with makeup and nail polish. "So, I found you a few long-sleeved shirts and sweaters and a couple more pairs of jeans. Oh, and a really cute pair of pajamas."

"You bought me *more* clothes?"

"And Faith too. It's getting cold."

"Reagan, I got plenty."

Shopping had been as much therapy as necessity. Her mid-morning call from The Project's director had wreaked havoc on her nerves all day. As Reagan navigated the roads to Lexington, her boss had spoken of budget cuts and a renewed push in Washington to eradicate wasteful spending. Apparently The Appalachia Project's funding was now in question. If patients weren't going to utilize the clinic, the program would be shut down. They had sixty days to improve their numbers or the director would have no choice but to pull the plug. "Well, now you have more."

"Shirley and me always shared a couple pairs of clothes between us. I guess I never knew it could be like this."

This is exactly what she wanted for Jenny— amazing new experiences, positive mentors, an education, good, nutritious food, and pretty clothes. Now she needed to make sure the young mother and her baby got to keep everything they had. Although Jenny had a child of her own, the state of Kentucky still considered her a minor. In the eyes of the law, she and her infant daughter weren't free to just up and leave without parental permission. For the next twelve months, Reagan needed to make certain she could stay in The Gap, but without a decent place to live and the protection of their security team in the hostile little town, there weren't a lot of safe, feasible options for her and the girls. "It can be so much better. I can't wait to show you."

"I don't know how. I guess maybe if Shane were here."

She didn't want to think about Shane. There was already too much on her mind. Today was supposed to be a happy day—the kickoff for Jenny's girls-only birthday weekend. With threats at a minimum, Chase was at home keeping an eye on the pill safe while she showed Jenny the time of her life.

"Oh, the stylist is ready to wash my hair."

"I can't wait to see you. Faith and I are going to start heading back to the hotel. We'll stop by the salon in about twenty minutes. Our dinner reservations are at five—right after Faith eats, so hopefully she'll sleep."

"I'll see you soon."

"Okay." She hung up and pulled out her keys as she neared the exit. Dropping them, she stopped and bent down awkwardly with the baby and her bags, frowning when she spotted the man in the brown leather jacket walking several steps behind her. She'd noticed him in a few of the stores she'd been in over the last couple of hours.

They made eye contact, and he moved into the candle shop. Turning, she kept going, reassuring herself their brief encounters had only been a coincidence.

~~~~

Reagan sampled more of the delicious *crème brulee* she and Jenny were sharing. During the last hour, she'd had the pleasure of watching Jenny enjoy another new experience—a three-course meal prepared perfectly by an amazing chef.

"And they put cucumbers on my eyelids like you see in the movies." She grinned as she scooped up more of their dessert. "I felt like a *real* city girl." The excited teenager hadn't stopped talking since Reagan stepped into the hotel's salon to pick her up.

"You *look* like a real city girl." Jenny was beautiful, wearing her red cap-sleeved button blazer and sleek black slacks. Her skin glowed from her mini facial, and her blond hair, now cut in long layers, had subtle highlights and lowlights, adding flair and sophistication.

"I can't believe I've actually been to a spa, and tonight I ate *filet mignon!*" She grinned again. "I don't know how I'll ever want anythin' else now that I've had what you and Shane have given me."

"We gave you a chance. *You* ran with the opportunities."

"I want to make you proud." She looked up from under her lashes.

"Mission accomplished." She set down her spoon.

Jenny smiled as Faith started fussing in her carrier close to the table. "Looks like we finished just in time." Jenny unsnapped the baby from the seat. "Hi, Faithy." She kissed her cheek and earned a smile. Jenny grinned again. "Did you wake up a happy girl?"

Reagan studied the young mother and her daughter in the glow of candlelight. For all the setbacks and disappointments she'd faced since her arrival in The Gap, she was certain she and Shane had done one thing perfectly right. She needed to find a way to get Jenny and Faith out of here. Jenny no longer belonged in Black Bear Gap. She and Faith both needed to be in a place where they could continue to thrive. "Should we go?"

"Yes."

She waved to their waiter, setting the already-signed check at the edge of the table, and they walked out.

"Perfect," Jenny said as they moved into the lobby and the elevator doors slid open, letting out a group.

"Let's head up. We'll play with Ms. Faith and make her nice and sleepy, then we'll order snacks."

Jenny's eyes widened. "Like from room service?"

"Definitely." She loved Jenny's enthusiasm for the things she'd always taken for granted. During her childhood, she'd yearned for affection and understanding, but she'd never done without the creature comforts Jenny was only now experiencing. She pushed the button for the third floor and did a double take when she spotted the man in the leather jacket she remembered from the mall sitting on the couch reading a newspaper. She moved to step out, but the doors closed her in.

"What's wrong?"

"Nothing." She smiled reassuringly, sliding her hand over Faith's back as the elevator car climbed. "Nothing's wrong. I just thought I saw someone I know."

Jenny frowned. "From The Gap?"

She had no idea who the man was or where he was from. "No."

The door opened on the third floor, and they stepped out. Reagan let them into their room, glanced both ways in the hall, then bolted the lock with an unsteady hand and slid the security bar in place for good measure. She no longer had any doubts that she was being followed.

CHAPTER TWENTY-SEVEN

REAGAN TURNED RIGHT TOWARD THE GED TESTING CENTER, placing a steadying hand on the cake box and pretty bouquet of flowers she and Faith had picked out in celebration of Jenny's big day. She glanced at the dashboard clock, knowing she and the baby would be waiting a good ten minutes, but Faith was fed and sleeping, and she was eager to celebrate Jenny's huge step toward independence.

Her gaze wandered to the rearview mirror, as it had more than a few times, searching for the black car she remembered seeing on her ride home from Doctor Schlibenburg's. She found herself wondering if the vehicle that had followed her belonged to the man with the leather jacket. She hadn't seen him since the night she stepped into the hotel elevator, but she wasn't about to believe he'd just disappeared.

She never mentioned the incidents in Lexington to Chase. She didn't plan to say anything until she had a solid plan in place for herself and the girls, especially with the director's frequent e-mails pressuring her to find a solution to their nonexistent patient load and his not-so-subtle hints that avoiding any further conflicts with community members was in her best interest. If Chase mentioned this new issue to the director, he might shut them down even earlier, and she wasn't ready to be on her own in The Gap without someone from Ethan Cooke Security.

The urge to call Shane and share all of the crazy

new developments had been hard to suppress, yet she had. It had been nearly a week since he left—a rough transition for all of them, but Jenny didn't seem quite as weepy. They were finding a new routine that included Chase, but it wasn't the same. Their new bodyguard was a great guy. He took turns making meals, but he wasn't hands-on with the baby, nor did he offer to help Jenny with her studies the way Shane always had. Instead, he tirelessly worked on reports and spent several hours on the phone with someone or other out in Los Angeles—on occasion speaking in Farsi.

In the six days since Shane's departure, she'd slept little and worried often, her conversations with The Project's director constantly weighing on her mind. She'd done her best to try to improve damaged local relationships by stopping by the market more frequently and suggesting a bonfire with a marshmallow roast and hot chocolate, but no one nibbled at the idea the way they had the food swap several weeks ago.

At this point, there was little hope the residents of The Gap would decide she wasn't some conniving government liar sent here to screw with their jobs. Every day that ticked by was a reminder that time was running short to find a way to get Jenny and Faith out of here.

She rubbed at the tension squeezing her shoulders, the excitement she'd managed to drum up for the day diminishing with the burden of her thoughts. Turning into the parking lot, she frowned when she spotted Jenny pinned up against the alley sidewall by the young man she could only assume was the infamous Terry. "You son of a bitch." Jerking the SUV to a halt, she yanked open her door. "Hey! Get your hands off her!"

Terry turned, sneering. "Well if it ain't Hot Doc to the rescue."

"Let me go, Terry." Jenny struggled to free herself.

"I'm thinkin' the doctor should come make me." He laughed.

Reagan steamed forward, shoving at Terry, slamming her heel into his toes. "Let her *go*."

"Ow!" He released his grip on Jenny.

"Jenny get in the car." She stepped closer to Terry. "You keep your hands off her." She whirled around, ready to leave, and was yanked back and shoved against the wall, ignoring the jarring smack to her shoulder. "You keep your hands off me too, you little bastard."

He gripped her arms tighter, holding her in place. "That's not real Christian of you now, Fed."

"Reagan." Jenny got back out, crying, starting their way.

"Stay in the car," she shouted, staring into Terry's dilated pupils, realizing he was high on something.

"Don't be bossin' my girl around. If she wants me she's welcome to come on back." He loomed closer to her face, any traces of humor leaving his eyes. "Where's my daughter, Hot Doc?"

"She's at home with the bodyguard," Reagan lied.

"You tryin' to keep me from my kid?"

"What I'm about to do is call the cops and file a report." She pushed against him.

Terry shoved her back for the second time. "I wouldn't be makin' a fool mistake like that." He squeezed her arms until she whimpered. "The Gap ain't real happy with you these days. Lots of people are wantin' you gone. You've been nothin' but trouble since you got here. It'd be a darn shame if you disappeared."

"Messing with a federal employee isn't a good idea.

If you're smart you'll remember that."

He hooted. "She's a feisty one." His smile vanished. "You stole my kid and my girl, and I'm thinkin' I might be fixin' to take 'em back."

"Your threats are pathetic." But she swallowed fear, studying the sores on his face and his rotting teeth.

"Oh, I'm not threatenin', I'm promisin'. Jenny and Faith only wake up in that cabin every day 'cause I'm lettin' it be that way. You start involvin' the cops in what's mine and Jenny's business, that might not be happenin' no more."

"You leave Jenny and Faith alone or I *will* involve the police. That's my promise to you."

A slow smile spread across his face. "Don't say I didn't warn ya."

She fought to free herself from his bruising fingers, got in the vehicle, and backed out with a screech, tossing Jenny a hot look. "What is he doing here, Jenny? I thought we agreed you were going to stay away from him."

"I didn't tell him I was gonna be here."

"Then how'd he know you were going to be at the testing center thirty miles away from The Gap?"

"I don't want to talk about it." She turned her body and stared out her window, her breath rushing in and out.

"Jenny—"

"I'm not talkin' to you, Reagan."

She took a deep, steadying breath, gripping trembling hands against the wheel, saying nothing more during the tense forty-minute ride back to town. Finally, she followed the last twist in the road to the cabin and pulled into the spot next to Chase's vehicle.

Jenny wasted no time getting out, grabbing Faith's carrier from the back and hurrying inside.

She swallowed, shaking her head, knowing she'd handled the entire situation poorly. Raising her voice to Jenny wasn't right. Accusing before she knew the whole story was wrong as well. Sighing, she shouldered her purse and Faith's diaper bag, then grabbed the cake, flowers, and gift. This wasn't the way she'd wanted the day to go. This afternoon was supposed to be a celebration of Jenny's accomplishments. Stepping inside, she smiled at Chase sitting on the couch with his laptop on his thighs. "Hi."

"How'd it go?"

"Um, fine." She set the stuff on the entryway table and sat on the cushion next to him. "Uh, we had a small run-in with Terry."

He frowned, sitting up. "Jenny's ex?"

She licked her lips. "Yeah. He was at the testing center when I picked her up. Shane told him to stay away from Jenny here on the property, but it wouldn't hurt if we keep an eye out for him anyway."

The crease in his brow deepened. "Did he threaten her?"

She rubbed at her still-throbbing arms, remembering Terry's promises. If she told Chase about the incident he would probably insist they involve the police. Chase didn't know Jenny or understand the delicate dynamics of her situation. She couldn't trust and confide in him the way she had Shane. She wasn't taking any chances that their new bodyguard might call the authorities and give Terry a reason to follow through with what he'd said. "No but I think from now on you should be with Jenny and Faith here on the property and whenever we go out." There would be no more solo trips for her and the girls. "I don't want him anywhere near Jenny or the baby."

"Of course."

She smiled her relief, certain Chase was more than capable of keeping Terry at bay. "Thanks." Standing, she went back for the goodies she bought, put the flowers in a makeshift vase, and cut two slices of cake, setting the items on a tray along with the present she'd had wrapped. "There's cake in the kitchen," she said to Chase on her way through the living room.

"Thanks."

"Sure." She straightened her shoulders and walked to Jenny's room. "Jenny?"

"Go away."

She pressed her lips together and fought with the doorknob anyway.

"I said go away."

"I heard you." She set the tray on the dresser as she looked at Jenny curled in a miserable ball in the center of her bed. "Jenny, I—"

"I passed all seven sections—with distinction." She sat up, wiping at her cheeks. "Just in case you cared."

Her guilt doubled, well aware she'd ruined Jenny's special day. "Congratulations." She nibbled her bottom lip as she and Jenny stared at each other in the awkward silence. "Faith and I picked out some things for you today."

Jenny tossed a glance toward the dresser with red-rimmed eyes. "I'm not much in the mood for cake and flowers."

"Honey, I'm so sorry for snapping at you. I shouldn't have."

"I didn't know he was gonna be there."

She sat next to Jenny. "I know. I'm sorry for assuming otherwise."

"I haven't talked to him since Shane told him to stay away."

"That's good. I'm *so* proud of you, sweetie." She

wrapped her arm around the teenager's slumped shoulders. "And excited for you. You're so smart, and you're turning into such a beautiful, stylish, capable young woman. You've become such a wonderful mother to your little girl."

"Thanks." Her face crumpled again with another bout of tears.

She sighed, pressing her forehead to Jenny's shoulder for a brief moment. "I really messed up."

She shook her head. "It's not that. I can see why you thought what you did."

"Then what?" she encouraged, sliding Jenny's hair behind her ear.

"Shane forgot."

She closed her eyes. "He didn't forget, sweetie." She pulled her closer. "He's incredibly busy."

"He's been gone almost a week, and we haven't heard nothin'—anything from him."

She stared into Jenny's sad eyes, her heart breaking for the girl. "Concert tours aren't exactly low key, I imagine. They're probably traveling all the time, and it's undoubtedly more than a full-time job keeping Cally safe."

She nodded. "I'm just thinkin' maybe he forgot about us already."

She shook her head, kissing Jenny's temple. "He hasn't forgotten you anymore than you've forgotten him."

"Maybe."

"I can promise you he hasn't."

"I just miss him so much."

She smiled sympathetically. "I'm sure you do."

Jenny swiped at the tears on her cheeks. "What about you? Do you miss him?"

If she wanted Jenny to communicate honestly she

needed to do the same in return. "Yes."

"A lot?"

She needed to be honest, but she didn't have to wear her heart on her sleeve. "Enough."

She pulled a tissue from the box on her bedside table. "Maybe you can come to Los Angeles with me and Faithy when we go."

She stood and grabbed the plates, handing Jenny her piece of cake, hoping to change the subject. "Here you go."

"Thanks." Jenny took the dish and sampled a section of the pale-purple frosting flower. "Mmm. Good."

Reagan helped herself to her own slice, nibbling at the white cake. "It *is* good."

Jenny settled back against her pillow, crossing her ankles. "So why won't you come with me and Faithy? You and Shane can see each other again. Maybe he could take you out on a date or somethin'."

She swallowed her bite, ignoring the rush of longing for even one more minute with him. "What Shane and I had was special while he was here, but now it's over."

Jenny paused with more cake on her fork. "It doesn't have to be."

"Yes it does." She sat on the bed again.

"He's got a thing for you, Reagan. Trust me on that."

She thought of Shane's phone conversation with the woman named Amber. "'Things' fade."

Jenny swallowed her bite, holding her gaze.

Reagan leaned forward, setting her plate on the side table. She didn't want to talk about Shane anymore. He was gone, but she still had plenty of problems to deal with right here. "I need to ask you about something."

"Yes, I do think you should call Shane."

She rolled her eyes as she smiled. "My question has nothing to do with your buddy."

She smiled back. "Okay."

She pressed her lips together and expelled a long breath through her nose, unsure of how Jenny would react after an already shaky afternoon. "Does Terry use drugs?"

Jenny frowned. "He might, I guess. He didn't when we were screwin' around, but he's different now."

"How is he different?"

"The last couple times I've seen him he was angry and kinda paranoid."

"But he's never mentioned anything specific to you?"

Jenny's gaze left hers. "Not exactly."

She took Jenny's hand. "This is really important."

"When I first came back to get Faith, he—he wanted me to steal pills from the clinic." Her lips wobbled. "I didn't. I never wanna break your trust."

Reagan nodded. "Okay."

"But that's why he's been gettin' so mad at me—that time with Shane and today."

Her heart sank, realizing the tough situation Jenny was in. "What kind of pills does he want you to take?"

"Anythin', really—prescription stuff."

"Did he ever ask you to get him pseudoephedrine?"

"No. Nothin' specific. He just wants whatever I can get—probably so he can sell it."

"Has he mentioned anything to you about meth?"

She shook her head.

"Are you sure?"

"Yes, I would tell you."

"The reason I'm asking is because I noticed he has

sores all over his face. They look like meth mites."

"I don't know what that is."

"Meth users often feel like bugs are crawling all over their bodies. They pick at their skin until it bleeds."

Jenny grimaced.

"I want you to stay away from him—all the way away from him. No phone calls, no e-mails, no contact whatsoever. He's dangerous. If he asks you for anything else or bothers you in any way I want to know immediately."

Her eyes filled. "He said he'd hurt you if I said anything."

"He won't hurt me." She thought of Terry's threats while she'd been pinned against the wall. "Has he said anything to you about wanting Faith?"

Jenny frowned. "No."

"Okay." She sighed, the weight on her shoulders growing exponentially as the urgency to get Jenny and Faith out of The Gap grew. "Jenny, what would you say if I said I wanted to take you and Faith with me when my contract is up here in Kentucky?"

Her eyes widened. "You want me and Faith to come with you to New York?"

"Well, I don't know if I want to go back to New York, but I want you to come with me wherever I go—and not just for a visit. I would want you and Faith to live with me permanently. We could enroll you in college and I could help you with Faith until you're through school."

"Are you askin' for real?"

"Yes."

"I—I never thought I'd ever really get out of here."

"I'll help you if you want it."

"Yes, I want to go. I want Faith to have more'n

this."

She nodded. "My contract doesn't end for nine more months, but what if we could go sooner?"

"If we could go tomorrow I would start packing right now."

"And it wouldn't bother you to leave your mother and sister?"

She shook her head. "Mommy's nothin' like you, and Shirley's already got her mind set to marryin' Michael Rogue as soon as Mommy will give her blessin'. I'm bettin' Shirley's the one who told Terry where I was gonna be today."

The thought had crossed her mind as well.

"Next time I speak to her on the phone I'll be tellin' her to keep her trap shut."

She nodded. "That sounds like a good idea. I'm going to talk to an attorney so we can figure out what we need to do, then I want us to speak to your mother and see what she thinks about the whole thing."

"What if she says no?"

"We'll figure out what our options are. I want you to let me worry about the details for now."

"Okay."

Her mind raced with all the things there were to do, but she stood and handed Jenny her gift. "You should probably open your present. Faith really wanted you to have this."

Jenny grinned, looking toward the crib. "She did, huh?"

Reagan smiled back. "Definitely."

"I wouldn't want to go and disappoint my baby girl, even if she's sleepin'." Chuckling, she took the wrapped box and opened it. "It's a camera. It's a really *nice* camera."

"I want you to be able to take pictures of Faith.

She's growing so fast."

Jenny stood and threw her arms around Reagan. "Thank you."

She hugged her back, holding on. "You deserve it. You've been working so hard for this moment. You passed with *distinction*. Charge up the batteries, because I'm going to take a picture of The Gap's newest graduate."

"It's kinda hard to believe I actually passed my GED."

Reagan shook her head. "I'm not surprised at all." She took out her phone, holding it up, focusing on Jenny with the flowers and half-eaten piece of cake in the background. "Smile. This will have to do for now."

Jenny smiled.

She snapped the photo and examined the shot. "Perfect."

"Will you send it to my e-mail?"

"Sure."

"I'm gonna check my inbox before Faithy wakes up."

Jenny had checked her e-mail every day since Shane left. "Use my phone if you want."

"Thanks." Jenny logged in, gasped, and laughed. "He sent me a message." She beamed. "Shane sent me a message. Look."

Break a leg, kid, Reagan read on the screen. She smiled, her heart melting.

"He didn't forget me."

"Of course he didn't." She kissed the top of Jenny's head. "I'm going to go make some phone calls. I'll be up in the loft if you need me."

"Okay. I'm gonna tell him about my new camera and the flowers and cake."

"Have fun. Congratulations, graduate. I'll see you at

dinner."

"See ya."

Reagan picked up the tray as Jenny's thumbs flew over the keys. She stepped into the hall, glancing into Shane's empty room that still smelled like him. She glanced toward the bed where they'd spent their final night, wishing desperately she could forget about him. Swallowing, she closed his door, not wanting to remember anymore.

~~~~

Reagan settled in behind the desk in the loft as the sun sank along the horizon of trees—another eventful day coming to a close in The Gap. But at least she was certain Jenny was committed to leaving. Now she could move forward with her plan to get the three of them out of here.

She opened her laptop, punching in her password, and accessed her contacts, reaching for the phone just as the clinic line rang. "Black Bear Gap Clinic, this is Doctor Rosner."

"Doctor Rosner, this is Cliff Yancey."

Her eyes widened with surprise. "Doctor Yancey. It's nice to hear from you." She picked up a pen and grabbed a pad of paper, more than ready to talk shop. "How was your honeymoon?" She frowned when the line stayed silent. "Hello?"

"Doctor Rosner, I can't help you with your patients."

The pen fell from her fingers. "I can't—" She shook her head. Was this *really* happening? "Cliff, I was counting on this. You said you—"

"Some things are better left alone. I've deleted the files you sent to me. Goodbye, Doctor Rosner."

"But—" The line went dead, and she hung up, resting her forehead in her palms. "Damn it." She knew she was asking a lot. Over the last few weeks, she'd come to the realization she'd stumbled onto something *big* when she diagnosed four men with progressive massive fibrosis, but that didn't mean she was going to give up. People were *dying*. Hard-working men and women were going off to the mines every day, trying to earn a living for their families, and their lives were being cut short by shoddy safety practices. Apparently she would be standing up to Corpus Mining alone, but that would have to wait until later. Jenny and Faith were her priority right now.

Shaking her head, she reached for the phone again as her e-mail announced an incoming message. She clicked over to the open screen, hoping Cliff might have written to offer some sort of explanation for his unexpected out, but frowned at the address instead.

"Who's this?" She clicked on the unopened message and gaped, staring at big blue eyes, shiny black hair, and a sweet peaches and cream complexion as Mable Totton smiled in the picture accompanying her obituary. Her breath backed up in her throat, and she slammed her computer closed as she rushed to her feet.

How? Why? She walked to the window on weak legs, gripping the sill as darkness loomed in the distance. She listened over the pounding of her heart, craving to hear Chase's deep voice muttering into his phone, but as she looked down to the quiet living room, she realized the big space was empty. Rubbing at the goosebumps covering her arms, she went back to the phone, picking it up, wishing to be anywhere but here, dialing a number she knew well.

"Good evening, Shurman, Shuster, and Finch."

"Um, yes, I was wondering if Marsha Finch might

be available."

"I'm sorry, ma'am, she's in a meeting."

"This is, um, this is Doctor Reagan Rosner." She brushed unsteady fingers through her hair. "Can I leave a message?"

"Yes, Doctor Rosner."

"Can you please have Marsha call me on my cellphone—she has the number—as soon as possible? It's extremely important. I need help finding a good family attorney in Kentucky right away."

"I'll send this on immediately."

"Thank you."

She hung up and turned away from her laptop, hurrying downstairs. Faith's muffled cries carried down the hall and she walked faster, welcoming the noise of Jenny's sweet baby girl.

CHAPTER TWENTY-EIGHT

REAGAN STAYED A FEW STEPS AHEAD OF JENNY AND CHASE as they walked the final muddy hundred yards to Jenny's family home. Luckily the sun had come out and the temperatures warmed a bit after three days of pouring rain. The inclement weather and the Hendley's disconnected phone line had prevented Reagan from reaching out to Jenny's mother for a much-needed conversation. Marsha Finch, her former malpractice lawyer, put her in touch with one of Kentucky's best family-law attorneys; now, she just needed Mrs. Hendley to hop on board with their plan and do what was best for her daughter.

The small group passed a row of tall pines, and the dilapidated white house came into view. Reagan scanned the trash and broken-down vehicles littering the yard, the plastic wrap covering windows in lieu of glass, and sighed her relief that Jenny no longer lived there. Turning, she smiled, studying the pretty teen with her shiny blond hair tied back and her slender figure showing off her new designer jeans, sweater, and hiking boots while she held Faith in the front pack. "Looks like we're here."

"It's been a while since I've been back. I've been poor my whole life. We sure never had much, but now that I have what I do and know what I want, I don't want to be here anymore."

She wrapped her arm around Jenny's shoulders. "There's nothing wrong with wanting more."

Jenny nodded. "I guess we should go knock."

"Chase, if you don't mind, we'll have you wait out here."

"Yeah. Sure."

He looked good—*really* good—as Jenny had pointed out, with his ball cap tucked low on his head and his shades in place, but she imagined it was Chase's excellent physique in his black Ethan Cooke Security zip-up jacket and snug blue jeans Jenny had been admiring. "Thanks. We shouldn't be too long."

"Take your time. I'll enjoy the view," he said as he took his water bottle out of the small backpack and drank deep.

"Me too," Jenny mouthed as she swept her gaze up his body, rolling her eyes dreamily as he turned his back to them.

Reagan swatted at the teenager's shoulder, earning a huge grin and small giggle. "Let's *go*, Jenny."

"Okay." Laughing, she led the way up crumbling concrete steps, composing herself before she knocked. "Mommy, it's me, Jenny," she called as she rapped her knuckle against rotting wood.

Mrs. Hendley opened the door in an oversized t-shirt and baggy jeans. "Jenny, what're you doin' here?"

"Reagan, Faith, and me came up for a visit."

She closed the door slightly. "I don't want nothin' to do with that baby of yours, Jenny."

"Mommy, look at her." Jenny turned to her side and adjusted Faith's tiny wool hat, exposing Faith's sweet face. "She ain't the devil. She's my pretty baby girl."

Mrs. Hendley stared at the baby. "She's cute enough, but she's a Staddler."

"No, mommy, she's *mine*. She's as much Hendley as she is Staddler."

343

"You get kicked out or somethin'? Are you wantin' to come back?"

"No, I'm wantin' you to let me move out of The Gap with Reagan."

Reagan barely suppressed a wince. She'd been hoping to ease Jenny's mother into the idea. "Mrs. Hendley." Smiling, she moved up a step. "It's nice to see you again."

"Doctor, I don't think I'm takin' too kindly to you bein' here, turnin' my girl into a Fed."

"Mrs. Hendley, I'm simply a physician trying to help the people in Black Bear Gap."

Jenny's mother crossed her arms, eyeing her suspiciously. "Sounds like you're more trouble than help."

She let the insult roll off her back. "Apparently so."

"That's not true," Jenny defended. "Reagan's a wonderful doctor. She saved me and Faith's lives. She's helpin' me raise my girl. I took the GED because she and Shane helped me. I'm gonna go to school for nursin', Mommy. I have a chance to get out of here and make somethin' of myself."

"You've been prayin' to our Lord and Savior about your sins?"

Jenny nodded.

Mrs. Hendley opened the door. "Come in, I guess."

They walked in to the room with worn furnishings that were new long before Jenny was born.

"I ain't got nothin' to offer for drink."

"That's fine, Mrs. Hendley. We don't want to take up too much of your time." She sat next to Jenny on the couch, unzipping her jacket in the stifling heat by the coal stove. "First, I want to tell you how incredibly proud of Jenny I am. You've raised an intelligent, sweet young woman."

Mrs. Hendley gave a decisive nod. "I'll thank you kindly."

"I'm hoping we might be able to work something out so I can bring Jenny and Faith with me when I leave The Gap. Jenny's an amazing mother and excellent student. I have no doubt she'll do very well in a nursing program."

"Where would you be goin'?"

"I live in New York City—"

"That's a mighty long way—a big place too. Full of sinners."

There was a fair share of "sinners" right here in The Gap, but Reagan kept her thoughts to herself. "New York is certainly large, but with a place that big comes a lot of opportunities. With a bit of hard work on Jenny's part she has a real shot at giving herself and Faith a wonderful life."

"I passed my GED, Mommy—with distinction."

"You've always been a smart girl—too smart. It get's you into trouble."

"Mrs. Hendley, Jenny is capable of making a huge difference in other people's lives. College will give her that chance." She licked her lips, ready to play her hand. "And she would be far away from Terry's influence."

"He's been botherin' me, Mommy. I've been keepin' my distance, but he's still causin' trouble."

Mrs. Hendley nodded. "That's what happens when you lay down with the devil, child."

"I don't want to lay down with him anymore. I want to make somethin' of myself."

"You got yourself real fancy stuff—nice clothes and fine words."

"I'm tryin'. I'm tryin' real hard to change my sinful ways, Mommy."

Mrs. Hendley looked from Jenny to Reagan. "What would we have to do to make it so Jenny could leave?"

Reagan suppressed a hopeful smile. "I've spoken with an attorney—"

"I ain't got no money for lawyers."

"That's okay. I'm paying for the advice."

Mrs. Hendley nodded.

"My attorney shared two avenues we can pursue. We can either put Jenny under my guardianship, which can take a bit of time, or we can schedule a date with the judge and ask him or her to deem Jenny an Emancipated Minor. You would have to come with us and tell the judge you agree that Jenny no longer needs to remain under your care."

"I ain't been takin' care of her for a while now."

"Yes, but my attorney thinks it would be best if we keep everything legal. It will help Jenny when she applies for college. As a single mother she'll be able to get Pell Grants and other financial assistance."

"Jenny's really goin' to college?"

"Oh, definitely."

"I'd like to think on it some. Big decisions are always worth prayin' on."

"Wonderful." She smiled. "If you don't mind, I'll have my attorney move forward and schedule an appointment with the judge. We'll hike up again or call when we have a date."

"That would be fine." She stood. "Although the phone's been out until I can pay up on the bill."

Jenny got to her feet. "Mommy, would you want to hold Faith?"

She took a step back, shaking her head. "She's still not welcome by me. You're gonna get on out of The Gap and get you an education. That's as Christian as I can be where that baby of yours is concerned."

Reagan saw the flash of hurt in Jenny's eyes. She took her hand, giving a squeeze of support. "We should probably get home before Faith's ready for her next bottle."

Jenny nodded. "Bye, Mommy."

"Bye now. You come on back with a date."

"We will. Thank you, Mrs. Hendley." They walked out into the cool temperatures and started back down the hill with Chase.

"How'd it go?" he asked.

"I think that went really well." Better than she'd expected.

Jenny shrugged. "Yeah."

"Your mother hurt your feelings."

"There's nothin' wrong with Faith," Jenny said in a rush of hot words.

She took Jenny's hand again. "You're absolutely right. Faith's perfect; we both know it. It's unfortunate your mother doesn't."

"It makes me so *mad*."

"It makes me mad too, but you know what?"

"What?"

"You're getting out of The Gap."

She grinned. "I am, huh?"

"You bet." She tugged Jenny against her, wrapping her close with one arm.

"We should celebrate. Let's do makeovers and eat junk food."

She needed to go into the clinic, just in case she had a chance to report a patient visit for the director, but today Jenny needed her more. "I think that sounds great. Chase, are you up for makeovers and junk food?"

He smiled. "I'll let you ladies have fun with the makeup, but I'll never turn down junk food."

"Perfect." She roped her arm through his, hoping

that maybe for once, things might be all right. "Let's go home."

~~~~

Shane let himself into his hotel room, walked to his bed, and collapsed back, groaning as he rubbed at his tired eyes. Cally's concert tour had been two non-stop weeks of insanity. The singer's management had booked her schedule to the max, leaving little time to eat, let alone sleep.

Sighing, he pulled his phone from his jeans, opened his e-mail, and grinned. Jenny had sent him one of her daily messages: *Look what you're missing...* And today she sent pictures as well. He flipped through, smiling at the photo of Faith with a pink bow secured in the few strands of blond hair on her head. He chuckled at the slightly blurry selfie of Jenny and Reagan sticking out their tongues with their eyes crossed. They both looked great with their hair curled and makeup in place.

He flipped to the next picture and his smile faded, turning into a long steaming breath as he looked at Faith laying between Jenny and Reagan on Jenny's bed, the three of them smiling for the camera. His heart ached; he was missing them like crazy. His days and nights were pure madness, yet he thought of them constantly. But it was Reagan who haunted him most, making sleep nearly impossible. Every time he closed his eyes she was there, staring into his gaze, smiling sweetly as she had when he lay inside her their last night together in The Gap.

Swallowing, he studied the beautiful woman, longing to run his fingers through her shiny hair and feel her soft lips give against his. His gaze slid over the silver and sapphire bracelet secured around her wrist, slightly relieved that she still wore the jewelry he'd given her. In the weeks he'd been gone, she'd made no attempt to contact him—no calls, texts, or e-mails. He checked his watch and dialed Chase's number.

"This is Rider."

"Hey, it's Shane."

"Hey man, how's Madrid?"

"Fucking *brutal*."

"Ah, the good old days."

He smiled. "You bored yet?"

"I don't know if 'bored' is the right word. Ethan's keeping me busy, and Reagan, Jenny, and Faith are definitely entertaining, but I have to admit this duty sucks."

"It takes some getting used to." He heard the laughter in the background. "Sounds like there's some fun going on out there."

"We're going to play some apple game, which I've been assured is a hell of a time. Reagan and Jenny are throwing sundaes together for us first. We're celebrating."

"Oh, yeah?"

"Jenny's mother agreed to a court date so Jenny and the baby can leave with Reagan when her contract is up."

A weight lifted off his shoulders. "That's amazing."

"They're certainly happy about it."

"Is everything else good?"

"Yeah, pretty uneventful."

Jenny and Reagan hooted again in the background. "Any more problems with Terry?"

"No. It poured fucking buckets here for the past few days, so today's the first time we were actually able to get out of the cabin. We hiked up to Jenny's house. The one thing this place has going for it is its views."

Reagan's sexy legs flashed in his mind. "There are definitely some good ones."

"Did you want to talk to Reagan?"

He never wanted to *stop* talking to Reagan, so it was better not to start. "Nah. Let the ladies have their fun."

"Here you go, Chase. You said you wanted big," Reagan said on a laugh.

Chase chuckled. "Jesus. Thanks. My sundae's here, man."

Shane clenched his jaw as he heard Reagan's voice and the easy way she spoke to his coworker. "I'll let you go then."

"Talk to you later."

"Yeah." He hung up, scrubbing his hands over his face. Things were good in The Gap. They were happy, celebrating...and he wasn't there. He looked at Jenny's message again. *Look what you're missing...*

He was well aware that he was missing out on everything.

CHAPTER TWENTY-NINE

REAGAN SAT AT HER DESK IN THE CLINIC, SCANNING DATA ON one of the places under her consideration for relocation. With an upcoming court date in place for Jenny's anticipated emancipation, she'd spent the last few days researching nursing schools all over the country. She wanted to narrow down her options to three to talk over with Jenny and share with the judge. Luckily her profession afforded her and the girls the opportunity to move anywhere they chose, but she had yet to look into employment for herself. The idea of responding to STAT calls and Code Blues was as overwhelming as securing a new home in a new state with two people depending on her.

The phone rang at her side, and she absently picked it up as she bookmarked the University of Iowa's College of Nursing page. "Black Bear Gap Clinic. This is Doctor Rosner."

"Get out," someone hissed in her ear, as they did at least three times a day and on occasion in the middle of the night.

She slammed down the phone, her heart beating faster as she blinked in the dim light, realizing she'd lost track of time and that the sun had set. "Damn," she whispered, closing her laptop as she looked over her shoulder toward the porch light on at the cabin. Ever since she'd realized she was being followed, she'd kept her hours at the clinic short, making certain she was never alone after dusk.

She gave a weary look to the phone and rushed to her feet. Since the night of their hike to the Hendley's, she'd been barraged by creepy calls. The messages varied to some degree, but they all had the same theme: She wasn't welcome here. She was as eager to go as they were to see her gone, but that wasn't an option at this point.

Grabbing her keys, she did a visual check of the safe and turned off the remaining lights, chastising herself for not paying attention to the clock. She closed the closet and whirled, screaming when a loud bang echoed off the waiting room window. Her breath heaved as she crept slowly toward the noise, whimpering and jumping again when a shadow passed in front of her office window.

She hurried into the pediatric exam room and shut the door, jamming a chair under the knob and picked up the phone, dialing the cabin.

"Hello?"

Fisting her hand, she swallowed, fighting to school her breathing. "Hey, Chase, it's Reagan. I uh—I didn't realize how dark it's gotten. I didn't bring a flashlight. Do you think maybe you could peek your head out the front door and wait for me?"

"No problem. Dinner's just about ready. I tried that beef stew from the pile of recipes Shane got from Sophie."

The thought of eating sickened her already shuddering stomach. "Mmm. Sounds good. I—I just need to grab my laptop."

"I'll be waiting for you. I have the door open right now."

"Okay, great." She hung up, hesitating before she moved the chair out of the way, afraid of what might be on the other side. Rushing into her office she yanked the laptop off her desk, not bothering to grab the charger, and bolted out the door. She sent Chase a wave and locked up, then walked quickly, her eyes darting about in the dark.

"Take your time," Chase called.

Not on your life. "I don't mind hurrying. Dinner sounds delicious." She dashed up the steps and walked inside.

Chase closed the door, turned, and frowned. "Are you okay?"

"Yeah. Definitely." She smiled brightly, toeing off her shoes.

"You're pale."

She was sweating too and doing everything in her power to hold back the need to shake. "I feel great."

He held her gaze, his eyes narrowing as he studied her, then shrugged. "You're the doctor."

"I am." She moved to the windows, yanking the curtains closed, certain that the man in the leather jacket was watching her every move. "It's *really* chilly out there tonight. This should help keep in the heat."

Chase stared at her. "Are you sure you're okay?"

"Mmm." She nodded. "Absolutely." She wanted to tell him about the terrifying phone calls and quiet taps against her bedroom windows in the middle of the night and tonight's loud bang at the clinic. She yearned to spill her guts about the endless intimidation tactics but smiled instead. She was so *close* to securing Jenny and Faith's future outside of The Gap. She wasn't about to start mentioning anything to Chase now with their court date less than a week away and the director constantly breathing down her neck. Soon she would tell Chase everything, but not until she held the legal documents in her hand that guaranteed Jenny and Faith were leaving with her. "I'm going to—"

"You've gotta see this." Jenny came down from the loft with Faith in her arms, wearing a smooth tinfoil crown on her head while Faith wore pink and black pajamas and her cat-ear headband.

Halloween. She'd forgotten.

"Come look at this." Jenny yanked on Reagan's wrist, dragging her upstairs to the computer. "Look what I found." She bounced on her feet.

Reagan winced even as Jenny supported the baby's neck and Faith laughed. "Why don't you give me Faith?"

Jenny handed over the baby and sat down, wiggling the mouse. "It's him. It's Shane."

Reagan leaned closer to the monitor, looking at the paparazzi shots of Cally Carlisle with Shane at her side. In one frame he wore jeans and a black polo as he opened the main hotel door for the singer. In the next he stood inches from her in a black suit with an earpiece in place and his wrist close to his open mouth as if he spoke into some sort of device while Cally signed autographs from the safety of the metal barriers separating her from her fans. Finally, he climbed the stairs of Cally's private plane, his eyes shielded by sunglasses, his tough build accentuated by jeans and a brown bomber jacket.

"Isn't this *cool*? Shane Harper, *our* Shane, is all over the internet standing next to Cally Carlisle."

Her heart hurt as she studied his striking face in the first two paparazzi shots. "It's pretty neat."

Jenny whirled in her chair. "Pretty neat? It's way more awesome than that. I'm gonna e-mail him right now."

The phone rang, and Reagan automatically tensed.

"Jenny, it's for you," Chase called. "It's your sister."

Reagan pressed her lips together, releasing a quiet

breath through her nose, trying her best to relax. She was home now. She was safe in the cabin.

"I'll be right back. Oh." She paused and turned, grabbing another tinfoil crown, securing it on Reagan's head. "There. Now you're ready for our Netflix ghoul fest. I made the cookies too."

She didn't know if her nerves could handle the ghoul fest Jenny had planned for the three of them after Faith headed off to bed. "I can't wait."

"It's gonna be awesome." Jenny dashed off for the phone.

Reagan glanced at Shane's handsome face once more on the screen and closed her eyes, longing for him. Then she turned away. "Should we help Chase with the table, sweetie?" She took the baby's hand in hers, kissing Faith's fingers.

Faith blinked up at her and smiled.

"Aw, you sure know how to make a girl feel better." Faith cooed.

Chuckling, she kissed the baby's forehead. "Let's go be helpers." She walked down to the dining area, snagging the spoons Chase set in the center of the table. "I'll take care of this."

"You have your color back."

She smiled. "I really am fine, but thanks for your concern."

"Is Faith having stew too?" He smiled at the baby.

She shook her head. "Afraid not. She still has a couple more months of just formula ahead of her."

He grimaced. "Bummer."

Chase worked constantly and was serious more than he wasn't, but on occasion his sense of humor shined through. She grinned. "Luckily she doesn't seem to mind."

"I would. Have you smelled that stuff?" He

shuddered.

Reagan laughed.

He touched his finger to Faith's chin. "She's a beautiful baby."

"She really is. She looks just like her mom."

"Reagan, I need to talk to you." Jenny hurried in, taking Reagan's hand. "Sorry, Chase, I really need to talk to Reagan."

"I guess we'll be right back."

"I'll be waiting," he said as he set the bowls on placemats.

Jenny pulled Reagan down the hall, the excitement of the last few minutes clearly gone.

"What's the matter?" Whatever it was, she knew she wasn't going to like it.

Jenny shut them in her room, and Reagan hurried over to the curtains, closing them with a snap.

"Reagan." Jenny leaned back against the door. "My sister just called."

"I know."

"She's sayin' some stuff—really awful stuff."

She sat on Jenny's bed, preparing herself for the next blow. "Like what?"

Jenny puffed out a long breath. "Well, lot's of people are talkin' about some girl in New York—Mable or something like that."

Her stomach clutched as her past came back to haunt her for the second time in less than a week.

"They're saying you did somethin' wrong and killed her, and that's why you left and came here."

She rushed to her feet, certain she was going to vomit. "I didn't—I need to—"

Jenny gripped her arm before she could bolt out the door. "There's more, Reagan." Jenny held her gaze, her eyes full of apology. "Shirley said some of Henry's

356

kids are tellin' folks you had their daddy burnt to a crisp because you didn't want anyone findin' out you were wrong about the black lung stuff too. They're thinkin' you're tryin' to cover up that the doctor in Lexington is right."

She shook her head, trying to take it all in. "*What*?"

"That's what they're sayin'. Lot's of people are belivin' it, and they're pretty mad."

She walked back to Jenny's bed and sat slowly as her world completely fell apart. Someone had done their homework and effectively turned the tables on their deception, further cementing her as the lying bad guy. "I wanted Henry to have an autopsy so we could prove that he *did* have progressive massive fibrosis. I wanted his family to receive proper compensation."

"I know that." Jenny sat next to her. "I know the truth, Reagan."

Every day something new and disastrous seemed to happen. Doctor Schlibenburg, Terry, Henry, the man in the leather jacket, the constant stream of phone calls. What was next? "I don't even have the *authority* to order a cremation; only next of kin can do that."

"People who think you could or would do such a thing are stupid." She rested her head against Reagan's shoulder. "I thought you should know."

"Thank you for telling me." She kissed the top of Jenny's head.

"Let me take Faith." Jenny took the baby, snuggling and smiling at her daughter, but not before Reagan caught the hint of worry in the teenager's eyes.

Reagan straightened her shoulders with the last of her strength. "I don't want you to worry about this for one second. I'm going to clear this up with Daisy first thing tomorrow. I want you to go have dinner."

"What about you?"

She forced a smile as she struggled to keep herself together. "I'll be out in just a couple of minutes. I believe we have a ghoul-packed night of fun ahead of us." Watching movies and choking down beef stew and cookies was the last thing she wanted to do, but she would for the young woman sitting at her side.

"I told Shirley to remind everybody that you saved my life and Faith's, and that you tried to save Henry too."

"Thanks," she said over the tight ball in her throat. Jenny's unwavering support was her final undoing. "I'm going to wash up." She stood and walked to her room, catching a whiff of Shane's scent in the hall. Would it never go away? Locking her door, she curled her hands into her robe hanging on the back of the door as she pressed her face to the soft cotton, quietly giving in to her tears.

~~~~

Mable's small hand guided the pink crayon over the piece of paper with sure strokes, then she dropped it to the table. "I don't want to color anymore."

Reagan smiled as she completed the Statue of Liberty's torch. "How come?"

"Because I'm dying."

Reagan's eyes whipped up, watching Mable's peaches-and-cream color fading. "What's wrong, sweetie?" she asked as she adjusted the bed, laying the little girl flat in preparation for resuscitation.

"I'm bleeding to death because you're careless and didn't pay attention. Now my mommy's all alone." She closed her eyes and flat-lined while Mrs. Totton screamed among the chaos of the crazy emergency room.

Reagan sat up, gasping in her bed, covered in a panicked sweat as Mable's voice echoed in her head. Dizzy with grief and fear, she lay back against her pillow, waiting for the nausea to stop churning and her heart rate to settle.

When she'd headed off to bed after Jenny's fright night, she'd expected a nightmare or two, but nothing as horrendous as the three she'd woken from in the last couple of hours. More rattled than she'd been in months, she lay still, listening to the sounds in the night. Her eyes darted to the door when she heard the creak down the hall then toward the window when the breeze rushed against the glass, every foreign sound sending her heart into another frenzy. Since Shane left, she had yet to sleep a full night. The stresses of her secret torments were starting to take their toll.

Rolling to her side, she plunked a pillow over her head and pressed the soft case over her ear, willing away the bad memories that wouldn't let her rest. She sat up when Faith's tiny, barking cough caught her attention. Frowning, she pulled back her covers and walked to the next room as Jenny moved toward Faith's crib.

"She sounds awful." Jenny picked her up. "And she's hot."

"Let me see." She took the baby from Jenny, pressing her cheek to Faith's as the baby fussed, wheezing in every breath. "She has croup. We'll bring her into the bathroom and get it really steamy."

They hurried into the bathroom, closing the door, and turned on the shower to hot.

Faith cried harder, each wail a horrid barky sound.

"It's okay, sweetheart," Reagan soothed, feeling the baby's forehead again, noting her pink cheeks and ears in the dim glow of the nightlight. "She's burning up. I'm going to have Chase go over to the clinic and get us some Tylenol." She settled the baby in Jenny's lap. "Keep her upright just like this and talk to her. Try and keep her calm."

Swallowing, Jenny nodded. "Hurry back. I'm real scared."

"She's going to be fine." She closed the door behind her and stifled a scream when she bumped into Chase standing topless in shorts in the dark. "God, you scared me."

"Sorry. Is Faith all right?"

"She has croup and a fever. I need you to go over to the clinic and get me Tylenol Infant Drops from the cabinet."

"Sure."

"Thanks." She went back into the bathroom, walking into a plume of steam as Jenny sang and rocked the baby. "How's she doing?"

"She still sounds bad."

She listened to Faith's pitiful cries and wheezing breaths. "Chase went to get us some fever reducer." She shut off the shower. "We're going to wrap Faith in a blanket and bring her outside. The steam and cold will help relax her airway."

"What if they don't?"

"Let's take it one step at a time."

They walked out to the living room, and Reagan grabbed a blanket from the couch, securing it around Jenny and Faith. "Let's go sit on the swing." She glanced out the door, staring into the shadows intensified by the light of the porch. "Come on." Glancing around uneasily, her muscles relaxed when Chase started back their way, the beam of his flashlight bobbing with his steps.

He climbed the stairs, handing off the medicine. "I hope this is what you wanted."

"Yes. Thank you." She opened the box, took the syringe from the packaging, and dosed out the proper amount for Faith's weight. "I don't like giving meds to babies Faith's age, but she's pretty hot." She squeezed the liquid down the inside of Faith's cheek, the baby wheezing worse than when they'd started the steam treatment. "Jenny, I want you to go in and get Faith's car seat. I think we should probably take Faith in to the emergency room."

"Why?" She clutched Reagan's arm. "You're a doctor."

"And I don't have what I need here for croup. Get the seat, pack a quick bag with formula, bottles, diapers, and a couple changes of clothes, then we're going to go."

Jenny hurried inside with tears streaming down her cheeks.

Reagan rocked the baby, trying her best to keep her calm. "You're okay, baby girl. You're okay." But with each struggling breath she silently urged Jenny to hurry.

Chase sat next to her on the swing. "Is she going to be all right?"

"She's struggling. I need Jenny to stay calm, but the sooner we can get her into the ER the better."

He nodded. "I'll get the keys."

"Thanks."

Chase walked inside, and seconds later a twig snapped somewhere in the woods. She paused mid-rock, standing when Jenny and Chase reappeared. "Let's go." She settled Faith in the car seat, sitting in the back with the baby, eagerly watching each mile bring them further away from The Gap as Chase pushed the speed limit toward the nearest hospital.

CHAPTER THIRTY

SHANE LINED UP HIS SHOT AND SMACKED THE EIGHT BALL into the corner pocket, winning the game. "I believe that's another free beer." Grinning, he gave Amber a high five as Tyson and his date complained.

"You forgot to mention that you're a fucking shark. The both of you," Tyson accused.

"You never asked." Shane chuckled when his coworker gave him the finger as he headed to the bar to order up another round of drinks.

"I'm going to the girls' room," Amber said, walking away in skin-tight jeans and a barely-there halter-top, showing off her spectacular body. He and Ethan's former temp were pals, but after three and a half weeks of pure misery, he'd dabbled with the idea of changing their status from pool partners to friends with benefits. Amber had hinted more than once that she was game for a bout of casual sex, so why the hell wasn't he interested?

He gave his cue a bad tempered toss to the edge of the table and did a double take when he spotted the slender woman with long brown hair moving toward the bar. She turned, and he half expected to see Reagan. "*Damn* it."

Rubbing at the back of his neck, he sighed, glancing around the familiar surroundings of one of his favorite hangouts. It was his first night out with friends since his return from Madrid over a week ago, and he didn't even want to be here.

He'd been eager for good music and beer and the football games playing on the monitors by the bar, yet as he stood among the noise, he craved board games or watching some foolish movie full of teenage angst while he sat in a cabin with Jenny and Reagan in the middle of nowhere.

Over the last several weeks, he'd gone about his days and nights without some teen crisis to handle or frequent interruptions from a fussy baby in need of a bottle or diaper change. He hadn't sat on the porch swing with the gorgeous doctor, breathing in the scent of her shampoo while the breeze blew and she fascinated him with all of the thoughts crowding that big brain of hers.

He still hadn't heard a word from her since their non-goodbye at the airport. Nothing. For three days there hadn't been any communication from Jenny either. No one-liner e-mails or three-page novels, which left him worrying that her desire to keep in touch was fading. He relied on her updates and looked forward to the pictures of Faith. She was his lifeline to the people he still wished he was with.

More than once he'd mentioned to Ethan he wanted his duty switched to head back to The Gap, but Ethan had told him about the director's threats to pull the program altogether. They were in a wait-and-see holding pattern and it was driving him fucking *crazy*.

A laugh floated on the air, and he whipped his head around, looking for Reagan. "Son of a bitch." He couldn't take it anymore. "I'll be right back," he tossed over his shoulder as Tyson returned with drinks, making his way to a somewhat quiet corner of the bar. He searched his contacts for Reagan's number, hesitated, and dialed.

Jamming his hand through his hair, he waited to

hear the voice that was never far from his mind.

~~~~

Reagan rested her head against the hard wood of the hospital's rocking chair as she moved her leg in a gentle rhythm. She glanced down at the baby finally asleep in her arms, closing her eyes herself, praying that Faith would sleep for more than the twenty-minute stretches she'd been averaging over the last three days since the Pediatrician admitted her for treatment and observation.

Seventy-two hours had passed in a whirlwind of worry and tests after Faith's fever spiked to a dangerous one-hundred-four-point-three mere minutes after they arrived at the ER. All blood tests came back normal, and her fever was now low-grade, but the poor baby had been diagnosed with a double ear infection and a stubborn case of croup that refused to ease, offering the miserable baby and her exhausted mother little relief from Faith's first bout with illness.

Reagan had done her best to soothe Jenny's terror and Faith's discomfort, but both had proved to be a challenge as her own energy and belief that everything was going to be okay waned. At some point they would leave St. Christopher's Medical Center. The doctor assumed they would go home tomorrow if Faith had a good night, but Reagan's problems wouldn't be over. They would just be different and just as dreadful.

Luckily they had Chase. He'd been a lifesaver, bringing by fresh clothes and good food from the downtown restaurants, spending a couple hours mid-morning and afternoon with them at the hospital. The help was welcome, his kindness incredibly sweet, but Chase wasn't Shane. For three days she'd yearned for

Shane's hugs and understanding and his knack for making her laugh. But he wasn't here and wouldn't be again, so she'd carried on, ignoring her longing for a man who had a life of his own thousands of miles away. He protected the rich and famous—a far cry from guarding a pill safe in the mountains of Eastern Kentucky.

The baby moved, and her eyes flew open. She rubbed Faith's back, settling her against her chest for another bout of fitful sleep.

She yawned, and her phone rang. Cursing, she grabbed it before Faith or Jenny could stir. "Hello?"

Music and laughter filled the background. "Reagan, it's Shane."

She smiled, and her heart stuttered from the sound of his voice. "Shane."

"I haven't heard from Jenny for a few days, so I thought I would check in and see how things are going."

She glanced toward the teenager dead asleep on the couch close to the crib, then at the wheezing baby resting in her arms. "They're great. We're doing really well. How about you?"

"I'm good." There was a small commotion, and Shane chuckled. "Thanks," he murmured. "Tonight's my first night off since the concert tour. Me and a couple of buddy's decided to head out for a beer."

"Sounds like fun."

"It's not bad. This last week I was out on a movie set in the middle of the desert, so a Sam on draught tastes pretty damn good."

Talking to him, hearing his contentment was worse than missing him every day. "I should let you get back to it."

"Hold up. How are the girls?"

She kissed the top of Faith's head. "Busy. Growing. We're starting to look into nursing schools for Jenny."

"Yeah, I heard about that. When I talked to Chase...last week? No, I guess it was the week before, he told me about your court date coming up. Jenny sounds pretty excited."

Reagan frowned. She knew Jenny and Shane communicated, but not Shane and Chase. As she listened to the noisy background of Shane's surroundings, she'd never been surer that keeping the issues she'd been plagued with in The Gap to herself was the right choice. He was happy in California, but he was too good of a man not to come running back to try and help. Shane didn't belong to them anymore. "She is. I'm sure she'll let you know when everything's decided."

"I'll be waiting. So, how are you?"

"Great," she continued with her deception. "I'm really good—happy. I haven't felt this settled in a long time."

Seconds passed in silence. "That's good." He cleared his throat. "Well, make sure you tell Jenny to e-mail me. She's missed a couple of days."

"I'll let her know you've been wanting to hear from her."

"You too. I thought I might hear from you sometimes as well."

She closed her eyes. He couldn't possibly know how much she yearned to reach out to him. She swallowed, fighting to clear any emotion from her voice. "I've been pretty busy."

"I guess if you have to be in The Gap you might as well be busy."

"Yeah."

There was another long pause. "I miss this—talking

to you. I miss sitting with you on the swing."

Her lips trembled, the dam about to burst, his words weakening her resolve. She couldn't do this anymore. Perhaps it was completely selfish, but she needed to share her burdens and hear him tell her everything was going to be okay. "Shane, things here in The Gap—I need—"

"Shane, come on," a female voice interrupted. "I'm waiting for my partner over here."

"Just a second," he murmured. "Sorry. What were you saying? I missed the last part."

I need you. She shook her head. "I—I just wanted to tell you how happy I am that you're settling back into your life."

"Thanks. I'm hanging in here."

"That's wonderful." She snuggled Faith closer, taking comfort as she gave it. "I'll let you go."

"Give Faith and Jenny a kiss for me."

"I will. Bye."

"Bye."

She hung up, breathing in several shaky breaths, as a tear coursed down her cheek. Why did he have to call? Why did he have to stir up her emotions when she'd been struggling so hard to put them behind her? He'd moved on. His happiness was undeniable, as was the fact that his beer with "buddies" was actually a date.

Setting down her phone, she closed her eyes, settling more truly against the seat, willing the sound of his voice from her mind until Faith woke her again ten minutes later.

~~~~

Shane walked Amber to her door just before midnight, surrounded by the scent of her perfume.

"Thanks for the fun." Smiling, she put her key in the lock.

"You're welcome."

"We'll have to do this again."

He shoved his hands in his pockets. "Definitely."

"Do you want to come in?"

He trailed his gaze down her excellent figure, knowing what she was offering and shook his head. "I have an early morning."

"Maybe next time."

"Yeah." He sent her a small smile. "I should probably—"

Amber cut him off as she stood on her tiptoes, touching her lips to his.

His hands flew to her arms, gripping her biceps, intending to pull back. *I'm really good—happy. I haven't felt this settled in a long time.* Reagan's words played through his mind, fanning the flames of hurt and anger. He cupped Amber's face and deepened the kiss, desperate to forget about Reagan. Doc's heart sure as hell wasn't breaking over him. Her mind wasn't constantly bogged down by thoughts of him.

Yet as he slid his tongue along Amber's, he felt nothing—no urgent need to dive any deeper and savor her taste. Determined to feel *something*, he wrapped his arms around her, waiting for the rush of desire that consumed him whenever he held Reagan close. When that didn't happen either, he brushed his fingers through her hair, but her shampoo didn't smell like Doc's. She didn't moan quietly the way Reagan did when he knew she had finally surrendered. Nothing about Amber was like the woman he couldn't stop *wanting*.

"Are you sure you don't want to come in?" she murmured against his lips.

He stepped back, staring into her pretty brown eyes—not blue. "I need to go."

"How about a date? Just you and me at someplace other than Smitty's?"

He shook his head. "I'm on duty for the next few days."

"So the next time you're not."

I'm really good—happy. Her voice echoed in his head like a fucking nightmare. He rubbed at his jaw he couldn't stop clenching. Reagan had sounded good. He was desperately in love with a woman in some Podunk town who'd already brushed him off. Whether he wanted to or not, he needed to move on. "Yeah, sure. I'll give you a call the next time I have off."

"Great." She went inside. "Goodnight."

"Night."

She closed her door and he walked away, hating the cool Doctor Rosner a little for being okay when he didn't know how he was going to live the rest of his life without her.

CHAPTER THIRTY-ONE

DUSK WAS SETTLING OVER THE GAP AS CHASE TURNED right off the main road and started the muddy climb toward the cabin. He swerved to avoid several potholes, the result of two solid days of rain, while Reagan sat in the passenger seat, smiling back at Jenny as she yawned for the third time. The pretty girl's fair complexion was marred by dark purple under-eye circles—the unfortunate affliction of the truly sleep deprived. "I'll settle Faith in if you want to take a shower and relax."

"I'm cravin' a warm bath, but I don't want to be too far away from my baby girl," she said, peeking at her daughter and adjusting Faith's blanket as she'd done at least two dozen times since they started home from the hospital.

"Faith's doing fine," she reassured, brushing her hand over Jenny's. "She rested relatively well last night, her fever's gone, the infection in her ears is responding well to the antibiotic, and her croup is so much better. Tonight we might actually get some *sleep*."

Jenny yawned again. "I'm so tired, but I feel like I might never sleep again. Sick babies sure get ya all shaken up."

She laughed. "True, but as your friend—and a doctor at that—I'm telling you Faith is definitely on the mend. If I didn't believe that we wouldn't be going home." She blinked, willing away her exhaustion.

"You're lookin' real tired yourself, Reagan." Jenny's brow furrowed. "Real tired."

She was dragging in a way that made her residency days seem like a cakewalk. "The last couple nights have been a bit rough."

"Maybe you should take a nap. I'll have a bath later."

She shook her head. "I need to catch up on a little work, which I can do while Cute Stuff sleeps." She'd hoped to have their relocation list narrowed down by now, and she wanted to give the mysterious thin white strips of paper that kept arriving in the mail another look, but Faith's croup hadn't given her time to do anything but get herself and the girls through the next wild ride.

"I don't know if I feel right about restin' when you're not."

"I won't be able to settle until I make sure I'm caught up on everything with the clinic. I haven't checked my e-mail in three days. I probably have a dozen voicemails waiting for me." She thought of her late-night call with Shane and Jenny's excitement when Reagan told her he was eagerly awaiting Jenny's next message. "Did you get in touch with Shane?"

"I e-mailed him this mornin' from your phone when you were talkin' to the doctor. I probably should've asked first."

She shook her head. "You know I don't care if you use my phone."

Jenny smiled. "My heart gets all gooey every time I think about you two talkin'." She made a pitter-patter motion against her chest. "He's missin' you," she said in a singsong voice.

Reagan ignored Chase's chuckle. "He misses *you* and Faith."

"I'm tellin' ya, Reagan, his 'thing' for you's not fadin' the way you're sure it is. I'm still thinkin' you should come with me and Faith to California. You can pick up where you left off."

"That *was* a pretty steamy kiss at the airport," Chase chimed in, tossing her a teasing grin.

Suddenly Mr. Serious wanted to be a funny guy. Reagan rolled her eyes at him. "You're not exactly helping me here."

He chuckled again.

"Chase is right, you know—steamy and really romantic. You two make a *perfect* couple. Someday I'm gonna find me someone who wants me the way Shane wants you."

She didn't want to talk about Shane or Jenny's misperceptions of what she thought Shane felt for her. Poor Jenny would be in for a rude awakening when she eventually stepped off a plane in Los Angeles and Shane introduced her to Amber.

Jenny licked her lips and ran a hand down her ponytail. "I um, I didn't tell him about Faith."

"Oh."

"I mean I said Faith'd had a bit of a cold, but I didn't tell him the rest." Jenny fiddled with her fingers as her eyes darted to Reagan's then to her nails. "He probably would've just worried."

"I don't think you did the wrong thing."

She met Reagan's gaze. "You don't?"

She shook her head. "I didn't mention it either."

Jenny expelled a long breath in what could only be relief. "Okay. Good. I guess maybe I kinda feel like I lied."

She cleared her throat, well aware she and Jenny had both kept the truth from Shane. "I want you to share your life and troubles with Shane if that's what you feel comfortable doing. He's a great guy who cares very deeply for you and the baby, but worrying him about something we had under control isn't necessary."

"Exactly."

She gave a decisive nod, easing her own conscience. "Exactly."

Chase tossed Reagan a look, frowning.

"What?"

"Nothing."

"You had plenty to say just a second ago." She batted her lash at him.

"Shane's a good buddy of mine. I think he would want to know if things aren't right."

"Faith's fine," she justified.

He shrugged. "You asked. I answered."

She didn't like Chase's answer. "He can't move on if he's constantly worrying about the girls."

He raised his brows as he concentrated on the road. "He can't or you can't?"

She frowned.

"Geez, guys, I didn't wanna make thing's all uncomfortable."

"You didn't." She smiled, ignoring Chase's last comment.

"Okay. Good." She sat back in her seat, checking on Faith. "So, I know you've gotta work, but maybe we could play a game or somethin' later—maybe kinda relax and settle back in. Now that we're goin' home and I have time to think about it, I'm gettin' real nervous about our court date tomorrow."

Jenny was anxious, but Reagan was eager to get their hearing with the judge over with. "We can do whatever you want, but I don't want you worrying too much. Your mother's on board with our plan. This is more of a formality than anything. You want to leave, I want to take you and Faith, and your mother isn't objecting. My attorney sees this as pretty open and shut."

Despite her reassurances, concern still filled Jenny's eyes.

"I promise, sweetie," she said, giving Jenny's hand an encouraging squeeze.

She nodded. "If you say it, I'll believe it."

"Good." Reagan smiled. "So what do you want to play?"

"I don't know."

"I'll let you decide. If you want, I can make us a snack first."

Jenny wrinkled her nose. "Unless it's somethin' that doesn't need cookin' I should probably help."

Reagan grinned as Chase laughed. "I was thinking of trying my hand at brownies."

Jenny gave her a pained look.

"Or not."

"I'm not tryin' to hurt your feelin's, but seriously, Reagan, you're not much of a baker...at all."

"But I've mastered grilled cheese. There wasn't one burnt spot on anyone's sandwiches the other night. You've gotta give me that."

"You're learnin', but you've got yourself a long way to go. Kinda like my nursin'. We're just gonna have to keep helpin' each other."

"All right, a mini cooking lesson and—"

Chase slammed on the brakes, the jolt interrupting Reagan's thoughts as she faced front. "Oh my God," she shuddered out, staring in horror at the clinic's broken windows and DOCTOR DEVIL spelled out in bright red spray paint across the cabin's porch, but it was the white crosses with FED1, FED2, FED3, and FED4 staked by the burning animal carcasses that turned her stomach completely. "Chase—"

"Stay buckled," he said as he whipped the vehicle

around in a backup maneuver worthy of the movies and started down the road much faster than they'd arrived. "Call the cops while I get us out of here."

"But—"

"Call the cops, Reagan."

Knowing he was right, that there was no other choice, she pulled the phone out of her purse, dialing 911 with trembling fingers.

"Nine-one-one, what's your emergency?"

"Yes, I would like to report a vandalism at the Black Bear Gap Clinic in Black Bear Gap, Kentucky." Although what she'd just seen was so much more than that. The spray paint and damaged door from the night Shane was still here had been a fairly harmless warning, but the disgusting mess they just left behind was an unmistakable threat.

Chase took the phone from her hand as he turned left on the main road. "This is Chase Rider, head of security for The Appalachia Project. I need officers at The Black Bear Gap Clinic as soon as possible. I don't know. If you could have a squad car wait. Yes. Thank you. This number is fine." He hung up.

"What are we gonna do?" Jenny asked, reaching for Reagan's hand, gripping her fingers, as she clutched at Faith's car seat with the other.

"We're going to drive around for a few minutes until I get some backup," Chase answered, his entire demeanor changed as his gaze darted constantly from the windshield to the rearview mirror.

Jenny's eyes grew impossibly wider as she looked at Reagan. "Backup?"

"Everything's going to be okay," Reagan soothed, even as her own heart pounded. "We'll figure this out."

Chase drove another four miles toward Rock Creek when Reagan's cell phone rang again. "This is Chase

Rider. Thanks. We'll be right there." He flipped a u-turn and punched up his speed, making it back to the clinic as two police cars raced up the clinic road. Another cruiser stopped along the shoulder, and Chase flashed his lights, rolling down Reagan's window as he pulled over. "I'm Chase Rider, Head of Security."

"I'll follow you up, Mr. Rider."

"Thanks." He secured Reagan's window, and they began their journey up the endless five miles. "When we get the okay, we're going to go straight inside. Reagan, I want you to slide over to the driver's seat and come out that way. Jenny, I'll help you get Faith and we'll all go in together from there."

Jenny swallowed. "Then what?"

"I'll close up the curtains, and we'll go about our business, but I want you staying away from the doors and windows until I have a better idea of what's going on."

"What about Ethan?" Reagan asked.

"I'll wait for more information from the police, then I'll give him a call."

She nodded, her mind already spinning, trying to think of ways to handle damage control. Chase would call Ethan, and Ethan would call the director. After the conversation Ethan and the director were bound to have, it would be a miracle if she was allowed to finish off the terms of her new timetable. With the Mable and Henry rumors stirring, there was little hope of convincing anyone, let alone herself, that she would find her way back into The Gap's good graces. Thank God tomorrow was Jenny's court hearing.

They pulled up in the driveway to blue lights blazing as two officers walked the property in the fading light.

The officer who followed them came up to the

window. "They just radioed me. The house looks secure."

"Thank you," Chase said, then helped Jenny get Faith out of the back as Reagan finagled her way out the driver's side.

"Goddamn it stinks out here," Chase said, hurrying them to the front door, carrying Faith's car seat.

Reagan pressed her hand to her nose and mouth in defense against the overwhelming stench of the skunks smoldering in their yard as she climbed the stairs, staring at the wretched crosses, the intention unmistakable—grave markers for herself and the three people who lived with her.

Chase shut the door behind them, leaving the retched scent outside.

"Well, this wasn't exactly how I thought we would spend the rest of the day," Reagan said, toeing off her shoes.

"I wish I could say home sweet home," Jenny said as she looked around uneasily, taking Faith from her carrier and holding her close as the baby started to cry.

"Stay here while I get to the—" A knock interrupted Chase. "Who's there?"

"Jessie Hendley."

Reagan barely suppressed a groan as she stepped up to Chase's side. "It's Jenny's mother."

Chase opened the door.

Mrs. Hendley stood in her familiar baggy jeans and oversized t-shirt, plugging her nose. "What in the name of our all mighty *Lord* is goin' on around here?"

"Why don't you come in?" Reagan pulled her inside, attempting to keep the smell out.

"Mommy—"

"There be cops all over the place. And what is that—animals burnin'? Smells like skunk."

Reagan pressed her lips together as she nodded. "Unfortunately someone thought they would have a little fun at our expense."

"It don't look like no fun to me."

"No, it certainly doesn't. Can I offer you a seat and something to drink?" She made a sweeping motion with her hand, hoping to draw Mrs. Hendley's attention to the cozy surrounding of where Jenny and Faith lived.

"No." She stayed by the door, keeping her hand on the knob. "My phone's still not connected, and the rain kept me away, but I came to tell you I ain't goin' through with your lawyer's high ideas."

"Mommy." Jenny rushed forward. "Our meetin' with the judge is *tomorrow*."

"Hush now, Jenny." Mrs. Hendley pointed at her daughter. "You gettin' on out of here was supposed to be for the best, but I'm thinkin' this ain't the right decision after all. The Lord's been tellin' me different. I come down here and see that He's right."

Chase's phone rang. "I need to take this." He walked off to the kitchen.

"Mrs. Hendley, letting Jenny get an education is a wonderful choice. And quite frankly, Jenny doesn't appear to be welcome in this town anymore."

"If she comes on to church with me and I tell them she was lured away by the devil, they'll take her back, I'm believin'."

"I don't want to stay here, Mommy." Jenny grabbed the bottle from the diaper bag, giving it to Faith as the baby started to cry. "I want to take my girl on out of here and get my education."

"I've been prayin' mighty hard on this one, Jenny, and you'll be stayin' here." She turned and walked out the door.

"Mrs. Hendley." Reagan followed her outside. "I hope you'll reconsider."

"I was hopin' I was wrong about you, Doc Reagan, but I've a mind to believe that paint on the wall." She gestured to the words *DOCTOR DEVIL*. "You gone and made my daughter more sinful than she already was. You gone and killed some little girl with your quackery and desecrated poor Henry's remains. You, Doc Reagan, are Satan in disguise. That pretty face and fancy education hides the true heathen you are."

Reagan crossed her arms in the chilly air. This was so much *worse* than any nightmare she could have imagined. "Mrs. Hendley—"

"I've got nothin' more to be sayin'. Jenny's got 'til tomorrow to pack herself on up and head back to the house."

"What about Faith?"

"I guess she'll have to be bringin' her. Them Staddlers is better than you, and that's not sayin' much."

"I won't force her to leave. I still plan to speak with the judge."

"She's my girl, Doc Reagan. Not yours." She walked off, and Reagan closed her eyes.

"Damn it." She turned and went back in, walking to Jenny crying and sitting on the couch as Faith continued drinking her bottle.

"She's not gonna let me go."

Reagan sat down next to her, wrapping an arm around her shoulders. "Let's take this a step at a time."

"There isn't much need. I know mommy. She's set her mind to sayin' no."

"We're still going to see the judge. Hopefully we can convince your mother—"

Jenny shook her head adamantly. "No. I bet she

said stuff about how you were the devil."

Reagan swallowed.

Jenny rushed to her feet and started pacing. "When Mommy brings up talk of the devil that's the end of it. Even if somethin' has nothin' to do with the devil she brings it up." Tears poured down her cheeks. "I never got to go to birthday parties and the sleepover with my friend down the road because celebratin' such foolishness was the work of the devil."

"Jenny—"

"I've been thinkin' I should write a note sayin' I want you to raise Faith, and I should leave. I'm her momma. If I say it, the judge will listen. You'd be a good mommy to her. I want Faith to go on away from here."

Reagan stood in Jenny's path. "I'm not leaving here without you."

"I saw those crosses outside. It's not safe for you here. You need to be leavin'."

"I'm not going anywhere without you." She snagged Jenny's elbow, squeezing gently. "Period."

"If I run away you won't have much reason—"

"Stop it," she said sharply. "I don't want you saying or even thinking like that. I'm not leaving here without you. If you run away, I'll have to stay longer, because I won't go until I find you."

Jenny burst into another round of sobbing.

Reagan wrapped her up, holding on as her chest tightened until the fear and stress made it hard to breathe. "We're leaving together," she said as she ran her hand down Jenny's hair. "You, me, and Faith. I'm promising you I won't leave you behind." She eased back, looking Jenny in the eye. "You and Faith are my family. You two are *mine*. Your mother gave birth to you, but you're mine, Jenny."

Jenny nodded, sucking in several shuddering breaths.

"Go wash your face. We've got brownies to make and games to play."

"I don't think I want to make brownies."

She didn't want them herself, but Jenny needed as normal an afternoon as Reagan could give her. "Either you help me or I'm making them on my own."

She wiped at her tears with her shoulder. "I don't think we can handle the house burnin' down too."

Reagan smiled despite the turmoil.

"I guess I'll go wash my face."

"That's a good choice." She took Faith. "Take a few deep breaths and collect yourself."

Jenny nodded and walked away.

She waited for Jenny to shut herself in the bathroom and sat down, closing her eyes as she rested her forehead against the baby's, taking several shuddering breaths of her own as she rocked.

"Reagan?"

She looked up, realizing Chase was staring down at her, and she rushed to her feet.

"I talked to Ethan."

"What did he say?"

"Not a whole lot at this point. I'm going to talk to the police when they're finished up and call him back. He and the director will decide what to do from there."

Of course they would. Because one disaster today wasn't quite enough. "Thanks for letting me know."

"I'm not sure what the plan is from here—"

"Oh, come on, Chase," she scoffed. "I think we both do. The director's going to close up shop and leave me here with two girls and no security."

"We're not going to just leave you here alone."

"For how long? Is your boss going to give up one of

his men for the next year if that's what it comes down to? Jenny's mother is going to fight me." And more than likely win.

"I don't know how we'll handle it, but we will."

She didn't have much hope for anything. "Right. Thanks." She walked off to her room, not sure of what to do anymore.

~~~~

"It looks like another win for you," Reagan said as she tallied her final score on the bottom of her Yahtzee sheet.

"I guess so." Jenny smiled, but it didn't reach her eyes.

"Are you up for one more round?"

Jenny shook her head, putting the dice back in the box. "I think I'm gonna take Faith to bed."

"What about a bowl of cereal first?" Jenny hadn't eaten much—not that she had either, even though they'd taken the time to tackle Sophie McCabe's recipe for roasted pork tenderloin and garlic mashed potatoes while the brownies they baked cooled.

She wrinkled her nose and pressed a hand to her stomach. "I'm not hungry."

"How about a game of UNO—best of three?" She'd spent the last several hours trying to preoccupy Jenny and banish the troubled look from her eyes—first in the kitchen, then with movies and games and playtime with Faith, but despite her best efforts, Jenny spent much of the afternoon and evening in tears.

"No thanks."

"Okay." She stood, taking Jenny's hand as the teenager's eyes welled yet again. "We're going to find a solution." She tucked Jenny's long strands of blond hair behind the girl's ear. "I want you to get some rest and not worry too much." She was worried enough for the both of them. When she and Chase spoke after dinner, Ethan was still waiting to hear back from the director, and her conversation with her attorney had done nothing to ease her mind. Everything about their lives was in limbo.

Jenny sniffled and picked up Faith from the bouncy seat where she'd fallen asleep. "Do you think maybe you could sleep with us?"

"Sure, but I'm not quite ready for bed. I have a bit of work to catch up on. She wrapped her arm around Jenny's waist. "Come on. I'll walk with you."

Jenny burrowed herself against Reagan's side as they moved down the hall, then she settled herself and the sleeping baby in her bed.

Reagan covered them up, making certain the curtains were closed tight, and kissed Jenny's forehead, then her finger, touching Faith's nose. "I'll be in soon."

"Okay."

"Get some sleep."

Jenny nodded and settled on her side, snuggling Faith.

"Goodnight."

"Reagan?"

"Yeah?" She stopped, turning in the doorway.

"What if the judge makes me go back?" She sat up as tears trailed down her cheeks in the light of the dim lamp on the bedside table. "What if tonight's the last night I get to sleep here?"

She swallowed, making sure her voice was confident as she fought with her own tears. "It won't be."

Her lips trembled as she shuddered out a long breath. "But what if it is?"

She gripped the doorframe, desperate for strength. "I won't let it be."

"But—"

"I'll camp out in your mother's lawn for the next year if I have to."

A small smile creased Jenny's lips. "You'd do that for me?"

"There isn't anything I *wouldn't* do for you."

Her smile widened. "I love you."

"I love you too, sweetie." She blew Jenny a kiss and closed the door halfway before going to her room. She sat at her desk, struggling with the weight on her chest, the urge to cry never far away.

Sighing, she stared at the stack of mail, noting the envelopes with the familiar Canadian postmark. She grabbed the nondescript white business envelope addressed to her and tore it open, taking out a strip.

...progressive massive fibrosis rates are skyrocketing in smaller mines scattered throughout Appalachia.

She ripped open the yellow package next and fished out another slim white slip.

...under-diagnosis and simple prevention are the biggest issues miners face.

She lined up the ten pieces she had, switching them around in several combinations, trying to make the sentences read cohesively, but eventually she gave up and shook her head. She glanced at more envelopes among the pile, but didn't have the energy or desire to see if she could string together more of Doctor Schlibenburg's article—for surely that's what this was. Slowly more answers were coming, but that mattered little now. Jenny and Faith were running out of time to stay where she could keep them safe.

She glanced toward her windows, knowing the moon shined bright beyond the curtains and that the worst of the mess the vandals left behind had been photographed and taken away, but her problems still remained. In little more than twelve hours she and Jenny would meet with the judge. Jenny and Faith's fate rested in one man's hands. The next year of their lives would be dictated by someone who had the power to tell them they couldn't stay together.

Her phone rang, and she jumped, staring at the office line sitting at her side. She let it ring again and a third time, already knowing she would hear the retched hissing voice if she answered. With little choice, she picked up, not wanting to wake Jenny if she had actually fallen asleep. "This is Doctor Rosner."

"You're gonna die," someone whispered. "You, Devil Fed, is gonna *die*."

Her head whipped up and she rushed to her feet with the familiar wave of dread. "Shut up. Stop calling here, dammit. Stop calling here." She slammed down the phone, her breath heaving, unable to take any more. Walking to her bed, she pressed her hands to her face and gave into her tears, weeping with the heavy burden of true helplessness.

~~~~

Shane logged off of his computer, closing his laptop when his office line beeped. He picked it up, holding the receiver with his shoulder, and shoved the laptop into its leather sleeve. "Yeah?"

"It's Ethan. Can you come down to my office?"

"Sure. I'll be right there."

"Thanks."

He hung up as the phone on his belt rang. "What the hell?" It was almost seven thirty, and he was busier now than he had been at five. He glanced at the readout and answered, knowing it was late in Kentucky.

"Shane, it's Chase."

His shoulders tensed, noting the strain in Chase's voice. "What's going on?"

"Has Ethan talked to you yet?"

He rubbed at his jaw. "No. What's up?"

"We've had some issues around here today—several, but that's not why I'm calling. It's Reagan."

His stomach sank, and he steamed out a long breath. "What's wrong with Reagan?"

"She's been dealing with a hell of a lot."

He frowned. "I just talked to her last night. She sounded fine." More than fine.

"She's not."

"Go ahead and expand on that," he said impatiently as he stood, walking to the window, staring out at the lights of Los Angeles.

"She's pretty much been falling apart since the baby's been sick."

"Jenny said Faith had a cold."

"Faith was in the hospital for three days."

"*What*?"

"It was pretty serious—high fever, croup, and a double ear infection."

He fisted his hand on the glass. "Why the fuck didn't you tell me?"

"I figured Jenny had until we were talking earlier today, then everything went to hell. Jenny's emancipation might not be happening after all, and I think there's stuff going on around here Reagan hasn't

387

been telling me about. I just walked passed her room and heard her slam down the phone after she told someone to stop calling. Now she's crying—really crying, man."

I avoid crying at all costs. It gives me a headache. Closing his eyes, he grit his teeth.

"I don't know what went on between the two of you. It's none of my business, but she's a mess. I thought you would want to know."

He *knew* he never should've left. "Let me go talk to Ethan, and I'll get back to you. If anything else happens in the meantime I want to know."

"You've got it."

He hung up and scrubbed his hands over his face. "*Fuck.*"

"Bad day?"

He turned, looking at Amber smiling in the doorway, wearing a sinful black dress. "Shit, Amber, this isn't a good time. I have a meeting with Ethan, then I'm heading out of town."

"I thought we might be able to catch a late dinner."

"I can't."

"I guess not. Where are you going?"

"Back to Kentucky." He took her hand and pulled her into the room, closing the door. "Look, this isn't going to work. I haven't been entirely honest with you. There's a woman—a doctor in Kentucky."

She raised her brows. "And you two have a thing."

"Yeah. Or we did. We still might." He shook his head as he rubbed at the back of his neck. "I'm sorry."

She shrugged. "I wasn't really looking for anything serious anyway."

He gave her a hug. "Thanks for understanding."

She hugged him back before she drew away. "Catch me the next time you're in town."

"I'll call you."

She kissed his cheek. "Good luck with the doctor."

"I'll take it. I've gotta go."

"Bye."

"Bye." He moved down the hall and walked into Ethan's office, shutting the door. "What the hell's going on, man?"

"Take a seat."

He rubbed at the back of his neck as he sat in the leather chair across from his friend.

"I'm sending someone out to help Chase."

"I'm going."

"I figured as much, but I wanted to let you give me the yay or nay, since you weren't too thrilled to head out there last time."

"I'll go," he said again.

"I'll book your flight."

He bumped his leg up and down, riddled with nervous energy, ready to be on his way. "I just got off the phone with Chase. He said some stuff happened today."

"Things are heating up again." Ethan handed over the pictures of crosses, burning animals, and spray paint.

Shane stopped on the photo of *DOCTOR DEVIL* scrawled across the cabin porch, his stomach curdling with the idea that they were dealing with this while he was out here. Jenny had to be scared to death. "We need to get them out of there."

"Chase says the doctor is hell bent on staying."

He met Ethan's stare. "Reagan won't leave without the kids, and I guess the emancipation's in jeopardy. I didn't get all the details. It's a fucking mess, and I need to go."

"I just got off the phone with the director. He's

shutting them down in one week. He's giving Reagan time to deal with paperwork and final inventories and then it's over."

"Fucking-A." He stood, unable to be still. "I can't leave them there."

"Get packed. I'll see if I can get you a redeye."

"Thanks."

CHAPTER THIRTY-TWO

REAGAN OPENED HER EYES IN THE DIM LIGHT FILTERING IN around the edges of the curtains, moaning as she sat up slowly in her bed. She pressed her fingers to her temples as her head throbbed viciously, the way it always did when she fell asleep crying. Blinking, she studied the wrinkles in her shirt and the khaki slacks she never bothered to change out of and stood, fighting the small wave of dizziness as she walked to the bathroom. She opened the medicine cabinet and shook a Tylenol into her hand, swallowing it with a quick gulp from the tap. Turning on the shower next, she took off her clothes and stepped into the warm spray, closing her eyes and hanging her head, letting the steam and water work their magic on her painfully tense muscles.

She washed slowly, taking her time as she bathed her skin in lavender suds and worked shampoo through her hair, then rinsed and added conditioner. This was exactly what she needed—five blessed minutes to herself to pretend her problems didn't exist. For the next few moments, her issues with the town and Jenny's now-complicated court hearing were a dilemma for another day. But even as she told herself so, her lips trembled, and she pressed them firm, doing her best to shake off the need to weep as the weight of her constant worry sat heavily on shoulders that couldn't take much more.

Sighing, she turned off the water and dried herself, staring at her pale reflection in the mirror. She needed to start taking better care of herself. Her appetite had been off with all of the stress, and her energy was almost nonexistent. She could hardly care for Jenny and Faith if she continued on as she was now.

She pulled on her robe and went to the kitchen, making herself herbal tea in the quiet house, and grabbed a banana on her way back to her room. Sitting at her desk, she sipped the soothing chamomile and sunk her teeth into the sweet fruit for a healthy dose of nutrients, then started through the rest of the mail she'd abandoned last night. She sorted the junk from actual correspondences, craving some semblance of order, and picked up an envelope at random, opening the bill for her Manhattan storage unit and set it aside in her to-do pile for the day. She sipped tea again, ate more banana, and ripped into another Canadian postmarked envelope, ready to get back to Doctor Schlibenburg's shredded paper.

...Corpus Mining, among the other companies under the McPhee family umbrella.

She frowned. What other companies under the McPhee family umbrella? As far as she knew, there was only Corpus Mining. She picked up her pen, scribbling down *McPhee* and circled it when the phone at her side rang. Huffing out a breath, she braced herself as she picked up, not quite ready for another death threat or some other nasty comment. "This is Doctor Rosner."

"Doctor Rosner, this is Detective Reedy."

She blinked. "Detective Reedy."

"Good morning."

"Good morning, Detective. What can I do for you?"

"Well, I'm calling because we're at a bit of a standstill in Doctor Schlibenburg's case. My partner and I have decided to start back at the beginning and reexamine all of our information, which led me back to our conversation and you mentioning x-rays you left with the doctor."

"Yes."

"What exactly do the x-ray films look like?"

She frowned at the odd question. Didn't everyone know what films looked like? "Uh, large rectangles—green-tinged for detailed examination."

"And you're sure you didn't bring them back to Black Bear Gap with you? I know you mentioned you left in a hurry."

"I'm positive. I purposely set them on the coffee table by the couch."

"We've taken some time to follow a few different leads, but I recently went back to search the property and didn't see anything."

"The images should be in a brown film box."

"A box?"

"Yes. It says *Medical X-ray film* on it. I also wrote *Black Bear Gap Clinic* along the top in permanent marker."

"And you said they were in the living room when you left?"

"Yes. Eight images—front and lateral views of four patients' lungs. But I can't say what Doctor Schlibenburg did with them after I left. I didn't get a chance to talk to him again."

"I'll go back today and take another look. I'm sure I just missed them."

"I'm sure that's it." Although she didn't believe that any more than the Detective did. Someone took the images, along with Doctor Schlibenburg's life. She nibbled her lip, contemplating mentioning the black car she believed had followed her back from Berea and the man with the brown leather jacket she saw at the mall and hotel, but said nothing, thinking better of the idea. The last thing she wanted to do was put herself and the girls in an even more precarious situation—especially with the very real possibility she, Jenny, and Faith would be stuck in The Gap for several months to come without any sort of protection. "Please let me know if you have trouble finding the films."

"I'll be in touch."

"Thank you, Detective." She hung up and took the final two envelopes from the dwindling stack of mail and pulled the pieces of paper out.

Mine companies in Eastern Kentucky appear to be some of the biggest offenders of shortcuts.

...employees will pay in grave numbers for the lack of local, state, and federal oversight.

"Reagan?" Jenny knocked on her half-open door.

She gathered up the small slips and shoved them under her stack of bills. "Come on in."

"I'm sick."

She stood and walked to the pale girl. "What doesn't feel good?"

"My stomach."

She pressed her hand to Jenny's forehead. "You don't have a fever."

"Every time I think about goin' in front of the judge I feel worse."

She smiled sympathetically. "It sounds like a bad case of nerves, honey."

Jenny sat on the bed. "I don't know if I'm gonna be able to do this."

She sat next to her, taking her hand. "Of course you

are. I'll be right there with you."

"I guess I just don't see much point if Mommy already said no."

"This is an emancipation case. My attorney wanted to remind us both that just because your mother has decided to object doesn't necessarily mean the judge will. He'll be looking at what's best for you."

"Shouldn't your attorney be there today? I mean wouldn't that help?"

She shook her head. "She assured me it wouldn't make a difference. She took care of helping us file the appropriate paperwork. Judge Thompson will want to hear from you and me."

"I'm just feelin' all mixed up inside."

"About leaving?"

She shook her head. "No. I'm still shook up over yesterday, but I know for sure I wanna get out of The Gap more'n anythin'."

"Then we're going to go to court and hope the judge sees things from our point of view."

Jenny sighed. "I'm real afraid he won't."

"We'll give it our best shot, but no matter what happens today, you and I are leaving here together one way or the other." She nudged Jenny's shoulder with her own. "How about we focus on that?"

She nodded. "Okay."

"How do you feel about warm blueberry muffins for breakfast, then I'll braid your hair. I can make a pretty side French braid bun."

She raised her brow. "A French braid bun?"

"Sure. We'll pull down a few wisps right about here," She pointed just below Jenny's temples, "and add a hint of curl for a mature, capable, and sophisticated look."

"Will you help me pick out an outfit too?"

"Definitely. What about the fitted gray slacks with that white-cuffed shirt?"

"I could dress it up with some of my new jewelry."

"Perfect." She winked. "By the time we leave the judge's chambers he won't be able to say no." She hoped that was true.

Jenny smiled. "I guess maybe my stomach feels a little better."

"Well let's go fill it with food before Ms. Faith wakes up." She wrapped her arm around Jenny as they started down the hall.

~~~~

Reagan sat next to Jenny in the small room off the judge's chambers, wearing her black tailored slacks and matching nipped-waist blazer while they waited their turn to speak with Judge Thompson. She slid a glance at her watch again, this time with the pretense of brushing several strands of her loosely curled hair behind her ear. She was certain time had somehow slowed down.

Faith cooed as she sat on Reagan's lap, crinkling the butterfly in her favorite sensory book while Jenny flipped through yet another magazine too fast to actually read any of the articles among the pages.

Huffing, she set the issue of *Time* on the side table and picked up a copy of *Better Homes and Gardens*. "This is takin' *forever*."

Of course she'd been thinking the same thing but smiled wryly anyway. "We've only been here for ten minutes, and we still have a few more to go."

Jenny rolled her eyes. "I just want to get this over with."

The door leading to the courthouse hallway

opened, and much to Regan's dismay, Mrs. Hendley walked in wearing a knee-length green skirt and white blouse, with Pastor McPhee at her side.

"Mommy," Jenny said, sitting up taller in her chair as Chase stood from the last available seat.

"Got yourself all fancied up with makeup I see." Mrs. Hendley's voice tightened with disapproval as she shook her head. "Paintin' yourself up only leads to trouble, and you've already got plenty of that—"

"Jessie," Pastor McPhee interrupted with a hand on Mrs. Hendley's shoulder, "please be comfortable while we wait." He gestured to the chair Chase had vacated as he sent Reagan a courteous nod.

She returned his gesture, adding a small smile as she studied him, wondering what part he played in his family's dirty business, for surely he was a participant. At a minimum, he knew what was going on at Corpus Mining.

Faith cooed, and Reagan turned the page for the baby, helping her brush her hand down the faux red fur of the caterpillar's body. "Soft," she said close to Faith's ear.

"Shirley and me cleared out a nice space for you and your girl last night," Mrs. Hendley spoke up again. "Your sister's lookin' forward to havin' you back."

Jenny set down the magazine with a small snap. "I don't want to go back. I won't be bringin' my girl to your house."

"Keep it cool," Chase muttered as he stood close by in the corner.

The judge's secretary came out of her office. "Judge Thompson is ready to see you."

They stood as the hallway door opened again.

Reagan did a double take when Shane walked in with a duffle bag slung over his shoulder, looking gorgeous in khaki slacks, a white button-down, and a sage-green tie. "Shane," she whispered as her heart pounded with the rush of longing.

"Shane!" Jenny rushed forward and launched herself into his arms. "You're here! I can't believe you're here."

"Hey, kid." He hugged her back as he held Reagan's gaze across the room.

She pulled away, grinning. "What are you doin' here?"

"Did you really think I would miss your big day?" He took her hands, stepping back. "Looking spiffy."

"Reagan helped me."

Their eyes met again. "Hey," he said.

He was here. For weeks she'd yearned for him, and he was standing right there. "Um, hey."

"Sir, who are you?" Judge Thompson's secretary asked.

"Shane Harper, security for the Appalachia Project."

"I thought he was security." She pointed to Chase.

He dug in his back pocket for his wallet, flashing his credentials. "We both are."

"Sir, this is a closed-chamber session. You'll have to wait out here with your coworker."

"Actually," he walked over to the older woman and murmured something.

She nodded. "Okay. Everyone, come on in."

The group, minus Chase, walked into the Judge's chambers.

Shane bumped into Reagan's back in the cramped space. "Sorry."

"That's okay," she said as she looked over her shoulder, breathing him in, still in shock that he'd come back for Jenny's hearing.

"Have a seat, everyone," Judge Thompson said.

Jenny took Faith when she started to fuss and gave her the bottle they had at the ready as she sat in between Shane and Reagan on the couch.

"We've got quite a crowd here this morning," Judge Thompson commented, looking surprisingly solid for a man in his sixties. He put on his glasses and stacked the papers on his desk. "We're here for the Petition of Emancipation for Jenny Hendley."

"Which I'm not akin too no more, sir," Mrs. Hendley said.

"But I'm really wantin' to go, Your Honor," Jenny spoke up.

Judge Thompson looked from Jenny to her mother. "We're all here to determine what's best for this young lady. Jenny, I'd like to hear from you first."

She swallowed, looking at Reagan.

Reagan nodded her encouragement.

"Well, Your Honor, I just turned seventeen, and I've got a daughter of my own." She gestured to Faith in her arms. "I'm wantin' to leave The Gap since there's not much of a future here. I passed my GED with distinction because Reagan and Shane helped me with my studyin'. I want to go to college and become a nurse. I've already been practicin' my skills at the clinic with Reagan." She licked her lips. "I, um, I can make a good livin'. I want to travel with my baby girl and have a nice house and put her in a school that's better than the one I went to."

Judge Thompson nodded. "Thank you, Jenny." He looked at Jenny's mother next. "Mrs. Hendley, your daughter has ambition and dreams for herself and her daughter. I'm hoping you can give me reasons why you've chosen to object to the emancipation."

Mrs. Hendley squirmed in her chair as her cheeks

turned pink. "Well, Sir, I'm thinkin' the doctor there ain't a good influence on Jenny. She's got the devil in her with her quackery and dishonesty. She's been fillin' my girl with high ideas, and Jenny's sinful enough all by herself—goin' and lyin' down with that Staddler heathen."

Judge Thompson folded his hands on the desk. "What opportunities do you plan to provide for Jenny?"

"We've got a fine church about a mile away from the house, which our wonderful Pastor McPhee here runs. If you've got the Lord in your heart you've got all you need."

"What about education?"

"Jenny's got smarts. She can wait until she's of age, then go on to school if that's what she's wantin' to do."

"How will I do that, Mommy?"

"Jenny, I'd like to ask the questions," the judge said.

"Sorry," she murmured.

"Doctor Rosner, you helped Jenny file her petition."

"Yes, Your Honor, with the help of my attorney, Leona MacNamay."

"I've read through the paperwork." He leaned further forward in his seat. "What would an emancipation offer Jenny, in your opinion?"

She crossed her legs and gripped her clammy hands in her lap, well aware of the weight her response would have on Jenny's case. "Your Honor, Jenny and I met by a twist of fate. Jenny's sister, Shirley, sought my help the night Faith was born. Jenny struggled through a difficult labor that quickly turned into an obstetric emergency. During Faith's delivery, she presented with shoulder dystocia, which resulted in Jenny losing a significant amount of blood. She came to stay with Mr. Harper and me at the cabin while she regained her strength—"

"And left," Mrs. Hendley interrupted. "Jenny got her strength up and ran off."

"Yes, she did," Reagan admitted. "Jenny struggled with the overwhelming transition from childhood to parenthood, but being a young mother certainly can't be easy, especially when there's little to no support at home and few resources within the community. Jenny did leave for a while, trusting Mr. Harper and I to care for Faith, which we happily did. But the most important piece is that Jenny came back, determined to learn and help raise her daughter. Jenny is an amazing, warm, intelligent young woman who has taken on motherhood in a most admirable way. I'm very proud of her dedication to Faith and her desire to provide herself and her little girl with a solid future."

Judge Thompson lifted another sheet of paper. "You would take Jenny and Faith with you to New York City?"

"Actually, I'm not certain we would return to New York." She slid a look at Shane. "But wherever I go, I want Jenny and Faith with me."

"You're willing to take on the financial burdens that come along with two juveniles?"

"Absolutely."

"My concern then is employment. If you don't return to your position in New York, what will you do for income?"

"Your Honor, my credentials allow me the freedom to practice anywhere. I'm lucky to work in a lucrative profession and have several sizeable bank accounts that will keep us comfortable until I make a job decision. I would like to settle where we can get Jenny into a good school."

"Has an institution been selected?" The judge looked from Jenny to Reagan.

Her shoulders tightened, deeply afraid her inability to answer would cost them Jenny's freedom from The Gap. "Not yet, but—"

"Your Honor," Shane interrupted, "if I could, I believe I have a solution." He stood, handing over a sheet of paper he pulled from an envelope. "This is a copy of a notarized letter from Grant Cooke, Chief of Staff at Los Angeles General. He's guaranteeing Jenny full-time employment and a full ride to Los Angeles University, where Jenny can take nursing classes."

Jenny pressed her lips together as her eyes grew wide.

The judge scanned the paper.

"Also, Your Honor," Shane said as he presented another paper, "this is a receipt showing Faith's first year of childcare has been paid in full at the top facility in the Pacific Palisades area—close by my residence. Faith would be mere minutes away from my home where she and Jenny would have a room if they want one."

The judge frowned. "Are you seeking guardianship, Mr. Harper?"

"I'm offering Jenny another option. There's no future for her here, but there is in Los Angeles."

"And how would that include Doctor Rosner?"

Reagan held Shane's unreadable stare and cleared her throat, knowing he'd more than likely saved the day. "Um, my main concern is Jenny and Faith's well-being. If Jenny wants to pursue this opportunity I'm confident Mr. Harper and I can work out the details to suit everyone's needs."

"Mrs. Hendley, has this information changed your mind?"

"No, sir. My daughter ain't goin' off to live with some man in sin."

"Your Honor, this is not a romantic gesture in any way," Shane added.

"Jenny, how do you feel?"

"I feel like my dreams are comin' true. I'm gonna have a job. I get to go to school and give Faith what she deserves."

"Your Honor," Pastor McPhee spoke up, "I feel like I must speak up for Jessie, and by doing so for Jenny."

"Okay."

"As a man of God, and as a man who knows Jenny quite well, I'm going to speak from my heart. If I can be frank, Your Honor, I'm concerned Jenny's been led astray by unsavory influences. The Gap certainly isn't a large place, and opportunities are indeed limited, but Jenny's family is there, as is the community who has supported and loved her for all of her seventeen years. In my opinion, I'm seeing a young woman who's lost and under the influence of those who might not have Jenny's best interests in mind. No one loves Jenny more than God Himself and her mother. Jessie has a lot to teach Jenny and Faith in the ways of our Lord, community, and family. College and jobs will be waiting for her in a year from now when she's older and more capable of making sound decisions on her own."

"Thank you, Pastor." The judge looked at the papers again. "My concern now is the trouble at the Black Bear Gap Clinic Mrs. Hendley mentioned in her phone call with my clerk yesterday afternoon."

"Pastor was nice enough to let me use his phone at the church," Mrs. Hendley supplied.

Judge Thompson nodded. "Two cases of vandalism. One involving dead animals and crosses?" He looked at Reagan and Shane.

Reagan swallowed as her heart began to thunder. "Uh—"

"Your Honor," Shane spoke up again. "As a member of The Project's security team, I would like to address that."

"Go ahead," Judge Thompson invited.

"The vandalism issues in question are certainly troubling, but my coworker and I are confident that Doctor Rosner, Jenny, and Faith are safe under our watch. Both Chase and I are well trained as Close Protection Agents, as well as have backgrounds in Federal Law Enforcement. We're working with Doctor Rosner and the director of the program to ease community tensions. Extra measures are also being taken to ensure the safety of our principals.

"It says in my notes here you and Mr. Rider are with Ethan Cooke Security," the judge said, scanning the documents in front of him.

"Yes, Your Honor."

"That name speaks for itself. Thank you, Mr. Harper."

"You're welcome."

Judge Thompson stacked his papers again and Reagan held her breath, afraid that Shane's assurances weren't going to be enough. "After hearing everyone's thoughts, I simply can't come to a decision today."

"But—" Jenny said.

"A parent's rights are strong and binding. Mrs. Hendley has expressed her concerns; however, I'm gravely aware of the lack of opportunities here in the area for young women such as Jenny. Jenny has taken the GED and passed with distinction. Mr. Harper and Doctor Rosner are able and willing to provide both financial and emotional support to Jenny and Faith, as they've done since the birth of Jenny's daughter. At this time I don't believe Jenny is ready for emancipation, but a temporary guardianship is not out of the question until she becomes of age. I would like to review all of the evidence brought forward today with the help of a *Guardian ad Litem*. We'll reconvene in two weeks for a final hearing."

Reagan nodded. "Thank you, Your Honor." She'd wanted Jenny and Faith out of The Gap today, but at least Judge Thompson hadn't said no.

"Your Honor, I'd like Jenny to be comin' on home with me. She can bring the baby," Mrs. Hendley spoke up as she stood.

Jenny rushed to her feet. "No. If I have to go with you, I will, but Faith isn't goin' up to that house. It's cold and dirty and no place for my baby girl."

"She's gotten a little too used to the finer things." Mrs. Hendley shook her head.

"For the time being and considering the current unrest in The Gap, Jenny and Faith will remain in Doctor Rosner's care under the watchful eye of Mr. Harper and Mr. Rider. That will be all for today."

The group filed out into the hall.

"I'll be prayin' for your sinin' soul, Jenny." Mrs. Hendley walked off, with Pastor McPhee following behind.

Jenny stared after her mother.

"Are you okay?" Shane asked her.

Jenny nodded. "Those papers you gave the judge, you really want us comin' to live with you in California?"

"I would love to have you." He took Faith, grinning when the baby smiled at him. "Hey, Faithy. Hi pretty girl." He kissed her forehead and snuggled her close.

"Reagan, can you believe he's back?" Jenny came and wrapped her arm around Reagan's waist.

She gave Jenny a small smile as Shane looked at her yet again, his guarded expression impossible to read, but the tension between them was unmistakable. "This is quite a surprise."

"Are you comin' back to the cabin for dinner?" Jenny asked.

"Absolutely."

"Great." She beamed.

"I'll—I'll settle Faith in back with me." Reagan took Faith, clearing her throat when her arm brushed Shane's solid chest. She walked quickly to the Pajero, strapping Faith in, listening to Shane's familiar voice as he and Jenny approached the vehicle. She glanced his way as she got in the backseat, noting the size of his small duffle bag, wondering how long he planned to stay.

CHAPTER THIRTY-THREE

REAGAN SAT ACROSS FROM SHANE AT THE DINNER TABLE picking at her meal, remembering to smile from time to time while Jenny shared stories about the things Shane had missed during his almost month away. They'd been home for several hours, and she'd done everything in her power to avoid being caught alone, fearful Shane would try to corner her to talk. She wasn't ready for that.

She glanced up, her heart kicking up a notch as she realized he was staring at her. Pressing her lips together, she cleared her throat and looked away as she reached for her water. She'd just gotten used to his chair at the table being empty. *Finally*, she was learning how to live without him, and now he was back—for how long she had no idea, but it would've been better for all of them if he had stayed in California where he belonged.

She met his eyes again and looked toward the hall, craving the quiet of her room. She could smell the aftershave on his skin—the scent that was just now beginning to fade outside his room—and ached to reach out to him.

"I'm gonna get more milk." Jenny pushed back from the table. "Does anyone else want a refill?"

"I'll get it." Reagan stood before Jenny could get up just as Faith started crying in the bedroom. "I'll get Faith instead." She moved down the hall, walking to the crib, smiling down at the sweet baby in the dim light. "Who's awake in here?"

Faith's cries turned to whimpers.

She reached in, picking her up. "Are you lonely, honey?" She snuggled Faith close, kissing her forehead, and frowned when her sleeve grew damp. "Uh oh. You soaked through your diaper." She set the baby on the changing table, peeling off the wet pajama bottoms and took several warm wipes from the dispenser to clean her off. "You need a bath in the morning, but I think this will get us through until then."

Faith fussed.

"I know. You're tired, and this isn't a whole lot of fun." She changed Faith's diaper, found fresh pajama pants, then pulled the soiled sheet from the mattress, bringing the bedding and baby with her down the hall.

"Faithy, what's wrong?" Jenny stood. "She's not gettin' sick again, is she?"

Reagan shook her head, putting the dirty clothes in the washing machine. "She leaked through her diaper. I'm going to get her a little more bottle and put her back to sleep."

"I can do it," Jenny said.

"I've got it." She grabbed four ounces of formula and left again, sitting in the rocking chair, playing with Faith's tiny fingers as the baby closed her eyes.

Moments later, Jenny walked into the room. "Are you plannin' on stayin' in here all night?"

"I love rocking our girl." She smiled. "She's only going to be small for a little while."

"Are you avoidin' Shane?"

Her gaze met Jenny's in the shadows. "No."

"You haven't said much to him."

"You've said plenty."

Jenny grinned. "I guess I have been talkin' his ear off."

"And he's enjoyed every second of it."

"I missed him so much. We're gonna watch a movie. Are you gonna come out?"

"I think I'm probably going to go to bed. I'm tired."

Jenny frowned. "You're tired a lot. Maybe you need vitamins or somethin'."

"I take my vitamins."

"Maybe you need more."

She smiled. "I think I just need a couple good nights of sleep."

Jenny stepped farther into the room, wiping down Faith's mattress, and put on a new sheet. "You and me haven't had much of a chance to talk either. I was wonderin' how you were feelin' about Los Angeles?"

"I feel like I'm excited you have such an amazing opportunity."

"But maybe you don't want to live in California."

She didn't know what she wanted for herself anymore. "I want you settled and happy somewhere safe."

"You don't seem happy. You haven't for a while. Maybe you're seein' how much of a burden it is takin' on me and Faith—"

"I'm not going to let you finish that sentence. Go watch your movie. Be seventeen and don't worry so much for a change."

"Are you sure you won't join us?"

"Maybe next time." She waited for Jenny to head back down the hall before tucking Faith into her crib then went to her room. As she changed her shirt, she glanced at the phone that had yet to ring and the pieces of paper peaking from the small stack of bills she hadn't gotten around to paying, and stepped back out, moving down the hall in the opposite direction of where the movie played in the living room. She opened the side door and walked out, pausing in the faint light streaming from the porch as she looked toward the trees. Being outside spooked her, but she craved the night air.

Climbing the steps, she sat on the swing, staring off into the dark, finding relief in the cool brushes of wind across her cheeks while moonlight shined down from high above.

~~~~

Shane sat on the couch in the dark, staring at but not watching the movie as he thought of the woman doing her best to avoid him down the hall. Reagan hadn't said more than a handful of words to him since he walked into the room outside of the judge's chambers. She'd looked so pretty in her sexy tailored suit—and more than a little surprised when their eyes met among the small sea of people. He hadn't missed the way her mouth whispered his name as she stared at him, clearly stunned.

He rubbed at his jaw, remembering her overly bright smiles at the kitchen table and the way she'd barely touched a bite of the food on her plate. In the four weeks he'd been gone, she'd definitely lost weight.

He looked toward the hallway again, needing to talk to her. They both had things to say to one another, but the timing had yet to be right. She'd spent the afternoon and evening evading him, and he'd patiently waited, biding his time for the perfect moment. Eventually he would catch Reagan alone. His eyes locked on the porch when a noise caught his and Chase's attention. He relaxed when he saw the chains holding the swing in place move slowly back and forth.

Reagan must have snuck out the side door,

assuming he wouldn't notice, but she was about to have company. He stood, walking to the window, peeking out at her slim figure accentuated in her black yoga pants and white t-shirt as she stared off into the dark. Sighing, he opened the door, and her head whipped around. "Hey," he stepped outside, closing the door behind him, noticing her shoulders tensing.

"Hi." She cleared her throat. "I thought you were watching a movie."

He shoved his hands in his pockets, surprised that a month away could leave so much room for awkwardness. "I saw the swing moving through the window."

"Oh."

"Do you mind if I sit down?"

"No. No." She scooted farther over.

He sat, rocking with her in their usual slow rhythm, saddened that none of the typical ease between them was there. He'd been gone, and she had changed. "So the appointment with the judge seemed to go pretty well," he said, attempting to start a conversation. "It got a little dicey when The Gap stuff came up, but I think we smoothed it out."

"I can't take any of the credit. You did all of the smoothing."

He shrugged.

"It was nice of you to work stuff out for Jenny."

"The schooling and job idea came to me during my first flight east. Ethan helped me pull everything together by the time I landed in Lexington this morning."

"Hopefully the judge will see things in Jenny's favor, thanks to you." She sent him a small, uncomfortable smile, and silence filled the air again.

"I didn't want to force you into anything. Los

411

Angeles doesn't have to be set in stone. It just gives Jenny more options."

"She seems pretty excited."

The wind rustled through the trees, the only sound filling the tense quiet. Seconds stretched into unbearable minutes, and he couldn't take it anymore.

"Why didn't you tell me?" he blurted out.

She looked at him, then turned away just as quickly. "I didn't need to. Jenny told you. So did Chase."

"I'm not talking about the Emancipation in general. I'm talking about the rest—Faith's illness, the fact that the court date was almost a no go."

"Faith's mother changed her mind at the last minute, and there was nothing you could do to fix Faith's situation."

"I care about those girls, Reagan. I want to know what's going on in their lives. When I ask the one person I trust most in this world for answers, I expect the truth."

"Faith and Jenny are fine," she tossed back.

"Oh yeah?"

"This is exactly why I didn't say anything." She stood, walking to the other side of the porch. "I'm sorry you felt like you needed to come all the way out here."

"I *wanted* to come out here." He didn't know how to talk to this cool woman.

"Everything's under control." She turned her back to him. "Everything's completely fine." She gripped the railing as her breathing grew ragged.

"Reagan." He gained his feet, aware that she was on the verge of tears. "I want to help you."

"I'm okay. Really," she shuddered out. "I've been handling everything on my own."

"But you don't have to."

She covered her face and started crying.

"Hey."

She moved toward the stairs.

"Hey." He snagged her arm before she could walk away and shut him out again. "Come here." He wrapped his arms around her, holding her tight.

She sagged against him, crying harder.

"Come here," he said again, lifting her, taking her back to the swing, and sat, settling his cheek on top of her head as he ran his hand up and down her back.

She rested her head against his chest, sniffled, but then lost her composure and sobbed some more.

"We're going to figure this out," he murmured, sliding his palm along her arm, realizing her cool skin was covered in goosebumps. He lifted her and brought her inside.

Jenny stood, her face full of concern, but he shook his head, moving down the hall to Reagan's room and closed them in. "Let's lay you down." He awkwardly pulled the covers back and settled her under the warm blankets. Then he crawled next to her, resting his head on the edge of her pillow, staring into her troubled eyes. "What's going on, Reagan?"

"I'm tired. I've felt a little off lately, that's all."

He held her gaze, knowing they had a long way to go to get back to where they'd been before.

"You don't have to stay." She wiped her cheeks. "I just need a little sleep."

"What if I want to stay?"

She tried to pull back her covers.

He settled his hand on her shoulder. "Where are you going?"

"I need water."

"I'll get you some." He went out to the kitchen, and Jenny rushed up to his side as he filled a glass.

"Is Reagan okay?"

413

"Yeah. I think she's a little run down."

"She's been awful tired. She's not eatin' much either."

"We'll get it figured out. I don't want you worrying." He was worked up enough on his own. Perhaps he'd been expecting Reagan to confide in him with a reluctant tear or two like usual, but she'd cried— *really* cried—as Chase had heard her doing last night. "She's going to be fine."

"Now that you're back I think she will be." Jenny shifted uncomfortably. "There's um, there's stuff that's been goin' on—"

"Yeah, I know. Faith was sick."

She darted him a guilty look. "I didn't want you worryin'."

"I wish you and Reagan would let me decide what I get to worry about."

"I'm sorry."

"We'll talk about it tomorrow." He started walking away.

"Shane, I wasn't talkin' about Faith. There's other stuff," she said in a rush, gesturing toward the stairs.

He followed Jenny up to the loft, sitting next to her on the couch. "What's going on?

She sighed out a long breath as she crossed her arms, her discomfort obvious. "There's lot's of rumors spreadin' around about Reagan. Shirley told me people are sayin' she made some mistakes at work in New York and killed some little girl. That's why she came here."

"What?"

She nodded. "They're also saying she had Henry burnt up so no one would find out he didn't have black lung."

He shook his head in confusion. "What the hell does that mean?"

"He was cremated instead of havin' an autopsy the way Reagan wanted, but no one's believin' that. They're real mad."

He jammed a hand through his hair. "Damn it, Jenny, why didn't you tell me?"

She shrugged as her eyes filled. "I got the impression Reagan didn't want anyone knowin'. I think people sayin' stuff about that girl—Mable, I think, her name was—hurt her feelin's real bad. But I wanted you to know because it's wearin' on her. She doin' her best to take care of me and Faith, but I see it. I'm tryin' not to be a burden, but when Mommy said I couldn't go yesterday, I cried and cried, and she just hugged me and told me that everythin' was goin' to be all right and I was hers and she wasn't leavin' here without me."

I've been handling everything on my own. He clenched his jaw with the weight of helplessness, remembering Chase mentioning Reagan slamming down the phone. "Dammit." What else wasn't she telling anyone?

"She kept me strong when Faith was sick. She kept us together like she always does. But I think maybe you and me might need to be strong for her now with all this stuff goin' on at the clinic. I imagine you're probably mad at me, but I did what I thought was right. Now I'm doin' it again by sayin' what needs to be said."

He looked at the teenager, wise beyond her years in so many ways. "I'm not mad." At least not at Jenny, but he was certainly frustrated with the woman who'd shut him out of her life so completely. "Let me go check on her."

"Are you gonna spend the night with her?"

Luckily he'd missed Jenny's nosy questions. "I'm going to sit with her for awhile."

She hugged him. "I'm glad you're home, Shane. I'm

415

glad I might be able to go home with you."

"Me too." He eased away. "Let me get Reagan her water."

"Okay."

He walked down the hall, stopping in Reagan's doorway to find her sleeping. They wouldn't be talking tonight, but he stepped in and shut her door anyway. He'd been waiting for this moment for a month—to stare at her beautiful face, to breathe her in. He set the glass down and lay next to her, running his fingers through her soft hair. Eventually she would wake and he would have to go back to his own room, but he was here to stay. Reagan was going to have to get used to that.

CHAPTER THIRTY-FOUR

REAGAN SIGHED, OPENING HER EYES, REFRESHED AND AT ease for the first time in too long. Yawning, she snuggled in, savoring the warmth of her covers, then frowned, realizing the heat against her back was a body and the arm wrapped around her waist belonged to Shane. She rolled abruptly, and Shane's eyes flew open. "What are you doing in here?"

"Apparently not sleeping anymore."

She snagged his wrist, pulling his arm off of her stomach, and sat up. "You shouldn't've slept in here in the first place."

He scrubbed his hands over his face. "It's not a big deal."

He made her *want* and confused her just as much, which was a damn big deal. "Then I'm sure we can both rest assured that this won't be happening again." She tucked her hair behind her ears, still flustered. "How long are you staying, anyway?"

He shrugged. "I guess that remains to be seen."

"What does that mean exactly?"

"It means when things are settled around here, I'll go home."

She wanted a timeframe, an exact day when she would have to watch him walk away again. Just because he was here now didn't mean he wouldn't be gone later today or tomorrow. Sighing, she closed her eyes and pulled her legs up to her chest, resting her forehead on her knees.

He sat up next to her. "I thought you would be happy to see me."

"I don't know what I am," she admitted, her voice muffled as she stayed tucked in a ball.

"I missed you."

She shook her head, not wanting to hear his declarations. "Please don't."

"Don't what?"

She pulled back the covers and stood, briefly taking in Shane's magnificent naked chest and sexy face, with his hair a mess and a day's worth of scruff. "Go back there."

"Where?"

"To a month ago when everything was different." She tugged on a sweatshirt in defense against the chill in the room. "Let's just leave things exactly the way we left them."

"Which was?"

"We were friends who happened to share a few good nights in bed."

"Reagan—"

She held up a halting hand. "I don't want to hear about connections and intimacy. I really don't."

He freed himself from the covers and got to his feet. "We had both."

She shook her head adamantly, thinking of the woman calling Shane's name when they'd spoken on the phone. "No. What you had was a convenient scratching post for the last few days you were here." She pulled her hair back in an aggressive ponytail.

He stared at her with such blatant shock in his eyes that she had to turn away. "What the hell, Reagan? What's your problem?"

"I don't have a problem. You left. You moved on with your life. I'm trying to deal with mine." She took socks from her drawer and stuffed her feet into soft cotton.

"I'm not going to let you sit here and blow off what we had—have."

"*Had.* If there was anything there at all." She reached for her sneaker, and he yanked it away.

"Damn it. What's this about?"

"Our different perceptions of 'buddies.'"

He frowned, shaking his head. "Buddies?"

"Oh, just get out." She pushed him back, walking him toward the door.

He stopped dead.

She crashed into him, and he grabbed hold of her wrists.

"I'm not going anywhere until you tell me what you're talking about."

"It doesn't *matter.*" Why wouldn't he let this go? Didn't he realize this was pointless?

"The last time we spoke I was out with—is this about Amber?"

She tried to pull free of his hold. "It's not about anything at all."

"Amber's my friend."

She lifted her brows.

"Okay, for the sake of full disclosure, maybe we kissed once, and maybe we were going to try for a real date, but that's not what I want."

His confession was a stab to her heart. "Because you came back here?"

"No, because I don't want Amber. I want you."

She refused to believe it. "You know what, Shane? I think you should go home and go for it with your 'buddy.'" She yanked away from him. "Like I said before, we had sex. Since we're being so honest, I won't deny that maybe there was something there, but I'll get over it. Kind of like you did. Now go away." She turned from him, blinking rapidly as her lips trembled.

"I'm not going anywhere." He stepped around, facing her. "I kissed Amber and thought about you the whole time."

"Stop. *God.* Is that supposed to help?" she laughed humorlessly, shaking her head. "You're making this worse. Let's just put a pause on the whole honesty thing and move on."

"Dammit." He yanked her against him. "What I'm trying to say is I don't want to kiss her again. She didn't taste like you or smell like you or make that little noise in her throat that drives me fucking *crazy*." He stepped back, smacking into the desk.

Reagan winced as the small stack of bills and slim white slips fell to the floor.

He bent down, frowning as he picked one up, then another and another. "What is this?"

"Nothing." She moved to snatch them away.

He lifted his arm above her reach, holding her gaze. "What are these, Reagan?"

Sighing, she stared down at the floor.

"Reagan." He cupped her face in his hands, the way he used to, forcing her to look at him.

Swallowing, she closed her eyes, gathering what little defense she had left against him.

"*Talk* to me." He stroked her cheeks with his thumbs as his voice gentled. "Please. What's going on?"

"I think those are pieces of Doctor Schlibenburg's article."

He stepped away, rubbing at the back of his neck. "When were you planning on mentioning it?"

"I wasn't. I don't have the full article yet, so there's no point. The strips just started showing up in the mail."

"When?"

"The day after you left."

His nostrils flared as he clenched his jaw. "Chase should've known about this."

"I disagree." She crouched down, picking up the rest of the mess.

"Reagan, we can't help you without open communication."

She scoffed as she gained her feet. "You can't help me anyway."

"Our job—"

"Is to report issues to your boss, who then reports them to mine. I tried to make a difference in this community, but no one's interested. Doctor Schlibenburg's notes and black lung are the least of my worries right now. My only goal has been buying Jenny and Faith as much time as possible. Next week you and Chase leave, but the girls and I don't. If keeping my mouth shut kept one of you here in The Gap to ensure their safety, that was all that mattered."

"Reagan, I'm not leaving you here."

She couldn't allow herself to believe him. "Until Ethan calls you back to California?"

"Not even then."

She shook her head.

"I'm here until this is over."

"Okay," she relented, ready to drop the entire subject.

"I want you to let me back in." He took her hand, pressing her palm to his cheek. "I want you to tell me about your troubles the way you used to not all that long ago."

She swallowed. "Things aren't the way they used to be. I don't want to depend on you the way I did before. I've been handling everything just fine on my own."

"Reagan—"

"We should talk about this later. Now that you're here I want to get Jenny back into the clinic so she can practice." She opened her door and walked down the hall, ready for a quick breakfast and to get out of here.

~~~~

"Damn it." He jammed his hands through his hair as Reagan left him staring after her. What the hell had happened between them? He'd only been gone four weeks, but it might as well have been a year. He'd expected the initial awkwardness of yesterday while they reacclimated to living under the same roof again, but after she broke down in his arms last night, he foolishly thought they would wake up, talk everything through, and pick up where they left off—or close to it.

Clearly Reagan rebuilt the defenses it had taken him weeks to knock down. She didn't trust that he had any real intentions of sticking around, nor did she believe he thought the connection they'd shared had been anything special. And bringing up Amber had only made it worse.

Shaking his head, he pounded the side of his fist against the top of the desk. "You're a fucking idiot, Harper." He didn't *want* Amber. He didn't love his former co-worker. But the woman who'd just told him to go to hell... He wanted and loved her desperately. Now he just needed the opportunity to show her.

He snagged his shirt from the corner of the bed, tempted to follow her down the hall and demand they straighten this whole thing out, but that would do more harm than good. Reagan was going to need time. He pulled the covers back on her bed, reminding himself that they started off on rocky ground when they first met and they'd been fine—more than fine.

Eventually she would realize he meant what he said. Sooner or later she would confide in him and tell him about the little girl in New York and Henry. She could shrug off what they had all she wanted, but deep down he knew as well as she did that they were far from finished. If worse came to worse, he would wear her down the way he had before, but first he needed to talk to Chase about Doctor Schlibenburg's mysterious article and figure out what they planned to do next.

CHAPTER THIRTY-FIVE

REAGAN SPREAD DIJON MUSTARD ON ANOTHER PIECE OF RYE bread and set it on top of several thin slices of deli-cut ham, completing her sandwich. She grabbed a peach from the fruit bowl and made her way to the table as she looked toward the loft, listening to the quiet back and forth of Shane and Chase's deep voices.

They'd gone upstairs minutes after she and Jenny came home from their lesson at the clinic. Shane had handed off a sleepy baby to her mom, and he and his pal had disappeared. She glanced at her watch, fairly certain she had enough time to finish her lunch and be gone before Shane came downstairs...not that she was still purposely avoiding him like last night. Or maybe she was.

She huffed out a long breath, the admission to herself slightly lowering, but she needed time. If spending her days and nights hiding from Shane gave her the opportunity to gain a little perspective over her ever-changing situation, then she would do what needed to be done.

Yesterday he'd walked through the courthouse doors and turned her world upside down, again. This morning he'd shaken her up even further with his promises to stay and his declarations that she was the only one he wanted—promises and declarations she couldn't let herself believe. Shane left. For a month they'd gone their separate ways, and he found someone else. He assured her he didn't want Amber, but he didn't get to just come and go. He didn't get to kiss other women and decide which one suited him best. As far as she was concerned, she and Shane were through. Now if she could only convince her heart to be as practical as her brain.

She looked to the loft again, snagging her bottom lip between her teeth when he laughed. She'd *missed* that sound; she'd missed everything about him. Never had she met a man who felt so right for her, but he wasn't.

Determined to move on and do what was best for herself and her girls, she took a huge bite of her sandwich, with every intention of gaining back the few pounds she'd lost. Over the past weeks she'd let herself fall apart. The stress had gotten to be too much, but from this moment forward she was taking charge. She didn't need Super Shane to swoop in and come to her rescue. She took care of herself—she always had. And that wasn't about to change now. Pheromones and chemicals. That's what she and Shane had had between, and now it was finished.

She picked up the short reflective essay Jenny had written, something Reagan required after any practical experience in the clinic and began to read, getting lost in the thoughts of an exceptionally bright seventeen-year-old who'd had her first opportunity to practice needle sticks on an orange.

...performing a venipuncture on the orange was scary and exciting all at the same time. Although I had an amazing opportunity to try something new, I think I'm glad I'll be practicing on fruit for a long time to come.

Reagan chuckled as she polished off the remainder

of her sandwich. She read the last couple of sentences again, grinning and shaking her head, and took a bite of her peach.

"It's nice to see a smile on your face." Shane walked over from the last step, resting his butt against the edge of the table, and crossed his arms at his chest.

Her smile vanished, and she cursed herself for losing track of time as she stared into gorgeous green eyes. Ignoring the uptick to her pulse and quick rush of tingles in her stomach, she stood, taking her plate to the sink.

He followed her. "How did Jenny's lesson go?"

"Fine." She turned, clearing her throat and tucking her hair behind her ear, realizing he was standing too close.

"She said something about an orange."

"Yeah." She licked her lips, backing up into the counter. "She practiced a venipuncture today—a blood draw."

He winced. "Thank God I didn't have to be your reluctant patient this time."

She smiled sadly, remembering a time when things had been different between them.

He shoved his hands in his pockets and rocked back on his heels. "What did you have for lunch?"

"Oh, um, a ham sandwich and a peach."

He nodded. "I like seeing you eating. It looks like you lost some weight."

"Just a pound or two." She tossed her napkin in the trash. "I actually need to finish—"

He took her hand, still holding the piece of fruit, pulling them toe-to-toe.

"Shane." She pressed her palm to his shirt.

"I'm hoping one of these times when we make eye contact you won't look at me like I'm public enemy number one." He lifted her hand, biting into the peach, catching the drips of juice with one, two, three open-mouthed suckles along the sensitive skin of her wrist before the drops could roll further down her forearm. "Sweet."

"Shane," she shuddered out, her resolve to keep her distance crumbling.

"I want your eyes to light up when you smile at me. I want you to trust me."

"I do trust you. I'm counting on you and Chase to keep the girls safe."

He shook his head. "You know that's not what I mean." Someone knocked on the front door. "Stay here." He walked to the door, opening it slightly. "Can I help you?"

"Good afternoon, I'm Detective Reedy—"

"Detective." Reagan tossed the remains of the peach in the trash and rushed to Shane's side. "Please come in."

Shane opened the door wider.

"Thank you," the man said, his voice nasally.

"Detective, this is Shane Harper. He's part of The Appalachia Project's security."

"I'd shake your hand, but I think I'm well on my way to a cold." He sneezed into his elbow.

"Can I get you something to eat or drink?" Reagan offered. "Maybe some tea?"

"No, thank you." He sneezed for the second time. "Doctor Rosner, I came by to ask for your help again."

"Sure. Please come have a seat."

Detective Reedy started coughing.

"You know what? I'm going to get you a glass of water anyway. Staying hydrated is one of the keys to fighting a cold. Give me just a minute." She walked to the kitchen with Shane following behind.

"Is this the guy who was here before?"

She nodded as she filled a glass.

"Did you mention anything to him about your mail?"

"No." She looked at him as she shut off the faucet, studying his kind eyes and tough, sexy build in jeans and a casual long-sleeved tee, wishing desperately everything was the way it used to be. "And I'm not planning on it at this time."

"Doc, you're withholding potential evidence."

"I know." And she hated it but her situation had yet to change. The girls' futures were still in question at this point whether Shane was here for the moment or not, and so far everyone associated with the mine was corrupt. What if she handed off Doctor Schlibenburg's strips of paper and they "mysteriously" disappeared? And wouldn't the police start intercepting her incoming mail? She needed to wait until she had the whole article. Doctor Schlibenburg had had something to say. He'd died for whatever it was.

"I think—"

"How do I know you're not leaving?" she blurted out, still unconvinced by his earlier assurances that he was here until the end.

He blinked. "What?"

"How do I know you're not going to leave me and the girls here in The Gap the next time your phone rings?"

"Because I said I won't. I'm not going anywhere."

She held his gaze.

"I never should've left in the first place. I'm not going anywhere," he repeated as he took her hand. "I'm not."

She nodded, trying to pull away.

He held her hand tighter. "I might've made a

couple of mistakes over the last few weeks, but I've never given you a reason not to trust what I say."

He was right. They had their personal problems, but he was still a good man. No matter what happened between them he still loved Jenny and Faith. "No, you haven't." She pulled free of him and walked out to their guest. "Here you go, Detective."

"Thank you." He sipped the water, clearing his throat.

She sat on the couch with Shane taking the cushion at her side. "What can I do for you, Detective?"

"Doctor Rosner, I went back to Doctor Schlibenburg's home after we spoke on the phone, and I just can't seem to find the x-rays you left behind. Doctor Schlibenburg's house is spotless, so I'm surprised I can't locate them." The detective set a schematic on the coffee table. "This is the layout of Doctor Schlibenburg's first floor."

Reagan studied the various rooms, recognizing a couple of them.

"I'm wondering if you could go back through your visit with him again."

"Sure. Doctor Schlibenburg met me outside here." She pointed to the circular drive. "We went in through the front door and immediately to his living room after he secured the three locks. I sat on this couch and the doctor here by the lamp where he held the films up to the light. He gave me his opinion on each film as I handed them over."

"And you said he concurred with your diagnosis of—" He flipped through his notes, "progressive massive fibrosis."

"Yes. He concluded that all of the patients had varying degrees of the disease." She gave her attention back to the diagram. "The clock right here on the mantle signaled that my hour was up, and that's when he shoved me out the door."

"You said you asked him about an article and he got upset."

"Yes." She looked at Shane. "I was still sitting on the couch when I pushed him a bit about helping me further. That's when I asked him if I could have a copy of his work, and he got upset. I gathered my things, leaving the x-rays in the box right here on the coffee table. He dragged me toward the front entrance." She traced the path she'd taken with her finger.

"And you left the box there?"

She nodded. "I'm positive. I have a box just like it in the clinic if you want to see what I'm referencing."

"That would be great."

She stood, grabbing the sweater she'd worn back from the clinic off the couch, and she, Shane, and the detective made their way down the path to the office.

"I see you've had more trouble since the last time I was here."

"Yes. The Gap is eager for my departure."

"And why would that be?"

"Black lung isn't a popular diagnosis. It's even more reprehensible when specialists disagree with your findings and patient's jobs and retirement are put in jeopardy."

"Sounds like a volatile situation."

"It's certainly controversial." She unlocked the door and they went inside. "So, there are different types of film," she said as she walked toward the small area she used for x-ray. "But I chose the green tinge for finer detail. The images you're looking for are on this." She pulled a square of film free and held it up. "I brought them in a box just like this. I wrote Black Bear Gap right here along the top."

"Would it be possible for me to take one of these?"

"Sure." She handed it over.

"This has been very helpful."

"Good."

"I'm hoping this might help us make some progress with the doctor's case—maybe explore some new angles and generate some new leads."

"I hope so."

"His daughter calls every day hoping for answers, but we've hit a dead end, if I'm being honest."

She struggled with a wave of guilt, knowing she hadn't been completely straight with the detective since the beginning. Poor Effie Schlibenburg had to be beside herself. Pressing her lips together, she met Shane's eyes. "Um, Detective, if I could just have a minute with Shane."

"Certainly."

She gestured with her head for Shane to step over to the corner with her.

Shane followed, crossing his arms as he stood in front of her. "What's up?"

"You're staying here in The Gap?" she asked him yet again.

His brow furrowed slightly. "I'm staying right here with you and the girls."

"You're absolutely sure?"

"Yes, Reagan."

"You're sure because I—"

"I'm not going anywhere." He took her hand and gave a gentle squeeze. "I'll say it as many times as I have to until you believe me."

As he held her hand in his and she stared into his eyes, she did. Sighing, she nodded and stepped back to where the detective waited. "Detective, if you have another minute, I've thought of something I should bring to your attention."

"Okay."

She was taking a risk here. She couldn't give the detective the strips of paper, but she could give him something now that she was absolutely certain Shane would stay. She was trusting her instincts that this was the right decision. "I'm not certain, but on my drive home from Doctor Schlibenburg's, I think I might've been followed."

"*What*?" Shane said as Detective Reedy said, "Oh?"

"I, um, I never mentioned it, because as I said I'm not one hundred percent sure."

"Why don't you tell me about it anyway?" He grabbed his small notebook from his back pocket. "Sometimes the smallest of details leads to the break we're looking for."

She hoped he was right. "Sure." She narrowed her eyes, struggling to recall the vehicle that had been traveling behind her. "I know it was black."

The detective wrote in his notepad.

"Make or model?"

She shook her head. "I don't know. I remember it being a mid-sized car and in good condition. It might've been a Ford."

"Was the driver male or female?"

She thought of the man with the leather jacket. "Male."

Detective Reedy paused with his pen against paper. "You sound fairly definitive."

She nodded. "I've wondered if the driver might have been the man I saw at the mall and again at the hotel the girls and I stayed at in Lexington a few weeks ago."

"Jesus, Reagan. Are you *kidding* me?" Shane said as he jammed his hands in his pockets.

"A man followed you in Lexington?" Detective Reedy asked. "Can you describe him?"

She looked at the detective, avoiding Shane's scathing stare. "Mmm, mid-forties. Tall. Thin build. Brown hair." She frowned. "Maybe hazel eyes and a brown leather jacket. I haven't seen him since, so it is possible the car and the man are just random coincidences."

"I wish you would have spoken up sooner, Doctor Rosner."

"No kidding," Shane muttered.

"I'm afraid the situation here in The Gap has forced me to think of two girl's safety above everything else."

"The police are here to help, Doctor Rosner."

Keeping her mouth closed had seemed the safer of the two options. "Yes," she said, looking through the open door toward the trees, certain someone watched.

"If you remember anything else, please let me know right away."

"I will."

They stepped back outside just as Jenny opened the cabin door with Faith crying in her arms. "Reagan, when you have a minute I need you."

"Go ahead, Doctor Rosner."

"Thank you." She met Shane's hard stare and turned toward the house. Shane didn't have to like the choices she'd made; he just had to live with them.

~~~~

Shane waited for the door to close behind Reagan and looked at the detective as the man pulled a tissue from his pocket and wiped his nose. "Why are you so interested in the x-rays?"

"I'm trying to piece together the victim's last day."

"You've got a dead doctor on your hands who hadn't practiced medicine in over five years, and you're worrying about some other physician's films? That doesn't make much sense unless you think those x-rays have something to do with his death."

The detective didn't respond.

"You can be straight with me, Detective, or I'll go around you."

The detective's eyes sharpened on his. "And why would you want to do that?"

"Because of that." He pointed to the trashed clinic. "And because ever since Reagan started diagnosing black lung things have gone to hell around here."

"Mr. Harper, this is an official investigation."

"And the people in that house are my family. I'm not a fucking rent-a-cop. I was a US Marshall for six years. I know how the game works, so you can tell me what you have, or I'll go back inside, make a few calls, and find out in less than twenty minutes."

Detective Reedy held his gaze. "I've wondered if Doctor Rosner's sudden interest in black lung had something to do with Schlibenburg's death. The man lived off the grid for more than five years with little trouble—or so we believe. After speaking with several of his former colleagues I find it funny that a once warm, kind man with a large social circle moved out to the middle of nowhere, lived with a dozen locks on his doors and just as many motion sensors on his windows, and was more or less a recluse. Something tipped the scales for his unexpected retirement. Something tipped them further, and now he's dead."

"And you think that was Reagan."

"I can't find the films or any evidence of that paper Doctor Rosner has made mention of. I've checked safety deposit boxes and his home safe. There were thousands of dollars but no papers." He shook his head. "Maybe it doesn't exist."

Shane said nothing of the dozen or so strips of paper in Reagan's room. He and Doc were going to have a long conversation about just what in the hell was going on around here.

"At this point, I know Doctor Rosner made contact, apparently was more than likely followed home, and Schlibenburg was found dead a few hours later."

"How'd they do him?"

"The medical examiner says the shove down the stairs should've finished him, but when that didn't appear to take care of it the large statue dropped on his head did."

"So why isn't Reagan a suspect? For all intents and purpose, she was the last person to see him alive."

"The statue weighed more than seventy-five pounds and was in another room. Doctor Rosner appears to be in shape, but I find it hard to believe she picked up a marble figurine, lifted it six feet in the air, and let it fall."

He winced. "Jesus."

"It was gruesome. One of the worst scenes I've worked."

"I want to be kept informed. My partner and I need to know what's going on." Reagan sure as hell wasn't keeping them in the loop.

The detective nodded. "I'll keep in touch."

"I appreciate it." He started toward the house, scanning the woods as he stepped inside and walked down the hall where Jenny and Reagan sat on Jenny's bed while Faith lay on the covers, diaperless and crying.

"It looks like a little bit of a rash. We'll put this cream on her bottom and see how she looks at her next changing."

The clinic line rang in Reagan's room.

"I'll be right back." She moved into her bedroom.

"What's wrong with Faith?" Shane asked Jenny from the door.

"She's got a diaper rash. It's okay, baby girl," Jenny soothed as she spread white goop all over Faith's butt.

"Oh." He kept going, stopping in Reagan's doorway.

"Leave me *alone*." She slammed down the phone.

He stepped inside. "Who was that?"

"Wrong number."

He steamed out a breath through his nose, hating that she wouldn't talk to him. "Cut the shit, Reagan. I need to know what's going on around here—all of it." He closed her door. "This is the second time I've heard about these mystery calls."

She frowned. "Second time?"

"Chase heard you tell someone to leave you alone the other night, and now I have."

She licked her lips. "Someone's harassing me."

He leaned against the wall, trying his best to keep his calm. "What do they say?"

She pressed her lips together. "It started out as hang ups, then the classic heavy breathing, then it turned into 'go away, you're not wanted here' or sentiments along those lines." She gripped her hands together, her knuckles turning white.

"What else?"

She started pacing.

He stood straight again, growing more frustrated with the woman who continued to evade him. "What else, Reagan?"

"They threatened my life."

"Goddamn. Why the hell didn't you say something? You're getting death threats—"

"Lower your voice," she demanded, pointing to Jenny's bedroom wall.

"Fine," he hissed. "You didn't think death threats were worth a mention?" He clenched his jaw, shaking his head. "Damn, Reagan, I thought you were supposed to be a genius."

"Don't insult my intelligence," she spat back in a nasty whisper. "I've done what I've done for the girls."

"For the girls?" He moved closer to her, fighting the urge to shout. "You can't help them or take them anywhere if you're *dead*."

She stared him down, glaring. "It's not that simple. It's not black and white."

"So explain it."

She advanced, and they stood almost toe-to-toe. "There's a lot going on—"

"Yeah, you're racking up quite a list."

"What's that supposed to mean?" she tossed back.

"Sick babies, mysterious letters, being followed, hang-up calls, death threats, cremated patients, and a dead girl in New York." He saw the flash of hurt in her eyes, but his anger fueled him on. "Did I miss anything, or does that cover everything you're handling on your own?"

"Wow." She whirled away. "You're really something," she said turning back to face him. "You leave for a month and walk back in here expecting everything to be the way you left it. Well it's not. Not even close."

"Chase has been right down the hall. If you didn't want to tell him you could've picked up the phone."

"So could *you*! So could you, Shane," she lowered her voice again.

"I did. I called you, and you lied."

"What did you want me to say?"

437

"The truth, goddammit. I wanted the truth."

"You want everything? You want it all? Fine. I missed you and needed you, but you weren't here. Faith was sick, and I was scared to death." Her breathing grew unsteady. "Black lung and the mysterious letters are the reason Doctor Schlibenburg is dead. Someone murdered him because he was unfortunate enough to answer my call. I probably am being followed, which is why I'm a damn prisoner in this house. I don't go out without Chase. If I head over to the clinic, I make sure I'm home before nightfall. The hang-up calls terrify me. The knocks against my windows at night make me *sick*. Henry was cremated to cover up one hell of a conspiracy, which appears to get bigger by the day. Corpus Mining—they're dirty. They're one of the key players in this whole thing. I don't have anything definitive to prove it other than the insanely horrible safety records I have saved on my computer, but I *know*. Terry threatened to take Faith and make things hard for Jenny if I don't watch my step. The director's been breathing down my neck since the moment you left, making it nearly impossible for me to say anything about any of this or risk losing the girls' protection. And Mable Totton's dead because I made mistakes. A seven-year-old child died because I was careless. Is that what you wanted? Do you feel better now that you've got all the facts straight?" Her lips trembled as tears poured down her cheeks.

He didn't. He didn't feel better at all. "Reagan, I'm sorry."

"Does it really matter? Does it change anything? God." She turned away, pressing her hand to her forehead.

"I'm sorry." He turned her back to face him. "I had no idea you were dealing with all of this."

She shrugged. "How could you if I didn't say anything?"

He pulled her against him, wrapping her arms around him, and she stayed, holding on just as tight, then just as quickly pushed away. "We're not doing this. I'm not doing this with you anymore."

"Reagan—"

"*No.*"

They had a mess to clean up, but safety had to come first. "From now on I answer the clinic line."

"For the most part the calls come at night unless I'm in the office—and then of course just right now."

"So I'll stay in here."

She shook her head. "Absolutely not."

"You're welcome to sleep in my room, but I'm answering that damn phone, and I'll be intercepting any future knocks on your windows and dealing with Terry if there are any further issues. I'm going to talk to Chase, and we're going to talk to Ethan."

She huffed out a breath.

"Ethan's not the villain here, Reagan. He has obligations as well. He understands that I'm staying one way or the other. Furthermore, he can help us, so if there's anything you've left out I want it now, because I'm going to have him get started on this right away."

"The McPhee family has more companies. Corpus Mining isn't their only family-run operation. I don't even know what else they do. I haven't had a chance to look into it, but Doctor Schlibenburg made reference." She walked to the small stack of white slips. "Here." She handed over one and he read.

...Corpus Mining, among the other companies under the McPhee family umbrella.

"And I think the doctor that used to work for the mine—I think whoever killed Doctor Schlibenburg killed him too."

This just kept getting better and better. "I'll take care of it. From this point forward, you don't go to the clinic without Chase or me."

"I—"

"I'm not arguing about this. These are the security measures we're taking until we can get the hell out of here."

She sat down at her desk, pressing her fingers to her temple.

He crouched down in front of her. "I wish I had known. I'm sorry I left when you needed me most."

Her eyes softened. "It's over now."

"No it's not." He took her hands, well aware they were talking about two different things, but he wasn't going to let this go. "It's far from it."

"Shane, I can't—"

He'd be damned if she was going to walk away. "Have dinner with me," he said abruptly as an idea started taking shape. "Go out on a date with me."

She laughed incredulously. "Shane, did you *hear* what I just said? All of the problems I just listed off to you?"

"I heard you and we're going to take care of them. I'm going to talk to Ethan and Chase in a minute and we're going to figure it out, but nothing's getting solved tonight."

She shook her head. "I think we both know this isn't a good idea."

"I think it's a great idea."

"What we had has come and gone."

He shook his head. "I don't believe that. I'm not so sure you do either."

"I have to; besides, we can't leave Chase and the girls."

"So have dinner with me right here—just dinner, Reagan. We need to talk."

She nibbled her lip. "I don't know."

"I'll take care of everything."

"Shane—"

"Meet me at the table at seven." He brought her hands up to his mouth, pressing her knuckles to his lips. "We're not finished, Reagan." He kissed her knuckles again, holding his breath, waiting for her to refuse.

She sighed. "What would I wear?"

"Maybe a dress." He smiled. "We'll have fun."

"Fine. One dinner."

"You won't be sorry." He kissed her knuckles again and stood. "I have some work to do. I'll see you at seven." He left her room, looking at his watch, wanting to hand off the white slips to Ethan and Chase for one night. Tomorrow he would focus on murder and conspiracies, but for now he had less than four hours to pull together the most important evening of his life.

~~~~

"The detective was back again. He left with a box like the one I got rid of."

He sighed in his ear. "It's time to finish this."

"There are two now—two guards."

"You'll have to work around them. I want this handled."

"Consider it done."

CHAPTER THIRTY-SIX

REAGAN SAT IN FRONT OF THE MIRROR IN JENNY'S ROOM, applying a layer of clear gloss to her lips, still trying to figure out what in the world she was doing. Hadn't she told herself only hours ago that she was finished with Shane? He'd been back little more than a day, and her resolve had already crumbled. She'd cried in his arms last night, and today she'd confessed everything in a moment of anger, telling him all of the secrets she'd planned to keep to herself for a while longer. *Then* she'd agreed to a date on top of that. What was it about that man that made it impossible to walk away? But it was just one dinner, she reminded herself. They would eat, talk a little, and then it would be over.

"I wish I had hair like yours. It's so soft and pretty," Jenny said as she set the last curl in Reagan's mass of hair.

"What are you talking about?" She smiled, meeting Jenny's eyes in the mirror. "Your hair's beautiful. It's so shiny and healthy and the perfect shade of blond."

"It's that fancy shampoo and conditioner I got in my birthday box." She set down the curling iron and brushed her fingers through the coils of brown.

"Well, whatever it is, your hair is amazing, and so is your skin—it's flawless. You'll be the perfect California chick before we know it."

"California chick." Jenny grinned. "I thought I was gonna be stuck here my whole life, but we're really gonna be California chicks, huh? Or someday at least."

As much as she was still leery about a move so close to Shane, she was sure taking the girls to Los Angeles was the right thing to do. Jenny had opportunities waiting for her there. Reagan refused to allow her issues with the man down the hall to be an obstacle in Jenny's way. "Absolutely. Hopefully in a couple of weeks."

"If that Guardian person says you and Shane are what's best for me and Faithy. I mean, of course you are. You two changed me and my baby girl's life."

"The judge just wants to be sure." She slid a pair of Jenny's new silver dangle earrings in place, the perfect complement to the bracelet she wore.

"Do you think Shane will introduce us to Abigail Quinn and Sophie McCabe?"

"I'm pretty sure most of Shane's co-workers get together at Ethan's house fairly often—or at least that's what Shane says—so I imagine yes. They're supposedly family parties."

"Family." She grinned again. "I love that we're a family. She crouched down, resting her chin on Reagan's shoulder.

"Me too." She tilted her head, touching her cheek to Jenny's.

"Sometimes I think about what a miracle it is that you and Shane came to The Gap. I'm pretty lucky, ya know? First you two save my life and Faith's with it, then you saved us again by givin' us a chance. It's not every day a girl finds the perfect mom and dad, but I sure did."

Reagan's eyes filled and she blinked, completely touched by Jenny's words. "I think we all got pretty lucky, sweetie."

Jenny smiled at her in the mirror and gasped as her eyes wandered to the alarm clock on the bedside table.

"It's six fifty-five. You've gotta *go*."

Reagan grinned. "I hear traffic's pretty bad between here and the dining room."

Jenny laughed.

She stood, examining her pretty yet simple navy blue cinched-waist dress with beaded spaghetti straps in the reflection. "Do you think this is too much?"

"No way. You look amazin'." Jenny smoothed a couple of the curls at Reagan's back. "Your first date."

"An unusual first date."

"I think it's gonna be special."

She applied gloss once more and rubbed her lips together. "It's definitely a sweet gesture."

"Are you still mad at him?"

She turned, facing Jenny. "Why would you think I'm mad?"

"I wasn't bein' nosy, but this mornin'...the walls are pretty thin around here, and I heard you fightin'." She smiled sheepishly.

"I'm not mad at Shane. I think 'unsure' is a better descriptor."

"I believe him, Reagan. He doesn't want that Amber woman. He wants you." She took Reagan's hand. "Are you mad at me for tellin' him about Henry and that little girl?"

Clearly she and Shane shouldn't have wasted their time trying to argue in whispers this afternoon. "You have good ears." She smiled when Jenny blushed. "No, I'm not mad."

"I've been worryin' about you, and I know he can help."

"I'm not mad, Jenny," she reassured again. "I'm sorry I put you in a position where you felt like you had to keep secrets."

"You never asked me to keep secrets. I sorta got the

sense you wanted your privacy—especially about Mable."

"It's really complicated. Nothing here in The Gap seems to be simple."

"I just want you to be okay—and happy, especially with Shane."

"Sometimes I think I'd be happiest if Shane and I could just stay friends. It's easier."

Jenny frowned. "I don't know, Reagan. I don't think you and Shane have ever been just friends—at least not since I've been around."

"We've always been friends."

Jenny shook her head. "Friends don't look at each other the way you two do, with all that electricity snappin' between you." She sighed. "Someday I'm gonna have that, and if the guy's hot like Shane that would be okay too."

She laughed, wrapping Jenny in a hug. "I love you."

"I love you too."

She kissed Jenny's cheek as she eased back. "Thanks for helping me get ready and for giving up the living room for us tonight. You and Chase are good sports."

Jenny shrugged. "Chase is probably on the phone in his room speakin' Farsi or whatever, and Shane's lettin' me use his laptop. I'm gonna watch somethin' on Netflix while Faithy gets her rest."

She looked toward the crib where the baby slept soundly. "Have fun."

"Thanks. You too."

She opened the door. "Here I go."

"Maybe kissin' him wouldn't hurt. Like you guys did at the airport," Jenny added.

She grinned. "I'll take it under consideration." She closed the door behind her and walked down the hall, feeling slightly silly for wearing heels and a dress to eat at the dining room table, but the amazing homey smells wafting her way made her mouth water. She stopped in the doorway, staring at Shane dressed in black slacks and a white button-down as he lit the last of the candles scattered around the room, casting the space in romantic, muted light. She took in the pretty place settings and the vase full of twigs decorated with berries and wine glasses filled with ice water while music played. "This is beautiful."

He turned, smiling, and her heart melted. "You're beautiful."

She stepped further into the room. "This looks amazing, Shane."

"I wanted to give you something special. This is the best I can do in the middle of nowhere."

"It's perfect." She walked up to him, pressing a kiss to his cheek, touched by all of the work he'd put into the evening. "Thank you."

"You're welcome." He glanced at his watch and looked around. "Uh, we don't exactly have a commute to the restaurant."

She smiled. "No we don't."

He scrubbed at his freshly shaven jaw. "I kind of didn't plan anything out for this part of the date."

Her smile turned into a grin. He couldn't possibly know how adorable he was—and absolutely gorgeous. "That's okay."

"So, do you want to eat—or we could talk first if you're not ready."

"It smells great in here, and I am pretty hungry."

"Then come have a seat." He took her hand and walked with her to the table, pulling out her chair and pushing her in. "Hold on just a second," he said as he turned, doing something behind her back. "All set."

Smiling, he sat down across from her.

"I—" She stopped when Jenny walked past them, smiling, coming back minutes later with beautifully presented side salads and a steaming casserole.

"Here you go." She set the small salad bowl to the right of the placemat and the main dish in the center, then did the same thing for Shane.

"Thanks," Shane and Reagan said at the same time.

"Have fun." She wandered back down the hall.

"I thought she was watching Netflix."

"Tonight she's a waitress too."

She grinned, looking down at her plate.

"Tatter tot casserole. Again, the best I could do in the middle of nowhere."

"I love tater tot casserole." She sampled her fist bite of cheesy potato and salt-and-pepper chicken. "Very good."

"Yeah?"

She cut another bite and ate more. "I love it."

"I want to do this again—take you out—but to a real restaurant."

"I don't know if a real restaurant could top this." And she meant it. Shane had created a lovely evening.

He smiled. "We'll be able to eat somewhere by the ocean or in the city—wherever you want—if you decide to bring the girls out to California."

"I miss the ocean. I can't remember the last time I've been."

He paused with his fork in his salad. "So you're coming to California?"

"I think we would be foolish not to. Everything's set up for Jenny. And she's excited."

"Ocean dining it is." He took a bite and swallowed. "What about you?"

"What about me?"

"Are you excited?"

She shrugged. "Honestly, I'm overwhelmed."

He nodded. "I can imagine. I thought I could help, so I talked to a realtor today about renting and buying options in the Palisades area. I'm not sure what your budget is."

She shook her head. "I haven't given it much thought."

"I want you and the girls to move in with me, but I'm not going to pressure you."

She took another bite and set down her fork. "I don't know what I plan to do yet." All of this was happening so fast. She'd sworn herself away from Shane, now they were having dinner, and she and the girls were definitely moving to California.

"I thought it would be good to try to have something in place before we meet with the Guardian Ad Litem in a couple of days."

"You're right."

"If worse comes to worse and you don't want to move in, the three of you could stay with me while we get everything sorted out."

But then she wouldn't want to leave. "I think Jenny should have some say since she'll be working and going to school." She frowned as a thought occurred to her. "Does she even know how to drive?"

"I'm thinking not."

She winced. "The roads are so busy in the Los Angeles area."

"We'll get her squared away. I can teach her how to drive, and my buddy Stone buys cars pretty cheap, fixes them up, and sells them. I'll give him a call and see if he can keep an eye out for something safe and good on gas."

"That sounds like a good idea. I've been thinking

about Jenny's work and school schedule. She's so young. She's really just a baby herself. I'm hoping that once we get things settled with the judge we can talk to Mr. Cooke about finding her something part-time and maybe enroll her in a class or two a semester. With Faith that'll keep her plenty busy."

"Yeah. Sure. We can make those changes." He took a drink of his water. "What about you? I'm sure Grant would love to have you at LA General."

She truly couldn't tolerate the idea of walking back into an ER. "I might take some time off." She shrugged when he looked at her. "Like I said, I haven't thought everything through."

"I'll support whatever you want. Ethan pays us well, so we can do it however. Everyone's really good about covering each other's duties. I won't have to travel much, if at all, during the first couple of months while we get you ladies set up."

"I don't need you to support me, Shane."

"I know you don't need me to do anything, but that doesn't mean I don't want to." He finished the last piece of chicken on his plate. "Are you finished?"

"Mmm. I'm full. It was very good."

"Do you want dessert?"

"Maybe in a little bit."

"I made apple crisp. With Jenny's help," he admitted.

He turned her heart to mush. "I can't wait to try it."

"So, no dessert." He rubbed at the back of his neck. "I guess I never realized how important the whole driving part of the date was."

She laughed and he grinned.

"Do you want to dance?" he asked.

"Okay."

He stood, turning up Jewel's version of *Have a*

Little Faith In Me on his MP3 player.

She took his hand and walked with him to the center of the room, looking into his eyes as they held each other close, moving in a slow circle. "You know, normally I would agree with you about the whole commute thing. The drive does give everyone an opportunity to transition as the evening progresses, but I like this better."

"It's certainly not bad." He pulled her closer.

She rested her head on his firm shoulder, savoring his familiar scent and the way she could relax so easily in his arms. The song ended, but three more passed before she drew away.

"All finished dancing?" His gaze darted to her mouth as he asked.

She licked her lips. "Yes."

"How about dessert?"

"I'm still stuffed. How about I have a bite of yours?"

He held her hand, bringing her with him to the refrigerator. "Big bite or little bite?" he asked, grabbing a spoon from the drawer.

"Medium."

He scooped a sample, holding it to her mouth.

She tasted apples still slightly warm and the delicious crunch of oatmeal and cinnamon. "Mmm. Really good." She took the spoon and scooped some for Shane.

He accepted her offering, nodding. "I'm thinking Jenny and I are going to have to have big bowls of this for breakfast."

She frowned her disapproval. "You *do* know you're talking to a doctor."

He laughed. "Okay, a mid-morning snack." He put the dish back in the refrigerator. "Are you ready to call it a night? I know you haven't been sleeping well."

"Are you taking care of me, Shane? A balanced meal, good conversation, and early to bed..."

He smiled. "Guilty. I'd offer you a walk on the beach but since that's not an option..."

"This has been great."

"Good. We could watch a movie though if you're not ready for bed."

Lights off with Shane sitting next to her in the dark: bad idea. "I could probably use the extra rest."

He took her hand again. "I'll walk you to your door." They stopped in front of her bedroom as if they were at her apartment door in the city. "I believe this is your stop."

She smiled. "It is. Thank you. Tonight was truly perfect—maybe the best date I've ever been on."

He raised his brows. "Oh really?"

She grinned. "Really."

He lifted her hand, studying the bracelet he'd given her wrapped around her wrist. "This looks good on you."

"It's my favorite. Someone pretty special gave it to me."

"Someone special, huh?" He settled his hands against her hips.

"Mmhm."

The fun left his eyes, turning intense—her cue to end the evening.

"I should probably—"

"Kiss me. You should kiss me, Reagan." He cupped her face, brushing his thumbs along her cheeks. "I need to taste you," he whispered, capturing her mouth, drawing out the joining of lips as her heart beat faster and she melted against him. "I missed you." Their mouths met again. "You're the only one I want. You're the only one I thought of." He touched her lips again, teasing out a moan as their tongues tangled and she gripped his wrists. "You're the only one I want to be with." He moved in to kiss her, pausing and frowning as he looked towards Jenny's slightly open door. He pulled it shut as Reagan realized they had a spy. "Christ." He shook his head. "What's a guy gotta do to get a little privacy around here?"

She chuckled. "Close quarters."

"I guess." He smiled, kissing her chastely. "Think about what I said." His eyes darted to her lips. "I'll see you in the morning." He turned to leave and she grabbed his arm.

"Shane."

He turned back. "Yeah?"

What was she doing? What did she need to say? Why wasn't she letting him walk away? "I... Stay." She pulled him back, hesitantly touching the buttons on his shirt as they stared in each other's eyes. "Stay."

"Are you sure?"

She was sure this felt right. Swallowing, she nodded.

He took her mouth, hungrily, almost savagely, grabbing for the doorknob, walking with her inside as she pulled at his shirt. "God, I need to touch you." He unzipped her dress and lifted it up and over her head, groaning. "You're perfect," he said, making quick work of her bra, filling his hands with her breasts. "God, Reagan."

She closed her eyes, whimpering with the sensations of his calloused palms teasing her sensitive skin.

"God," he whispered again, his breath heaving as he took her breast into his mouth.

Moaning, she went after his shirt and he yanked it off, sending the buttons on his cuffs flying, as she fought to free him from his belt, slacks, and boxers.

He sent her panties to the floor, lifted her, and moved to the bed, falling with her, plunging deep, making her gasp as he filled her with his girth.

"Yes. Yes," she shuddered as he clenched his jaw, sucking in a sharp breath, pumping quickly before slowing his pace as he stared into her eyes.

"Slow."

She kissed him, still caught up in the frenzy of yearning, and he eased back.

"Slow," he said again, drawing out the pleasure. "I want to feel you, Reagan. I want to watch you." He arrowed deeper and she moaned. He kept his promise, and she built with each lazy thrust, her gaze held captive by his until her hands clutched at his back and she gasped, arching up with the flash of heat, then fell, her staggered cry swallowed when he took her mouth, sending her high again, climaxing with her the second time.

~~~~

Shane nestled his face against Reagan's neck as they both caught their breath. He kissed her soft skin where her pulse pounded, then her jaw, and then her lips swollen from his. "This wasn't the plan for tonight when I asked you to have dinner."

"I know."

He brushed the hair back from her damp forehead, unable to stop touching her even as he still lay inside her. "I don't hate that it happened, but sex definitely wasn't on the agenda."

She sent him a small smile. "I know, Shane."

"I missed this. I missed you."

"I missed you too."

Her eyes were still dark with passion, her cheeks rosy from the heat they brought each other. "I'm sorry I left. I never should've left."

She stroked her fingers up and down his back. "You needed to go. You had a job to do. I understand that. Ethan was depending on you."

He shook his head. "So were you."

"We knew all along you had twelve weeks in The Gap. You never made promises you couldn't keep."

"If I'd had any idea you were dealing with all this—"

"But you didn't. I didn't tell anyone."

"The stuff with Henry—that happened before I left."

She nodded. "The day you told me you had to go."

"Why didn't you say something? Why didn't you let me help you?"

"Because there was nothing you could do." She traced his ear with her fingertips.

"I could've shared the burden for starters."

"I didn't want you to. I know you, Shane. If I had mentioned Henry, you wouldn't have gotten on your plane. You would've given up your career for something I could handle on my own."

"You handle too much on your own." He thought back to her list of secrets, remembering the flash of hurt he'd seen when he brought up the little girl who died. "What happened in New York?"

Seconds passed as she stared into his eyes, then turned her head on the pillow, sighing.

He pressed another kiss to her neck in comfort and laced their fingers. "What happened, Reagan?"

"I killed Mable."

"I don't believe that."

She looked at him. "Not intentionally, but I did."

"Tell me."

"She and her family were in a horrible car accident. Her father was dead at the scene, and her brother died at the hospital. I'd just finished my shift when three calls rang down on my pager. The whole night had been crazy. I hurried to see if I could help right as Mable's ambulance pulled up—possible concussion. That was all it was supposed to be." She blinked as her eyes grew misty. "She was so pretty—big blue eyes and peaches-and-cream skin. Visually she looked good—just a bloody lip and a bruise on the temple. She conversed well and her physical examination was unremarkable except for the seatbelt bruising across her chest and hip. I put in for a CT scan—just to be cautious, but she was sixth in line behind the stabbings and gunshot wounds."

He gripped her hands tighter as her voice grew strained and her eyes more troubled.

"She and I colored while her mother dealt with the news of Mable's brother. She told me they were on vacation—on the way to the ferry to see the Statue of Liberty. She drew a picture of her family—four smiling faces—then she set down her crayon and said her stomach hurt. I felt her abdomen again and realized she had a splenic rupture. I called a code and we raced her to OR, but she bled out before Doctor V. could get in and repair her." She sniffled as tears slid down her temples.

"I'm so sorry, Reagan."

"I can still hear her mother screaming at me. She told me I killed her baby." More tears flowed.

"No you didn't."

She nodded. "She had undiagnosed mono, which can cause the spleen to enlarge. They think the impact of the crash started an undetectable slow bleed that eventually turned catastrophic, but I should've felt it when I palpated her abdomen. I should've paid more attention and looked closer for distention."

"You didn't know."

"I didn't." She sucked in a shuddering breath. "But if I could go back and change it... I would give anything to go back."

He ached for the kind woman whose big heart was clearly broken for someone else's child. "Of course you would."

"I almost lost my license, but then there was the formal investigation, which found me not at fault. I wanted to come here and make a difference. I needed to make up for losing a life that I should've saved."

"You've done so much for these people."

She shook her head. "I tried, but it doesn't feel like enough." She swallowed. "I don't—I don't know if I can do it anymore—practice medicine, especially in the ER."

"You're such a good doctor, Reagan."

"I'm not so sure. Mable died, and everything here has been a disaster. Maybe it's time to move on."

"I'd hate to see you give up something you're so damn good at, but I'm going to support whatever you choose. If you want to stay home for a while and figure out what's next, we'll make it happen."

She smiled. "How did I make it through the last month without you?" She wrapped her arms around him. "Why do you always know just what to say to make me feel better?"

"Because I love you." He stroked her cheek as he stared into her eyes.

"Shane—"

"I've never needed anyone the way I need you. I've never wanted anyone the way I want you."

She licked her lips. "I want and need you too. It scares me. I've always depended on myself, even as a little girl. Then you came along, and nothing's been the same since."

"Good."

She shook her head. "I don't know."

"It's good, Reagan. When you find the person you want to be with, I don't think anything *should* be the same. I love you," he said again waiting for her to say it back, absorbing the pain when she didn't. He cleared his throat in the awkward silence. "Okay. I guess—"

"I can't give you children." Her lips trembled. "I more than likely will never be able to get pregnant."

Was that what this was about? "So we'll find another specialist, and there's that in vitro thing. One of my sister's friends ended up with twins."

"But it might not work."

He cupped her face in his hands. "I don't care."

"I do. You're wonderful with kids. You should have your own."

"We have two at this point." He gestured to Jenny's wall. "And there's always adoption. I can live without making babies, Reagan, but I absolutely can't live without you. I *love* you."

Her eyes filled as her breathing grew unsteady, but she still wouldn't say it back.

He shook his head and pulled away as her silence ripped at his heart.

"Shane, wait." She wrapped her legs around his waist, holding him in place. "I'm sorry. I'm scared. I'm terrified, but I'm so in love with you."

He closed his eyes, sighing out a breath, resting his forehead against hers.

"There's so much going on." She kissed him. "But I don't want you falling asleep tonight thinking that I'm not crazy, madly in love with you."

"Crazy, *madly* in love?"

She nodded, smiling. "I'd definitely say crazy, madly."

He tucked her hair behind her ears. "Doc loves me so much she's crazy."

She chuckled. "Agreed."

He turned off the light and entered her again, savoring her long moan. "Let's see if we can add a few more descriptors to our list."

She gripped his ass and snagged his bottom lip. "Like 'wild.'"

He grinned as his hormones shot into overdrive. "I think 'wild' is a good one." He slid his fingers down, rubbing them against her, making her suck in a breath as he played her and nipped her jaw with his teeth. "But I think I'm going to try for 'insane.'" Moving his hand in firm, steady circles, he sent her over fast and hard. "Yup, I'm definitely thinking of trying for insanity, so you should probably hold on."

"I've always wondered what it feels like to be insane," she said breathily.

"Let's find out.

Their mouths met in a frenzy of passion, and he effectively destroyed them both with one hell of a ride.

CHAPTER THIRTY-SEVEN

A QUIET CREAKING NOISE REGISTERED THROUGH THE HAZE of exhaustion, waking Shane out of a deep sleep. He opened his eyes, reaching for Reagan, and realized she was gone. "Reagan?" He sat up.

"I'm right here," she said, standing by her dresser.

He blinked in the dark, scrubbing his hands over his face. "What are you doing?"

"I was thirsty." She drank more water from her glass. "Do you want a sip?"

"Yeah, sure." He took the glass she offered, swallowing a cool gulp. "Thanks."

Reagan reached in her drawer, pulled out panties, and put them on. Short shorts came next and a spaghetti-strap top.

"Now what are you doing?"

"They call this getting dressed," she teased.

Grinning, he set the glass on the side table. "Why would you want to go and do that? I'm just going to have to take those clothes off you."

She arched her brows. "You think so?"

"Absolutely."

"Mr. Harper, you're insatiable." She smiled, crawling across the bed. "You wore me out, and here you are ready to go at it again."

"Baby, I'm *always* ready to go." He yanked on her arm, pulling her down on top of him.

"Mmm." She captured his lips, sliding her tongue along his as she reached down, rubbing her palm over him. "Yes, you are."

He steamed out a breath as she kissed his neck and chest, his abs, and nipped at his hip. "Reagan, I—" He groaned, closing his eyes when her hot mouth went to work.

She added her hand and he clenched his jaw, fisting his hands in her hair as she torturously brought him to the edge. She picked up her pace, and he tensed.

"I'm going to cum, Reagan," he panted out, and she moved faster, finishing him off on a burst of pure ecstasy. "God. *God.*"

"How was that?" She followed the same path she'd taken down, making her way back up. "Was that okay?"

"When I can think straight I'll let you know." He pulled on her arm again and rolled her under him as she chuckled. "You know, Doc, I'm a big believer in tit for tat."

"Is that so?" She snagged her bottom lip between her teeth.

"Oh, yeah." He suckled her breast through her thin top and she arched, whimpering. "In fact, I'll have to insist." He started his own journey down, sliding her shirt up, toying with her nipples. She moaned, and he traced her belly button with his tongue, smiling when her stomach muscles quivered. "I'm—" The loud smack against the window startled him. "What the fuck was that?" He rushed from the bed, pulling on his boxers as the rapid banging came again.

"They're back," Reagan shuddered out, stumbling as she fought her way out from under the covers.

"Reagan! Shane!" Jenny's muffled holler penetrated the wall.

"Come on." He took Reagan's hand, closing the door behind them as they hurried into the hallway.

"Reagan." Jenny stepped from her room, carrying

Faith. "Someone was bangin' on my window." She flew into Reagan's open arms as Chase emerged from his room in sweatpants, holding his gun in his hand.

"There's shit on fire, man—animals again, I think. And there are fucking people in and out of the woods. I just called it in."

"I'm scared." Jenny burrowed closer to Reagan.

"It's okay, Sweetie," Reagan kissed Jenny's cheek. "We're safe here with Shane and Chase."

Shane met Reagan's frightened eyes as he went into his room, dragging on jeans, then took his gun from the top drawer and a magazine from the bottom, shoving a full clip into his weapon.

"What are we gonna do?" Jenny asked, gently bumping Faith up and down, running her trembling hand along the baby's back as Faith cried.

"We're going to wait for the police, just like last time," Shane answered. "Everything worked out fine then, and it will again," he continued, looking at Chase, both of them knowing tonight wasn't like the night a couple of jackasses painted up the clinic and destroyed a door. "When the cops get here—" The banging came again, and then the window shattered in Reagan's room, interrupting him. "Shit. Sit and stay right over here," he said to Reagan and Jenny, pushing them into the corner out of his and Chase's way as they took their stances on either side of the doorway.

Chase nodded, kicking in the door, pointing his gun with Shane following immediately behind, ready to shoot, but stared in horror instead at Reagan's rug going up in flames.

"Fuck! Grab something and lets put this out." They both yanked Reagan's towels from the rack and smacked at the hungry licks of fire, extinguishing the small blaze. Shane coughed as he breathed in smoke.

"We've got to get them out of here."

"I'll get the car seat and keys, and we'll get ready to go."

Shane nodded, grabbing his cell phone and wallet from the pants Reagan had sent to the floor not all that long ago on his way back into the hall, and closed the door. "We've gotta go," he said, holding Reagan's gaze. "Get Faith in her seat and call the police. Tell them about the fire and to hurry the hell up."

"Okay," she took the phone he handed over as another window smashed in the living room, followed quickly by another.

"Stay here!" He called as he and Chase hurried down the hall, slowing up, pressing their backs to the wall before cautiously entering the room in a race to beat the next round of flames spreading up the curtains.

"Let me wet these," Chase yelled, grabbing the blankets Jenny and Reagan typically covered up with when they watched TV.

"We need to get these off the wall before the whole fucking place goes up." Shane jammed his hand against the long rod, dislodging the metal poll from its holders.

"Here!"

He caught the sopping blanket Chase threw him and smothered the worst of the blaze as Chase beat out the rest. Coughing, Shane looked at the mess of charred walls through the haze of smoke. "We can't wait for the police."

"You're right. We can't. So let's go."

"Reagan, Jenny, come on!"

Reagan carried Faith in her car seat with Jenny moving a step ahead of them as they appeared from around the corner. Something pounded violently against the exterior of the house, and Jenny jumped, screaming.

"The police should be here any minute," Reagan told them. "I just hung up with dispatch."

"We can't afford to wait," Shane said.

"I'm not wearin' shoes," Jenny said as tears streamed down her cheeks.

"It doesn't matter," Shane reassured her, taking back the phone from Reagan.

"I don't wanna go *outside!*"

"Hey, you have to trust me and Chase." He took Jenny by her shoulders, doing his best to settle her down as her body shook beneath his hands. "Do you trust me?"

"Yes." She sniffled.

"We would never do anything to put you in more danger."

Jenny nodded. "I know."

"Take a couple of deep breaths and try to chill out. I need to know you're ready to listen to Chase when he takes you and Reagan out."

"What about you?" Reagan asked.

"I'll come with Faith."

She nodded.

"Jenny, you're going to take the front seat," Shane instructed. "Reagan, you'll get in the back and slide over to the driver's side. I want you ready to snap Faith's seat into place. We're going to do this fast."

Reagan nodded again, snatching up Faith's diaper bag and slinging the strap of her laptop case over her shoulder as sirens wailed and blue lights flashed through the broken windows. Three police cars pulled up in the driveway.

"It's about fucking time," Chase said.

"Okay, change of plans." Shane shoved a hand through his hair. "We're going to do a quick grab of the things you need—a change of clothes, bathroom stuff."

"I'm going out." Chase opened the door.

"All right." Shane turned his attention to the ladies looking at him. "Jenny, we'll start with you." He glanced out the window as Chase met one of the officers getting out of the car, pointing toward the woods and windows in the cabin. After a few moments, he jogged back inside.

"Let's get some stuff," Chase said, closing the door again with streaks of soot covering his stomach and chest. "They're going to process the scene and give us a call when they know what the hell's going on. Jenny, come with me and we'll get you what you and Faith need."

Jenny wiped her cheeks, following Chase to her room.

Reagan took Faith from her seat as the baby cried. "It's okay, sweet girl. It's okay," she soothed. "Shh, Faithy. Everything's all right now."

Shane pulled Reagan against him, wrapping her up as his adrenaline started to ebb. "Are you okay?"

She rested her head against his chest, nodding. "I'm fine, just a little shaken up."

"We're leaving. What do you want from your room?"

"Um, I guess a couple changes of clothes." She looked up, meeting his gaze. "What are we going to do?"

"Head into Lexington. We'll talk to Ethan and see what we can do about getting us the hell out of here."

Her eyes watered as she shook her head. "We can't go."

"We're not leaving them, Reagan." He pressed a kiss to her temple. "Let's get what we need and we'll figure out the rest at the hotel."

"Okay." She kissed his cheek and took his hand, walking with him into the bedroom as she settled Faith and he gathered clothes for her.

~~~~

Reagan sat by Jenny as she lay on the bed in their hotel room, feeding Faith in the crook of her arm.

"It just doesn't seem safe goin' back there." She sniffled.

Reagan handed the teenager another tissue, still trying to calm her down after the long, tense drive to Lexington with Chase following behind them in the second Pajero. They'd settled into the room over an hour ago, but Jenny was still too worked up to get some much-needed rest. "Shane and Chase are working it out. They're on the phone with Ethan right now."

"Do we have to go back when the sun comes up?"

She shook her head. "I'm not sure, but what I *do* know is Shane and Chase haven't let us down yet."

Jenny nodded. "I know." She balanced the bottle against her side as she wiped her eyes. "I imagine when I'm not so scared I might think Shane and Chase looked mighty fine kickin' in doors with their shirts off."

Reagan laughed, a good solid laugh. "Jenny Hendley, what would I do without you?"

Jenny gave her a small smile. "I'm just speakin' the truth."

She chuckled. "And I won't argue. Shane and Chase are certainly mouthwatering."

"But what about the guardian lady?"

And they were back to this again. Reagan suppressed a sigh. "My attorney's going to file an emergency hearing as soon as the court opens tomorrow," she reminded Jenny for the umpteenth time.

"What if that doesn't work? The *Guardian ad Litem* can't exactly come to the cabin and see that you take good care of me with the living room all burnt up." More tears fell. "She's not gonna let me go. She's gonna tell the judge and they're gonna make me stay with Mommy. Maybe we should really be thinkin' about you takin' Faith on back to California—"

She shook her head, pressing a firm hand to Jenny's arm. "Stop."

"Reagan—"

"We're not leaving you here," Shane said from the door of the adjoining rooms where he and Chase had been talking to their boss.

"I was just thinkin'—"

"That you need to get some sleep," Shane finished for her.

Jenny huffed out a breath.

"We leave together or don't go at all." He grabbed Reagan's hand. "I need to talk to you."

"Okay." She stood and pulled the covers over the girls as Jenny took the bottle from Faith's mouth and nestled up next to her little girl. "Snuggle in." She leaned over, kissing Jenny's forehead then kissed her finger, touching Faith's cheek. "Get some rest."

"I'll try."

"You're safe here. We'll be in in a couple of minutes." He kissed Jenny's cheek. "Good night." He turned off the lamp.

"Night, guys."

Reagan closed the door joining the rooms, her smile for Jenny disappearing. "God."

"Hey." Shane wrapped his arms around her.

She hugged him back, absorbing the comfort he

offered so freely. "What are we going to do?"

He slid his hand down her hair. "We're going to figure this out."

She shook her head as she looked up at him. "Optimism is for Jenny. I need real answers."

"We spoke to Ethan. He's going to fax documents to your attorney to send along with the emergency motion she's filing with the court. It's formal paperwork basically saying that as CEO of Ethan Cooke Security, he believes Jenny and Faith are no longer safe in the area. Chase and I added our two cents." He kissed her forehead. "That's a lot of weight coming from a security expert, former FBI agent, and an ex-US Marshall. Ethan is also going to get in touch with the officers who handled the issues up at the clinic and see if he can have them send something along too."

She sat on the bed, more than half sick. "What if that doesn't work? What if Jenny's mother spins it around to work against us?"

He joined her. "I don't see that happening. Jenny's directly affected by the violence in the area. All of that 'the town loves Jenny best' crap from the Pastor doesn't hold up against reality. If the town was so in love with Jenny they wouldn't have tried to burn her and her baby alive."

"Yeah, I guess—"

"Here. Come lay with me for a second." He pushed her down to the pillow, pulling her close. "I have a hard time believing any judge who's looking out for the best interest of a minor will think it's safe to let a young lady go back to a place where the house she's living in has been set on fire—twice."

She sighed. "You're right. I hope you're right."

"Hasn't anyone ever told you I'm always right?" He grinned as her eyebrow shot up.

"'Always' is a pretty definitive word."

"And one I'm comfortable with."

She chuckled and sniffed the skin of his neck as she kissed him. "Mmm. You smell much better than you did when we got here."

He laughed. "Thanks."

She smiled. "Sorry but it's true."

"A guy puts out a couple of fires and he's told he stinks. I took a shower. Chase is taking his turn."

"Did I forget to mention you're my hero?" She batted her lashes, kissing him again.

He grinned. "Suck up."

The water shut off in the bathroom. "Sounds like Chase is finished." He stood. "Let's get out of here before he walks out buck ass naked." He took her hand. "Come on. Let's go to bed."

"Okay."

They moved to their own room, closing the adjoining door most of the way.

Reagan tiptoed closer to Jenny and Faith's bed. "She's asleep."

"Of course she is. She's exhausted." He pulled the covers back and they settled under the blankets. "Goodnight."

"Goodnight." She kissed him. "I love you."

"I love you too."

Shane flipped off the lamp on his side of the bed. He pulled her close, and she gave him a smile.

"You really are my hero." She kissed him again.

"Get some rest."

"I will." She closed her eyes because she knew that's what Shane wanted and worried for the remainder of the night.

CHAPTER THIRTY-EIGHT

REAGAN SAT IN THE PASSENGER'S SEAT, GRIPPING SHANE'S hand in hers as he drove them toward the courthouse. The day had been a whirlwind of tense phone calls with the lawyer and a long morning meeting with Nancy Bloom, Jenny's appointed *Guardian ad Litem*. Luckily her attorney had managed to secure an emergency hearing in Judge Thompson's full docket, citing dangerous and unforeseen circumstances for their twelve forty-five appointment in his chambers.

"...think it went okay today. Don't you?"

"Yes," Reagan said, trying her best to stay patient with Jenny when her own nerves were frayed. From the moment Jenny opened her eyes this morning she'd talked incessantly. Quickly after lunch, Chase had taken his leave, heading back to The Gap to speak with the police and get the mail, but also to escape the constant chatter of a teenager on edge.

"I mean Ms. Nancy seemed happy about me havin' a job, and I think she likes that I'll be startin' school. And now that we're gonna be livin' with Shane—I definitely think that seems like a stable environment." She paused to apply lip gloss. "Hopefully she met with Mommy and saw that living in The Gap isn't good for me and Faithy. I mean—"

"Hey, Jenny?" Shane interrupted, looking in the rearview mirror.

"Yeah?"

"Do you ever stop talking?"

She huffed out a breath. "I'm nervous."

"We knocked Nancy's socks off. Look out the window for a few minutes...with your mouth closed."

"I'm just nervous," she grumbled, crossing her arms and stared out the window.

Reagan slid Shane a look, and they grinned at each other in the now blessedly quiet.

"Here we are," he said, switching on his blinker and parallel parked in the one open spot near the small courthouse. "Let me get out first."

Reagan nodded, flipping down the visor, checking her makeup for the most important meeting of her life while Shane helped the girls.

Shane opened Reagan's door with Jenny at his side and Faith's carrier in his free hand. "Ready?"

"To get this over with?" She blew out a long breath. "*Yes.*"

He took her hand, kissing her knuckles. "Everything's going to work out."

She looked at Jenny and gave a decisive nod, even though she wasn't so sure. "Definitely."

Jenny opened the door to the awaiting security guards.

"Good afternoon," the man said.

"Good afternoon." Shane handed over Faith's seat to Reagan. "Go on through, guys." He pulled out his identification. "I have a weapon."

"Remove it for me slowly, sir, and go on through the detector."

Shane took his gun from his holster, gave it to the officer, and walked through the detector, taking his pistol back on the other side."

"I know I'm not supposed to be talkin', but I thought I should tell ya I've gotta go to the bathroom."

Reagan looked from the mutiny in Jenny's eyes to

Shane's raised brow. "Go ahead. We'll wait right over there for you." She pointed to the small alcove.

Jenny whirled and pushed her way into the women's room.

Shane rubbed at his jaw. "There are few things I love more than a seventeen-year-old with her panties in a twist."

"We're all tired and on edge."

He steamed out a deep breath. "Yeah, I guess we are."

She walked over to the water fountains, setting down Faith's carrier while the baby slept soundly. She paced a step away, and back again.

"Take it easy, Doc."

She gave him a small smile. "I'm trying. This is it. Everything comes down to the next few minutes."

He hugged her. "It'll be okay."

"But look at us." She eased away slightly, gesturing to her clothes. "We're in jeans. We should've saved time to go the store."

"This is an emergency hearing."

She shook her head. "Still. We're not exactly presenting ourselves as two successful professionals showing up to the judge's chambers in denim and sweaters."

"Doc, we're fine—even in jeans."

She sighed.

"Hey." He pulled her back against him. "Unless Jenny's mother bought a new house, can suddenly provide her daughter with a college education, a job, and childcare for Faith, I think we've got this."

"I just keep hearing Judge Thompson saying, "A parent's rights are strong and binding.""

"Unless they interfere with a kid's safety, which in this case they do."

She nodded. "I'm terrified Mrs. Hendley still has the upper hand."

"I don't see how."

"We can't lose them. I don't know what I'll do if we lose them," she whispered, her eyes tearing up as she stared at him, confessing her biggest fear.

"We won't." He kissed her. "Judge Thompson letting Jenny stay with Mrs. Hendley doesn't make any sense."

Pressing her lips together, she relaxed against him—as much as she could. "You're right."

"I'm pretty sure we came to that conclusion last night."

She chuckled, kissing his chin as Jenny came out with her long hair smoothed and her lips slicked with more clear gloss.

Reagan untangled herself from Shane and took Jenny's hands. "Are you ready?"

Jenny nodded.

"Then let's go kick some butt," Shane said, picking up Faith's seat.

Within moments they made their way to Judge Thompson's waiting area. Reagan's muscles tensed further when her eyes met Mrs. Hendley's across the room. She gave the pastor a polite nod.

"Jenny," Mrs. Hendley said.

"Mommy." Jenny stepped closer to Reagan and Shane.

"I've a mind to believe the Good Lord will be seein' you comin' home with Pastor McPhee and me."

Jenny's frightened eyes met Reagan's.

"Why don't we see what the judge decides?" Shane commented as Judge Thompson's assistant walked into the room.

"Good afternoon." She smiled.

"Hello again." Reagan returned her greeting.

"Judge Thompson is ready to see all of you."

They filed in after Mrs. Hendley and the Pastor.

"Go ahead and have a seat," Judge Thompson said.

Reagan made eye contact with Nancy Bloom and took her seat on one side of Jenny on the couch, with Shane on the other. "Thank you for seeing us so quickly, Your Honor."

"Let's get right down to business. We're here for an emergency hearing for Jenny Hendley." He glanced over papers. "It looks like there's been quite a bit of trouble in The Gap since our last meeting a short while ago." He looked at Reagan, then Shane.

"I'm afraid so," Reagan replied.

"Ms. Bloom and I have spent the last little while going over the findings of her expedited report. After reviewing all of the information set before me, I feel confident I can make a sound decision. I will grant Doctor Rosner temporary guardianship of Jenny—"

"She's a murderin' heathen!" Mrs. Hendley shouted as she rushed to her feet. "Child killer is what she is!"

"Mrs. Hendley, I'm going to ask you to sit down, or I'll have you removed for contempt."

"I have a right to my say."

"And I have a right to put you in jail."

Mrs. Hendley sat down, glaring at Reagan.

Judge Thompson leafed through papers. "Mrs. Hendley, you've referenced Doctor Rosner as a murderer on several occasions—"

"She killed a little girl! Devil killer!"

Judge Thompson's eyes scanned a typed sheet. "I'm assuming Mrs. Hendley's outburst is in regards to the June seventeenth death of Mable Totton."

Reagan swallowed, hating that she was forced to relive her biggest mistake again and again. "Yes, I'm sure it is, Your Honor."

"The medical board found no fault."

"Yes, Your Honor." She made eye contact with Pastor McPhee and looked away, taking Shane and Jenny's hands in the support they offered. "I'm afraid Mable's death was an accident of the worst kind."

"Doctor Rosner, your background is nothing but impressive. Your former coworkers have nothing but wonderful things to say about you as a physician and as a human being in general. I don't see the need to prolong this case any further. Jenny has passed her exams with flying colors, she has gainful employment waiting for her, not to mention the opportunity for a college degree, along with two upstanding adults ready and willing to guide her through the often turbulent roads of childrearing and adulthood." He closed his file. "You are free to leave the state at your convenience."

"Thank you, Your Honor."

"Paperwork will be filed with the clerk and a copy will be sent to you."

"Thank you," Reagan and Shane said at the same time as they stood and left the room. Reagan immediately wrapped Jenny up in a hug as her eyes filled with the rush of relief. "It's all over. I can't believe this is really over."

"Don't you be thinkin' you'll ever be welcome on my doorstep again, Jenny Hendley. I'll pray mighty hard for your sinnin' soul," Mrs. Hendley hollered as Pastor McPhee pulled her down the hall.

The commotion quieted when Jenny's mother stepped outside.

Reagan pressed her hand to Jenny's cheek. "Are you okay, sweetie?"

"Yes. I just want to go home—to my new home in California."

"Let's go back to the hotel and see what Chase found out, and we'll book flights for tomorrow." Shane wrapped his arm around Jenny's waist.

She returned the gesture. "I'm sorry I was talkin' so much."

"That's okay. Next time I'll just put you in a sleeper hold and put us all out of our misery."

"*Shane.*" She bumped him with her hip.

"*Jenny,*" he said back, mocking her tone.

They looked at each other and grinned.

And just like that, Reagan had her happy little family back. Chuckling, she followed behind them, carrying the baby to the SUV.

~~~~

"I've never flown on a plane before. Okay, I've never actually even *stepped* on a plane before. When me and Reagan brought you to the airport it was only the second time I've ever been," Jenny went on as she had since they pulled away from the courthouse. Her nervous energy had turned into giddy excitement, which meant her mouth hadn't stopped moving since she apologized for talking too much the first time around.

Shane rolled his eyes at Reagan as he slid the keycard in their hotel door and let everyone in. "Here you go." He handed over Faith's seat to Jenny. "Why don't you go read to your daughter?"

"She's sleepin'."

"Read to her anyway or watch some TV for a while. You're driving me crazy, Hendley."

She blinked, her eyes full of hurt. "You don't have to be so grumpy about it."

He was being a cranky ass. Having the custody

issue resolved was supposed to have lightened the load some, but there was still plenty left on their plate to deal with. "I'm sorry."

She gave him a jerking shrug, darting him a look from under her lashes. "I guess it's okay."

He sighed, his guilt not quite assuaged. "Why don't you help me out and look up flights for tomorrow—something for mid-morning."

She beamed, her hurt feelings clearly forgotten. "Really?"

Ethan would book their flights as soon as he and Chase gave him the green light to send them home, but having Jenny search would give her something to do. "Sure. There are no direct flights, so try and find us the shortest layover."

"Okay." She took Faith, settling the baby in the center of the bed with a blanket and went over to his laptop, getting right to work.

"Keep an eye on the prices too. We've got five seats to book, so it wouldn't hurt to check out a few of the different carriers."

"Got it."

"Nicely done," Reagan complimented quietly.

He clenched his jaw and rubbed at the back of his neck. "That sleeper hold was getting real tempting."

She smiled.

He tossed out a humorless laugh. "You think I'm kidding."

She took his chin in her hand giving a gentle jiggle. "Of course you are."

He wrapped his arms around her waist, resting his forehead against hers, unable to shake the edgy feeling turning his mood sour. "Okay, I am."

Kissing him, she laced her fingers at the back of his neck. "What's wrong?"

He shrugged.

"You've been my rock. Let me be yours for a little while."

"I guess I'm just ready to get the hell out of here. I want to take you ladies home and put this behind us."

"Mmm." She kissed him again. "That sounds good." She brought her mouth to his for a third time. "We'll be taking off before you know it."

There was a noise outside the door. Seconds later it opened, and Chase stepped in with his phone at his ear. "Yeah. I'm here now. I'll call you back." He hung up. "How'd it go?"

"I'm proud to say we have two bouncing baby girls."

"Awesome."

"I'm lookin' for our flights home." Jenny grinned.

Chase frowned, looking at Shane.

"She's quietly searching, Rider."

Chase smiled, nodding. "Do you have a minute?" He gestured toward the adjoining room.

"Yeah." He was anxious to find out how things had gone in The Gap.

"Uh, do you mind if I join you?" Reagan asked.

"No, come on in." They walked into the next room, and Shane partially closed the door. "So what's up?"

"A few things. I got some unexpected news."

Shane's shoulders tensed, trying to read Chase's typically intense stare. "Oh yeah?"

"Terry Staddler's in the slammer."

He raised his brows in surprise. "No kidding?"

"What for?" Reagan wanted to know.

"Drug possession and attempt to distribute— methamphetamines. Apparently, he's been in trouble a lot lately. This is his second arrest in just a few days."

Another problem to check off the list. "Hopefully

the asshole will do a little time and leave Jenny and Faith alone. What else did you find out?"

"Not a lot. The cops are still trying to figure out who tried to torch the cabin. They did a small perimeter search hoping to find something, but any footprints got lost in the underbrush, and there didn't appear to be a whole lot of evidence left behind except for the shit they used to shatter the windows."

"Did anyone give you the plan from here on out?" He'd been so busy trying to get back into Reagan's good graces and dealing with Jenny's custody hearing he felt out of the loop.

"Ethan's been playing phone tag with whats-his-face in Washington. They finally touched base about an hour ago. The director wants a final inventory from Reagan by tomorrow evening at the latest. The police have been assigned to keep an eye on the property until movers come to pick up furnishings and equipment on Friday."

"I need to get back there today then." Reagan started toward their room. "I should see if the director e-mailed me."

"Hold on just a minute. I picked up the mail." Chase held up three opened envelopes. "I hope you don't mind, Reagan, but I wanted to see what we had."

She came back to join them. "No, that's fine."

"Did Ethan get a trace on whose been sending them?"

"Not yet. He's thinking the Mine Safety and Health Association links that came via e-mail and the stuff coming snail mail are probably from the same person, but so far the e-mail account appears to be a dummy and the postmarks are from Nova Scotia and New Brunswick, so there's not much to go on there."

Shane walked over to the table reading the small

rectangles Chase dumped out. There were no strips with one or two sentences this time, only names—names all three of them recognized.

McPhee
Pattell
Jacobson

Shane frowned. "What the hell is this?"

Chase shook his head. "I don't know. Ethan's still trying to track down more information on the McPhee's. He's been working on it since you handed the stuff off yesterday—" Chase's phone rang, and he looked at the screen. "This is him right here. Hello? Yeah." He picked up a pen and squished the edge of a fast food bag flat. "No kidding."

Shane moved closer as Chase scribbled.

Several mines. Conditions poor. Same doc. COPD.

"I'm not sure," Chase continued. "Okay. Let me call you back." He hung up.

Shane shoved his hands in his pockets, reading Chase's writing again. "What's up?"

"After 'a lot of fucking digging'—and that's a direct quote—Ethan found out the McPhees have their hands in several small mining sites throughout Eastern Kentucky. Supposedly the health and safety conditions are as bad, if not worse, than Corpus Mining's."

Reagan shook her head. "How is that not public information?"

"It is if you look hard enough," Chase replied. "Not long after Senior McPhee died, his boys got dirty. They use the name 'Stygian Corporation' as the front for the other eight locations, which are bought and sold regularly among a close group of other big-name families."

"To confuse ownership," Reagan said.

Shane nodded as it all started to make sense. "If the Mine Safety and Health Association is constantly trying to keep track of who owns what, it makes it nearly impossible to issue infractions and hold anyone criminally liable."

"Exactly," Chase and Reagan said at the same time.

"Crooked bastards."

"There's more." Chase tapped his notes. "Doctor Rosner, I'll give you one guess as to who oversees the medical care for all nine mining operations."

"Doctor Hargus."

He winked, pointing at her as he clicked his tongue. "You're good. After a bit of hacking, Ethan was able to find that any referrals Doctor Hargus makes for lung issues are sent to the one and only Doctor Jacobson."

"I'll bet." Her nostrils flared as she pressed her lips firm in disapproval.

"The very few patients Doctor Hargus has referred over the past few years have initially been diagnosed with COPD, allergies, or pneumonia, which Doctor Jacobson backed up one hundred percent of the time."

"Which is why black lung doesn't appear to exist in Eastern Kentucky." She pressed her fingers to her temple. "There are probably dozens upon dozens if not hundreds of undiagnosed cases." She touched the three rectangles of paper on the table. "Doctor Schlibenburg was going to expose the whole thing, but someone found out about his plans."

"That would explain why he went into hiding," Chase agreed.

She swallowed. "And why he's dead."

Shane glanced at the name of Corpus Mining's first doctor. "I wonder what Pattell had to do with the whole thing? Why did Schlibenburg give him a mention? He's been dead a long time."

"Doctor Patell died about a year after Senior McPhee," Reagan said, picking up the paper.

"About six months after Stygian was formed," Chase added.

Shane narrowed his eyes as he tried to keep all of the information from the last day straight. "And wasn't that about the time Corpus Mining started having trouble with the Mine Safety and Health Association?"

"I think so." Chase opened his laptop, calling up the files they'd copied over from Reagan's computer. "Yup. Their pretty safety records were starting to go to hell right around that time."

Reagan pulled out one of the chairs and sat. "By all accounts, Doctor Pattell was an amazing physician and family man. He must've known things weren't quite right. What if he didn't like what was going on?" She took Shane's hand. "His wife insisted he didn't kill himself. The librarian I spoke to said she couldn't think of anyone who would want to harm him. He'd been the physician on record for years—a good family friend. No one would suspect the McPhees had anything to do with murder."

Shane exchanged a look with Chase, not liking where this was going. If their theories were correct, two doctors were dead, and the one sitting next to him knew as much as the deceased had.

Reagan stood. "Shane, I think we need to talk to Detective Reedy."

He looked at Chase again, taking his phone out when Chase nodded. "Okay. I'll give him a call."

"Are you going to head down to the clinic?" Chase

wanted to know.

Shane clenched his jaw as he met Reagan's gaze. "I guess we have to."

"I'll give Officer Swift a call and let him know you'll be on your way."

He would feel better if he and Chase were handling this together, but this wouldn't be the first time he'd worked with someone outside of Ethan Cooke Security to pull off a duty. "I appreciate it."

Chase dialed and walked toward the bathroom as Shane selected the detective's number from his contacts.

"Detective Reedy."

"Good afternoon, Detective, this is Shane Harper, security with The Appalachia Project."

"Hello, Mr. Harper. What can I do for you?"

He sat on the edge of the bed. "We've stumbled on some new information we need to share with you."

"I'm in Berea right now. I can head down to the clinic—"

"We're actually staying in a hotel on the outskirts of Lexington. We had more issues last night." He reached out, grabbing Reagan's hand as she paced in front of him and pulled her down on his lap, wanting her to relax.

"Oh."

"But Doctor Rosner and I are heading down to close up the clinic. We're leaving for Los Angeles in the morning." He looked at his watch. "We can meet you at three."

"I'll be waiting.

"We're a good ninety minutes out depending on traffic."

"That's fine. I'll probably get there just before you. I'm giving Schlibenburg's place another once over. I can't find the damn films."

They had more than likely been destroyed. "We'll see you in about an hour and a half."

"See you then."

He hung up.

"What did he say?"

"That he'll meet us."

Reagan stood from his lap. "Let me get my laptop—"

"Are you goin' to The Gap?" Jenny asked from the doorway.

"We won't be long," Reagan reassured. "I have to submit my inventory."

"And grab the few things I couldn't fit in the Pajero," Chase added as he headed back to join them. "Faith's pack-n-play and a couple other things are still there."

"But I don't want you to go." Jenny stepped farther into the room, her eyes full of concern. "It's not safe."

Reagan took her hands. "I have to give final pill counts to the director."

"But—"

"You've done enough reading to know how much trouble I can get in if I can't account for discrepancies with a controlled substance."

Jenny nodded.

"Besides, Shane will be there, and Detective Reedy and another officer." She kissed her cheek.

"Officer Swift's on duty until seven," Chase confirmed. "He said everything's been quiet and to come on down."

"See? We'll be back long before seven." Reagan hugged her.

They didn't have time for this. Shane wanted them to do what needed to be done and get back. "Did you find the flights?" he asked Jenny.

She nodded.

"Good. You and Chase can call Ethan and get us squared away."

"Okay," she responded quietly, her eyes still unsure.

"You do want to go to LA tomorrow, right?"

"Yes."

"Then we need to get ready." He pulled the keys from his pocket and gave his attention to Chase. "I'll call when we get to The Gap and make contact with Officer Swift."

"Sounds good. We'll hold down the fort around here. Jenny, Faith, and I are going to the post office to ship most of our stuff home."

He nodded. "We'll be back soon. Make sure you give Chase a hand," he said to Jenny, giving her a friendly nudge.

"I will."

"I know you will. We'll be back soon." He took Reagan's hand. "Come on. I want to be heading back before it gets dark." He closed the door, ready to finish this and put Black Bear Gap, Kentucky behind them for good.

CHAPTER THIRTY-NINE

SHANE HUGGED THE CURVE AND STRAIGHTENED OUT THE wheel as they rolled into The Gap. He glanced at Henry and Daisy's house and the beat-up pickup in the drive, then toward the boarded-up, derelict buildings that had shocked him once upon a time. They passed the gas station and mini-mart where the same group of men stood to the side of the door filling their lungs with smoke and their stomachs with endless cans of soda. He looked Reagan's way as she sighed, staring out the window. "What's wrong?"

"I can't believe this is the last time we'll drive through here."

He frowned. "You sound sad."

"Kind of." She met his gaze. "I really wanted to help these people. After Mable's death I needed to do something good. I was going to make a difference and maybe make up—just a little—for being so incredibly wrong."

"Reagan—"

She shook her head. "I was going to heal a community in need and maybe heal myself in the process."

He took his eyes off the road again, noting the hint of pain in hers, hating that she still blamed herself for a horrible tragedy everyone else had deemed an accident. "Mable's death wasn't your fault."

She expelled a long breath. "In some ways I understand that. I'm just saying," she shook her head

485

again, "I'm sure I'm not making any sense."

He knew the woman at his side well enough to understand that she saw her less-than-successful experience in The Gap as a failed penance. "I'm hoping someday you'll be able to let yourself off the hook for something that was never your fault." Taking her hand, he kissed her knuckles. "And you did help these people—as much as they would let you."

"I wish I could've done more. There's so much *need* here—heart disease, diabetes, black lung."

"You can't help someone who doesn't want it." He pulled his hand from hers to turn on the dirt road, heading toward the cabin. "Who knows? Maybe someone in Washington will try something like this again."

"Probably not, but maybe."

"I guess we'll have to see." He pulled his cell phone free of his pocket. "I'm going to let Officer Swift know we're here." He selected the number Chase had sent him, waiting through one ring.

"This is Officer Swift."

"Hey, this is Shane Harper with The Appalachia Project. I'm about four miles out."

"I'm just finishing up another perimeter search. I was telling Chase how everything's been real quiet."

"That's good to hear. Has Detective Reedy shown up yet?"

"No. Other than Chase I haven't seen anyone today."

"Okay. Thanks." He hung up.

"Is Detective Reedy there?" Reagan asked.

"Not yet," he replied, dialing another number. Officer Swift said the day had been quiet, but he would feel better knowing Reedy would be there as well.

"This is Detective Reedy."

"Hey, it's Shane Harper."

"Hi, Shane. I'm about five, maybe ten minutes out."

"Great." He glanced at the dashboard clock, reducing his speed slightly to give the detective time to catch up. "We're just ahead of you."

"I'll see you shortly then."

"Sounds good." He hung up. "Reedy's about ten minutes out."

"I probably won't need much more than that in the clinic." She tucked her leg under her right in the seat. "I haven't prescribed pills since the last time I did my counts, so it's really just about double-checking and giving the more expensive equipment a once over, which you can do if you want."

"Yeah. Sure. I'd like to get this finished up fairly quickly so we can be out of here before sunset." He looked toward the sun already sinking along the horizon.

"Why don't I help you with the stuff in the cabin, then we'll go over to the clinic."

"Sounds like we have a plan." He slowed further as he pulled into the driveway, glancing toward the Kentucky State Police cruiser parked in between the clinic and the cabin. He returned Officer Swift's wave and scanned the area despite the trooper's assurances that all was well. Satisfied after his own assessment, he sent off a quick text to Chase.

We're here. Place looks secure. I'll let you know when we're heading out.

Putting his phone away, he smiled at Reagan. "Ready?"

"Absolutely."

He slid his forearm against his gun before he

opened his door, got out, and went around to Reagan's side. "Let's do this."

She nodded, and they made their way to the cabin, unlocking the door and letting themselves in.

"PU." Reagan wrinkled her nose, stepping further into the smoky stench of the common area.

Shane stared at the boarded-up windows, soot-covered walls, and charred, tattered remains of the curtains, realizing just how close he and Chase had come to losing control of the fire. He took the first couple of steps up to the loft and walked down the hall, doing a visual sweep of each room, making certain he and Reagan were the only ones inside.

"Wow, Chase did a great job," she called as she moved his way, joining him outside of Jenny and Faith's room. "There's hardly anything left."

"Good," he said glancing toward the tail end of the police cruiser through Jenny's window. The faster they packed up, the sooner they could leave.

"We're going to have to wash everything when we get home." Reagan started opening and closing empty drawers.

"I do have a washing machine."

"We'll certainly be putting it to good use." She moved to the next dresser, doing the same thing she'd done with the chest of drawers. "I want to make sure Chase didn't forget anything."

"Sure. I guess I'll take care of the pack-n-play."

"Let me finish the drawer checks and I'll help you with the rest."

"Okay." He grabbed the pack-n-play and activity mat Chase had wrapped in trash bags and went outside, starting toward the Pajero.

Officer Swift got out of his vehicle. "Can I give you a hand?"

"I appreciate it, but I think I've got it." He went around to the back, setting down the stuff, and popped the trunk as Officer Swift joined him from the other side.

"Do you have much left in there?"

"Nah. Just a few things—mostly the baby's stuff." He lifted the pack-n-play and set it inside. As he did, he noticed the small hole in the waist of the officer's uniform. He zeroed in on the soot pattern and the drops of drying crimson, recognizing the signs of a close-range gunshot. His eyes darted up to the man's face as he moved to reach for his weapon.

"Not so fast, Fed." Officer Swift, or whoever the hell he was, pulled out the taser and fired, sending Shane to the ground in a helpless heap.

Shane groaned as his muscles tensed with the surge of searing electricity. Before he could recover from the shock, something smacked against the side of his head. The pain was instant and intense, and the world went dark.

~~~~

Reagan peeked in the last of Jenny and Faith's drawers and pushed them back in place, satisfied that Chase had done a thorough job. She moved to her own room, grimacing as she breathed in the nasty stench of smoke, stronger in the boarded up space. She glanced at the melted alarm clock among the mess on her torched area rug, set her laptop case on the bed, and opened the first of her drawers, ready to inspect them all.

When she and Shane drove through town a few minutes ago, she'd experienced a wave of regret, finding herself saddened to leave The Gap behind. Her entire life had changed here. She and Shane had met for the first time right outside, and Jenny and Faith had been thrust into their care not long after. When she signed on to oversee the clinic in Black Bear Gap, she had no idea she would find her family.

Now that she was back among the ruins of a place she wasn't welcome, she was eager to do the inventory, speak with Detective Reedy, and get the people she loved out of Kentucky.

The side door opened.

"We're going to have to give Chase a medal. He really did a great job," she moved to the desk and peeked in more drawers, frowning when Shane didn't respond. "Shane?"

She turned and gasped, stumbling back as she stared at the police officer pointing a gun at her. It was the same man who'd worn the brown leather jacket and followed her around Lexington. "Where's Shane?"

He smirked. "He's busy. Where's your laptop?"

Her heart thundered in her chest as she looked toward the bed, struggling to remain calm. "Right—right there."

"Open it and access your files."

She took a shaky step to comply and stopped. "Where's Shane?"

"He's napping. Now get the laptop."

Her gaze darted from the gun mere inches from her face to the spatters of blood on the waist of his uniform, and her stomach roiled with the retched pangs of wild fear. "I want to see Shane," she shuddered out.

He took another step closer. "You're not really in a position to bargain."

Shane was bleeding somewhere. "Did you kill him?" Her voice broke. "Did you kill him?" she asked again, not certain she could bear to hear the answer.

"Did you hear the gun go off?"

There was more than one way to murder a man. "I won't put in my password until I see for myself that he's okay."

"I heard you were a pain in the ass." He yanked the case from the tangle of sheets. "Let's go." He gestured with the weapon.

"Where is he?" she asked, hurrying down the hall, taking the steps outside quickly. "Where—" Her heart stopped, and her breath caught in her lungs when she saw the soles of Shane's shoes by the back tire. "Shane! Shane!" She ran to where he lay crumpled on the dirt, pressing her lips together against the need to weep as she crouched down, touching her trembling fingers to his neck.

His pulse beat steady and strong, but she worried about the nasty contusion and trails of drying blood along his temple. "Shane, wake up," she whispered, sliding her hand over his hair, willing him to open his eyes, too afraid to roll him to his back. Then she noticed the taser probes still embedded in his side. She grabbed hold of the first, pressed firmly on the surrounding skin beneath his shirt, and pulled quickly, dislodging the first barb. Sniffling, she yanked the second free.

"See? He's fine—"

"He's not *fine*." A tear tracked down her cheek with the weight of utter helplessness. She needed to clean his wounds and get him to the hospital for a CT scan.

"He's good enough. Now get up. We're going for a walk."

She touched Shane again, looking toward the road, wondering where Detective Reedy was. He should've been here by now. "Where are we going?"

"Just get up." He tapped her shoulder with the barrel of the pistol. "You got to see your bodyguard, now you'll do what I say, unless you want a bullet in his brain."

"No." She rushed to her feet, glancing down at Shane, wanting to stay with him as much as she wanted to put distance between him and the animal holding her hostage. If Shane regained consciousness now, he would die before she could do anything to help.

"Walk this way."

They moved down the overgrown path she and Shane had taken the day they found the old hunting cabin. She kept her eyes to the ground, on the lookout for bear traps as her mind raced, trying to think of a way to get back to Shane. She froze in her tracks when something among the brush caught her attention. Gasping, she hurried toward the man dressed in a white t-shirt and boxers, sprawled out and bleeding from the waist. Her gaze trailed over *SWIFTY* tattooed into his left forearm. *This* was Officer Swift, and he was bleeding to death. "You shot him."

He shrugged. "It's a rough day to be in The Gap."

She pressed her fingers to his weak pulse and lifted his shirt, rolling him slightly, studying the entry and exit points of his wounds. She then struggled to tear at the hem of his top in an attempt to apply pressure and staunch the bleeding.

"We don't have time for you to play wilderness doctor."

"He's going to die." She tossed him a look, finding some of her cool as her brain automatically clicked into professional mode.

"You're *all* going to die, so I wouldn't worry about that too much." He pointed the pistol at Officer Swift's heart. "Get up and get moving."

Reluctantly she did as she was told, keeping her eyes open for anything she could use as a weapon. Two men needed her help. "How long has Officer Swift been laying there?"

"For a few minutes. Since he hung up with your buddy. I guess that's what you get for not paying attention." He chuckled. "I snuck up right behind him like a sleek cat. I've got wilderness skills none of these sissy city boys have." He snorted out another laugh, shaking his head. "Pulled his gun before he had a chance to turn. Sure as hell didn't have much time to get myself ready." He gestured to his stolen uniform. "Made it into the cruiser just before you drove up."

Reagan clenched her jaw, repulsed by his disregard for another life.

"Now I want you to listen real careful, Doctor Rosner. Real careful," the man said as they stopped in front of the small hunting cabin she recognized from the day she and Shane went on their boat ride. "You're going to hold this gun." He smiled as their eyes met. "We're going to hold the gun *together*," he clarified. "I see that sparkle in your eyes. You think I'm stupid enough to let you put a bullet in me?" He shook his head as he pressed his chest to her back and forced her to grip the gun between his gloved hands.

She pushed against him in an attempt to knock him off balance, trying her best to turn, more than ready to shoot him, but his size made her efforts laughable.

"Nice try." He held her tighter against him, preventing her from moving. "Now fire it." He bumped against her. "Fire it!"

She slammed her eyes closed and pulled the trigger, the deafening sound echoing into the forest.

"Good. Now go inside." He pushed her up the

steps, and she walked into the small musty space absorbing a new wave of dread as she stared into Doctor Jacobson's cool eyes.

"Doctor Rosner." Doctor Jacobson nodded cordially as he leaned casually against the wall. "Go ahead and have a seat."

With no other choice she sat in the rickety chair by the old table, darting a glance at the pen and blank piece of paper. "Why are you doing this?"

"You didn't really think we were going to let a loose end leave the state did you?"

She stared at him, not bothering to comment, fully aware there was no point.

He smiled. "I've got to give it to you: You're tenacious, a real go-getter." He punctuated his statement with a sarcastic fist pump. "You've certainly kept us on our toes over the last few months. More than a few times you made me sweat, Doctor Rosner." He shook his head with a laugh. "But now we're here, and you're going to write a little note. You're going to tell everyone how you just don't have the will to live."

She swallowed. "*What?*"

Doctor Jacobson's partner pointed the gun at the back of her head.

"Pick up the pen, Doctor," Doctor Jacobson repeated, "and tell everyone how you can't live with your mistakes anymore. Tell them that the guilt over the little girl—"

She glared, fighting back a fresh wave of anger and fearful tears. "You did that. You spread those lies about me."

He shrugged. "I had my brother do a little digging." He gestured to the man with the pistol. "We got the rumor mill rolling at the mine, and Billy started dropping subtle hints along with his sermons at the church, and the rest, Doctor, is history. Such an unfortunate blemish for someone so dedicated." He shook his head mournfully. "Anyway, you need to tell everyone how you couldn't stand dealing with the death of that little girl and so many misdiagnoses here in The Gap. You'll also need to mention how you had Henry cremated before anyone could find out about his COPD. *Write* it, Doctor Rosner, or your boyfriend will die now instead of later."

Tears tracked down her cheeks as she wrote what the doctor told her to.

"Excellent. Now I want you to add that you had to kill what's-his-face—"

"Shane," Doctor Jacobson's brother added.

"Shane," Doctor Jacobson repeated, "because you couldn't live, but you couldn't let him live either."

"No." She rushed to her feet. "I won't write that. You leave him alone. You leave Shane alone, dammit."

"You, Doctor Rosner, should've left *this* alone. We warned you several times—phone calls, dead animals, and graffiti, yet you kept on going. Your constant need to help has caused more harm than anything. Henry suffered. Doctor Schlibenburg died a most horrible death—"

"You didn't have to kill him," she spat, clenching her fists. "He wasn't going to help me."

"There are few guarantees in life, Doctor, but killing a man will certainly keep his mouth shut." He grinned. "And just think—you led us *right* to him."

She shook her head, pressing her lips firm against the need to weep.

"Doctor Schlibenburg was going to rat us out." He clicked his tongue in disapproval. "He was going to blow our little network wide open with his paper, but Doctor Schlibenburg understood our warnings loud and clear and hightailed it into hiding. You, Doctor Reagan, helped us track down our biggest threat, and now you're the only one left."

"He was an old man."

"Now he's six feet under." He pointed to the chair. "Sit down and finish up your note, or the next step will be going after the blond and her baby."

"Jenny and Faith," the man supplied again.

"Whatever," Doctor Jacobson said.

"What about Officer Swift?" She stalled for more time, certain Detective Reedy had to be here by now, hopefully helping Shane.

Doctor Jacobson shrugged. "He got in your way, so he had to go too. You don't have to write that. We can't spell everything out, or things will start looking a little suspicious. A double murder-suicide?" He whistled through his teeth. "They'll be talking about Doc Reagan for years to come."

Doctor Jacobson's brother chuckled.

"*Write*, Doctor Rosner."

With no choice, she scribbled down the words as tears streamed down her cheeks.

Doctor Jacobson came over, scanned the words and smiled. "Perfect. Now access the x-rays in your files."

She hesitated, holding his gaze.

"Access the files, Doctor Rosner."

She swallowed, knowing she was running out of time. "How do you live with yourself?"

"Quite comfortably. Some people go to medical school to help others. I went because I like money. My practice keeps me comfortable, but the coal companies keep me in my yacht. A couple million a year is a small price to pay for the assurances of the wrong diagnoses. COPD, emphysema brought on by a lifetime of smoking, and let's not forget the occasional allergy." He shrugged. "It works well for everyone involved."

"Except for the patients and their families who are suffering."

"They're going to die anyway."

"God," she scoffed. "You're disgusting."

"On that note, let's finish this off. Type in your password, access the files, and I'll take care of the rest."

"I won't."

"Well, then Shane's going to die."

She raised her eyebrow. "He's going to die anyway."

He came up behind her, yanking on her hair "Open your files."

She whimpered against the bite of pain. "You're going to kill me. As soon as I open this I'm going to die."

"You *do* have an exceptional IQ."

"So why would I do it?"

"Bud, go take care of Shane."

Bud opened the door.

"No!" She rushed halfway to her feet and fell back in her chair as Doctor Jacobson still held her hair in his grip. "Okay. I'll open it." She started typing in the password. "You know you won't get away with this. There are other copies."

"The ones at Doctor Schlibenburg's were confiscated, but let me guess, you left a file with the other guy?" Doctor Jacobson looked at Bud. "Well, what's his name?"

"Chase."

"We're going to go take care of Chase next."

She pulled up the files.

"Delete them."

Her finger hovered over the button.

"Delete them, Doctor Rosner."

She hit "delete," watching her images vanish.

Doctor Jacobson laughed. "Perfect. Gunshot residue on your hands, which will match the murder weapon and your fingerprints on the computer. You took the cop out because he was in the way, and you killed your lover because he wasn't going to live if you couldn't. Then you came back and ended your own life right here. It's really quite ideal. Bud, go ahead and begin."

Bud moved toward the old propane line, and a quiet hissing noise filled the room as he twisted it on.

"Bud's going to sit with you until you lose consciousness."

"Is this what you did to Doctor Pattell?"

"Pretty much, but we took care of him in his car in the garage. Authenticity counts." He shook his head. "It's a shame you bleeding hearts just don't get it. Luckily our secrets will die with you." He moved toward the door. "Bud, don't forget to give Officer *Swifty* back his clothes when you're finished.

Bud nodded.

"Come on over to Willy and Billy's after you finish up with Chase. Corpus Mining and Stygian are officially in the clear—that's something to celebrate." He opened the door. "Well, goodnight, Doctor Rosner."

Bud slipped on a mask as the doctor stepped out.

"It was a pleasure working with you. Now I'm going to go take care of your lover. He'll have died just minutes before you. Authenticity count." He winked, smiling, as he pulled black gloves from his pocket and put them on, then caught the gun Bud tossed to him.

"Leave him alone!" she screamed, hurrying to the door as it closed. Bud knocked her back. "I'm not dying in here!" She shoved him and he pushed her, sending her sprawling to the floor. The scent of rotten egg filled her nostrils and she gagged, standing, breathing in the air that wasn't so powerfully tainted. She covered her mouth and nose with her shirt as she swept the room, trying to figure another way out. The window was boarded, but she spotted a small crack exposed to the outdoors, walked over, and started pounding. "Help!" She rested her head against the wall, covering her face with her arms, giving into her tears, putting her mouth to the small opening, sucking in fresher air.

"Help!" She needed to think, and quickly. The headache and nausea of overexposure were already beginning to take their toll in the small space. She didn't have much time, maybe a minute or two before she would pass out. She did her best to suck in as much clean air as possible, stumbling, falling as the room spun around her.

CHAPTER FORTY

SHANE OPENED HIS EYES, GROANING, THE PAIN IN HIS HEAD agonizing as he watched two blurry figures walk off. Blinking, confused, he recognized Reagan's voice as his gaze traveled up the backs of her leather shoes and jeans, then her gray sweater, squinting as the police officer pointed a gun at her head. Then they disappeared among the trees.

Officer Swift...who wasn't Officer Swift... He remembered the bullet hole and bloodstains in the waist of the police uniform, and his brain started clicking back into gear. Rushing to sit up, he held his forehead in his hands, waiting for the torturous drumbeat in his skull to subside.

"Shit," he muttered, slowly gaining is feet, battling waves of nausea as he reached for his phone, but it was gone. "Damn it." The world spun while he felt around for his missing gun and rubbed absently at the minor discomfort along his side where the taser barbs had impaled him. "Fuck."

He blinked to clear his hazy vision and ran toward the house, the impact of each jarring step unbearable as he took the stairs in twos, well aware that Reagan was getting further away from him with every second ticking by. It was tempting to abandon protocol and follow her into the woods, but if he wanted her back he needed to play smart. He wasn't foolish enough to ignore the fact that he was in rough shape and needed help.

Wandering around the living room, he searched for the house phone among the filthy chaos of burnt embers, then climbed the steps to the loft and dialed Chase.

"Yeah?"

"I need backup. Someone knocked me out. They have Reagan."

"Where the fuck is Swift?"

"Probably dead. The fucker who tased me then clocked me was wearing his uniform. There was a bullet hole in the side of his shirt."

"Jesus. I'll call the police. Where's Reedy?"

"I don't know. I don't have his number. It's on my phone. I can't find it."

"I'll take care of it."

"Hurry." He hung up and turned too quickly, catching himself against the arm of the couch before he fell. When the dizzy spell passed, he rushed down the steps and into the kitchen, grabbing a knife from the butcher block—not ideal, but it would have to do.

With his weapon in hand, he took off toward the trees, halting mid-step when a gunshot echoed somewhere in the close distance. "Reagan." He fought to breathe as his world simply stopped. "No. God. *No.*" He jammed a trembling hand through his hair, the shocking pain jarring him back into action, and he walk-ran as fast as his head would allow him to move in the direction of the sickening sound.

Branches snapped and leaves crunched beneath his feet as his breath heaved and he stumbled on, sweating with the effort to hurry. The undergrowth grew thicker with every inch he gained, making his hellish journey all the more challenging. He faltered when he spotted an arm peeking from the tangle of brush and decaying logs, and for one horrific moment he thought Reagan lay on the ground before he realized he'd found Officer Swift.

Crouching, he read *Swifty* inked into the man's arm and felt for the almost non-existent pulse, studying the man's grayish pallor, taking in the extent of his blood loss. "Hang in there, buddy. Hang in there," he muttered and kept going. Reagan was alive—he needed to believe that. As soon as he found her and got her back, they would deal with the fallen policeman.

He picked up his pace, gaining his bearings when he realized he was heading toward the abandoned hunting cabin. Trudging on for what felt like miles, he finally spotted the edge of the small wooden structure. Ducking down, he cautiously moved closer, needing to figure out if Reagan was even in there. He stood, advancing slowly with his eyes scanning for bear traps and his ears tuned, catching the muffled sounds of a male and female voice the closer he came to the door. He shuddered out a breath, embracing the rush of relief. Reagan was right here, and she was alive.

The door opened suddenly, and Shane hurried back, moving further into the trees.

"Well, goodnight, Doctor Rosner." The well-built blond man walked down the steps. "Now I'm going to take care of your lover. He'll have died just minutes before you. Authenticity counts." He winked and smiled as he pulled on the black gloves he took from his pocket and caught the police-issue Glock someone threw to him.

"Leave him alone!" Reagan screamed, her voice growing muffled when the door closed.

The blond chuckled as he reached for his phone with his free hand, dialed, and put it to his ear. "Willy, it's Steven. Everything's been taken care of—or will be after we deal with the bastard in the driveway and the one in Lexington. The x-rays were deleted."

Shane followed, quickly closing the distance between himself and the man who could only be Doctor Jacobson. He dropped his knife as he tripped on a branch, cursing his less-than-graceful footwork when the asshole turned. Rushing forward, Shane took advantage of the momentary confusion, and knocked the doctor down, sucker-punching him in the face.

"Son of a bitch," the doctor spat, throwing his own punch, knocking Shane's head back.

He saw stars with the quick shock of pain against his chin and blinked them from his vision, afraid he would lose his on-top advantage as he fought for the gun Doctor Jacobson tried to point his way. Reagan's muffled cries for help spurred him on, and he sent his fist forward again, causing a fountain of blood to spew from Doctor Jacobson's nose. "You fucker," he grunted out, plowing his hand into his face for the third time, knocking him unconscious.

"You fucker," he repeated, breathless as he grabbed the gun and gained his feet. He jogged back to the small hunting shelter and wrapped his tender knuckles against the door, moving to the corner as the impersonating officer opened up, wearing a gas mask. "Come here," Shane said through his teeth, jerking on the man's arm, forcing him down the stairs while he pressed the Glock into his chest.

"You shoot you kill us all."

Shane caught the whiff of gas and punched the man in the stomach, fighting off his mask as he moved behind the asshole and hooked his arm tight around the man's neck, using his bicep to cut off his oxygen supply, sending him to the ground in a heap, well aware that Reagan no longer called for help.

"Reagan!" He hurried up the stairs, coughing as he

breathed in the putrid smell of propane, finding Reagan lying on the floor curled in a ball. "Reagan!" He rushed to her side, rolling her to face him. "Reagan."

She blinked, looking up at him through glassy eyes.

"Come on." He scooped her up, stumbling his way down the stairs as police cars screeched to a halt in the distance. "Take deep breaths," he encouraged, walking quickly away from the cabin, knowing it could blow at any second.

She closed her eyes as her head lolled back against his shoulder.

He gave her a shake as the relief of finding her was short lived. "Take deep breaths, Reagan," he demanded now, struggling not to panic, terrified he was too late after all.

"I need oxygen," she croaked out as men started hollering in the woods.

"I know. Let's get you out of here." He looked up quickly, almost falling, consumed by another wave of dizziness as Detective Reedy ran their way.

"Jesus Christ. What the hell's going on around here?"

"Where the fuck have you been?" Shane demanded as he continued down the path.

"I had a blowout. I tried calling you, but no one answered."

"I was busy being unconscious."

"Reedy!" someone hollered.

"Over here," Reedy yelled with his hands cupped around his mouth.

"Officer Swift," Reagan murmured. "He needs help."

"You missed Officer Swift."

Reedy shook his head. "They found him. They're carrying him out now—ambulance is on the way."

Reagan coughed, resting heavy against Shane's shoulder.

"Your perps are bleeding back by the old hunting place, but we need the oxygen in the clinic now. She's barely conscious."

"Where are the keys?"

"I don't know. By the Pajero probably."

Reedy ran to the SUV, stopping quickly, gesturing to two officers standing at the edge of the woods before he picked up the keys by the back right tire and rushed inside the clinic. Moments later he appeared with a small oxygen tank.

"Full stream," Reagan said as Reedy secured the mask on her face

"Keep your eyes open, Reagan," Shane murmured softly.

"Let me breathe first," she muffled through the plastic covering her mouth, taking slow deep breaths.

She was still struggling. Who knew exactly how long she'd been trapped in the fumes? "I don't want to wait for the ambulance," Shane said.

"I'll be okay." She opened her eyes. "I didn't pass out."

"You were just about gone when I got there."

Reedy opened the back door to his car. "Get in. I'll get you to the hospital." He radioed in as Shane settled them in, and they rushed down the road with sirens blaring, passing the ambulance coming up on the way.

Shane clutched Reagan close with hands not quite steady, kissing her temple, realizing how close he'd come to losing the love of his life. "Are you okay?"

"I think so." She touched his face. "You're concussed."

His head screamed, and he could easily vomit from the pain, but none of that mattered. "I'm fine."

Forty long minutes later, they arrived at the hospital with two gurneys waiting. "I'm not going anywhere until I know how she is," Shane said as he lifted Reagan from the backseat and laid her on the bed.

She lifted her mask. "Go get your head scanned, Shane."

"I don't—"

"*Go.*"

Her demand gave him little room to argue. "Okay." He hopped on the gurney, letting the team of doctors and nurses wheel him away, when all he wanted was to stay with Reagan.

~~~~

Shane's nurse pushed his wheelchair toward Reagan's room—far too slowly, in his opinion. Tapping impatient fingers against the armrest—in time with his still throbbing head—he counted off the doors.

"Hold your horses, Mr. Harper. We're just about there."

"Great. Thanks," he added, tossing her a quick smile, realizing his response came out more tersely than he meant. "I appreciate all your help, Trina. Really."

Her eyebrows shot up on her pretty ebony face as she pressed her lips firm, answering him with an, "Mmhm."

"Give a guy a break here. I need to get to Doc. She's my one true love."

Shaking her head, she grinned. "You've been a pain in my butt today, Mr. Harper, but you've got charm—more than any one man has a right to."

He chuckled. "Thanks."

"That wasn't necessarily a compliment."

He tossed her a pained look. "Aw, Trina, don't go and hurt my feelings."

She let loose a goose-like honk of a laugh. "Too much charm indeed."

He and Trina had more than one go-around throughout the evening. First she'd snatched the phone away from him in the radiology department. He and Chase had been mid-conversation when she took the receiver, slamming it down in its base while scolding him for helping himself to hospital property without permission when she was trying to get him ready for his tests. Then they'd exchanged words when he insisted he'd waited long enough to see Reagan and could walk himself down the hall to check on her, but Shane quickly realized Trina held the power here at St. Christopher's Medical Center when she told him to sit his handsome butt in the wheelchair so she could keep her job or she would have the doctor mark his charts and keep him bedridden for the next twenty-four hours.

"Your lady certainly has her hands full with you."

"She loves it," he said as he turned in his chair again.

"I imagine she just might."

They passed another door and one more before they finally stopped. "See? Here we are."

"Let's go in."

"What ever happened to knocking?"

Clenching his jaw, he gave a quick rap with tender knuckles against the wood and rolled himself forward, not interested in the formalities of being polite. He'd waited—not so patiently—for at least two hours to see Reagan. Despite several reassurances from the medical team that Reagan was fine, he needed to get a look for himself.

"Let me help you, Mr. Harper." Trina guided him through the doorway.

"Hey," Reagan's face lit up as she set down her magazine. "There you are."

He smiled, relieved all over again. Here she was, safe. "Hi."

"Look at you," her voice dripped with sympathy, and her eyes softened as she sat up and reached out her hand to him. "You're in worse shape than I am."

"That's okay." He grabbed hold of her warm fingers when Trina rolled him to her bedside. Kissing her knuckles and wrist, he studied Reagan's coloring, which appeared as flawless and gorgeous as usual. He relaxed further, noting the typical sparkle in her pretty blue eyes instead of the terrifying listlessness he'd observed when he picked her up off the nasty wooden floor. "You're good? You're going to be all right?"

She nodded.

"I tried telling him, but he's been heck-bent on seeing for himself." Trina patted Shane's shoulder. "You've got yourself a fine man, Doctor Rosner."

Reagan smiled. "Yes I do."

"I'll leave you two alone."

"Thank you, Trina. Seriously."

"You got it, ace." His ball-busting nurse winked. "I'll be in to check on you two a little later," she said as she left.

He held Reagan's hand tighter, pressing more kisses to her skin as the door closed. "How are you?"

"Good. Really good, actually. Getting me out into the fresh air and giving me the oxygen at the clinic made a huge difference. I have very low levels of CO_2 in my blood."

He nuzzled her knuckles against his cheek, unable

to stop touching her. If he'd been a minute or two later, he would've lost her. "What about a hyperbaric chamber? Maybe—"

She smiled. "I don't need that. They're going to keep me on oxygen for awhile longer," She pointed to the tubes pushing air into her nose, "and keep an eye on me overnight."

He stared into her eyes, flashing back to the image of her lying limp and curled up in a ball—as he had too many times to count. "God, I feel sick."

She touched his cheek. "That's your concussion."

"No." He shook his head, holding her gaze.

"Come here." She patted her bed. "Come lay down with me."

He stood, bracing the rail, still slightly dizzy, and got in bed with her, dressed in an identical johnny. "We need to do something about these outfits."

She grinned. "You look cute."

"Chase said he would bring us clothes."

"I wouldn't mind real pajamas." She wrapped her arms around him, kissing his neck and jaw. "How's your head?"

"Fine."

She tilted her head with her brows raised. "How's your head, Shane?"

He sighed, resting against the pillow. "It hurts like hell. Trina gave me something, so the pounding is finally down to a dull roar."

"I'm sorry he hit you. I'm sorry I couldn't help you."

He read the regret in her eyes. "Everything worked out."

"Yes. We're both going to be okay." She tilted his head closer, inspecting. "The doctor told me you have a mild concussion. He also said you were a pain in the butt in radiology."

509

"Bull." Chuckling, he wrapped her up tight, needing her. "Okay, I might've helped myself to the phone, and I *may* have suggested that they were taking too long." He stared into her eyes, stroking her cheek. "I needed to see you. I couldn't be away from you for one more minute, Reagan."

"I'm right here."

"Thank God." He gently pressed his forehead to hers. "Thank God."

She took his hand, holding his palm to her cheek, and kissed him. "We're all right," she whispered.

He nodded.

"What did Chase say before your nurse took the phone away?"

He winced. "You heard about that too, huh?"

"I heard about all sorts of things." She batted her lashes.

He grinned. "I still have a job to do," he justified.

Sighing, she shook her head. "What did Chase say?"

"That Officer Swift is in critical care. They life-flighted him up to Lexington. They're hoping he'll pull through."

"The colder temperatures probably saved his life."

"Detective Reedy told Chase they have Jacobson and his brother in custody, and they're actively investigating the McPhee's. Reedy's really damn excited about all of the information Chase sent his way. If there's any justice in this world they'll all go down for a long, long time."

"And hopefully the people in The Gap will finally get some help."

The doctor came in. "Mr. Harper, what are you doing in here?"

"I'm not leaving," he said. "How's Reagan?"

"She's fine." He turned his attention to Reagan,

patting her arm. "We're going to check your levels again in a couple hours, Doctor Rosner, but at this point I'm very happy with the results of the last blood draw. I have no reason to believe there has been any damage to your organs. Your CO_2 saturations are extremely low considering the amount of time you believe you spent in such a small space."

"See? Everything's okay," she said quietly, bumping his arm with hers.

He could hear Reagan and Doctor Holmes' reassurances a thousand times, and would still want to hear them a thousand more. He nodded. "When do we get to go home?"

"I'll be releasing you and Doctor Rosner tomorrow as long as you have a good night, but plane rides will have to wait forty-eight to seventy-two hours."

Shane steamed out a quiet breath with the news.

"I'll order another blood draw, Doctor Rosner, and assess you both further in the morning."

"Thank you."

There was a quiet knock at the door, and Jenny walked in with Faith and Chase. "Is it okay if we come in?"

"Of course it is." Reagan smiled and held out her arms.

Chase took Faith, and Jenny rushed over, hugging Reagan tight as she sniffled. "I was real worried about you. Real, real worried."

"I'm okay, sweetie."

Jenny eased back, giving Reagan a once over. "You look all right."

"I am—promise. I only have to stay overnight."

"What about you?" Jenny said to Shane, walking around to his side of the bed.

"I've got a headache."

"You look a lot worse than Reagan." She grimaced. "A lot worse. That's some egg you've got on your head."

"Gee, Hendley, thanks." He gave her shoulder a gentle push.

She smiled. "I bet it's makin' you grumpy, huh?"

"Nah, I'm just a little sore."

She hugged him more gently than she had Reagan. "I'm glad you're okay." She kissed his cheek. "I was worryin' about you too."

He held her tight, thinking of how the whole day could have gone down. Everyone in this room could've been victims of a few assholes' greed. "Everything's okay now. We're all fine," he told her as much as himself. "Tomorrow we're going home."

Reagan frowned. "We're not flying."

"No, we're not. We're extending the rental on the Pajero for all I care. I just want us out of here. Can you make that happen, man?" He looked at Chase.

"Yeah, I can make that happen. Get some rest." He set the duffle bag on the small table to Shane's side. "The ladies and I will be by to pick you up as soon as we get the word, and we'll go."

Shane and Chase bumped fists. "Thanks."

"No problem."

Reagan grinned, smiling at the baby. "Are you guys going to be okay tonight at the hotel?"

Chase and Jenny looked at each other.

"Sure. We're gonna go to the store and pick out some travelin' food and get everythin' ready. I'm gonna take care of you two for awhile." She hugged them, kissed their cheeks. "Don't you worry about a thing." She took Faith from Chase. "Come on, baby girl. Tomorrow we're finally goin' home."

Reagan blew Jenny and Faith a kiss "We'll see you in the morning. Thanks, Chase."

"You've got it."

"Bye," Shane called as the door closed behind them. "You know, Jenny's really got her head on straight."

Reagan smiled. "Yes, she does. I can't wait to watch her and Faith thrive—*really* thrive."

"The adventure starts tomorrow."

"We can wait."

He shook his head. "No we can't."

"It probably wouldn't hurt to give yourself another day."

Traveling would suck, but getting the hell out of Kentucky was more important than being comfortable. "I need to take you away from here. I have to."

She nodded. "Okay."

He kissed her. "I hope they don't think I'm leaving this bed."

She kissed him back. "I'd like to watch them try and make you." She settled in the nook of his shoulder, resting her head on his chest. "I love you, Shane."

"I love you too. Let's get some rest."

"Okay. Goodnight."

"Night." He closed his eyes, counting his blessing as he held the woman he loved close, knowing his good friend was taking care of his and Reagan's girls. In just a few hours he was bringing them all home.

CHAPTER FORTY-ONE

THE SALTY BREEZE TANGLED REAGAN'S HAIR, AND SHE laughed with Shane as her stomach lurched deliciously when the Ferris wheel started its ascent back into the darkening sky. Los Angeles twinkled bright in the distance, and the Pacific crashed against the sandy shores below. "This, Mr. Harper, is *fun*."

"Good." He grinned, kissing her forehead as he wrapped his arms tighter around her, pulling her impossibly closer against his side. "You're not bummed that we blew off dinner?"

"Are you kidding?" She pulled back slightly. "The burger and fries were great." Somehow they'd ended up on Santa Monica Pier instead of at the high-end restaurant in the city where Shane had made reservations. They'd ridden the rollercoaster and zoomed around in the scrambler, Shane wearing a button-down and slacks and she a little black dress with heels.

"This wasn't exactly the ambiance I was going for on our first real date night."

She glanced around at the blaze of colorful lights and listened to the screams and laughter of people enjoying the iconic California tourist stop on the surprisingly mild November night. "This isn't our first real date night." She grabbed his tie, inching his face forward, kissing him and smiling into his gorgeous green eyes, certain she couldn't be any happier. "I believe we had that in The Gap." She kissed him again.

"And this is *almost* just as perfect."

He chuckled. "You certainly don't ask for much."

"Not when I have everything I want and need."

His eyes softened as he smiled. "I'm sorry it's taken me almost a month to get around to taking my girl out."

She smiled back. "We've been busy settling in."

He cupped her face in his hands, stroking her cheeks with his thumbs, sending her heart racing with his tender touch. "I'm so glad you're here with me, Reagan."

"I don't want to be anywhere else."

"I love you."

"I love you too."

He pressed his lips to hers as the Ferris wheel stopped at the top, letting on more passengers. Moments passed as Shane deepened the kiss, slowly, sweetly, and she moaned, clutching at his shirt. He eased back when their seat jerked slightly and they began moving toward the bottom. "I think it's our turn to get off this time around," he said, nibbling at her jaw.

"I guess all good things have to come to an end."

"So I've heard."

Their bucket came to a stop in front of the man who opened the safety latch and let them out.

"Thanks," Shane said as he took Reagan's hand. "So, what do you want to do next?"

"I don't know. I think we've been on all of the rides."

"How about a walk on the beach—or would you rather go home?"

She wavered, the pounding surf just yards away tempting her, but Jenny had her hands full at the house with pre-Thanksgiving preparations. "I think we should probably head home."

He glanced at his watch and nodded, walking with her toward the parking lot. "So, Doc, I didn't get much of a chance to hear about your first day at work." He slid his arm around her waist as they made their way to his Mercedes. "You were too busy screaming on the kiddie rides."

"I didn't scream." Grinning, she bumped his hip playfully.

He looked at her, his eyebrow raised.

"Okay, maybe I screamed *once* on the Pacific Plunge."

He groaned. "I might've screamed too." He patted his stomach. "I'm glad we went on that before we ate."

She laughed as he chuckled.

"Tell me about work," he said next to her ear.

"It was good. Amazing, actually." She grinned with the rush of excitement, thinking of her new position as part-time physician at Southern California Teen Outreach.

"Amazing." He nodded. "Not a bad way to start new employment."

"I really think I'm going to love this. And working three days a week is pretty great."

"It's a good gig if you can get it."

She nodded her agreement, thrilled that she could work and make a difference and still have plenty of time for Jenny and Faith. "I saw six new patients today. Four of the young ladies are pregnant. I've scheduled appointments with them for next week. We're going to sit down with a counselor and make sure they understand that they can still finish school."

"You'll do a hell of a job." He pressed on the key fob and opened her door for her.

"Thanks."

"You're welcome. They're lucky to have you."

"I guess so."

"I know so."

It would take time to completely rebuild her confidence as a physician after Mable and her time in The Gap, but someday she hoped to be as sure of herself as Shane was. She smiled. "Thank you."

He winked. "Any time." He kissed her again before she sat down. "All set?"

"All set."

He closed her in and hustled around to his side. Getting in, he turned over the ignition. "Okay, tell me more," he said as he fought his way into traffic.

"Let's talk about you. How did it feel to finally be back in action at Ethan Cooke Security in a non-concussed, non-paper-pusher capacity?"

"Good." He took her hand. "Busy—just the way I like it, but I liked it better knowing that when I got off the plane from San Francisco this afternoon I was coming home to you and the girls."

"Mmm." She brought his knuckles to her lips. "I liked seeing you pull in the driveway."

"Speaking of driveways, ours will be crowded soon. Stone thinks he'll be finished with Jenny's new car by Christmas, easy."

She grinned. "She's going to be so excited. She's doing so well, Shane." Her eyes welled with pride. "She's just taken off—she and Faith both."

"They're great kids."

"Did you see her face yesterday when she deposited her first paycheck? The pride?"

"I did."

"I think two days a week is working out well for her."

"Agreed. I'm glad she's decided to go for her RN."

"Me too. Just think, come spring semester our girl will be on her way." She sighed. "Everything's finally settling into place." And tomorrow the four of them would spend their first Thanksgiving together—along with dozens of Shane's co-workers at the Cookes' home.

A long silence filled the car while she enjoyed the pleasure of utter contentment.

Shane gave their laced fingers a gentle squeeze. "So, I heard from Detective Reedy this afternoon."

She looked at him, sitting up straighter. "You did?"

He nodded. "I didn't want to ruin our date, so I thought I would wait to tell you."

She tucked her hair behind her ear with the small stirrings of tension. "What did he say?"

"Well, Officer Swift went home this morning. His infections cleared up, and he's expected to be back at work by the first of the year."

"Thank God for that."

"They've figured out who was sending Doctor Schlibenburg's article to The Gap," he said as he took a right toward the quiet neighborhoods of the Palisades.

"Oh yeah?"

"One of Schlibenburg's former assistants had copies of his work and the data from the Mine Safety and Health Administration. Apparently Doctor Schlibenburg called him hours before he died and said if anything happened to him he wanted you to have the information."

She sighed. Doctor Schlibenburg's useless death still bothered her. "I just wish it would've helped."

"Oh, it's helped. Doctor Hargus has lost his medical license and is facing criminal charges right along with the McPhee's, Jacobson, and his brother. And Doctor Yancey, the guy from Nashville—"

"I know who Doctor Yancey is." She smiled. "I reached out to him for help."

"Right. He contacted Detective Reedy yesterday and shared that he and his wife's lives had been threatened when they got back from their honeymoon, which only adds another nail to all of the bastards' coffins."

"I should give him a call."

"Doctor Yancey's going to get together with some of the other physicians in the region and start attacking black lung head on."

She lifted her brows, intrigued. "Really?"

His gaze darted to hers several times. "That's what he said."

"That's wonderful."

He clenched his jaw. "I, uh, I wasn't sure if you would want to head back out to Kentucky to help."

She shook her head. "I'm staying right here with you and the girls."

"Good." He expelled a deep breath of what could only be relief.

"I'm home, Shane. I'm home," she repeated, stroking his hand.

He nodded. "I got some other news."

"What's that?"

"Terry's looking at two to five years, so we won't have to worry about him for awhile."

She closed her eyes in relief. "I would have to say everything's just about perfect."

"You did a lot of good in Kentucky, Doc. A lot of good. None of this stuff would've happened if you hadn't stood up for the people there."

"It was my job."

He shook his head. "You went way above and beyond. You're a damn good woman, Reagan."

"Thanks."

He pulled into the driveway next to her new car. "Here we are."

"Here we are." She smiled, staring at the sweet little California ranch they were making theirs together.

"Are you ready?"

The lights glowed warm and inviting through the big picture windows. "Yes. I imagine Jenny could use a hand with the pies."

He got out, and she met him at the hood of the car. "Come on." He took her hand and walked past the front door to the latch on the fence.

"What are we doing?"

"I wanted to show you something."

"Oh, okay." She moved with him through the small backyard and stopped short, staring at the new porch swing swaying slightly and the candles burning in prettily decorated paper bags set around the brick patio. "What have you done?" she smiled.

"I thought we could use a swing. What do you think?"

She laughed. "I think I love it."

He grinned. "Yeah?"

She nodded. "Definitely.

"Let's go test it out." He tugged on her hand.

"Okay."

They sat down and he cuddled her close.

She kissed his cheek and settled her head on his chest. "This is perfect."

"Kind of like The Gap."

She shook her head, taking in the winking stars and quiet whoosh of cars driving by in the neighborhood. "This is so much better."

He slid his palm up and down her arm. "This was one of the best parts of being in Kentucky—sitting with you out on the porch listening to you share all of those fascinating thoughts in that big brain of yours. I missed it when I left."

"Mmm," she agreed, snuggling closer, never wanting to be without him again.

"So it only seems right that I should ask you to be my wife right here."

She sat up slowly as his words sunk in.

He opened a small box, revealing a stunning band of silver and diamonds. "Will you marry me, Reagan? Will you help me raise our girls and grow old with me right here in our house?"

"Shane," she whispered as tears spilled down her cheeks and she stared into his kind green eyes. "Yes." She threw her arms around him. "Yes, I'll marry you."

He wrapped her up, kissing her neck. "I had no idea that when I pulled into that Podunk town I was going to find everything I've ever wanted." He eased back. "I love you."

She sniffled, pressing her palms to his cheeks. "I love you too—so much."

"Let me put your ring on you."

She held out her left hand and watched him push the jewelry on her finger. "It's beautiful."

"I—" Shane glanced up and grinned. "We have an audience."

Reagan looked over her shoulder toward the window in the kitchen, where Jenny held Faith. Laughing, she gestured for her to come on out.

Jenny rushed outside. "You said yes!" She bounced Faith. "Reagan said yes, Faithy!"

Faith smiled.

"Congratulations." Jenny beamed at them and hugged them both.

"Thank you," Reagan smiled, certain she might

never stop.

"Do you like your new swing?"

"I love it. You two certainly surprised me." Reagan tugged on Jenny's arm. "Come sit down with us and give it a try."

Jenny sat sandwiched between them in her casual designer clothes, standing Faith up on her thighs as the sweet baby cooed, staring at the flickers of candlelight.

"How'd the baking go?" Shane asked.

"Good. Two apple crumb and two cherry pies are coolin'.' I can't believe we're goin' to the Cookes' for Thanksgivin'."

"It'll be one hell of a show."

"You'll get to show off your new ring." Jenny rested her head against Reagan's shoulder. "When do you think you'll get married?"

"As soon as possible," Shane and Reagan said at the same time.

They looked at each other and laughed, linking their fingers on the back of the swing as they gently rocked their little family in the peace and quiet of the warm Los Angeles night.

ABOUT THE AUTHOR

Cate Beauman is the author of the best-selling series, The Bodyguards of L.A. County. She currently lives in North Carolina with her husband, two boys, and their St. Bernards, Bear and Jack.

www.catebeauman.com
www.facebook.com/CateBeauman
www.goodreads.com/catebeauman
Follow Cate on Twitter: @CateBeauman

THE BODYGUARDS OF L.A. COUNTY

Morgan's Hunter
Book One: The story of Morgan and Hunter
ISBN: 978-0989569606

Falling For Sarah
Book Two: The story of Sarah and Ethan
ISBN: 978-0989569613

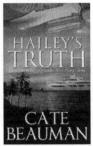

Hailey's Truth
Book Three: The story of Hailey and Austin
ISBN: 978-0989569620

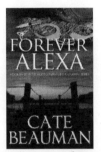

Forever Alexa
Book Four: The story of Alexa and Jackson
ISBN: 978-0989569637

Waiting For Wren
Book Five: The story of Wren and Tucker
ISBN: 978-0989569644

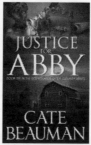

Justice For Abby
Book Six: The story of Abby and Jared
ISBN: 978-0989569651

Saving Sophie
Book Seven: The story of Sophie and Stone
ISBN: 978-0989569668

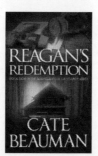

Reagan's Redemption
Book Eight: The story of Reagan and Shane
ISBN: 978-0989569675

COMING SUMMER OF 2015

Answers For Julie
Book Nine: The story of Julie and Chase
ISBN: 978-0989569699

42591921R10327

Made in the USA
Lexington, KY
28 June 2015